THE BONDS THAT BIND US
BOOK II

The Corrupted Prince

S.A. GONSALVES

GRENDEL PRESS

Trigger Warnings

ɷↄ

This book contains subject matter that may be
triggering or unsuitable for those under sixteen
or with mental health illnesses.
Sensitive subject matter includes:

Graphic depictions of violence.
Allusion to sexual assault.
Mention of suicide.
References to violence against minors.
Mention of cult-like activities.

To my husband, Steven.
Thank you for standing by me through all the
good times, chaotic times, and everything in between.
I wouldn't have made it this far without you.

But remember...
I'm proud of you, too

❧

To Angelo
I'm twelve years late, but you would
have loved these books.

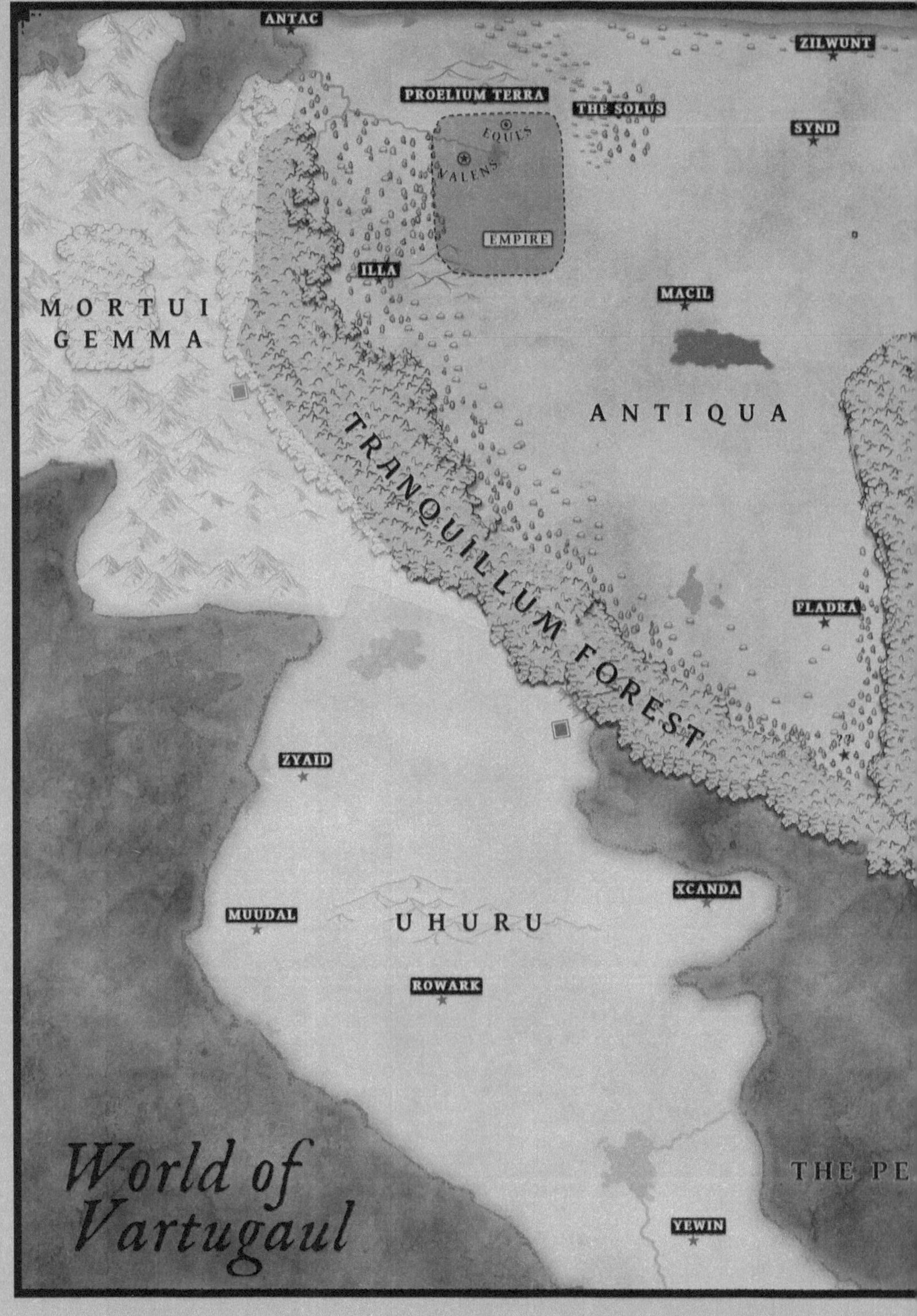

ANTAC
ZILWUNT
PROELIUM TERRA
THE SOLUS
SYND
EQUES
VALENS
EMPIRE
ILLA
MACIL
MORTUI
GEMMA
ANTIQUA
TRANQUILLUM FOREST
FLADRA
ZYAID
XCANDA
MUUDAL
UHURU
ROWARK
World of
Vartugaul
YEWIN
THE PE

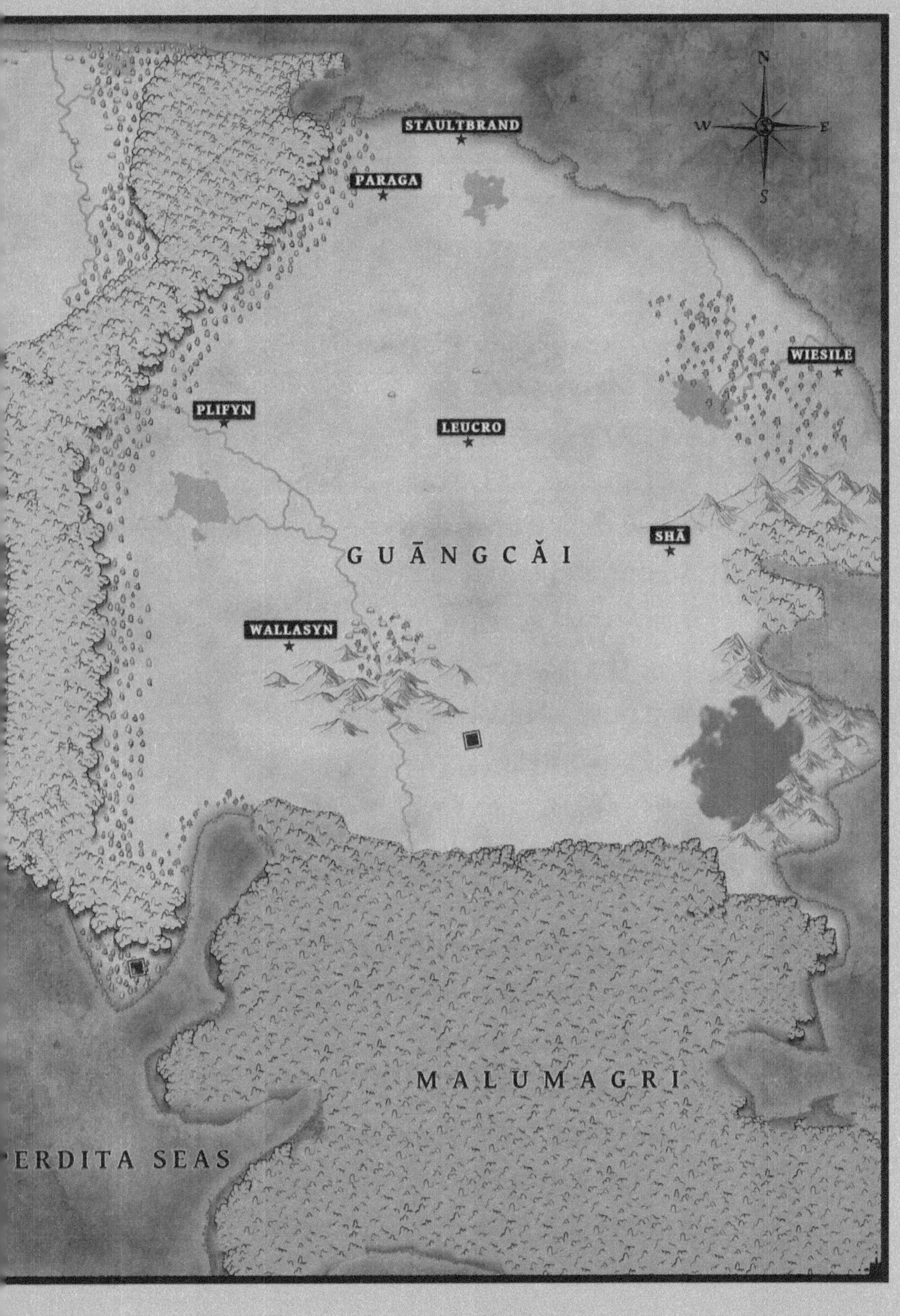

STAULTBRAND
PARAGA
WIESILE
PLIFYN
LEUCRO
SHĂ
GUĀNGCĂI
WALLASYN
MALUMAGRI
ERDITA SEAS
N
W
E
S

| TABLE OF CONTENTS |

I	THE PRINCE, THE PRISONER & THE PUPPET	1
II	GREY EYES IN CHAINS… AGAIN	8
III	A LITTLE TOO CLOSE FOR "BROTHERHOOD"	19
IV	YOU DIDN'T START THIS JOURNEY AS QUEEN	31
V	BLACK ASH & FIRE	48
VI	NO ONE WILL KNOW YOUR NAME	57
VII	THE OTHER BROTHER	73
VIII	A FALLEN KING	84
IX	NOTHING HEALS LIKE FLUFFY PILLOWS	92
X	CAN YOU LOOK SURPRISED WITHOUT EYEBROWS?	100
XI	MADNESS RULES MADNESS	112
XII	IT'S NOT MY BLOOD	120
XIII	JOIN THE FESTIVITIES	129
XIV	JEALOUSY, FEAR & DESPAIR	141
XV	THE VOICE KEEPS YELLING AT ME	151
XVI	SWEET RAIN, BURNT WOOD AND…	160
XVII	TWO LEAVES & ONE TREE	167
XVIII	DON'T LET THE MUD HIDE YOUR LIGHT	175
XIX	ASHES, ASHES, WE ALL BURN	185
XX	WOULD YOU HAVE HID & WATCHED?	197
XXI	RETURN WHAT IS MINE	212
XXII	WHAT'S DONE IS DONE	225
XXIII	WHAT DOES TRUST MEAN TO YOU?	235
XXIV	SOMEONE SHOULD CUT THE GRASS	244
XXV	THE PLACE SHE NEVER CALLED HOME	253
XXVI	POISONED, TAINTED HEART	262

XXVII | MIDNIGHT STAR 271

XXVIII | THREE SHOTS IS ENOUGH 283

XXIX | EXCEPTIONALLY RECKLESS 295

XXX | A DEMON BEFORE THEM 315

XXXI | HALF HEARTED, HALF TRUTHS 326

XXXII | A WOMAN & TWO MEN WALK INTO AN INN 341

XXXIII | FIRE & CARNAGE. ICE & HAPPINESS. 353

XXXIV | THAT HORSE HOLDS GRUDGES 371

XXXV | WE'RE BOTH VERY TRAGIC 379

XXXVI | THE TOWN BY THE SHORE 391

XXXVII | BACK TO THE BEGINNING 397

XXXVIII | THE BEST DISGUISE IS ME 411

XXXVIX | THE SOUL CAN HEAL 420

XL | TWO SIDES OF THE SAME SEED 435

XLI | BLOOD DOESN'T EQUAL FAMILY 441

XLII | THE SEARCH IS OVER 456

NAMES, WORDS AND TERMINOLOGY OF VARTUGAUL

ACKNOWLEDGEMENTS

I

The Prince, The Prisoner & The Puppet

| GALAHAD |

GALAHAD watched in horror as twenty or so Captains and Validus rushed towards them from behind the black curtains of the throne room.

Quickly, they grabbed Sulwyn, forcing her hard onto her knees. They shoved a drenched cloth into her face, no doubt poisoning her. She struggled valiantly but her body started to slacken. Galahad made one step towards her before a hand grabbed his shoulder, then another grabbed his wrist. More grabbed his legs and torso. They surrounded him, holding him in place, but he would not give up. He could not let Artaxiad take her, separate her from him. He just needed to take another step.

And another.

His hand reached out, grazing her fingers.

A sharp pain radiated through his head and dazzling stars erupted before his eyes. Someone had tried to knock him out with something rather hard. He tried and failed to keep standing, one knee on the black-and-white tiles. The spots of red stone taunted him like blood drops, his own blood dripping from his head and falling atop them.

There was no choice.

He would need to release any power he had. Show them who he truly was and what they were dealing with. That sandy, gritty throb of blackness danced around the edges of his eyes. The rise in power thrummed through him.

And then it all stopped.

Sulwyn's gaze, in her last moments of consciousness, connected with his and she shook her head. Then she was falling to the ground, arms securing her limp body just as another hard strike lashed his head and all he could hear was King Artaxiad's laughter echo around him just before blackness swallowed his mind.

❧

| DAIJIRO |

Daijiro bid Galahad and Sulwyn goodbye before he rushed off to the Solus, Sulwyn's void-dark grey eyes haunting him. Such defeat. Such confusion. But he could understand it.

He had listened to the few words he could hear just before Sulwyn cut Queen Pandora's throat. Slashed her in such a vicious way, it confused him. It wasn't like her to be that violent. Even when she killed the first Validus Leader, Caldwell, in rage; it was desperation, not animalistic. There was something so incredibly wrong with all of it, but there was nothing he could say about her disastrous plan to make a move on the Empire.

He'd tortured and beheaded his own father, but this was different. Sulwyn made that evident with the look in her eyes. So empty. Despite the fact that her parents left her to die at birth. Despite the fact that they destroyed the High City for their own gain, erecting the Empire in its place. Despite the savage twist of the knife as it slashed through tender flesh.

"Ah, Sulwyn," he mumbled, passing a hand over his face just as he entered the underground tunnels of the Solus. Immediately, he made his way to the only cell that was heavily guarded, the door still open, unable to lock without his key.

Daijiro's eyes fell on Gwydion's kneeling form within the Pain Cell walls. His disguise as a humble scholar and friend of the people long gone. Instead of the soft grey tunic and pants, short brown hair and glasses framing kind brown eyes and an approachable face. Instead of all of that, it was a Devinal of all things, that knelt before him.

The real Gwydion's long black and indigo hair was a mess down his back and shoulders. The flowing purple and blue robes of silk and cotton were dirty from being dragged by the Validus to this very cell. His violet eyes pierced Daijiro's crimson ones in a look that could never be considered kind and he carried magic power stronger than any of them had seen.

Silence spread between them, neither moving, neither speaking. Something like a burning itch sat at the pit of his stomach every time he saw Gwydion's smirk. There was more to him than just being a Devinal. But he couldn't figure it out and that annoyed him more.

Daijiro could not leave the Solus yet. He would talk to Sulwyn soon, but for now, he needed to focus on the task at hand. He could not trust anyone else to handle Gwydion, especially if he tried to escape with his unknown power. He knew Gwydion was humouring them. It had been far too easy to bring him under arrest. They didn't know how strong he was, but he had kept the main castle of the Empire, Valens Muros and the maze of a prison, the Solus, under magic for years without anyone noticing. And if Sulwyn was right, he was more involved with bringing Raghnall, better known as the Steel Warrior, to the Empire than they realised, something that shouldn't have been easy in the first place as he was head of the fallen High City's army and mentor to Sulwyn herself.

Unease rippled within him.

"Sir!" called a voice as a man with yellow eyes wearing the Validus uniform jogged towards him. Daijiro turned his eyes to Demir for a fraction of a second, returning them to Gwydion watching his smirk grow confident.

Demir bowed but stepped closely, whispering in his ear, "The king has taken Sulwyn captive…"

"What?" Daijiro turned to look at him, eyes wide. It hadn't even been an hour since he last saw her. Why? There was no way Artaxiad could have figured out that it was Sulwyn who killed the queen. Her plan was haphazard at best, based on a vision she had and wild emotions. But they were still careful. What the hell was Galahad doing?

Daijiro stared at Demir. He was a pest and ultimately trying to earn favour wherever he could get it, even though he was already a member of Validus Uferor En. But he knew he also had a sense of honour, and after going on a mission with Sulwyn, he seemed to keep her in high regard—even if he didn't know her truth.

That she was forced to come to the Empire and act the part of their Blood Princess. That for whatever reason, she was betrayed by the man who had saved and raised her, the ever-revered Steel Warrior. And though that in itself was suspicious, it didn't change the fact that they travelled across Vartugaul, doing their best to keep it safe under their titles as Steel Warrior and Kintana.

Demir cast a glance at Gwydion but continued to whisper, "He's going to make her queen…"

A faint pulse ticked against Daijiro's eye. What a sick bastard. "Where the hell is Galahad?" he asked quietly, still staring at Gwydion, who hadn't moved, though his head was downcast.

"He went with her. They were called to meet with the king in the throne room shortly after it had been transformed for mourning. But it seems the king had other plans. They were separated. Knocked the prince out and locked him in the upper dungeons for now… I don't know where they took the Lady Princess."

Daijiro sneered. "How many of our men did that take?"

"About twenty…"

"Looks like he's already made his move," Gwydion interrupted unexpectedly, looking up.

"What do you know?" demanded Daijiro.

"Artaxiad has a fascination with power and blood. His *desire* for it is unmatched. It only makes sense that he would aim for Sulwyn now that

Pandora is dead—he's no longer blinded by his ambition. This is his chance to reach a higher strength with her by his side."

"What is that supposed to even mean?" He seethed.

Gwydion shrugged, an annoying smirk across his features.

"She is not someone to be underestimated." Daijiro stepped forwards. He signalled for Demir to move back.

"I don't believe so either. But neither am I, and I think you've been doing that for a while now. Guarding me all alone? You have admirable confidence… or stupidity."

"I won't make sacrifices for your cause. I am more than enough." Daijiro stepped forwards again, but soon, a strange sensation, like cool water, trickled over him. He glanced at Demir, who shivered, unaware. It took him a second to realise that the magic barrier around the Solus was fading. Daijiro growled, his frustration growing as he rushed towards Gwydion and kicked him hard in the gut.

Winded, Gwydion fell back and clenched his stomach in pain as he laughed in strangled breaths.

"Irritation is all over your face, Daijiro. You remind me of someone I knew once upon a time." But Daijiro couldn't care less about who he reminded him of. Artaxiad had taken Sulwyn while he was stuck here dealing with this garbage. He knew Galahad couldn't show his power, but Daijiro had no worries with that. Had he stayed, he could have stopped it. So Daijiro aimed his fury at Gwydion's face, holding him in place and punching him hard enough that he bruised his own knuckles in the process.

"You should have learned stronger magic to aid you. As a Velyūn, a half-bred Velikat and human man of all things, you have that right…" Gwydion coughed, spitting out blood and smirking. But Daijiro could only stare, looking at him like he'd never seen him.

"I know what a Velyūn is. Just like I know Zalika is one as well. It's not that difficult to discern once you know what you are looking for." Daijiro's hold over Gwydion faltered for a second, inhaling deeply for a breath. He sat up quickly, butting Daijiro in the stomach with his head and forcing him back.

"Tell Galahad it's only going to get harder from now on. He'll know what I'm talking about." He stood swiftly, the chains around his feet and arms melting into nothingness. "This was your only chance to kill me, Daijiro. Remember that."

"NO!" roared Daijiro, putting two and two together much too late. The barrier finally shattered, and with it, Gwydion shifted, disappearing altogether.

Daijiro shrieked in rage, rushing forwards and smashing the cell walls, over and over, earning more blood from his knuckles.

❦❧

<h1 style="text-align:center">|ILDRI|</h1>

The air tingled, nudging her skin in cold and warm waves, building and building until it no longer tingled.

It burned.

Ildri shifted in her sleep against the hard, cold floor, trying and failing to ignore the burning that now shifted and became a cool wave from the tip of her head before slowly pooling down. She bolted awake, standing quickly while breathing in the stale air of the small, solitary cell around her—the Pain Cells.

The magic around the Solus was lifting along with her own magic, taking in the nature that had been blocked for almost twenty-four years. Peeling away, layer after layer, until finally, it shattered. A sudden surge of magic erupted in the distance until that, too, was gone. Someone removed the barrier and shifted themselves out of the Solus. But Ildri couldn't let herself wonder too long on that matter.

Because now, she was free, and soon, the rest of them would be too.

| GALAHAD |

The trial to convict Gwydion was canceled the following day, and the fact that Gwydion had escaped left everyone in even more confusion. There were many people who refused to believe he murdered the queen. Once news spread that Zander, Pandora's brother, had disappeared as well, everyone was quick to conclude that he was responsible for her death instead. He was the better option. He had reason to betray her as she murdered their parents when they took the High City. They made him out to be the enemy instead of Gwydion—including Artaxiad.

Galahad and Daijiro sat within the Proelium Terra, rows and rows of carved stone benches filled with the Privileged who lived and benefited from the Empire, including any bloodshed that we may. All looked up at Artaxiad's form as he stood at the edge of the precipice.

"My people, it has been a few days since your former queen has passed. The search for her brother will continue until we have justice. As we mourn, we cannot show weakness. We are strong. We are mighty. To continue providing you with this might and this protection, I have named Sulwyn our new queen!"

Galahad clenched his jaw, hands balled into fists. Artaxiad had lost his mind; even the Empire was shocked by his words and rash actions, but soon, they started to applaud, unsure of all else and having no choice but to follow.

"Distraught by loss, she is recovering. But she is young, and she has proven herself. Alongside me, we will continue to lead you in confidence! Do look forwards to the near future. I will have a grander announcement to give you, followed by a wonderful night to come. To lift our spirits and to spread throughout the land that no group or treason can bring us down!"

II

Grey Eyes In Chains ...Again

| TARU |

THESE were not voices he was familiar with. They were calm yet urgent, soft yet powerful, one but many. And they all kept hissing the same thing over and over.

"Danger..."

"Danger..."

"Danger!"

He shot up, his body heavy, arms waving wildly around him, dirt pitching up. He placed a withered hand to his erratic heart, breath coming as if he had run for miles and miles.

"Sulwyn..." the man whispered, sitting for just a few seconds, but was distracted, jumping up and yelling into the dark, the campfire already out.

"I am not abandoning you!" Taru turned to the small rock he had been sharing stories with during the last few nights. After Galahad and Sulwyn had left the fog town, the other residents began to quickly pack up and leave after the truth of their leader Tamesis was revealed, as well as the horrors he had inflicted upon the Kurome clan, Galahad's clan. Shortly after, the abandoned town was flooded with Empire personnel, including Néosan and King Artaxiad himself. They scoured the town for days, searching for secrets or anything they could find.

With the fog gone, the town was easy to find. And though Taru knew he was capable of handling the situation if he stayed, he decided against it.

His shoes were scared.

"I will find you again, and besides, I could never forget *you*." He turned dramatically to a large tree with wide branches and purple leaves. "I told you, I was only trespassing for a little while. Travelling, as it were. That means I can't stay forever. And definitely not now." His ability to hear the soul in any object made others think he was crazy. But Taru was far from that… though still a little crazy.

Taru quickly began to pack up his small camp, washing his thin, wrinkled face and lilac tufted hair in the river. He glanced at his reflection. He was paler than he would like, always fond of his dark olive skin like a tree. But there was nothing for it when he was on the run. Soon, he whistled for Hana, his horse companion of the last few years. She trudged through the trees sleepily, her bright blue eyes visibly upset and glaring into his mismatched grey and light brown irises. Just as Taru was about to mount the horse, he hesitated and ran back towards the small rock, picking it up and taking it with him in his already heavy bag.

"What's one more, hmm?" he said to Hana, who only neighed as if she were sighing at his antics. "We ride for the Empire…" he then said seriously, and they always seem to come out great. And Hana took off at a gallop.

கை

It was dawn some days later by the time he reached the Empire, and the security around the walls was unusually high. This slowed his progress tremendously. Lines upon lines of sellers, guests and Privileged alike coming back from their journeys covered the land in front of him. By the time he passed through three levels of checking, prodding, and questions, he was finally in front of the large iron doors, the vast, black stone walls stretching out forever on both sides, displaying the sheer size of the Empire and what they had achieved.

It had been many, many years since he had been, since the good years of the High City, if not longer. The iron doors loomed over him, casting them all into dark shadows in the rising sun.

"Visitors are being monitored. State your purpose," said a bored Néosan through the smaller door for singular entry.

Taru dismounted Hana, walking closer to hear the door better. "I am an old friend of the prince; I am here on his request." The Néosan looked at him properly for the first time and with slight apprehension.

"Name?"

"Taru… and this is Hana," he said brightly, addressing his horse. The Néosan looked him over skeptically, but Taru knew how he appeared: old and feeble. A few seconds later, the guard passed him off as a nonthreat.

"I don't really care what your relation to the prince is, but word of advice? Friend or foe, the prince is in a rage and may kill you." He smirked, but his eyes were terrified. The man opened the doors to let him in. Taru smiled and nodded, leading Hana through, but his face darkened as soon as he passed the eyes of the Néosan.

He waited for his escort to Galahad. As soon as Taru hit the streets of the Empire, he knew something was terribly wrong. He knew much about the Empire, the people that lived there, and how they carried on. But darkness hovered over them all. The source was the looming castle of Valens Muros far in the distance.

Privileged and Common Ones alike wore clothes of dark red and black, keeping their heads down and their bodies tense.

Someone had died.

Taru paused, wondering if it was Sulwyn, but the Néosan shoved him along, the people barely looking at him.

"The path isn't a long one, but faster on horse. Ride it," he grunted, obviously annoyed that his job was to guide this old man to the prince. Taru silently obliged, watching as the second castle, Eques Muros, came into view. Activity was high around the castle, preparations being made for something he didn't know, Néosan of every level running in and out.

As they reached the open back area of grassy fields, Taru left Hana to her own accord and followed the Néosan through Eques to the upper floors.

They stopped just shy of a door that led off to the right. "That is where you will find the prince. Don't do anything that would get you killed, which right now could just be breathing." He chuckled as if it were a funny joke. They were clearly thrilled with whatever Galahad's behaviour had become. "We don't want to wipe you off the floor..." The Néosan saluted before going back the way he came.

Taru hated this castle.

Everything here was too loud and whiny. The carpet was upset; they hated all the boots. The mirrors were tired of seeing uniformed men and women gallivanting through the halls. And the walls were tense. Tense with the fear building within Eques. Even though the door protested at being knocked (it was rather upset; it had been slammed too often in the last few days), he knocked anyway.

Within a hair's breadth, the wooden door was yanked open, and Taru was now face-to-face with the adopted prince of Vartugaul, Galahad, who looked worse for wear.

Taru first met Galahad many years ago when he was still a boy, and his clan had not been destroyed and killed off save for a few survivors. Back then, he had read Galahad's soul, noting that the time would come when he would have trouble controlling his power. But it had elevated and grown far too quickly in a short amount of time since he saw him over a month ago. Taru kept his guard up, studying Galahad's multicoloured eyes of indigo, scarlet, and violet. Eyes with three colours, the signature trait of the Kurome clan, always dazzling but, in Galahad's case, always haunted.

"Taru?!" Whatever hostility he had been holding melted away upon seeing Taru in front of his door, in Eques no less. Galahad pulled him into the room.

Taru looked around. Tables upturned, the sofas on their sides, the chairs smashed against the walls. Galahad's unique sword lay across the bed as if waiting to be used at any moment. The room was trashed, things littering the wood floor and carpets. He looked back at Galahad.

"Sorry, please… sit. Why are you here? How did you get here?"

"Hana," he said, simply taking one of the surviving chairs (it was terrified) and placing it upright again to face the darkened grate.

"Hana?"

"My horse."

Galahad took a deep breath. Taru could sense the danger, watching as he clenched both fists with knuckles that were cut and bruised. His shoulders tense, his demeanour edgy and barely holding back whatever hostility he carried.

"Why have you come *here*, Taru, to the Empire?" he asked solemnly.

"Sulwyn…" But at the mention of her name, Galahad's face darkened, his expression murderous. Taru's face fell. "What has happened?"

"Pandora is dead. Sulwyn is queen," he grunted.

Out of everything Taru had been imagining, this was not one of them. How did things get this far? Pandora was dead?

"Sulwyn's soul reached out to me, with the aid of the Seers past. She is in danger, and they can only help her so much," said Taru gravely, but before he could say more, the door burst open and a small girl with long indigo hair ran in.

"I knew it! I knew it was you! I heard Hana!" she squealed and tackled Taru.

"Arsinone! You can't run into his room unannounced!" reprimanded another voice.

"But he's my grandfather, Ez!" She hugged Taru tighter, and he hugged her just so.

"Oh! My child, my dear, dear child," he cried, patting her head.

"At least something nice is happenin'…" Eztli said, looking on.

"Have you seen anything?" Galahad asked, impassive to the scene before him. Taru observed them over Arsinone's shoulder. Eztli's eyes were wide with terror, but she held it in, her stance strong.

"We haven't been allowed to see her yet… We don't even know where in the castle she could be."

"Dungeon. We know she's underground somewhere… And it's not in the lower or upper," chimed Arsinone, "but I can't hear her. Something is wrong with her."

Taru watched Galahad close his eyes, tensing for a second, a tremor running through his body as he fought against himself.

"You've come all this way, Taru, but I'm sorry I cannot stay with you right now…" Galahad started, his eyes closed tightly.

Taru watched Eztli beckon Arsinone forwards to follow her out of the room quietly.

"I'll see you later, Gee-Gee," whispered Arsinone, carefully watching Galahad as well. Both girls took their leave quickly.

"Please make yourself at home and get some rest. You must have travelled far. I'll see you later…"

"When *was* the last time you saw her?" Taru asked quietly. He knew exactly what he was doing, trying to tread as carefully as he could. But knew that Galahad had already started losing control for some time now. At least since they reunited in the fog town, he could see it. Galahad's control had been slipping, his power progressing faster than it should have, and this incident was only making it worse.

He breathed through clenched teeth. "A week ago… The night Pandora was killed by Sulwyn…"

"Sulwyn did? Does Artaxiad know? Is that why he has her?"

"No, he doesn't. He's been fooled by a Devinal left to run free," he ground out. "He's taken her because he has a sick infatuation with her. And he's keeping me—us—from her."

Taru looked at the black voids of Galahad's now-opened eyes. Almost all the colour was gone now, just bits of it bleeding through the centre.

"I need to leave, Taru. I'm sorry." Galahad turned abruptly, crossing the room and slamming the door shut. Taru could hear his clothes complaining further and further away, leaving Eques altogether.

≈

| S U L W Y N |

The colour of blue and black flittered through her mind, easing in and out along the wind and the trees. She watched a small, older man riding atop a black horse with a blue sheen. Like how her own horse, Ki, shone red in the sun. What was Ki doing right now?

A cool draft blew past her, sending a fit of shivers across her skin. Her body weighed on her, right down to the bone, with confusion the only distraction. A subtle drip echoed in the distance, water hitting stone.

Drip.

Drip.

Drip.

It was oddly calming yet irritating at the same time. But soon, that sound faded into the background, giving way to the numbness in her hands and arms. Sulwyn tried to move but only the sound of chains echoed around her.

Chains?

She moved her heavy arms again, but the rattle was there. Slowly, she opened her eyes. Something that should have taken a fraction of a second took her minutes. Light in the far distance swam into her vision, burning her sensitive eyes. She blinked a few times, urging the burn away. Each time she blinked, her eyes came into focus, until finally, she realised she was in the back of an enormously large stone space.

A prison cell.

But this was not like the ones in the lower or upper dungeons of Valens, nor was it like the ones in the Solus. Was she still in the Empire?

Soon, her body began to catch up with her mind. How did she get here? What happened? Sulwyn looked down, catching the short black and red fabric in the flickering light. What the hell was this dress, and why was she so exposed?

"Has she awakened?" asked a voice in the distance too far for her to see.

"The king administered more last night, but he should be around to do so again soon. She's been knocked out the whole time."

"Artaxiad?" Sulwyn muttered. As she sat in thought, her memories came back to her in a whirl of patterns, sound and despair.

The night was full of colours and magic that wasn't really magic. She could see Kione's bewildered face as Eztli piled tarts atop a plate for him. Saw Galahad's air of shyness and unsureness when they first met for the night. Felt Daijiro's eyes on her as they danced gently to the sounds of tinkling music, Daijiro's hands like fire against her skin.

It would have been a peaceful night had the Empire not defiled Caldwell's memory. Had they not captured and tortured Arsinone. She could see the warm blood coating her hands and drenching her dress in these cold memories.

She had killed her mother and queen, Pandora, but Pandora had planned for Sulwyn's survival, not just abandoning her in a burning house as she originally thought.

Sulwyn heaved, a panic rising in her chest.

"Should she be here though?" one of the men whispered, bringing her back to the present.

"Well, it's a little odd for her to be *here*. She lost a mother as well. But the king said it was in her best interest. Distraught with sadness..."

"You think being queen would give you special treatment... Wouldn't that be better spent in a bed?"

Being queen? What did that mean?

"But why does he want to rule alongside his daughter? Isn't that a little..."

"No one to trust better than she, no?" finished one, but soon they both stopped talking as footsteps could be heard in the distance.

"Has she awakened?" called a voice, and Sulwyn instantly recognised it as Artaxiad's. She let herself fall limp. Artaxiad had made her queen? The sick, twisted…

Memories of walking into a large white room flashed through her, Artaxiad sitting on a throne next to Pandora's that was draped in black.

He spoke smoothly. "It's been long enough. I think she will be safe coming back with me…" A few seconds later, she could hear the jangle of keys and the sound of an iron door opening. Sulwyn closed her eyes, sagging further.

It took everything in her not to flinch at his touch as he grabbed her chin in his hand. With this action, she was vividly reminded of how he kissed her before she passed out. Many men had surrounded her and Galahad, keeping them apart while they held the drugged cloth to her face. Where was Galahad? The last thing she saw was him kneeling on the ground, blood coating his brown hair and dripping down the side. A stark contrast to his pale skin.

And his eyes.

His eyes that threatened to turn black. She couldn't allow that. Didn't allow that, she was sure.

"Even down here, you are as beautiful as ever, Sulwyn…" His voice brought her back as he moved his hand towards her neck, his palm on the side as if she was his lover. She tried her best not to throw up or to headbutt him at his closeness. He brought his hand back up, holding her chin with his fingers, and she acted in kind. Sulwyn lolled her head, opening her eyes for a fraction of a second before she rolled them back.

For someone who had just lost his wife, he looked ecstatic.

"We can't be too careful, now, can we?" His arm brushed her, beckoning someone forwards. His hand left her face and she flopped down once more.

"Sulwyn, dear, precious Sulwyn, do you know what your title is?"

She hesitated. Why was he asking her something like this? What was she supposed to say? She clenched her jaw, choosing to slowly shake her head instead.

"That's okay… because I am here to teach you. You are *my* queen now, Sulwyn, and the queen of Vartugaul."

Sulwyn tried her hardest to stop her body from shivering from the icy fear that ran through her. He had lost his mind. Absolutely and devastatingly so. And she was screwed, so beyond screwed. She opened her eyes weakly; enough to see one of the Captains place a small, ornate wooden box next to Artaxiad.

"This is medicine. It will help you with your grief and confusion. This ordeal has taken its toll on us all. It will make you stronger. Fit enough to rule alongside me."

Sulwyn wanted to fight, but she would get nowhere being chained like this. Terror dropped into her heart, spreading more ice through her veins. A sharp pain made its way into her neck and she gasped, opening her eyes widely to see Artaxiad place a small syringe with a dark green residue back into the box. But there were three others, an orange, a purple and a blue one. What the hell were these?!

"There, there… All good things have to hurt a little at first, right? Even if I borrowed the knowledge, Gwydion isn't the only one who can study science."

Gwydion?

He had gotten these things from him?

Wasn't he the enemy? Artaxiad should have been angry with him, but that's not what it sounded like.

What happened to Gwydion?

Artaxiad injected the second, orange in colour, and Sulwyn's thoughts slowed. By the time he injected all four, she was limp. Her consciousness trying and failing to stay awake. She heard the rattle of keys again before she slumped into Artaxiad's arms.

The chains had been removed.

A tingling numbness snaked through her, her mind on the border of consciousness but not yet falling into it. Artaxiad lifted her up and cradled her into his chest. As he walked, the air touched her skin, which now pulsed hot and cold. The terror never left her, and instead of staying in the safety of this dungeon, she was being carried along stairs, up to wherever it was he was taking her, alone.

Finally, her mind gave in, and the remaining tension sagged out of her. The last thing she heard was Artaxiad's deep chuckle.

III

A Little Too Close For "Brotherhood"

| GALAHAD |

FOR most of the day Galahad wandered through Tranquilium Forest that bordered Antiqua and the Empire. By the time he came back to Eques, it was night, and he had missed all of his duties as he had done when Sulwyn was in a coma, which wasn't that long ago. And though he knew he shouldn't be acting this way now; it was impossible not to.

He'd been right there.

Just a few steps, and he could have taken her from Artaxiad's grasp. But as soon as he saw her shake her head, he knew he had lost. In the end, she had protected him, kept his power secret and let herself be taken. Anger seized him and he lashed out along the halls of the first floor, hitting a black vase and watching it shatter.

Now she was trapped with Artaxiad, stuck like a possession, and he couldn't do anything about it. Not unless he was prepared to turn the entire Empire against her, and before he could get that far, they would all be killed.

Galahad made his way up the flights of stairs, slightly aware that everyone dashed out of his way as he walked. Taking a deep breath, he opened his door to see Arsinone, Taru and Eztli all having tea.

"What are you doing?" he asked scathingly. It irritated him to see something so mundane happening when he was here, frustrated at his immobility.

"Waitin' for ya…" Eztli said abruptly, just as Nori came through the doorway, curtsying quickly.

"He's decided it!" she said breathlessly, edging slightly away from Galahad and more towards Taru.

"Boy, stop making the sheets angry!" barked Taru unexpectedly. They all looked at him as he confronted the pillow.

Galahad begged everything and everyone around him for patience. "*What* has been decided?"

Nori looked at him, caution in every movement she made. "The king… In two days he's holding a small coronation for Sulwyn to ascend as queen… and…"

He could see she was afraid to continue. Watching her like this, knowing he was the cause of this, tore at him more. "Continue, Nori… please." He took a seat in one of the chairs that Taru had repaired.

She breathed out. "He specifically called for us to be her attendants that day…"

Tension rose along his spine and neck. Though that fact should have thrilled him, he knew Artaxiad was not stupid, no matter how unstable he had become. He would never allow anyone that could be on her side near her without reason. What was he playing at?

"Even if this is a trap, I'm gonna see her. We must be present for the coronation anyway," Eztli said from her corner.

"Me too!" Arsinone added, her uneven eyes, one orange, one brown, both fierce.

He couldn't stop them even if he wanted to. "I can't protect you if you choose to go. I've been banned from Valens," Galahad snapped irritably.

"As it is, that ban doesn't apply to me," said a voice behind him. Galahad sensed him and relief washed over him. But he would never admit to it.

Daijiro told Galahad what happened in the Solus and about Gwydion's escape that had been hidden from the public, as well as Artaxiad's plan to reach higher power, but unsure how.

"When did you get back?" Galahad turned to look at Daijiro, his blond and white hair tied back in a mess. He was dirty, travelling for as long as he did. His pristine yellow and black clothing was in need of repair. Even the sash he wrapped around his waist was worse for wear. But Daijiro just leaned against the door frame casually, his hands still bandaged from when he tried to beat Gwydion and the Solus walls. He wanted them to heal naturally as punishment for letting Gwydion escape.

Daijiro had been sent out to look for Zander, but Galahad knew he was only searching for signs of Gwydion or Diesirae. He had also gotten Kione out of the Empire and into hiding for now—who was also using this chance to try and find Diesirae, his sister. He knew Kione felt responsible because she was his kin.

"Who's that?" Daijiro disregarded his question altogether and pointed at Taru.

Galahad looked at the old man, frowning a bit at the apprehensive look he gave Daijiro.

"Taru, Arsinone's grandfather and an old family friend. He—" But before he could mention his ability to read the history of a soul, Taru cut him off.

"I haven't seen one of you in a long time," he huffed, but soon turned his attention to one of the teacups.

Daijiro eyed him suspiciously but turned back to Galahad. "I got back not too long ago. Already made my report to our lovely king about how we've passed on a message that a new queen will be appointed in the days to follow to the surrounding towns. But I came back earlier and let the Néosan do it instead. They don't need me, and I shouldn't be away from the Empire long. I thought you should know, though. Valens is heavily guarded, particularly the room next to his own."

"Sulwyn must be in it now," said Galahad, standing as if to go there, but Arsinone jumped up instead.

"We should be heading back. I'll try and listen for her now that she's out of her prison…" Arsinone said, kissing Taru on the forehead. Eztli and Nori took their leave, waving to Taru.

"Taru, have you had dinner?" Galahad asked, but his thoughts were elsewhere.

"No, not yet… just this tea and snacks…" he answered simply, but Galahad could see the understanding in his eyes. "I've already called for Arsinone to wait. They can guide me to the kitchens."

"Don't draw any attention to yourself," Galahad whispered, holding the door open for him.

As soon as he was out the door, Galahad launched himself at Daijiro and pushed him against the now-closed door. Daijiro looked up at him, not in surprise or fear, but concern.

"You've gotten worse." He kept his arms up in surrender. Galahad's hands gripped his collar tightly. "Is there a reason you have me pinned to a door? I do assure you, I'm not *that* attracted to you. Though if you are interested…" Daijiro said nonchalantly.

"Can I trust you?" asked Galahad, his voice more like a plea than anything. The last few weeks were chaotic, but Daijiro had proved time and time again that he was definitely not one with the Empire. But in his state, he needed to be sure. He needed someone on whom he could rely. Someone he could trust to watch him.

"I won't sell myself to you. You can trust me if you want to." He relaxed his arms, bringing them to his side.

Galahad knew it made no difference; his eyes were fully black. He knew more than Galahad ever wanted anyone to. "Are you a threat to her?" His grip tightened.

Daijiro smirked, but his crimson eyes were serious. "You really like to hear me talk, don't you?" Daijiro looked him over before guiding his eyes back up to his.

Silence spread between them until finally, Galahad let go, stepping back. Daijiro readjusted his tunic before he held his palm forwards and forced

Galahad painfully down to his knees with that troublesome ability of his. Daijiro sat on the wooden floor, cross-legged, watching him, but his ability to paralyse without touch never wavered.

"I can't let you be the only one having fun. I've told you before. I'm not a good person... I've seen a lot of bloodshed and caused just as much, if not more. Far more than you in both aspects." He smiled widely; eyes feral. "Your temper rivals mine, but where you try to suppress it and for obvious reasons, I let it run wild. I stopped caring about what happened to anyone around me, what I've done or haven't done. I'm not like Caldwell. I don't have that sort of regret. But meeting Sulwyn... and getting to know you... Well, I might not die for you... I can't say I'd die for her either, but I'll fight for both of you." He paused, looking at Galahad carefully. "I swear it on my mother." He released his hold on Galahad, standing and reaching his hand out. Galahad hesitated for just a moment before grasping his arm. Daijiro pulled him up, slapping him on the shoulder.

"At least until I'm bored, and I promise, I'll try not to misbehave." He winked.

৽৵

| SULWYN |

Sulwyn lay in silence as maids with voices she didn't recognise moved about the room, tidying and cleaning and whatever else it was that needed to be done. She had no memory of what happened in or after she left the cell or when she got to this room on this bed. She didn't even know if any time had passed at all until she started to listen to one of the maids speaking quietly.

"I heard it's tomorrow..." said one maid.

"Well, it's smaller, right? Much smaller than the first coronation... A few hundred people or so, but it's supposed to be really elegant."

Something within Sulwyn was rising, like deep hate and a sort of itch that she could never reach from the inside of her soul. But she continued to listen, lying there on the soft bed.

"I heard he's announcing something else…" she continued, pausing before lowering her voice further. "They say the king's gone crazy, lost his mind completely…"

"Enough!" yelled Sulwyn, sitting up and staring at the maids in the distance. They were a bit further than she thought, all frozen in terror. "We don't pay you to run your mouth. You are here to work, not slander the Empire!" she continued to shout, the hate in her subsiding, the itch a little duller now. She frowned, waves of dizziness crashing into her, the room swaying.

"Awake?" Artaxiad asked, coming from a door far on the left. Sulwyn glimpsed the hall, but it wasn't a hall. It was another bedroom, and she now realised she was in Pandora's old room, connected to Artaxiad's. This room was fairly large. Her bedroom doors were wide open, displaying a massive sitting and dining area, the door Artaxiad had come through, another door off to the right, and many other doors she figured were closets scattered around. But most of Pandora's personal effects had been removed, the room clean and clear.

He smiled, seemingly proud of her outburst, before dismissing the other maids. They dashed out quickly, looking back for a millisecond before closing the door.

"It's becoming of you to act with such authority." He walked forwards, his dark black robes trailing behind him. "Tomorrow is a big day for you. Not as grand as your initial coronation, no, but special all the same. We must save it for a bigger event in the next few weeks." His dull green eyes looked at her as if she weren't truly there. A scar ran from one eye down his cheek, while another crossed through from his nose to his ear. Who had given him that?

She breathed deeply, but words and thoughts would not formulate much for her. The hateful irritation from before had died down completely, and instead, a wave of calm at seeing Artaxiad rushed through her.

"Then I need to be presentable." She heard the words she spoke, unaware of thinking them.

"Indeed, and so I've brought some extra help. Tonight, they will help you bathe. You are still weak from your coma and with grief, as are we all. Come, let me bring you to the bathing room."

Artaxiad crossed over, licking his lips as he came beside her bed and uncovered her. She had been changed into a dark red nightdress, a little more exposed than she would have normally liked, but the thoughts would not hold and floated away. Artaxiad bent over, placing her arm over his shoulder and his arm under her legs. With a quiet grunt, he lifted her off the bed, holding her delicately as he crossed the room to the other side into a large bathing room.

A knock sounded from one of the doors. He gently placed her on a small, decorated chair that sat in front of an old, white vanity. She faced the bathroom door, waiting.

"I'll be back tomorrow to escort you. Take your time and let yourself be pampered." He smiled sweetly, turning to leave. "Take good care of her," she heard him say, chuckling as he left the room and closed the door with a snap.

One girl with brown hair and dark skin and another with light brown hair and pale skin walked into the bathing room carrying soaps, washes and towels. The girl with dark skin looked familiar, but the other she was sure she had never seen before.

"Eztli and Robyn at yer service." They curtsied respectfully, placing all the objects down on the marble top. Sulwyn watched them with a stony glare as they bustled around, drawing the bath and adding fragrances. Soon, both women stepped towards her to help her undress, leading her to the tub. As she raised her leg carefully into the water, the girl named Robyn squeezed her arm tightly, pain shooting through her.

Sulwyn flinched, knocking the girl's arm away. "Be careful! How long have you been here that you can't even assist me properly?" she snapped.

The girl looked at her but quickly bowed in shame. "I'm sorry, I was trying to make sure you didn't slip..."

"Are you talking back to me?"

"Sulwyn…" Eztli whispered.

Sulwyn snapped her attention to her instead. "How dare you address me by name? I am not your friend. You are not someone I know. I am the queen, and I expect you to treat me as such!" The sharp slap that followed echoed throughout the room.

Eztli's eyes were wide, tears welling up, but soon, she blinked them away and bowed deeply. "I do apologise."

"Just do your job…" berated Sulwyn.

ഏ∽

Sulwyn awoke in the middle of the night in the centre of her large, soft bed. The space between starting her bath to this moment was completely blank. What happened?

A knock sounded on her door before opening, someone peering in, followed by the snap of a closing door. A few minutes later, the door opened wide, and Artaxiad strode in, his face set in hard lines.

"I see you're awake. What is the last thing you remember?"

Sulwyn stared at him, her mind coming up blank. "I was going for a bath…"

He looked at her solemnly. "Remember, Sulwyn. It pains me more to do this than you can imagine." He called for someone beyond the door.

A Néosan and a maid came in, one carrying a familiar, ornate wooden box, another carrying a long, thin metal whip.

"Good help is hard to come by, and I can't have you murdering them on a whim. You must be corrected." He took the whip and swished it slightly. "You may leave us," he addressed the two. They bowed and took their leave.

"I don't understand," Sulwyn said, a strange, cold wave of prickliness running through her. Had she killed someone? How could she not remember that? Who did she kill? She vaguely remembered both the maids, remembered slapping the one named Eztli. Had it been her? Pain shot through her chest, but soon it dulled into nothingness as she looked up at Artaxiad's eyes. Dead and calm.

"It hurts me more, my queen."

He pulled the sheets back, exposing her delicate blue nightgown, and brought the whip down onto her bare legs. She grunted in pain, the cold metal burning thin white lines, enflaming into pink onto her skin.

"Explain your reasoning!" she demanded, and somehow this triggered a dangerous shift in Artaxiad.

"You may be queen, but I am still the king, and I expect you to show me some respect." His words, similar to her own from where she couldn't remember, were cold as he whipped her again. He reached forwards and roughly turned her onto her stomach, aiming for the back of her legs. Sulwyn screamed, confusion rising in her until even that was clouded as he moved the whip to hit her back.

What seemed like hours was only a few minutes until he was turning her around again, and she lay flat on her back. She wasn't bleeding, not that she could tell with her body on fire from the pain. But she had experienced worse.

When?

Muddled memories of a time when something similar had happened flashed through her, but the more she thought about it, the more it hurt to think until a needle jabbed into her neck, ending her struggle.

"You need a bit more patience, Sulwyn. A bit more control. I am here for you, don't forget that. My word is your strength."

She heard a lid snap close. Four pricks had gone into her neck. Her skin tingling and growing numb. All thoughts were mumbling into one. His hand reached out, hot against her face, stroking her cheek.

"Soon, we will be together, properly. Where we can raise a stronger Empire."

"Together?" mumbled Sulwyn. Wasn't that a bad thing?

"Yes, together. But for now, *I* will display patience, despite how much you call to me. With your eyes, and your... But I will stop here for tonight. Do not disappoint me again, Sulwyn."

Artaxiad left the room, and Sulwyn lay there, trembling from the pain and the burning and the assault of whatever those needles were. Soon, any thought she had faded, as did her consciousness.

§

| DAIJIRO |

"What happened to you?" Daijiro grumbled, looking up as the door bounced off the wall. Nori rushed after Eztli into Daijiro's room.

He kept staring from where he sat, reading in the far corner. Though it wasn't as large as Galahad's, it still had a decent array of space and a sitting area. And unlike Galahad's, his bedroom was hidden behind a door at the opposite end. He seemed to like everything in open spaces. Daijiro did not. He detested being exposed.

"I don't remember saying I wanted you all in my room, every day, all the time. I thought that's what the prince's room was for."

"The prince is sleeping for once, so we came here," said Arsinone, popping up behind Eztli and shutting the door gently. Daijiro sighed, looking at Eztli properly.

"What happened to your face and… Is that blood?" He stood, realising she was on the verge of tears.

"Sulwyn…" She started crying now, earning a look from all of them. Before she could form the words, the door crashed open again, and Galahad walked in, pale and sweating, until he collapsed onto the carpeted floor.

Daijiro threw the book somewhere behind him and strode across the sitting area, stooping down next to him and bringing a hand to his face. "He's cold. Bring me blankets, magic-girl, and light a fire," he demanded, and she took off back into the hall. "Little one, tell me what happened. She doesn't look like she's going to speak any time soon." He motioned to Eztli, who sat on the floor next to them.

"I can just show you…" Arsinone said, her eyes boring into his.

He admired her, knew her story, and found her quite capable for a ten-year-old who had the mind of someone far wiser. "Go ahead."

Arsinone reached forwards, touching his forehead, but froze, staring at him with wide eyes.

He looked at her carefully. She had seen something in him. But soon, she was composed and reaching forwards to touch Eztli. He smirked at her but closed his eyes.

He could see Sulwyn in front of him through Eztli's eyes. She was submerged, for the most part, in a large tub full of water and bubbles with fragrances wafting around them. He felt the subtle sting on her face. She had been slapped not too long ago.

Eztli looked from Sulwyn to another maid, but she hadn't been paying attention to what the girl had said until Sulwyn was beckoning the maid closer.

"What did you say?" she hissed, pulling the dress of the girl and bringing her to eye level.

"Just, you reminded me of our late queen... in terms of... well, everything."

"Forget her. I am your queen now, and I think it's about time I show the rest of you your place." Sulwyn pulled the maid forwards and into the tub with her.

"Sulwyn!" yelled Eztli, forgetting herself and covering her mouth.

Sulwyn glared at her. "Bring me that knife," she ordered, pointing to a small dagger that hung along the wall among other collections.

"What for... my queen?" Eztli asked, carefully stepping back.

"Unless you want me to use it on you, you will give it to me now." Sulwyn stretched out a long, slender arm, the muscle lost when she was in a coma. Eztli noticed many new cuts and welts that hadn't been there before. In fact, they were only a few days old, some bright red as the water irritated them.

The maid sat still in the tub, her clothes soaking, her legs hanging over the edge as her head was pressed against the porcelain at a weird angle.

Slowly, Eztli reached for the knife, handing it to Sulwyn.

Sulwyn brought her lips close to the girl's ear, but bore into Eztli's eyes. "You can pass this message onto any of the other help, including yourself, that I will not sit by and listen to you slander me or the Empire," she hissed.

Before the girl could scream, Sulwyn slit her throat and shoved her under the water. Red dyed the tub, climbing into the maid's clothes and dripping onto the floor. It seeped into the water, sticking onto Sulwyn.

"I'll need you to draw me another bath."

IV

You Didn't Start This Journey As Queen

| DAIJIRO |

EZTLI was beside herself in tears once Arsinone broke the connection, pulling the memories from Daijiro. A prickling coldness ran through him, but he had to attend to the matter at hand: Galahad.

Nori had gotten a fire going, warming the room quickly. Daijiro dragged Galahad closer to it, getting him warm before placing a palm on his forehead. Unlike Arsinone, Daijiro could not hear a soul, thoughts, or anything like that. But he could feel brain activity.

Just like he could control the nerves, muscles and feelings in the body, he could do the same with the mind. It was harder, a more precise practise, but it worked all the same. It was his highest form of torture, and that was why he oversaw the Solus. But he could only achieve *this* by touch.

Galahad's mind was definitely working, almost in overdrive, and so Daijiro prompted him to gain consciousness. Galahad gripped his wrist tightly, his eyes black and his expression dangerously wild until Daijiro could see recognition in his eyes, and he faltered.

"What happened to *you*?" Daijiro asked, at a loss.

"I don't know… Pain, like lashings? Flared everywhere." Galahad sat up quickly, lifting the fabric of his pant legs, exposing his skin. There were faint ghost lines of red that were quickly fading.

Daijiro sat cross-legged, bracing back on his arms, the plush cream rug enveloping his hands and his silk robe like a sea behind him. "Interesting... Little one, what have you learned?" He turned to Arsinone.

She answered immediately as if she had expected this. Besides Daijiro, she was the only calm one. "Artaxiad punishes her if she disobeys him or acts out of line. She got in trouble for killing a maid named Robyn."

"She killed a maid?" Galahad's eyes had already returned to their tricoloured state of navy, violet and ruby, but with it, he looked exhausted.

"In the same way she killed Pandora... but with less heart and no regret," Daijiro muttered darkly. He was unsettled. This was not Sulwyn. Her eyes were void of herself, and it made him even more uneasy, nervous even.

She was a light. A strength to others, she reminded him of why he came to the Empire before he had forsaken everything and given up his goal. He would not let them turn her into someone like him.

"There were small marks on her neck..." Daijiro said, thinking back to Eztli's frantic memory. From what he could see, Sulwyn was being poisoned in some way, and if she didn't act how Artaxiad wanted her to, she was tortured.

She was being conditioned.

He looked at Eztli. "She didn't recognise you?" he asked for reassurance but knew the answer before she shook her head. "Tomorrow, all three of you are going to help her get ready, right? I think we need to stir her memories. No one battles better than she does mentally. Tomorrow, we need to get her brain working."

They looked confused but nodded anyway.

"Ez, come, let's go... it's late..." Nori urged softly, throwing a sheet around Eztli's shoulders. They left the room, Arsinone trailing behind them, but she took a moment to turn back and look at Daijiro. He caught her stare but waved her off.

৩৵৶

| GALAHAD |

Galahad decided to stay the night in Daijiro's room for Taru's safety. He had almost attacked him when he started to receive burning strikes across his legs and back. If it happened again, he couldn't be sure he'd be able to control himself. It wasn't until early morning that he woke up thrashing before rolling off the couch and onto the floor with a heavy thump.

The same stinging pain coursed through him, this time over his stomach and arms. He reached forwards, rolling the tunic up his torso to see angry red lines quickly fading.

What the hell was this? Had someone used magic on him without his knowledge? But the only person out to get him that he knew of was Gwydion. If it were someone else, he'd have a hard time finding them.

"That was about a half hour long." Daijiro's voice came from his left.

Galahad watched him step over the back of the couch, settling onto the seat like a cat.

"That's how long it was last time." He breathed out deeply, a wave of exhaustion flowing through him. "You know more about magic. Am I cursed?"

"The magic-girl would have been able to tell if you were. You're looking for the wrong answer. Your clan would be ashamed."

Galahad glared at him, but soon, Daijiro was sliding off the cushions and beside him onto the wooden floor.

He looked at Galahad pointedly. "I thought about our conversation the day before, you know, during that time we were so intimately close?" He smirked when Galahad continued glaring. "I meant it..." He started using a finger to draw invisible lines over the wooden floor.

"I'm glad you haven't gotten bored yet..." said Galahad, but it took him a few seconds to realise that the lines Daijiro was drawing were not just absent-minded movements but actual lines that burned gold over the wood before fading out. Daijiro glanced up at him.

"I'm showing you something interesting to help distract you from your pain, but the one who's actually being whipped is Sulwyn, not you. So, stop bitching about them."

"What?" And then Galahad finally registered what he was writing.

They were lost letters from the Kurome clan, his clan.

"When you become close to someone, really close to them, you may share in their pain. At least, that is what I heard," Daijiro explained.

Galahad was sharing Sulwyn's pain. How could he have forgotten that? There were people in his own family that had this bond, though rare. Siblings, friends, even those that didn't get along. When a connection was strong, they started to share their emotions, but Sulwyn wasn't from his clan. She wouldn't be able to feel his, which was fine with him. He focused on Daijiro's eyes, something vulnerable in them.

"How do you know this? How do you know our letters?" A sense of paranoia and terror skittered deep within. Someone who wasn't one of his own knew this much. Much more than he ever let on, even during the fog town when Tiergan, his traitorous uncle, screamed the truth of his past and the torture Galahad suffered at his hands.

"I may have come to the Empire after you, but I knew exactly what you were when I first saw you. I don't talk about other clans' secrets. That would be a disservice to my own... And we didn't have that kind of relationship." He smirked, but his tone softened. "My mother taught them to me." Galahad raised an eyebrow, but Daijiro continued, "She used to be a teacher. Her specialty was medicinal herbs and everyday magic. She taught your clan, and in turn, learned a bit. But never much. Your people were especially secretive. She gave it up after she met a man and had me."

Galahad was quiet for a moment until a name stirred in his mind. "Seila?"

Daijiro's eyes wavered, but he concentrated on keeping the glowing letters still, his palm over them. "So, you have heard of her."

Galahad watched him smile, and it was different. It was reminiscent of a time when he must have known something similar to happiness, like how Galahad felt when he talked about his own parents.

"My parents learned some things from her. I heard about her through their stories. They travelled a lot and stayed with Velika in their youth, and in turn, she would visit. I never heard anything about Velyūn though, so I failed to notice you were one."

"As your clan has secrets, so does ours. Not as strongly, though. This is really all I know about yours."

"And your father?" Galahad asked slowly, but Daijiro stopped writing, letting the glow fade. The room seemed a little darker now despite the rising sun.

"I killed him." His voice was rough, anger beneath it. His eyes met Galahad's, considering him as the silence stretched between them. "I heard everything about you in that town, not that it was difficult with that maniac screaming half of it out. I guess I can share." He smirked, but it was dark. "They met when my mother was travelling. And for whatever reason, he stuck with her, eventually making her fall in love with him. As a Velikat, she's naturally alluring. No doubt he was drawn to it, being just a normal human. She brought him home to her village, but the rest of them were against it. Too many times, human men came and took their women only for them to end up dead once they were sold for their blood."

"Blood?"

"Some people believe it can heal, enhance or control if ingested. But it doesn't. Our power doesn't flow like that. It can't be taken and used. Maybe it could be recreated using other means, the ability to allure and persuade and control, but never could our blood be used to copy that. That ability dies as soon as it's out of the body.

"My mother wavered in her choice until she realised she was with child. She settled, and the rest accepted begrudgingly. It would be a few years after I was born, during Artaxiad's Ascendancy, that she would learn my father was a devoted follower of the king, even part of the original rebellion that Artaxiad and Pandora had started. She was afraid, but she was also blinded by what she thought was love. Even when he abused us both, tried to kill us whenever he was intoxicated or not, she never gave up." Daijiro leaned back against the couch, his dark eyes somber.

"My powers weren't what they are now. She tried to keep them hidden from him, and so I lived in fear, stunting my growth. There are many things I'm still learning even after all these years, like that fire thing to remove the arrow from Sulwyn's shoulder..." He trailed off for a second, looking past Galahad to something he couldn't see.

"I was fifteen, hunting for food. When I came back the next morning, our village had been destroyed. My people killed, my mother dead. And the only person left was that man who she loved so much," he spat out bitterly. "He killed her with his own hands. Led Artaxiad and his Néosan to our village, the only one left with our people, and slaughtered them all. That had been the plan all along. To infiltrate the last of our clan.

"When I came home, panic flooded his eyes, and I relished in it because he knew. He always knew I was stronger, but because of fear and my mother's love, I couldn't touch him. But she was dead, and there was nothing left to protect him. I watched him run, thinking he had a chance. If he could make it to Artaxiad's men, he would be safe. But he never arrived."

Daijiro looked at Galahad now, fully unhinged as he relived that moment. "I caught up to him with ease. A mere human such as himself had brought us down. A mere human like Artaxiad dared touch us, using the cover of night. We were an old village. We barely had anyone who could fight a war. I used my power properly for the first time on him. The terror... the shock that flooded him. It was beautiful. Years I had been waiting, and I made sure he felt that as I tortured him for days until he begged for mercy. Crawling and crying. Pleading and apologising. Screaming and whimpering... Then I cut off his head and went into hiding."

He stood, holding out his hand for Galahad to take. "I trained for a year. Requested an audience with Pandora and bought my way in with the heads of a hundred Néosan, bidding my time for the right moment. But just like Caldwell and anyone else, I eventually lost my way."

Galahad reached up, taking his arm to stand.

"I want Artaxiad dead, but it doesn't matter to me if I get the finishing blow. I know you and Sulwyn have just as much against him as I do. As long as I can be part of it, I'm content."

Galahad had no words. He was thirteen when Daijiro first came to the Empire, still in and out of the lower dungeons. In all the time they had been here, he had never heard Daijiro talk this much. Didn't expect this sort of story from him. He knew there was darkness, but he didn't realise how twisted it really was.

"We're both very tragic." Daijiro's tone was lighter now. "Do you want a hug? This is a brotherhood now after all, remember?"

Galahad didn't think he was serious, but he did it anyway. He stepped forwards and brought Daijiro into a short but strong hug.

"Oh..." Daijiro muttered quietly but hugged him back all the same. They stepped back, the moment a little awkward, but the bond was there. Galahad now knew Daijiro had a reason for being here, and though the way he acted was a little unconventional, it was highly effective.

"I don't think I need to go in-depth about the connection you have with Sulwyn. How could you forget that? You're a pretty shitty prince... in both aspects."

Galahad kicked his shin. "We need to come up with something soon, Daijiro. She can't stay there for too long. Even if it means becoming an enemy of the Empire."

"Relax, I'm obviously smarter than you. We do it my way first. I'm not all 'blood first, talk later'. I have a plan."

࿇

| SULWYN |

Sulwyn awoke from a chill that ran through her. She had gotten in trouble again, but she couldn't remember why. She looked down at her arms. She was not whipped hard enough to bleed, but thin, red welts marked her arms and her stomach. She pushed her nightgown down to cover herself better.

It was not his fault. The king was right, and she was wrong.

Slowly, she rolled off the bed, her skin pulling and tightening with pain. The room had been readjusted, furniture in different places to make it look new again. In the far corner, there was a small, opened box tucked under one of the large wardrobes outside the bedroom. The more she stared at it, the more the shapes began to focus.

In the box, there were a few old but well-kept children's dolls sitting atop other boxes. Sulwyn found herself slowly sliding off the bed, crawling across the dark, plush rugs, out the shady oak door, and onto the burgundy wood floors until finally, she was pulling the box out.

These were the dolls she had seen in her office all that time before. As someone who openly detested children, why did she have these? Sulwyn picked up one of the dolls. It was porcelain, with dark black hair and large, round grey eyes. Though the skin tone was all wrong, it reminded Sulwyn of herself.

And then it was covered in blood, oozing out of the neck.

Sulwyn yelped, tossing the doll back into the box where it lay innocent and clean. Pain shot through her head and her chest, but she pushed the box away and back under the wardrobe. She paused; on her right hand was a black metal ring on her index finger. What was this ring? But on her left hand, there was a patch of skin on the same finger that was untanned from the sun. As if something had been there the whole time.

"Where is my silver ring?" she asked aloud to no one, but what ring was she even talking about?

Bells tolled in the distance, five ringing out across the Empire. Today was her coronation as queen. It seemed like it was only yesterday that she had her coronation as princess. But that memory came to her in blurred fragments. The more she thought about it, the more her head throbbed. So she stopped. What did it matter anyway?

A knock sounded on the door before three maids came in, one holding a dinner tray, the other two trailing behind. She recognised Eztli from before, but the other two only stirred slight recognition.

"Good evening, our queen." Eztli curtsied swiftly. The other two looked at each other before following suit. "We will be assisting ya for the evenin' until it is time for yer coronation."

Eztli strode over, placing the dinner set onto the small dining table that sat in one corner of the room near the fire. The maid turned to her, looking down at her with something like confusion. "Do ya need some assistance?"

"No. I made it over here. I can make it there," Sulwyn snapped. She didn't need some maid's pity. Sulwyn used the wardrobe to help her stand, the pain still in her legs and back from the night before. But she had faced worse pain.

When?

"We hope ya enjoy this dinner. I had a personal hand in it." Eztli smiled and gestured at the small table.

Sulwyn walked over, trying to ignore the pain with every movement. All the other dinners she had were elaborate, but this one was light and simple.

A rich, creamy soup with bits of carrots and chicken sat at the centre of the silver tray, alongside a small leafy salad and buttery bread. How pathetic. She was a queen! But another, stronger thought was rather content with this. She dipped a spoon in the ceramic bowl and tasted the soup.

It was familiar and homey and made her chest pang uncomfortably, but she kept eating it until there was nothing left on the tray. She observed the maids bustling about, going through the dresses in her wardrobes and the jewellery and shoes. She wouldn't be able to wear a short dress or anything that didn't cover her arms. But it was her fault. She had been wrong.

"We shall get you nice and fresh before we choose your outfit if that is okay with you, my queen?" spoke the softer-looking one.

"What is your name?" Sulwyn asked, frowning at the same time. How could she ask such a silly question? Why should she even care?

The girl's angled green eyes widened slightly, but soon she was curtsying again. "Nori, my queen." She stayed down until Sulwyn waved her off.

"And you? You're a bit young to be tending to things such as this…"

"Arsinone, my queen. I promise my lack of age doesn't stop me from doing my duties." She smiled politely, quickly curtsying.

Sulwyn stared, her dark blue hair tied back into a long ponytail, the maid's dress slightly too large for her.

As she looked at all three of them, her thoughts flowed like mud. No matter how much she tried to focus on them, on the conversation and anything around her, she was trudging through dirty sludge. It irritated her greatly, the anger building and moving her thick thoughts aside. She was to be queen. None of these people mattered.

"Well, let's get to it. We only have four hours. I must stand out," she snapped.

Eztli and Nori nodded quickly, rushing to her and helping her towards the bathing room.

Sulwyn stiffened. The last time she had been in here, she had found herself back in bed, and she was punished. But no matter how much she tried to recall those events, nothing came to mind, and she only knew what Artaxiad had told her.

"The water should be nice and warm," Nori said. Sulwyn realised she had dissociated, sitting on the small stool that rested in front of the ornate vanity. How many spaces of her memory were blank? And why couldn't she remember anything before this room?

Artaxiad and the other maids spoke of her previous coronation as princess, but when had that even happened, and what had happened to Pandora?

"How did Pandora die?" she asked quickly as they sponged her skin.

Eztli dropped the soap into the tub, splashing herself. She paled, watching Sulwyn, who only stared, waiting. Eztli reached back into the tub for the soap, her dark skin contrasting against the porcelain. "She was murdered, my queen…" she said quietly.

"And the murderer?"

"Still at large…" Eztli whispered, but she stood straighter, smiling brighter. "We should also wash ya hair, add some nice fragrances. There is also this bath mix that can soothe yer body. Would ya like to try it?"

Sulwyn looked at the small pouch in her hand, considering it until she nodded her consent.

Eztli poured some of the green powder into the water, stirring it in and allowing the smells to waft around them.

Sulwyn stiffened. She had smelled this before and the effects were immediate, a soft, healing sort of tingle wrapped around her, numbing her wounds. "Where did you get this?" she demanded, surprised at how haphazard she sounded.

"It was gifted to you by the prince," said Nori, "to calm the muscles for today."

"The prince?"

A bell tolled in the background three times. Three hours left until her coronation as queen, and then she could properly rule alongside Artaxiad.

A chill ran through her despite the warm water and the soothing bath mix.

Her hair had been dried and curled loosely for the night, her face made suitable for the event with golds and dark browns and pinks. As Sulwyn sat waiting for the maids to bring her dress, excitement thrummed in her despite the last couple of days. She was always worrying about the trouble she would get into next. Worried that Artaxiad would be angry with her. But she was sure she was doing an excellent job. Sulwyn barely yelled at these maids throughout the night. And she didn't have to either; they were excellent help. She would have to tell Artaxiad she wanted them to be hers.

"Here we are!" Eztli announced, coming back into the room.

Sulwyn turned around to see her carrying a long dress draped with a black velvet cloth.

Nori stepped forwards, helping her remove the velvet to reveal a beautiful, long dress made of black lace.

Sulwyn's nerves relaxed a little, seeing the long, thin sleeves. Though the welts on her skin had gone down significantly after the bath, she couldn't be too sure. She didn't want anyone to question how she was being treated by their king.

But a tight congestion in her chest and confusion in her mind erupted as she looked at the dress closely. Though the dress was black, many tiny jewels of blue, purple and red coated the bodice, and with it, the memory of two men she couldn't remember flashed through her.

Who were these men to her?

"This dress was not in my closet..." Sulwyn started, her voice low.

"No, it wasn'. It was gifted to ya by the prince and the All-Command as a coronation present." Eztli looked at her pointedly. The congestion grew, but Sulwyn brushed it off. It was a dress and a gift. It would be rude not to take it, especially when it was so beautiful.

Sulwyn nodded in acceptance and let the maids dress her completely.

Sulwyn walked arm in arm with Artaxiad down a long hallway with lush red carpets. A path she knew she had walked down many times before yet couldn't remember when. Artaxiad had no qualms with her dress, and as he walked, his mood grew brighter still. Well, if he was content, what did it matter when she had been here before?

"Don't rush, my queen. Take your time and lean on me. You are still rather unwell," he cooed.

She nodded, excitement rising in her as they got closer and closer to the door until they were just in front of it.

A manservant greeted them, knocking on the large wooden door as a voice unseen to them called the guests to attention. Soon, light streamed through the opening doors, elaborate fanfare reaching her ears. Cheers and clapping greeted them as Artaxiad waved and led Sulwyn down the stairs. Slowly but surely, she made it all the way. The people parted before them while they walked towards two large thrones.

Artaxiad gestured for Sulwyn to sit as he remained standing, turning to greet the people on his small precipice.

"My people. The last week has been very difficult. I appreciate the effort you have all gone through to show mourning for our late queen. Pandora was by my side, our side, from the very beginning. Knowing her was our honour." The people nodded their heads, solemn and confused. "As I said before, we are strength. We cannot show weakness, and though it is hard, we must keep our heads high. To prevent those that are undeserving from taking this opportunity to cause strife among our grief and to help us lead the way, I present to you Queen Sulwyn of Vartugaul." He stepped to the side, letting them all stare at her fully.

Though the crowd was clapping, she noticed that many looked rather bemused, confused or worried. Did they think she was not worthy? Did they think she could not lead them well alongside Artaxiad? Unrest itched deeply within her soul. How dare they?

But Artaxiad stepped carefully in front of her, a small syringe with just blue liquid in his hand. "I know that look, Sulwyn, but it will not do well to upset the people. They need to accept you first. Accept us. So, let's stay calm for the night, shall we?" Subtly without notice, he pressed the needle against her neck. A stinging pinch and the flow of cold liquid went through her. Quickly, he pulled it away, folding it into his sleeve and using that moment to adjust her curls.

The energy she had before began to fade and her body slackened against her will. Sulwyn could vaguely hear Artaxiad justifying her behaviour due to illness and shock from the recent events. Once he finished talking, the music started playing again. Artaxiad jovially excused himself to speak to some of the elite that lived in Valens.

Sulwyn watched people mingle and dance around her, all eating, drinking and laughing. But she needed to sit here. There was no reason for her to go down there with those people who didn't even know her. She ruled *over* them. She didn't need to be *with* them.

"Would ya care for a drink or some food, my queen?" Eztli asked, who was swiftly at her side. The maid showed her a tray of small tarts and a blue drink that smelled like fruits. Wordlessly, she took them from her, realising she was famished and only had soup earlier on.

"Thank you…"

Eztli looked shocked for just a minute before she curtsied. "My pleasure. Please, if ya need anythin' else, let me know." She turned, going back to refill her tray and continue through the crowd.

Sulwyn quietly ate her tarts, sipping the drink. She had this drink before during her first coronation. She smiled slightly, looking out into the crowd and faltered. A man with golden blond and white hair weaved through the crowd, but as quickly as she had noticed him, he was gone. She was soon distracted when another man with black hair and light brown skin came up to her, bowing and asking for her hand to dance.

Sulwyn looked around to see Artaxiad glancing at her. He contemplated briefly before nodding his permission. With that, Sulwyn reached out her hand and let the man take her to the dance floor.

She looked up at him, forgetting his name as he spoke it. She had never seen him before and was quickly tired from the dance. He had said words to her, but she had drifted out of the conversation. By the end of it, he bowed politely but moved on and blended into the crowd. Others began to ask her to dance after confirming they could. But now, the irritation was rising in her after the fifth dance.

As she turned to escape, another man gracefully took her hand and led her towards him.

"I have danced enough. I will not be led around like a common wom—" She stopped, looking up at the man with blond-white hair from before. His dark red eyes pierced her own.

"Now, my queen. Please give me this last dance of yours before you rest. I will be gentle," he purred, leading her lightly through the other dancers. The smell of something like sweet rain and burnt wood flowed around her, confusing her. Where were these smells coming from?

"What is your name?" she whispered, though something deep within her knew she knew once upon a time.

He smirked, and it sent flutters through her. "Daijiro, your All-Command at your beck and call," he whispered back, and a strange pull came over her, releasing the tension in her mind just a bit. She found herself moving closer to him. Even as one song ended and another started, she didn't want to stop dancing with him. He looked at her darkly.

He bent down closer to her, his lips by her ear, earning a shiver. "This is too easy, Cailín. Where did the fight go?"

Sulwyn stiffened, her grip stronger in his hands. She pulled back, affronted. Anger flared within her veins, but something else did too. Something strong and nagging, but she didn't want to confront it. "Who do you think you are? Talking to me like that?" she challenged, but the look in his eyes sent a tremor of fear through her, bloodlust that she could never match buried within it.

"At one point, I was your enemy. The next, I was your fiancé. What would you like me to be now?" he continued to purr, but she could hear the urgency in his voice, his eyes darting around quickly. "I'm upset, Cailín, that you could have forgotten me of all people. We've shared so much in the last couple of months."

Something was wrong. Sulwyn tried to pull away from him, but he held her tighter, and soon, it was as if she were bound by chains, unable to move against his will. He looked at her, his eyes fierce and wild and a little panicked.

"Listen to me, Sulwyn. You did not come this far to be tarnished by trash. You are a star. *The* Star. And there are many people waiting for you to guide them. Like me, many people who had been lost, have been found because of you. You didn't start this journey as queen." He leaned his head forwards, placing his forehead against hers. A tingling pain and heat seeped through her skin at his touch. "The faster you get back to being you, the faster we can move on. And it's not only me that needs you. There's a rather angry man who needs saving too."

Sulwyn forgot everything she was feeling before. Her need to escape, her anger, the annoyance of being insulted. Instead, she couldn't breathe. Something was trapped within her, trying to escape.

"Who...?" she asked breathlessly, just as she spotted Artaxiad in the distance. He was now slowly but surely making his way over.

Daijiro looked at her carefully, his forehead pulling back, his hand brushing her cheek. "Galahad, our prince of many things."

Sulwyn froze, and in her mind, blue, purple and red eyes looked at her with care and worry. The same emotions reflected in him as the man who was just in front of her, but in her moment of confusion, Daijiro had taken off. She looked around, around the people, around the entire ballroom, but he just vanished before her.

Artaxiad stepped up to her, eyeing her curiously, but she knew he was angry. "Who was just here with you?" he asked, smiling sweetly.

Sulwyn hesitated, warning bells echoing in her mind. "I don't know. I think he builds something for us. Are you here to dance with me as well?" She smiled quickly. He looked at her but took her hand in his and led her to dance. Sulwyn continued to smile even after they finished, and he led her back to her throne, but her heart was in turmoil.

Even as she sat, trying to gather her thoughts, she was interrupted. Many hours had passed, and now Artaxiad was back in front of her, addressing their guests.

"I thank you again for coming, and with this, our night has come to an end. But as I mentioned before, I have a few surprises for you all."

The crowd listened intently, all a little happier from the lull of food and drink.

"In this challenging time, it is important to unite and carry the strength of each other, to create a stronger bond. As you all know, we have yet to assign another Leader in Caldwell's place. I intend for Sulwyn to take this place once she recovers."

Sulwyn started at the name Caldwell, a dull ache running through her. Who was Caldwell, and why did she need to replace him? But her thoughts were disrupted when Artaxiad continued, hushing the applause.

"But to maintain our full strength and peace, I have more news. In three weeks, when the moon is full… To wholly bring our newfound bond together, Sulwyn and I shall be wed and you are all welcome to attend!"

V

Black Ash & Fire

| GALAHAD |

"MARRIAGE?!" Galahad exclaimed; fists clenched. He had nothing left to destroy, his room shattered once again, and Eztli, Nori and Arsinone looked on in fear. Taru and Daijiro were not with them. No one was there to help him. Seething, he could barely see the girls in front of him.

"Galahad, please... He said in three weeks!" Eztli started. "There still be three weeks to get her out. And from what we've learned, he hasn' tried to consummate anythin'. He hasn' touched her besides the punishments."

"THAT'S NOT GOOD ENOUGH!" he roared, his vision blackening for a fraction of a second. He heard Eztli gasp, could see her look down at his hands in fear, but he couldn't acknowledge it. Not when the thrum of his own blood deafened him. "You need to leave," he barked with everything he could muster, but Arsinone stepped forwards.

"There is time. He wants to make her the Leader to replace Caldwell, which will mean she can't stay in Valens with him all the time."

"And then what? We can't take her from Artaxiad without him coming for us. Without him sending the entire Empire out to find us if we run."

"Then we kill him," came Daijiro from behind, stepping into his room. He looked maddened; a look Galahad forgot he could make. The wild, murderous look that he carried with honour was back.

"How?" gritted Galahad.

"I haven't gotten that far..." Daijiro said, but he, too, glanced at Galahad's hands. Finally, Galahad looked down to see that the skin around both hands had started to blacken like ash crawling its way past his wrists, his nails growing sharp and black as well.

"What is this?" he choked, horror and fury rising.

"Arsinone, silence him," came Taru's severe tone unexpectedly behind Daijiro.

He looked at Arsinone as she reached into his soul and pressed on it. Soon, everything was dark, and he crumpled.

❧

Galahad shot up from the floor.

The room was dark, the fire out, and silence pressed against him. He looked around and spotted only Taru sitting in the dim moon light on the floor in front of him, regarding him cautiously.

"You are a danger to everyone," Taru started gravelly and more severe than Galahad had ever heard from him.

Galahad looked down at his hands, his skin free of the ashen black that had crawled into it, his nails their normal length. From the lore he'd been taught, there was a true form of the Demon Father of their clan. Only awakened and used on two occasions, though he couldn't remember what they were now.

But the drawings showed a man burned in black from his fingers to his elbows, hands elongated with sharp nails and darkness spread from his feet to his knees. Thin, large, black wings of ash like a shadow and eyes as black as night. A true demon.

Was that what was to become of him?

Could he even control that?

He was not born that. No one was meant for that besides the First Children. But aside from that, why? Why were his powers escalating so quickly? Too quickly for him to adjust, to control and rein.

"Taru... what do I do?"

The old man pondered, looking at him carefully. "I have had my suspicions for a while now since we met again in the fog town. Based on when I first saw you as a child until now, this is not how your powers should be, not yet. They have transgressed. And I am afraid you may have been tampered with, forcing your powers to be like this."

Galahad stared at him. "Is that even possible? Who could have done that and how?" But even as he said it, his heart sank. There were blank spaces in his memories from his past. Times when Tiergan had taken him for punishment and altered his memory. Had he been doing something more? But Tiergan could only pull memories and roughly heal. He would have needed help to achieve something more than that. How had he learned to pull memories in the first place? That wasn't a clan trait...

"Can Arsinone read blank spaces in a soul?" Galahad asked, but Taru's eyes darkened.

"Keep in mind that Arsinone is a child. A special child descendant of mine, but a child, nonetheless. If there is someone or something that has managed to affect you so, she can read it, but it may affect her too. When Arsinone reads a soul, she feels it, just as I feel it when I read the history. Your power is too great, and I do not want it to hurt her. She is not ready to see your soul yet. I am also afraid that if you give in and keep giving in, you will lose pieces of yourself until it is all gone."

"Lose myself?" he whispered. Impatience and rage rose in him once again, but seeing Taru so serious in front of him helped keep it at bay just a little. "Tiergan is out of the question. You said they raided the town. If he didn't already escape somehow, he's dead. The only other person who was there besides Artaxiad is Nero, and I don't know what he is doing or where he is."

"The way everything is going, I'm sure he will arrive soon. For now, you will need to control your anger. If you want to help Sulwyn, then save yourself first. Just hold on a little longer." Taru reached forwards, his rough palm patting Galahad's hand gently.

༄

| SULWYN |

"Are you ready?" Artaxiad asked as Sulwyn turned to face him. He was dressed practically instead of elaborately for their first visit to the Solus as an engaged couple. It was time for Artaxiad to make his yearly visit and this time, he wanted Sulwyn to show him around. But ever since her coronation, a gnawing feeling had been nipping at her.

It had been an entire week since she became queen, two weeks until their wedding, which still took Sulwyn by surprise and gave her mild discomfort. But if this was what was needed, so be it. They needed to maintain peace no matter how it was achieved. This is what he told her, and this is what she would do.

"Where is my ring?" she asked nonchalantly. Artaxiad looked up in glee as they walked side by side out of Valens to their horses. Ki was nowhere to be found.

Who was Ki?

"A bonded ring? The time will come, my queen, but you must wait patiently as I am waiting for you." He smiled slyly, but she shook her head, trying to ignore the deep disgust that flitted through her, though she was unsure of why.

She had no idea what a bonded ring was but knew that couldn't be right. "While I look forwards to that, that was not what I meant. I'm talking about my other ring." She lifted her right hand and he held it, looking at the lighter spot of skin where the sun had not reached. His expression darkened for a fraction of a second, but soon, he reached into his pocket.

In his hand was a wide, smooth, silver ring that looked rather worn with travel. It was scratched in several places but shone with care nonetheless.

"I didn't think you would notice. I gave it to you a while ago, do you remember?" he asked, slipping it onto her index finger.

She smiled upon seeing it but faltered. "I'm sorry, I don't remember…"

But Artaxiad nodded, gesturing for her to mount the chestnut brown horse as he mounted his white and black one. "In time, Sulwyn, let us first go about our duties. There, you will meet one of the Validus who will explain your duties as Caldwell's replacement Leader." He took off with Sulwyn close behind, but all she could hear in her mind was the name Caldwell.

"What happened to Caldwell?" she yelled as they galloped through the city.

"He died for treason," Artaxiad said shortly.

His comment ended the conversation, but the pain in Sulwyn's chest pounded in rhythm to the galloping. Confusion obscured her thoughts.

As they rode closer, Sulwyn could see the tall, iron walls that imprisoned their criminals in an unescapable maze. A large, square entrapment for those who defied the Empire since the fall of the High City and after.

By the time they had reached the Solus and dismounted, Sulwyn was sick. Her head was throbbing and her skin had a sheen of cold sweat. A fever was building and radiating through her skin, but she didn't know why she would have one. She hadn't done anything to catch an illness, but it had been chaotic in the last few days. It must be stress and unrest.

"Sulwyn..." Artaxiad said, pulling her to the side and touching her forehead. Instantly, she recoiled, looking at him with hate, but soon it was removed with confusion. Artaxiad's expression fell, and he pulled out a small box from within his dark grey coat. He removed the syringe with blue transparent liquid.

"You have been doing better, Sulwyn. I didn't think I'd need to keep using these so frequently," he hissed, and before she could protest, he plunged the needle into the side of her neck.

But Sulwyn was already used to it. The blue one wasn't so bad. It helped clear her thoughts so that she could do her duties more efficiently as the king needed them.

"Good girl..." he breathed over her face, looking at her with hazed green eyes, his hair and skin so like her own. He moved his head closer, his lips inching near hers. Sulwyn couldn't think about it, only accepting the prelude of what was to come, as was her duty.

But the smell of sweet rain and burnt wood wafted around her, stronger than before, though from when she didn't remember. Red eyes stirred in her memories, and she found herself pulling back and looking past the king. Artaxiad grew livid, turning to where she looked as they both watched Daijiro strut forwards from out of the entrance of the Solus.

An impatient grunt sounded from Artaxiad, but he turned back to Sulwyn, forcing her head closer and kissing her aggressively. Repulsion rose in her for a second like vomit until it was pushed down by the cover of emptiness that plagued her these days. Instantly, the smell evaporated, replaced with the burn of a feral hatred. The sudden intensity of it made her pull back from Artaxiad quickly.

The king looked like he wanted to slaughter everyone around him but reined it in, turning to Daijiro once more. "Where is Demir? I want to introduce her as Uferor En's new Leader."

Sulwyn looked at Daijiro again and faltered, finding the source of bloodlust and hate until, just as suddenly, it was covered with a bright smile and his eyes were on Artaxiad's.

"He is coming. We've been having problems with the prisoners. I came to greet you first." He bowed stiffly.

Artaxiad waved him off, passing through the entrance, beckoning Sulwyn to follow him down the rocky path surrounded by large trees to the second door.

But Sulwyn walked cautiously and stared at Daijiro, watching him rise slowly, his eyes meeting hers. And instead of the look he had given her at her coronation, that had been full of softness and mild confusion, it was replaced with hate and panic.

She needed to ignore him.

He had no business looking at her like that.

What was he to her?

Itchy irritation clawed deep in her soul as his eyes bore into hers.

A prickling that wouldn't rest.

Who was he to look down on her like that, to claim closeness to her when they danced?

To even hold her like that?

How dare he.

"Avert your eyes," she commanded, but Daijiro never broke his gaze and followed her instead.

Artaxiad glanced back at them. A wave of fear washed over her, but not for herself. Who was she afraid for?

"I said avert your gaze," she snapped louder, stopping just before the second entrance to the Solus.

Artaxiad paused, looking at them both. "Sulwyn." He stepped forwards, but she held up her hand, shoulders back, standing tall.

"I can deal with him. I will be just behind you, my king." She spoke to Artaxiad delicately and looked at Daijiro harshly.

Artaxiad smirked, pleased at her tone. "I trust you, Sulwyn, carry on." And with that, he continued into the prison, leaving Sulwyn and Daijiro outside.

"Why do you keep staring at me? I am your queen, and you will respect me," she snarled, conflicting waves of emotions rolling over her. What was wrong with her? Hate, repulsion and confusion continued to build within, but at the same time, so did her fever. It continued to rise and rise, and now she tried not to vomit.

"Respect? That is something you earn, Sulwyn. You, of all people, know that. You are not the queen of Vartugaul, not like this," he spat, his own anger matching hers, scarlet eyes piercing.

"What do you want from me?" she yelled, but the ground tipped, and the burning fever and throbbing pain flared within her.

"Cailín?" Concern wiped the hate from his features as he steadied her, but her limbs wobbled. "Sulwyn!" he hissed, recoiling at the touch of her skin. She watched him look around quickly before picking her up and bringing her to the side of the walls and out of plain view.

"What's happening?" she huffed, needle–like pricks lacing her body alongside waves of fire and ice.

"Look at me," Daijiro whispered, never letting her go, only cradling her closer, silencing her cries of pain in his chest.

"Don't… You can't touch me like this, Daijiro! If he sees us—" She froze, Daijiro's eyes as wide as her own. Why did she say that?

"Just focus on what you see," Daijiro said finally, breaking her out of her confusion as the fever hit its peak and the world fell around her.

Her vision was clear. The sound perfect. Though her mind was muddled in confusion, she could remember that she previously had a vision this clear. But before she could think about it further, her new vision materialised within her.

Sulwyn was standing in the dim halls of the Solus, underground where the Pain Cells were located. The cells that held the last four men and women of the High City. The scene blurred, affected by the poison in her, but she kept walking, hearing a voice in the distance.

Slowly, she inched around the corner to see the cell at the end open, a torch held by a hooded person just high enough for them to see within. They remained at a distance as if worried the person inside might pull them in. Sulwyn stepped forwards, remembering that no one could see her as this was something that had yet to be. As she walked closer, the words became clear.

"I still don't trust you," a man spoke, the same man that currently held her as this vision ran through her.

"The feeling is mutual," a rough, low female voice spoke from within the cell, "but we have a common interest, and I promise to make it worth your while. Plus, I'm the only one who can keep the other three in check." Sulwyn had heard this voice before but could not remember who it belonged to. It made her think of sand, hot sun and warm bowls of stew.

"I assume you have a plan?" he asked, a smirk in his voice.

"Just leave it open, and you'll see in time what is coming."

As suddenly as the vision started, it began to dematerialise, but before it could fade completely, the same female voice sighed.

"*Finally...*" the woman spoke in her mind, and now there was endless blackness before her. "*I have been waiting for you to come to the Solus. I knew you would, sooner or later. Especially with what has been happening.*"

"*Who... I know you?*" Sulwyn was quieter than she intended, but the voice heard her all the same.

"*You do. But you're still battling something I can't help you with. So, I will leave you with a gift.*" The more the voice spoke, the more a memory floated to the front. Night sky, Daijiro watching her by a wall as she sat in the grass across a dark woman from the Pain Cells. She was the only one who had any sanity due to her magic as Devinal.

"*Why should I trust this?*"

"*Why shouldn't you?*" she countered. "*In due time, an acid rainstorm will come. And when it does, it will wreak havoc across the Empire. It will be up to you to do what you think you need to. It's the only thing I can give you right now.*"

VI

No One Will Know Your Name
| SULWYN |

DAIJIRO followed closely behind Sulwyn as they both caught up with Artaxiad. He turned to greet her; his smile leery until he caught Daijiro behind her.

"I hope you settled your differences…" he said dangerously, but Daijiro only bowed.

"I have apologised for offending our queen and am lucky enough that she has forgiven me for the moment," he spoke, earning a look of surprise from Artaxiad.

Sulwyn remained impassive. The fever had burned away the poison that Artaxiad had put in her, but it didn't clear her mind completely. Some of her memories had come back after her vision, now realising it was Ildri that spoke to her. But she was no closer to understanding how to remove the effect Artaxiad had on her than before. He had been controlling her with whatever it was he had gotten from Gwydion, and she let it happen. She didn't know how long this flash of clarity would last, but she would hold onto it for as long as possible.

She glanced at Daijiro just as all three of them made their way through the tunnels to the outside centre of the Solus. He held a finger to his lips, brushing his other hand against hers. A wave of revulsion crashed through her, the one that was trying to conform her to be the second

Pandora, but she fought it down, and to aid her efforts, she knew Daijiro was trying to use his own allure for her. The smell of sweet rain and burnt wood wafted around her, breaking the confusion into smaller, more bearable pieces. It seemed to melt it away, just a little.

Demir ran forwards, bowing to Artaxiad and turning to Sulwyn. She saw him glance at Daijiro, who subtly shook his head.

"My queen." He bowed to her, that deep itch stabbing her. She was losing grip on her true consciousness.

"You made me wait. They tell you in advance that your king and queen are coming. Are you looking down on me?" she asked, aware of the other inmates looking at them from cell upon cell above. She glanced around, spotting some familiar faces. But in her haze, she forgot them until she glanced at one that was empty—Zander's cell. Wasn't he Pandora's brother?

What happened to him?

"Forgive me, my queen. The ones in the Pain Cells have been acting up."

"The Pain Cells?" called Artaxiad, his expression unsettled.

"Yes," Daijiro started, looking at him instantly. "They have been much more vocal in these last few weeks than ever before. I am hoping that it will settle once they are out for their scheduled day next week."

A dark look crossed Artaxiad. "Bring me to them."

Daijiro nodded, leading them back through the tunnels. As soon as they entered the area with the Pain Cells, yells and murmuring could be heard. All four of them were speaking nonsense or making sounds that had no relevance to anything.

"*Kintana…*" whispered a voice, startling Sulwyn, bringing back memories of Arsinone and thankfulness that she hadn't hurt her in these last few weeks. But this voice didn't belong to her and wasn't from the soul. It whispered around her unheard, carried through by magic: Ildri.

"*You have seen my message. Wait for us…*"

"Didn't we come here to check the Solus and get information on what it means to be the Leader of Uferor En?" snapped Sulwyn. She could hear a chuckle from Ildri praising her distraction.

If Ildri could use her magic, then it confirmed the barrier over the Solus was gone. What had happened to Gwydion? Who was Gwydion again?

Sulwyn looked over to Daijiro, who responded with a sly grin. He had heard it too.

But she made a mistake. Artaxiad had caught them.

"It seems I underestimated you. You are not ready to be a Leader just yet."

"No!" she yelled, but that made it worse.

"I only wish the best for you," he grunted, grabbing her wrist.

"I have done everything you have asked of me!" She tried to pull free from his grip, but it was stronger than she could have imagined.

"Daijiro, Demir, you are dismissed. Return to your posts," he called, and she turned back to see them glance at each other. She looked at Daijiro. A flash of anger crossed his face, his fists clenched.

"You disappoint me, Sulwyn. I need to be firmer with you." He yanked her away from the Pain Cells and across the hall towards the other side, where rooms for extra guards and equipment were located. He shoved her into one of them, locking the door behind them.

All the strength she had gained from her vision had waned as it normally did, but she kept consciousness for as long as she could to avert Artaxiad's attention. Now she had no strength to fight back and could only watch helplessly as he pulled out that infernal box once again.

"You are the queen of Vartugaul, Sulwyn. *My* queen." He caressed her cheek, pushing her hair back to expose her neck. Without warning, he injected the orange one. The one that made her limp to do his bidding. The green one, the one that stripped her of her own thoughts, leaving her only able to listen to his command without question. And finally, the purple one, the one that erased her heart.

Though the blue one had already been used, the one that made her calm or should have, it didn't matter. She couldn't fight all four.

Not now.

Not yet.

ѦѦ

Sulwyn woke up back in her room that connected to Artaxiad's. It was night, the area lit by few candles. She tried to turn onto her back, but the pain from the whip had kept her in place. She had made her king angry, but she couldn't remember why. How many days had passed since she was left here?

They had gone to the Solus. She was going to be a Leader, but now she wasn't, and she didn't understand why. What had she done? She was a good queen, and soon, she would be a good wife.

Disgust rose in her before she pushed it down. There was nothing wrong with this. This was the only way to maintain peace, to maintain a hold on the Empire and all of Vartugaul.

A knock sounded on her door before the three maids from before slipped in, bringing food on a tray. She heard her stomach rumble, but she didn't have the energy to move, the cuts hurting. The last time this happened, Galahad snuck the food into her cell.

Galahad.

She froze, forcing herself to turn and sit up, but her head pounded into her eyes.

"Queen Sulwyn?" called Eztli, placing the tray down as Nori lit more lanterns until the room was fully illuminated.

"Had I been asleep, I would have you punished." The words came out, but she didn't remember thinking them. She frowned but was distracted once again by the smell of food. Sulwyn stood carefully, walking out of the bedroom and straight to the dining table. "How long have I been in this room?" she asked, taking a seat and tucking into the soft beef stew and rice.

Eztli hesitated. "A bit o'er a week, my queen..."

"A week?!" exclaimed Sulwyn, dropping her spoon.

"The wedding is in five days, my queen." Eztli bowed, but Sulwyn could not process it. A week? She had been out for a week? Or had she?

"What… what happened this past week?" Sulwyn asked carefully, the rise in emotions confusing her.

"Our king visited you twice daily to administer the medicine to help you recover…" started Nori, but she hesitated.

"Have I done something?" Sulwyn asked quietly, unsure why she was asking that and asking them of all people.

Eztli looked at her. "Not really, no."

"If you lie to me, I will hurt you," she threatened, but they were hollow words.

"Arsinone…" Eztli said. Sulwyn turned to look at the girl, realising she hadn't said anything since she entered.

Arsinone walked forwards, turning around and lifting her dress. A large, deep purple bruise sat in the middle of her small back. Tears welled up immediately as Sulwyn looked at the bruise. But her distress fought with the smugness she felt from their fear.

This was wrong.

It was all wrong.

"It's okay, Sulwyn…" Arsinone whispered.

Nori quickly grabbed Arsinone and pulled her to the side of the room. "You cannot speak to the queen like that!" Nori hissed, glancing back at Sulwyn. But she couldn't hear them anymore. Instead, she looked at the ring on her finger that caught the firelight. She had forgotten something so very important.

"Please, my queen, let us change ya for the night. Ya been in that nightdress for the last few…" Eztli started, drawing her attention away from everyone onto her.

Silence spread between them as Sulwyn finished her food before she let Eztli and Nori bathe her. As she was stepping out of the warm water, the light caught her leg, and with it, the burn on her calf.

"If you don't mind, my queen..." Nori said, casting an unsure glance at Eztli. "Where did you get this burn?"

Irritation rolled under her skin, but at the same time, something else she couldn't place tingled through her. She stepped onto the lush black rug, wrapping a towel around herself before looking down at her leg.

"When I was a baby..." she started but stopped. An older man's face crossed her mind.

Ice-blue eyes bright and smiling at her as he placed the ring on her finger.

Then, eyes that were cold and empty as he looked at her with emptiness before she fell to darkness.

His wide eyes void of life atop other dead bodies in the lower dungeons, and the foreboding that she had missed something so important struck her hard.

"There was no scar," she whispered, looking at Eztli with wide eyes.

"I beg yer pardon, my queen?"

Clarity.

She had clarity and would uncover as much as she could right now. Since coming to the Empire and seeing Raghnall's body, she knew she was missing something. Knew there was something wrong with his reason for surrendering her in the first place. "When you led me to the lower dungeons, how many days had it been since I had entered the Empire?" she asked quickly, gripping Eztli's shoulders.

"Um... I believe it was just o'er a week," the maid answered, utter confusion crossing her face.

"Nori, magic has its own limitation apart from magic that is tied to the life and death of the Devinal that used it. If there was magic in a cream used to hide scars for exactly a week, it would function until its time was up, right?"

"You..." Nori began, but she nodded vigorously.

"He had no scar. He had NO scar!" Sulwyn yelled, coming out of the bathing room and into the living room. But before she could venture this idea further, Artaxiad came into the room. Sulwyn froze, schooling her features immediately.

Not this time. She would not lose this time.

"You are doing well today, it seems. I would love you to join me and a few others for dinner tonight to discuss other details about the wedding."

Sulwyn smiled. "Of course, my king." But Artaxiad looked at her suspiciously, so she did something drastic. Sulwyn fumbled the towel, letting it fall to the floor as if it slipped from her grasp. Artaxiad's gaze was on her quickly, slightly bemused but lust written all over his face. Pricks of anger bit through her, but she breathed slowly, willing it to pass.

"My queen!" exclaimed Nori, but she stopped as Artaxiad held up his hand.

"I want her in something purple tonight. See that she looks the part." He eyed her again, touching his lips with his fingers in anticipation.

જ્જ

By the end of the night, Sulwyn was exhausted. Fighting again against Artaxiad's poison would be her undoing, though he only administered two of the four tonight before dinner. She could not think clearly enough to escape, but she made sure to act the part she was given. When the guests had taken their leave, Sulwyn turned to Artaxiad, sipping her tea.

"Have I earned enough trust to be a Leader once more?" she asked, hoping the answer was yes. She couldn't see any other way out of this than being allowed free rein, to get away from his influence. But it looked like she asked the wrong question. He could sense her intent.

"Sulwyn, I do not appreciate the tone you have taken with me tonight. Not only does it look like you are disobeying me, but you are belittling me. I am not to be taken lightly." And she realised now where the words she had spoken during these last few weeks had come from. These were the things he had been saying, the things she was forced to mimic and act like.

At first, she thought she had taken on a bit of Pandora's persona, but Pandora was more willed than that. Even Artaxiad didn't talk back to her.

And though she was killed, she was still a force to be reckoned with in everyone's mind.

Who killed her?

"I had no intention of doing so…" she started, but it was too late, and for whatever reason, Artaxiad was now livid. He stood and shoved the plates off the table. The tinkle of breaking glass and ceramic echoed off the walls of the richly furnished dining room. The mess on the floor was a great contrast to the heavy, dark hangings and golden trinkets along the deep, earthy-brown walls. Servants came out, but Artaxiad shooed them away except one.

"Bring it," he ordered, and the woman dashed out quickly. Soon, she returned with the long, thin whip before taking off in a scurry.

"Just days before our wedding, and this is how you treat me?" he asked, yanking her out of the chair and shoving her back onto the dining room table. Broken plates ripped the skin along her spine, but the pain enflamed further when he brought the whip down onto her legs. "I have done nothing but care for you. Be patient with you! And yet you still defy me!" he bellowed, whipping her harder, his expression wild and manic. Sulwyn tried to shield her body to no avail. Though this whip did not have magical properties like the one Caldwell used, it hit much harder. *Artaxiad* hit much harder.

He dragged her off the table and flung her onto the floor, ripping the hem of the dark plum dress away from her legs and torso, her underslip the only thing protecting her skin.

"Why. Do. You. Defy. ME?" He lashed her with every word until she screamed. The old scars from his previous hits flared as new ones joined them until the skin broke and bled. Air burned at the open wounds, the broken plates cutting into her deeper.

How had she ended up here? As her consciousness slipped, a voice called to her.

"You must bring luck, Sulwyn…" Caldwell coughed, his blood coating her hands at what she had done. Red covered his bright white clothes, seeping into his

white hair, his stark blue eyes full of tears. The large, carved-out mountain of the Proelium Terra melted away from her until she could only see Caldwell, standing in front of her with his sister by his side, finally, at peace. All of his self-inflicted scars of penance healed. But as soon as he and his sister walked away, another face came to her.

"Sometimes, we must sacrifice ourselves to achieve more. To save more. But Sulwyn, this isn't the choice you need to make," Raghnall said, kneeling in front of her. Here he was younger. Less lines, his icy eyes bluer and his hair blacker than silver.

She had just turned six when he finally told her the truth of how her parents had left her for dead, how he had found her abandoned in their burning house, raised her and hoped beyond hope that the peace would restore itself. That the Empire would fall. But she could see he knew that couldn't happen.

Not without him.

And not without her.

She held their blood, which meant she could hold their strength and the ability to wield it for good and take it back from what they had created.

"Sulwyn, we can run. We can stay safe. This isn't your battle," he said sadly, but she knew he knew her decision.

"If I can do something about it, then I will die trying to do it," she said fiercely for a six-year-old, until his face faded, replaced with one similar to hers, if she had red hair.

Pandora lay under her, slit neck bleeding onto her hands, warm like Caldwell's. "Don't endanger the people you think you trust. It doesn't end with me. Artaxiad is just as terrible, if not worse. And he will come after them all, one way or another. And after him, there are more..." she whispered the last part.

And then Sulwyn watched Pandora take her last breaths until finally, she spoke once more, whispering so Gwydion couldn't hear her, "I knew..." She choked in barely a sigh, her eyes full of anger and tears and pain. "Raghnall had been tracking us before you were born."

King Artaxiad!" yelled a Néosan bursting through the doors. Sulwyn's blurry gaze swept over a man she had never seen, watching his eyes widen at the scene in front of him. Sulwyn knew she was covered in blood, Artaxiad hovering over her, his lips close to hers. She could see his anger at being interrupted once again, but he moved back.

"You have ten seconds to explain why I shouldn't kill you," started Artaxiad, but they could hear the wind lash against the window alongside tiny tinkles of glass. Tonight was the night Ildri foresaw.

"Shardstorm, my king," the Néosan said, but Artaxiad looked like that wasn't good enough. "But there are acid clouds in the distance…"

Artaxiad stood. Having a glass sandstorm and acid rain at the same time could create something far worse. "Sound the weather alarm. Get everyone inside who hasn't already gone in. I'll see to my horses. I can't have them run."

Sulwyn couldn't help but smirk at that. Out of all the things this man actually cared about, it was his damn horses. He turned to her; his face blurry as she lay pitifully on the ground. "I am not done with you, Sulwyn. And to ensure this doesn't happen again, I have no choice but to kill the youngest maid in your service."

"No…" Sulwyn said weakly, but she couldn't move. Everything in her was numb. Her mind, her skin, even her hair. All of it, dead.

She had killed her mother, and her mother knew Raghnall had been there. When Raghnall first found her, he said the fire was in the farthest corner of the house from where he had located her. He thought it was strange but never addressed it further, but Pandora had done that purposely. Had left the chance for her to be saved up to the goddess of the moon. To stop them. But not just them.

Gwydion.

Gwydion, who knew more than he was letting on.

Gwydion, who was a Devinal.

Gwydion, who Pandora was suspicious of.

Sulwyn's purpose was clear.

She needed to take back Vartugaul from all of them. There was no sense in her failing here. She didn't come this far to die at the hands of Artaxiad, be it physically or mentally.

"Sulwyn! Sulwyn, please!"

And then Arsinone's inner voice stuttered; she had been knocked out. Someone had gotten to her and was bringing her to Artaxiad. She needed to go. This girl had been tortured enough in the last month by her hands, and by Pandora's.

Sulwyn forced herself up. She could hear Artaxiad in the distance, shouting commands to ensure minimal damage to the Empire. "Bring the girl!" he roared.

Her skin burned, but she stood, taking off the ridiculous high heels and casting them aside. She would end this today. She had to. Whatever Ildri was going to do would give her that chance.

Sulwyn stumbled out of the room, but not before she stopped to grab a decorative short sword from the dining room walls. She dragged the blade across her palm, ensuring it was sharp enough as the blood welled up and continued.

"You!" called a Néosan, rushing towards her, but Sulwyn cut his throat and watched him fall. Soon, one by one, Néosan noticed her making a bloody path through the halls.

She was done with this.

Her anger willed her forwards.

Anyone who tried to stop her, she would slay.

As luck would have it, few people were left down this path as they tended to the emergency needs of the castle.

Finally, she reached the exit, pushing the doors forwards. She was nearly knocked over from the force of the wind, but she pressed on, stumbling down the long set of stone steps. One long path led off towards the main street, another led towards the stables. The sand and bits of glass lashed against her cuts, burning them. And finally, a sound she never expected to hear as large bells echoed across the sky in a strange pattern.

The Solus had fallen.

Ildri must have sensed the storm and timed it to work in their favour. With everyone hiding inside and with Ildri at the helm, it would be easy to take over the Solus. She hoped they would get away, far away, before anyone could get them.

A sense of foreboding hit her. There were real criminals in the Solus who would escape into the unsuspecting. But she couldn't think of that now because she found Artaxiad frantically locking the iron doors to the stables. Desperate to hold on to the one other thing he had control over.

As she got closer, the shardstorm calmed slightly, the eye of the storm surrounding them. She could see the wind and sand encompassing them, blocking out any witnesses. She could blame this on the prisoners and the weather, and no one could prove it.

"Sulwyn?" He saw her now, just as she spotted Arsinone being tied to one of the Solar Orb posts. How she had wanted to destroy those. Something else he had cared about. His obsession with the Lost World. With things he just couldn't have. But Sulwyn could barely focus on that. He had intended for Arsinone to die in the shardstorm and the acid rain, slowly and painfully. The Néosan tying her looked up in confusion, but she made her way towards them.

"Sulwyn, I order you to stop!" he called, but hesitated when she looked at him.

"You're an idiot, Artaxiad. Didn't Caldwell ever tell you? I'm one of the few who can build immunity to poison. Did you think those would not apply? All you did was help me. Did you think I wouldn't fight it? Did you think I wouldn't break free?" She slowly stepped up to the Néosan, looking him in the eyes as he wavered, sword out. He moved to stab her, but she rushed him, catching him in the stomach. However, the sudden movement sent her mind whirling into blackness for a second, allowing herself to get stabbed in the thigh.

Sulwyn fell to her knees, the energy knocked out of her. Artaxiad laughed, relief all over his face. "You can't beat me, Sulwyn. All I need is to up your dosage. I was being lenient. I like your flair and your defiance. I kept it low on purpose. I didn't want to marry a sculpture. That wouldn't be any fun in bed, would it?" He leered, and though seething anger clawed in her, she couldn't stand. She looked out into the shardstorm, the eye protecting them for now. She needed to get Arsinone to safety first, but movement caught her eye as a figure stepped out of the swirling sand.

"Is that what you were doing?" called Daijiro, stepping into the light, his palm held out forwards, no doubt holding Artaxiad in place with his strange power. Sulwyn looked at Artaxiad, his eyes wide in disbelief at being on the receiving end of Daijiro's ability.

"You? Of all people? You... We have given you everything!" he roared but stopped, bending over and clutching his chest. The air was crushed out of him as Daijiro curled his fingers a little.

"You also took everything from me." Daijiro's blood-red eyes flashed with fury, his voice bordering on insanity. Then he closed his hand into a fist. Artaxiad snarled, struggling to breathe. "You never wondered what it was I could do exactly? I'm not limited to binding people against their will. Because that's not what I just did, is it? What I gripped now was the nerves in your heart. Do you want to experience it again?" He smirked, and Artaxiad screamed.

Lightning flashed around them, followed by the roar of thunder. Galahad stepped out from the storm, dragging two Néosan who had been trying to hold him back. Sulwyn stared. His eyes were still their tricoloured glory as he walked up to her, kneeling beside her.

"I'm so sorry it took this long..." he whispered, hugging her gently. He turned to untie Arsinone, leaning her against the pole.

Sulwyn had no words for him, only nodding as he helped her stand. Another of Artaxiad's screams filled the air.

"Pitiful. You've destroyed so many people. So many clans and you can barely manage this? Is this the person that Vartugaul fears? The man who has fallen to his own mind. Lost in lust and power? Your daughter is far stronger than you," continued Daijiro, his eyes dangerous.

"My daughter?" he whispered, and looked up, sweat beading along his brow.

"Did you forget that's who she is?" called Galahad, and it was only then that Artaxiad noticed him. "Have you grown so delusional that you didn't know that she is your kin?" he asked calmly, but Sulwyn shivered at his tone.

Daijiro stepped back, making a fist once more, and the sound of cracking bones reached them alongside Artaxiad's screams, his legs giving out as the bones in them shattered. "For good measure," he added darkly. "Well, I've had my fun. My vengeance was with *my* father, as should be yours." He turned to Sulwyn, who stepped forwards, letting go of Galahad.

She ignored the pain that flared with every step, broken shards of plate stuck in her foot. The bits of shards and sand that stung the cuts across her skin. Each step was made bearable by the suffering on Artaxiad's face. His black hair, tinged by that violet sheen they shared, fell into his eyes and stuck to his olive skin, which was a ghost of her own.

"You are a sickness. How dare you torture me, kiss me for your own sick pleasure. Attempt to control me, to make me your slave. Pandora was fiercer than you," Sulwyn said, but Artaxiad just laughed.

"Pandora lost her way a long time ago. She stopped being the woman once feared, a shadow of what she was, and in her last moments, she lost her mind. Talking about treason. Paranoia was etched in her eyes with her insanity."

"She knew Raghnall was tracking you. Did she ever tell you that? That's why I survived," Sulwyn gritted out. "But she was still poisonous, just like you. Nothing redeems her, but at one point, she was better than you." Artaxiad was furious, but she continued. "She also knew Gwydion was a Devinal but never told you that either. All these years and even your partner in crime kept you in the dark."

"Gwydion...?" Somehow, Artaxiad couldn't register his name correctly.

"Someone's addled his memory of him..." Daijiro said quietly. "Probably Gwydion himself."

"You've fallen, Artaxiad," continued Sulwyn, stepping right up to him and bringing the blade close to his neck. "I should kill you the way I killed Pandora." She seethed, hollow satisfaction vibrating through her as his eyes widened and his face paled further.

"You killed Pandora?"

"Is it really that unbelievable? As if I would come to your side like thousands before me. The Steel Warrior raised me, not you. I know life for its worth, and I know yours has none." But Sulwyn moved the dagger and instead stabbed him vengefully in the groin.

Artaxiad shrieked, but it carried nowhere, the eye of the storm slowly moving and bringing the wind again. Lightning illuminated the sky, the crack of thunder close behind.

"That's for the hundreds you had raped or hurt, you disgusting excuse for a human. Wanting to consummate with your own blood!" She pulled the dagger out slowly. Watching as he tried to contain his pain. "But your death isn't mine." She stood and tossed the short blade. She looked back at Galahad, who had been silently watching. Daijiro moved to collect Arsinone, carrying her on his back and taking Sulwyn's hand, pulling her gently away to the side as they watched Galahad draw his sword.

The black blade swallowed any light around them, the hilt sparkling instead. The sword was magnificent no matter how many times she saw it. While the blade was a void of darkness, the hilt represented the colour in his eyes. Ruby dyed the entire hilt as plum vines engraved themselves around it. And embedded in the corners, twinkling like a stormy sea, were navy crystals of some kind.

"I was ten when you destroyed me," came Galahad's voice in that same unsettled calm.

Artaxiad looked up at him, unable to escape or move, and for once, something like fear was in his dull green eyes.

"I marked you once." He traced the tip of his sword, scraping the crossed scars below Artaxiad's eye. "Something that gave me peace whenever I saw your face in my nightmares and in my waking moments, reminding me that you could die just like any of us. Reminding me of my parents' sacrifice. Reminding me of the screams and the fire and the terror you wrecked upon my clan. Of the voices of hundreds of lost souls in the dungeons. Reminding me of the people I had to leave behind, to bide my time." He stepped closer now. "Reminding me of the power I never gave you." The colours of Galahad's eyes melted away into pure black as Artaxiad roared in anger and fear mingled into one.

"Everything you have worked for. We will destroy. Until no one knows your name," Galahad whispered, moving quickly and plunging the sword into Artaxiad's chest straight through his heart. Galahad twisted it with cruel vengeance, pushing it straight out of his back.

Artaxiad choked, the gurgle of life and blood mixing into one as he looked on in disbelief, his eyes beholding Galahad's black ones until they moved to find Sulwyn's grey ones. Blood spluttered out of his mouth, drowning his lungs and throat, stuttering his breath just as the acid rain began to fall, the wind resuming its relentless attack on them.

And then Galahad ripped his sword out of Artaxiad's chest as they watched his pitiful body fall forwards.

The man who brought the High City to its knees.

Still.

Ruined.

The king of Vartugaul was dead.

VII

The Other Brother

| SULWYN |

"HOW are we going to hide this?" Panic laced her words. The poison that thrummed through her wanted to cry out in despair at what she had done, what they had done. But her heart and mind screamed to fight the thoughts that were not her own, knowing this was the only way. What she originally sought to do. She stumbled, dizzy from the effort.

"Breathe deeply," started Daijiro, catching her elbow and lifting her to her feet.

But she couldn't do it. There was nothing left in her. Her knees hit the sand-covered ground. She had left death in the hallways, and it was obvious that Artaxiad was murdered by a sword.

"She's panicking..." Arsinone whispered, lifting her head from Daijiro's back.

"Sulwyn, listen to me..." Daijiro put Arsinone carefully onto the ground and shook Sulwyn's shoulders.

Sulwyn's mind was in and out, too many thoughts. Her eyes wandered, passing over Daijiro, over Arsinone and over to Galahad, who stood staring at Artaxiad's lifeless form.

Did he feel better?

Would this make it better?

"Sulwyn!" Daijiro hissed, slapping her lightly but enough that she snapped her attention to him.

If she was panicking, it was nothing to the look he gave her. She didn't even realise Daijiro could show such despair. She narrowed her eyes. Why was he reacting this way to her panicking?

"Listen to me," he demanded, a glint of hysteria in his eyes. "We didn't do this without a plan. But I need you to help us."

The rain pelted Sulwyn harder, itching her skin but helping to clear her mind, and finally with a deep inhale, she roared. So much like the one she let out all that time ago in the middle of a pond at night.

Her scream echoed around them, trapped by the sand and acid rain. Casting out as much of the confusion as she could for now. This was no time to be questioning her decisions. The moment was now.

Startled, Daijiro leaned back. He turned to Galahad, who finally brought his attention to them.

She forced herself to stand, everything burning, but everything clearing just enough. "I killed… I killed a lot of Néosan in the castle on the way here. If we're going to make this work, they need to be removed, and quickly."

"I've already managed to reach Nori and Eztli…" Arsinone said from her spot on the ground. "They will clean the halls, but someone needs to help them bring the bodies here. The rest are coming." She pointed in the distance.

"The rest?" asked Sulwyn, but Daijiro smirked. She watched his own panic subside after hers did. She would have to figure that out later.

"No matter how powerful Ildri is, in her state, she wouldn't have been able to escape the Pain Cells alone. There is only one key, and I have its confidence, remember?" He smiled darkly, pulling the key out from under his clothes before dashing back to Valens the way Sulwyn had come. Was what she saw in her vision the moment they planned this? But before she could think about it further, she heard her name.

"Kintana," came a voice from the sand, barely audible over the rising wind. But Sulwyn realised the wind was wrapping around not just Ildri, but the other three prisoners from the Pain Cells. The last remaining men and women of Raghnall's High City Guard. While her memories were still jumbled, she did remember what they looked like the first time she saw them.

They were not the same now.

Eleri, known as Twenty-Seven to the Protectors and Néosan, was the first one she met when she was assigned to the Solus. Made to observe their two hours outside time that they had once a month. Eleri was Raghnall's second-in-command during the High City reign, but she was reduced to a shadow of herself during her time in the Pain Cells. After over twenty years they all were. However, Eleri's bright blue eyes seemed far more aware than the last time and her blond hair that trailed the ground was cut to her shoulders.

She didn't know the names of the other two. Only knowing them as their arrest number. The vast number of scars on Forty-Two's faded brown skin shone brightly in the dim light. His grey and black curly hair tied back into a short nub. Orange eyes observing everything around them. She realised how different the former High City would look to them. Wondering how things had changed. Sulwyn hoped this would not be too much information to receive.

She moved her attention to Thirty. When she first saw him, he appeared relaxed and nonchalant. But now his angled hazel eyes blazed with anger and confusion. Though his skin was still pale, it seemed to flush a little as his rage burned through him.

Being a Devinal, Ildri must have assisted in healing their minds. She could only help them so far when they were all imprisoned, but now she could help them all heal while she healed as well. And it seemed to be working. They all looked like they were adapting.

"Ildri…" Sulwyn said, a little wary.

"The only way you escape is if we take the blame." Ildri cast a triumphant glance towards Artaxiad's dead body. "Which won't take long. I used the cover of the shardstorm to hide us further within, and the acid rain was luck. But I will let it fall, and with it, the Néosan and others alike will swarm these streets and eventually make their way here."

Just as she said this, Daijiro, along with Nori and Eztli, dragged the six Néosan out. Sulwyn was lucky that Artaxiad had only strayed as far as the stables.

Daijiro grabbed the blades from the Néosan and turned to Ildri, a moment of hesitation in his eyes. "Don't make me regret this, Thirty-Six."

She smiled, though there was a hint of venom in her dark yellow eyes. "Our interests are the same, as you have pointed out. Keep our star safe, and we have a deal."

Daijiro smirked. "I look forwards to meeting the rest of you properly. Until next time." He tossed the blades at their feet. They picked them up unfamiliarly at first, but soon, their grips strengthened and their stances solidified.

All of them turned their gaze to Sulwyn, Ildri bowing before her. "Are you ready?"

"Wait, where will you go?!" But before she could get a response, the wind started to slow and the sand floated in the space around them.

Using the last bit of coverage, Galahad whipped his sword towards the ground, the blood of Artaxiad splashing against the sand and cobblestone before he wiped it and sheathed it.

Eztli picked up Arsinone quickly, and Nori followed suit, their escape planned, running back through the stables and into the castle through another path.

Soon the sand began to crumble around all of them, and the wind vanished, making way for the acid rain. Sulwyn gasped, trying to ignore the burn of each raindrop that seeped into her open wounds.

Immediately, the blare of a horn and the stomp of feet and rain on metal reached their ears. Coming from behind them, through the streets from the direction of the Solus, were hundreds of Néosan and Captains alike armed for the acid, and a fight. They broke off into groups, spreading along the streets until finally, one parted and made their way onto the grounds of Valens and towards the back where they stood.

"Until we meet again, Kintana... If this trip doesn't kill me first." Ildri winked.

Another horn sounded closer to them, signifying their catch. A Validus Sulwyn didn't know the name of jumped off his horse before he stumbled at the sight of their dead king and the carnage of Néosan. Sulwyn hadn't noticed, but Daijiro and Galahad had already stepped back somewhere behind her.

"What happened here!" the man exclaimed, but before he and his men could form a barricade around the four prisoners, Ildri's eyes flashed white. The other three reached out to touch her, and soon they all shifted and disappeared.

Sulwyn was in and out of consciousness once again. Hushed voices surrounded her until a burning pain went through her so rapidly that she screamed.

"Be careful!" hissed Nori, reprimanding Eztli.

"I'm sorry!" she grunted but stopped. Sulwyn looked at her with wide eyes, and the room seemed to freeze. Though the urge to reach out and hurt them went through her, it passed like a short breath, her own will squashing it.

"Sulwyn!" called Arsinone. She sat up suddenly, taking in the room around her. She was back in Eques Muros, the second castle dedicated to Captains and Validus. Her eyes darted around at all the plush blue fabrics and gold hangings—it was Daijiro's bedroom.

"Don't move too much." Nori grabbed a bunch of pillows and stacked them behind Sulwyn, who forced herself up and braced on the soft pile of fabric.

"I can't heal your cuts because the acid rain trickled into them. They might be infected. I have to clean them first," she continued.

The fire crackled pleasantly, making the room stuffy and excessively warm. But the chill that ran through her was grateful. For once she had a normal fever, not one preluding a vision. However, something like fear rose in her, and she pushed away their hands and the blanket.

"Where are Daijiro and Galahad?" She moved to get up, but Eztli held her back. Without meaning to, Sulwyn yanked her arm out of her grip, stumbling out of bed. Eztli froze, fear in her eyes. "Where?" Sulwyn demanded, lacking sympathy at that moment. She was still battling the negativity of the poison and would have to make it up to them another time. But she knew something was wrong.

"They were summoned," Nori said at once, casting a glance at Eztli, who was now furious.

"Don't keep things from me, Eztli," Sulwyn growled, fear and anger rising. "Artaxiad is dead. Who could summon them?"

"Nero," Eztli muttered, and Sulwyn stilled.

"Nero?"

"He started to travel back to Antiqua from Guāngcǎi a few weeks ago. Had heard about the queen's death and the next steps taken by Artaxiad. Once Gwydion left and Galahad... Well, Nero is the only other person in the Triarchy, the founder no less," Eztli finished, defeated.

Wordlessly, Sulwyn rummaged around the room, finding clothes and shoes; all Daijiro's, the shoes far too large for her, but she would have to make do. As much as she would gallivant without shoes, her feet were screaming, swollen and bandaged from cuts.

"Sulwyn, please wait!" Eztli called but flinched when Sulwyn turned.

"Don't tell me I need to stay here. How long was I out?"

"Just the night, it's almost dawn..." Nori answered from the bed.

"Please, they wanted ya to stay here. So many things have happened to ya in a short amount of time. It's going to catch up to ya!" pleaded Eztli, but her voice trailed away under Sulwyn's glare.

"The Empire does not die just because Artaxiad and Pandora have. I cannot sleep here. The longer we wait, the more danger will come upon us. Artaxiad was vile, but he kept the control he created. Everyone will be in danger. Evil doesn't sleep." And with that, she turned, opened the door and shut it with a snap.

Once she made her way out the winding stairs and cold halls, she was exhausted. The twilight air doing nothing to help her. She would need to find a horse. There was no way she could make it there on foot in her condition and it would take too long.

Sulwyn made it to their stables, but before she could go in, the trotting of hooves on grass met her ears. She turned to see Taru and his horse alongside Ki.

"Ki!" she shouted in glee before turning. "Taru!"

"Queen?" he asked, but his horse just bucked irritably. Sulwyn recognised this horse from the dream she had. Upon seeing her next to Ki, she realised they must be the same breed of horse.

"Hana, this is Sulwyn," Taru said affectionately.

"Nice to meet you, Hana." Sulwyn reached forwards slowly, and Hana moved to greet her, her head nuzzling her hand.

"You must move quickly, Sulwyn. The storm is not over yet," Taru said severely, putting a hold on any questions she had. "No, the storm isn't coming for you," he reprimanded, a metal bucket near one of the horses.

"I'll see you later, Taru," Sulwyn said just as Ki knelt for her to get onto his back. After a brief struggle, she managed to sit astride, and soon they were taking off back towards Valens.

Though the sun had yet to rise, the number of people in the streets was intense. Néosan and Protectors alike were patrolling the area, and the Privileged demanding answers. By the looks of it, the announcement of Artaxiad had yet to be made. Sulwyn looked around quickly, wondering where Kione was right now, but was distracted by the sound of yet another horn in the distance. An escapee must have been found.

Sulwyn picked up the pace, urging Ki faster as they weaved between people trying to get out of her way.

Soon, Valens loomed before her, and though her body protested, she jumped off Ki and ran straight towards the large, black front doors. She was met by Néosan, who only hesitated for a moment before they let her in.

She crossed the lavish gold and white antechamber, brushing past more Néosan, Captains, and Validus alike. Some maids and manservants hovered the area, taking in the needs of the others visiting. But soon, a hush fell over them as they noticed her stepping between them as quickly as she could. Not knowing where she should go, she rounded a corner and almost crashed into Demir.

"Queen!" He hurriedly bowed, eyeing her oddly and staring at her strange outfit.

"Take me to Daijiro and Galahad." He stared at her incredulously. "Please!" she wheezed, extremely out of breath from the journey. He must have pitied her but he nodded stiffly.

They travelled along the first floor past the ballroom and the dining room, which were still destroyed, and many other rooms until they turned another corner and only one room was left. She hadn't noticed before, but Valens was now clear to her. She remembered every path they had taken, unlike before when she first came to the Empire. The only way Ildri could have gotten out of the Solus is if Gwydion removed his magic barrier, which he must have done here as well.

"They are in there…" he muttered, but he didn't leave. Instead, he took post at the beginning of the hall, yellow eyes fierce and waiting.

"Thank you…" Somehow or another, it seemed she had earned his respect, even if he was a little snot. She wondered if that would change once he knew her truth.

Sulwyn stepped forwards, fear rising in her along the quick beat of blood rushing in her ears, but she would not hold back. Instead of knocking, she flung the door open and stopped.

"Raghnall?" she whispered, until reality sunk in. He looked strikingly like him, but if he were twenty years younger with dark blond hair and a bit more height. His eyes were light brown instead of whitish blue, stern and guarded instead of warm.

"Fortunately, no," he replied, standing straighter as he took her in, a brow raised at her odd ensemble of clothes, no doubt.

"Sulwyn," said Galahad quietly, eyes boring into her with the look she knew he would give her. The one that was silently screaming, *"Why didn't you stay at Eques?"* mixed with something else... something like fear.

Nero. The man who aided in the attack against Galahad's clan, who had tried to torture and force him to reveal his powers. Sulwyn's gaze darkened as she watched him. Until she noticed Daijiro opposite her, his eyes in silent warning.

Sulwyn took a deep, calming breath against her erratic heart. "I believe we haven't had the chance to meet. I have heard stories of you, Nero. The pleasure is mine." And though she wasn't wearing a dress, she curtsied all the same.

As Nero stared at her, a nagging itched her mind. She had forgotten *something* yet again, but she needed to focus on the task at hand.

"Your story is the only one missing. They insisted I let you rest given the circumstances, but you've made my task easier for me," Nero said, ignoring her greeting and keeping his emotions impassive at her arrival.

"And what story is that?" demanded Sulwyn. He was straight-cut. His grey jacket fitted and tightly buttoned all the way to his neck, black pants lacking any sort of crease. While he looked like Raghnall at first glance, she saw nothing of him in this man. The only thing they shared were some physical traits. And somehow, it seemed Nero was thinking the same thing.

"You hold his stance. Not something one should revel in, especially at his betrayal." He spoke calmly, his voice clearer than Raghnall's, with practised emotionless tones.

"You'll be glad to know that I don't see it in you."

Nero stared again, nothing betraying his thoughts. "Imagine my surprise when only a month ago, I received word that our queen was murdered. Soon followed by the news that their daughter, who had only just come to the Empire half a year ago, would now be queen and to wed her own father no less. And now, learning that the king is dead upon my arrival. How would that sound to you?"

"The most striking thing in everything you just said was the king wanted to marry his own daughter," Sulwyn retorted, and even she could tell that he was unsettled by that fact. But he quickly gained face.

"How did the king die?" he asked, walking closer to her.

The room they were in was small, something like a meeting room for lesser topics. Barely furnished with a small unlit grate to keep the winter winds away. And yet somehow, Nero made the room smaller. His presence was undoubtedly something. She'd give him that. But he wasn't Raghnall, and he wasn't Artaxiad.

Sulwyn didn't know what Daijiro and Galahad had said, but she would keep it simple and go from there. "I don't know if you've been informed, but there was a mass breakout from the Solus, and prisoners killed him. A Validus can attest to that. An unfortunate loss to the Empire so soon after the death of my mother..." She paused, trying to bring forth emotions of despair. Which was easier than she thought it would be.

She watched him flick his eyes from Daijiro to Galahad, no doubt looking for prompts from their actions. But soon enough, Sulwyn heard Arsinone.

"They went into detail about the Solus. Explained Gwydion was a Devinal, and he aided the escape plan. Daijiro and Galahad were out responding to the alarms. You were out because you feared for your father's life alone in the stables, knowing he would be a target."

Sulwyn smiled internally. "I didn't think it was possible," she started, getting her emotions to work with her. "I had said that it was Gwydion who murdered my mother. I watched him do it! I couldn't stop him! Not someone like him. But he twisted my father. Made him forget that he had killed her, that he carried magic as a weapon. How else would he have escaped? I knew it would only be a matter of time before he tried something else. To get our king out of the way!"

Daijiro and Galahad stared at her intently, but Nero spoke first. "And you didn't think to mention this to anyone?"

"Who would believe me? The distraught daughter trapped between trying to keep her people and king safe as he deteriorated in front of my eyes? Ask anyone! The king was many things, but trying to marry his own child? Does that not sound strange to you? Who else could have accomplished that save for someone like Gwydion, a Devinal of all things? He made my father torture me!" she howled, pulling up the sleeves to show the deep, red welts that were inflamed and stinging from the acid rain.

Nero stared at her. Seconds that seemed like forever as each beat of her heart passed until finally, he nodded. "I understand the severity of this situation, but I cannot allow you to be queen."

Sulwyn clenched her jaw, trying her best not to make eye contact with anyone other than Nero.

"The people will be in chaos come this morning when we announce the king's death so shortly after the queen. Though you were named the new queen by Artaxiad, as you said, some questioned his state of mind. Now that he is not here to defend it, they will panic and wonder if you hold any capability of leading, as well as hold doubts about you. As the leader and creator of the Triarchy, I will reside next to you until we can settle things properly."

VIII

A Fallen King

| SULWYN |

SULWYN, Galahad and Daijiro were escorted and followed by Demir to another room where they were to change and wait until the announcement was made. Demir bowed himself out just as a few servants came in.

The room was far larger than the one they had just been in. This one was white and grey with small windows and full of other rooms that held apparel and the like, a wardrobe for the elite that lived here. All three were escorted to their own rooms.

These maids were not any she was familiar with. If they had any questions, they kept it to themselves, bustling around as she sat waiting after they had stripped her down, giving her a deep blue chemise. Fatigue crawled through her, the poison slowly waning, allowing for exhaustion to properly claim her.

As she watched them, she noticed that they would not make eye contact with her. They all feared her. And rightly so. She was still queen even if no one agreed, and in these last few weeks, she had been a terror in the bare moments she was allowed to see other people. "May I clean your skin, my queen?" asked one of the girls, but soon a sharp knock sounded at the door, and Eztli and Nori came in. Relief washed over her. She figured they would follow her, given how she had left. And if Arsinone was somewhere in the castle, they would be too.

"She is our charge. Yer dismissed," called Eztli, who had much more authority than Sulwyn ever realised. They curtsied quickly and were clearly glad to be given the excuse to leave. Eztli shut the door behind them, and both Nori and Eztli turned to face her.

Sulwyn looked at them for mere seconds, when without warning, she broke down completely. Perplexed, the girls relaxed, their stiffness melting away as Sulwyn slid off the chair and onto the floor. But she could not stop the tears, not this time. Eztli rushed forwards, sitting in front of her.

It was like when she had first come to the Empire, waking up in that cell alone, confused and betrayed. Everything was a mess. The fear of being caught clawed at her, and she didn't know why. This is what she sought to do, one way or another. So why did she keep reacting this way?

A soft knock sounded on the door, and without waiting, it opened, revealing tricoloured eyes. Sulwyn looked up, unable to voice anything but sobs despite her efforts. Daijiro pushed his way in, past Galahad, looking at him pointedly.

"We need to talk…" Galahad said, but Sulwyn silenced him with a look.

"You, of all people, know it's not safe to speak here." Her tone was harsher than she wanted. Damn this poison! She grabbed the chair behind her and chucked it at the wall near the two of them, hearing a satisfying *crack*. She could sense the startled look they gave her, the moment when they all looked at each other, and it angered her more, but she needed to hold on. In less than twenty-four hours, the poison would be completely out, and she could finally be free again. Even if she was becoming immune, she was tired. She just wanted to stop.

"Can you do anything for her, Nori?" whispered Galahad.

"No!" Sulwyn demanded. "I'm done with this. With being controlled and willed and prodded. *I* will make it go away," she gritted out, shivering again. The fever climbed higher, fatiguing her more. But she still had a part to play.

"Sir?" called a man from somewhere outside of the room. Sulwyn caught Galahad's eye. He was tired, too, beyond tired and worn out, but his eyes only held warmth for her. He nodded before stepping out to address the Néosan, closing the door behind them.

"We need to get ya cleaned an' dressed," mumbled Eztli, moving to stand, but before she did, she wrapped her arms around Sulwyn's shoulders.

Sulwyn tensed at her touch, the urge to harm still there, but soon, she was able to wrap her arms around Eztli and pull her down into a hug. When was the last time she had embraced anyone like this? Something with so much warmth and comfort, it flowed into her. Battling the war within her.

"I'm right 'ere, sweetness." Eztli gently pulled away, returning to Nori's side as they started to go through the clothes in the room.

Sulwyn had almost forgotten Daijiro was there until he walked somewhere behind her. A grey blanket fell over her shoulders.

"It won't do anyone any good if you pass out now." He crouched down in front of her, his eyes burning. "We will talk once this is over. All of us." He reached forwards carefully, taking her hand in his, warmth sliding through her. She looked up at him; light, pulling waves of calm came from him. It was as if little bits of her anger and confusion were melting away. His allure as a Velyūn was always astonishing to her. Something that could make her feel at ease but could also sway someone to do his bidding. Daijiro smirked crookedly. "Just a little, just for now."

Sulwyn was draped in folds of dark blue, black lace rising over her neck and down her arms. Goddess of the moon, she still hated lace. But it was simple and modest for the occasion. And the only appropriate attire they could find at the last second. Galahad was in a jacket and pants of black and green, always the sole person to wear green after its ban when the High City fell. A "gift" he was given as it was the colour of his clan when Artaxiad slaughtered them all. Daijiro in burgundy and black. Regardless of the event, he still had a sash wrapped around his waist. This time it was also burgundy. She walked between them, feeling the warmth that emitted from both as she tried not to let cold dread freeze her.

Four long gongs rang in the distance as they made their procession out of the main entrance of Valens, off the castle grounds and towards the streets.

Privileged and Common Ones alike remained. Even though homes and stores were damaged in the aftermath of the storm, everyone stopped and stared, making a wide berth, as the line was led by Nero and other Validus carrying an ornate bed of wood with Artaxiad resting above it. They were to walk to the centre of the Empire, where a large fountain stood, bringing all of the streets together into a large circle. Though the distance was quite far to walk and her body dragged with each step, it felt like no time at all.

The centre of the Empire was much like the one in the fog town but far more exquisite, with blue and purple stones laid into the ground in a large circle. A large black marble fountain with an elegant statue of a horse and tree sat in the middle, the water tinkling gently out of the marble leaves into the white stone pool.

Sulwyn, Galahad and Daijiro followed just behind. Walking along the path as the sun broke over the horizon and cast them all into first light. Sulwyn glanced at the people around her, many staring at Artaxiad's lifeless body, but most staring at her.

She couldn't gauge their emotions, most in utter shock, some in disbelief. But some—some stared at her with hard eyes. Her stomach dropped each time she connected with one, but she withheld her emotions, maintaining the solemn look with which she had started.

Sulwyn only had about an hour of rest. Unable to think of much else, she used that time to sleep. She was weakened now, more than she had ever been despite her life as Kintana, the Blood Princess and the queen of Vartugaul. The only choice she had was to see this through and take her next steps carefully. Putting together everything she had come to learn in the last few months. She couldn't let this become a habit.

She was done with feeling this defeat at the hands of people she was meant to remove.

Her whole life, she had spent waiting for the opportunity to take a winning blow to the Empire. And they achieved it. She wouldn't let it go to waste.

The procession came to a halt, Artaxiad's body being laid to rest in front of the fountain for all to pay their respects to. He had been cleaned and changed into one of his most elaborate sets of clothes of golds, reds and blacks, his hair and beard trimmed and combed. The scars on his face glinted in the light of the rising sun. No one would know he had been stabbed and broken. No one could tell he had died in anguish and confusion.

"The people of the Empire!" called Nero loudly, much to the surprise of many. She heard Raghnall's name or Steel Warrior pass their lips in hushed tones. She couldn't blame them; they were strikingly similar. It ached her to see him.

"For those of you who do not know me, my name is Nero. I have known our king and queen since they first saved us from the High City. Assisted them in their needs and created the Triarchy to aid them further." At this, the whispers changed. They knew who Nero was. And as she looked at him, she saw the resemblance now, faintly in how he presented himself. Raghnall always had a way with people and could bring them together. Though where he did it with familiarity and strength, Nero did it with a sort of rigidness, strict and to the rule.

"As all of you would agree, strange things have befallen the Empire as of late. And as I try to get to the bottom of it, I ask that you have patience with me and our young queen." He gestured for Sulwyn to step to the front alongside him.

"Our leaders, Artaxiad and Pandora, had lived most of their lives here without their daughter. Someone they thought had disappeared forever. Finally reunited, their bond was met with tragedy. Their time together was too short. Sulwyn has their strength, but she is still a fledgling, new to leadership and overcoming all that has happened in her life," he continued, and even Sulwyn found herself pulled into his speech.

He was neither demanding nor condescending. He spoke like someone who held nothing but the people's best interest at heart, all the while maintaining that expressionless tone. He was asking for their permission to have him lead along side her. Not forcing it. Making it look like they had a choice in the matter when she knew they did not.

What a tactic.

Sulwyn would have applauded him if it weren't for the setting.

"If you will have me, I will stay here while she settles in and ensure that the Empire stays at the top as they have for these last twenty-four years." Silence met her ears until everyone slowly but surely began to clap. Not too exuberant or forceful, remembering that at the end of this, there was a dead king and a growing threat outside their borders. Nero bowed his head in thanks before addressing the situation at hand.

"Early this morning, during the cover of the storm, prisoners from the Solus escaped. We are working tirelessly to capture them and bring them back. If they wish to retrace their steps and turn themselves in, we will let them go back to the Solus in peace." His eyes darkened, looking out at the people. "However, if they fight us and refuse our rule, we will have no choice but to execute them on the spot.

"There are some more dangerous than others that have escaped, and as I have discovered, they are the ones responsible for killing our king. Our king, who put his people before himself in this storm, seeking order and guaranteeing coverage for those around him. Our *king*, who strove to protect us all. He was slain heartlessly during these dark days." He paused, and Sulwyn could see he was reading the crowd, ensuring his words struck them deeply. "These prisoners are nothing but selfish murderers and common miscreants. Hell-bent on destruction and revenge. And we will find them and give them the death they deserve."

Sulwyn stared at him. He lied about who had killed Artaxiad, or who they thought killed him. He was the leader of the Triarchy. There was no way he didn't know who those prisoners were. He also didn't mention anything about Gwydion. She turned to look at the people. All of them in despair and confusion.

Of course he wouldn't.

Since Artaxiad's death, Sulwyn's mind cleared with each moment. Things she had forgotten came to her as quickly as they normally had. Gwydion was a trusted Triarchy, and Artaxiad had managed to convince them all that Pandora's death was by her brother Zander, not Gwydion. Because why not?

And Nero wouldn't mention that the prisoners were from the Pain Cells. For all Sulwyn knew, the Privileged didn't even know those existed. And even if they did know, it wouldn't be public knowledge that there were four people from the High City king's private guard, led by Nero's brother no less. Artaxiad and Pandora were dead. Knowing Raghnall's prized comrades were still alive and now free would cause chaos. She could see why Artaxiad had held Nero in high regard, trusting him to create the Triarchy in the first place.

"But enough about those cruel prisoners. For this morning, we are here to celebrate the life of our king. The man who brought us this far, who carried us through his ambition and strength." Nero stepped away from the wooden bed, bringing Artaxiad into full view.

Just like with Pandora, a torch was given to her, and she stood to the side waiting, maintaining her look of sadness. Nero reached for another torch, but this time beckoned Galahad to come forwards. Galahad stiffened, a tic in his jaw. He took the torch from Nero and stood stoically next to her. He acted like when they first met in the upper dungeons. All emotion hidden. Everything broken.

As Nero reached for another torch and Néosan began to stack firewood around the podium, pouring oil along the way, Sulwyn secretly moved her hand to find Galahad's. He looked at her for a fraction of a second, eyes wide with relief. Slowly, his fingers laced with hers tightly before he let go and turned to face Artaxiad.

"We thank you, for leading us, for bringing us this far. May you be at peace alongside Pandora." Sulwyn joined Galahad and Nero, and in unison, the three of them dropped their torches onto Artaxiad's body, watching as it erupted in flames.

IX

Nothing Heals Like Fluffy Pillows

| SULWYN |

A wet cloth cooled the burning in her head, but the towel itched her skin. She reached up and shoved it off, the cold, wet towel slumping by her neck. A hand reached to pick it up gently, placing it back on her forehead despite her protests.

Sulwyn opened her eyes suddenly, greeted by dark blue, violet and deep red irises. Adrenaline rushed through her, the image of Pandora's room slipping from her mind, the green eyes that haunted her these last few weeks fading. She blinked the images away, pushing herself up.

"Sulwyn, it's okay to stay lying down," Galahad whispered, assuring her with his hands. He placed them gently against her shoulders, and she admitted defeat, sinking back under the covers. She could hear crickets chirping outside the window; night had fallen.

Once Artaxiad's body started to burn, Sulwyn had finally reached her limit and collapsed right in the centre of the city. She could hear the screams and gasps from those around her, and quickly, someone scooped her up and took her away, but it was neither Galahad nor Daijiro. In her moments of wake and sleep, she realised it was Nero, but his face remained unchanged. She knew he did it for show, and once they were safely behind the cover of many Néosan, he deposited her into Galahad's arms.

But whatever the means, she was back in a bed away from the horrors she had faced.

"How long have I been here?" Her throat dry. Galahad reached beside her for a pitcher, filling a glass with water and handing it to her.

"You're getting better at this… It's not the next day, just the night of." He smiled tightly; brows furrowed.

"You look terrible…" She drank the cool water, her throat content.

"You aren't that much better, Sulwyn," he muttered darkly, and everything unspoken passed between them.

"Tell me your story," she asked, leaning back down on the bed. Though she wished they were in his room in Valens, she settled for his room in Eques. He still had a view of a large tree just outside his green-curtained windows that bloomed with pretty orange flowers, filling the room with a sweet, perfumed scent. He looked at her carefully, considering. "I'm okay, Galahad… It's out now. The fever must have burned it away. It did so when I had a vision, though not as slowly as this…"

"You had a vision?"

"It already came to pass. Ildri had tied in a warning as well." She stared at him, willing him to speak. He sighed, giving in.

"Artaxiad threw me in the upper dungeons the night he took you, but no one bothered to remove the keys from my person, so I left soon after. By the time I was out, I had heard no word of you or Artaxiad. I went to Eques when Daijiro had just returned. Gwydion dissolved the barrier over the Solus and shifted location elsewhere." He clenched his fists, but Sulwyn reached forwards, taking his hands in hers instead.

"The next day, Artaxiad announced that Gwydion was framed by Zander and that Zander had escaped. No one knows where Gwydion went, but Artaxiad never questioned it, and so no one else did either. He's still at large, and we have no leads."

"And Zander?" asked Sulwyn, remembering how he had first told her he would help her achieve something great when she met him at his cell, and so he had. She never could have expected he was Pandora's brother.

But Taru had mentioned she had one during his soul reading for her, and she realised now, he looked strikingly like Pandora but with deep lines and worn, brown eyes and dark auburn hair.

"I don't know. We don't know how he escaped, and we're wondering if Gwydion took him with him to aid his story, but you had gone missing as well. It wasn't until Taru came did I realise how much trouble you must be in." He took his hands back and instead hid his face in his palms.

"I saw Taru in a dream…" she whispered.

"He said the Seers past sought him out to try and help you. That your soul was calling out," Galahad mumbled in between his fingers.

"What's wrong?" She could sense it since she first saw him. The darkness he carried had grown. Was it because of Nero? Because of her?

"Gwydion passed a message through Daijiro to me. 'It's only going to get harder from here on,'" he whispered, moving his hands from his face. She could see fear hidden in his eyes. "Taru also mentioned…" he started then stopped, as if saying it aloud would be his undoing.

This time, Sulwyn sat up, slowly but carefully. Her body was stiff, and the cuts pinched as she moved. She looked at him intently, waiting for him to speak when he was ready.

"It's becoming difficult…" was all he managed to say.

She knew there was more to this, but she couldn't push him if he didn't want to talk. And with Nero arriving, she figured he was reliving moments he wished he had forgotten. Things had been strained between them since they left the fog town. Many things left unspoken and unresolved. But she wanted to keep what they had right now without pushing him away and being patient with him as he had been with her.

"Tell me the rest," she suggested, and he nodded. After another pause, he continued.

"A few days ago, marked the one month that the prisoners in the Pain Cells have their day out. During this, Ildri approached Daijiro, admitting she was a Devinal and could sense the acid rain and shardstorm about to come. Because Daijiro is like you and can feel when rain will follow, he put faith in her. She said she could make the shardstorm worse, but she needed someone to get them out of the Solus."

She had seen him in her vision, everything making sense now. But Daijiro giving Ildri a chance was something she never thought she'd see. The moments she spent learning about Daijiro confused her still, especially through her current state of haziness. Though fueled by bloodlust, he had assisted her more times than she could count in different ways. His red eyes stood before her, in brief memory of when they danced both at the Summer Waning Gala and her coronation as queen.

What enigma was he?

"There is a lot more to him than you could imagine…" Galahad said softly, leaving Sulwyn bewildered. Their relationship had grown in her time away, more than when she was in a coma. Somehow this made her envious. They were sharing things with each other and not with her.

"I had a vision with Daijiro… When I was visiting the Solus. I saw him make a deal with Ildri. I know he didn't lock her cell. But what if he gets caught? He's the only one with the key…" Fear thrummed through her at the thought. That was a gaping hole in the story, but Galahad smirked.

"He's mass destruction, remember? She asked that of him and he let her do what she wanted, encouraged her to use her magic to destroy the other cells as well as her own. No one knows that the cells were made with basic Devinal magic. Only Ildri could break them out without the key, but she needed out of her cell first. She knew the storm was coming, and waited for the warning bells. They sound in the Solus too. That was the signal for all of us.

"But Artaxiad wasn't a fool, not completely. Though he didn't see Daijiro's betrayal coming, he didn't trust me. Néosan were always around me, which was why I was delayed in joining you sooner. But Daijiro managed to get to you before me, giving me time to deal with them under the cover of the storm."

"But Nero wasn't in your plans…" she started.

"No. He never sent word that he was coming. It wasn't until Eztli learned from the outposts that she let me know, but it didn't matter. He had left too late, and the storm delayed him. All we needed was that day. I can deal with Nero. I'm not the person he found all those years ago." He bawled the sheets between his fists, and Sulwyn saw the black rapidly start to cover the whites of his eyes.

But soon, he closed them and inhaled deep, shaky breaths. When he opened his eyes, the black had receded to a faint tint at the edges. Soon, he adjusted his gaze to her and waited.

It was her turn.

Sulwyn braced back against the soft pillows, taking his hand in hers once again, a tremor going through her.

"Poison," she said, and he nodded slowly.

"The night you..."

"Killed that maid? I remember now," she spat, but he squeezed her hand tighter.

"Eztli came to find Daijiro, and Arsinone showed him what happened. He suspected they were drugging you to bend your will."

There were many things about his sentence that confused her. Like why they went to Daijiro and not Galahad, or why his expression darkened just a bit, but she would ask her questions later. "Artaxiad said he had gotten them from Gwydion, that he wasn't the only one who studied in sciences."

"Gwydion?"

"These last few weeks have been a blur, but everything has been coming back to me bit by bit. Whatever it was I was being injected with could strip me of my mind, soul and heart. It... He made me do things I wasn't even aware of. Everything was hazy, I was so angry and irritated all the time, and if it didn't line up with what Artaxiad wanted, it didn't line up with me. It was like he instilled his will upon me, making me act like him."

"That's unsettling..." Galahad replied, but then he turned to the door. A moment after, it opened and Daijiro waltzed in.

"I believe we agreed we'd *all* talk?" His eyes flashed dangerously; no doubt upset that he had missed some of their conversation.

"What have you been up to?" asked Sulwyn, taking him in. Somehow, he seemed the better one out of the three of them.

"Nero's been interrogating me for the last two hours," he said nonchalantly, walking across the room and towards the bed. He plopped onto it, kicking his slippers off and placing his head next to Sulwyn's stomach. She looked down at him, a little nonplussed.

"And?" asked Galahad, an edge to his voice at the mention of Nero.

"He has no proof. I'm not a fool, and I'm not new to this either," he said darkly. "I cannot be interrogated, not by someone like him."

"But he has suspicions," Sulwyn said, looking between the two.

"He has suspicions about everyone," continued Daijiro. "From what I've heard of Nero, he's a try-hard. And this is the opportune moment for him to shine. Cailín, you may be queen, but you never won the people's favour. Artaxiad pushed you onto them, and they didn't truly trust his judgement. They all thought he'd gone a little mad from Pandora's death. But no one would defy him. However, you are still their daughter, and unless a better option is shown, you have the right to rule."

"But Nero won't stand for that," Galahad added. "Among all else, he follows the rules and the instructions given to him. If Artaxiad made her queen, she will stay as queen unless he can find something that overrules that. Which is probably what he's looking for."

"Like us being the real culprits?" she whispered.

"Let's not get ahead of ourselves." Daijiro chuckled. "He's going to have a demanding time with that while having to focus on stopping everyone who escaped from the Solus. Though I didn't realise Ildri was going to let *everyone* out. But it throws suspicion off more, I guess."

"We need to rein them back into the Solus…" Sulwyn said, knowing that a lot of those people were real criminals. She would not let them kill the innocent. She even hoped that by being imprisoned, they had learned some humility. But she wouldn't hold her breath for it.

"That's the plan," Daijiro replied, stretching. "Nero is sending us all out to find them."

"All?" asked Galahad a little wearily.

"All. That includes you, Cailín. Though Artaxiad never followed through with it, Nero has taken to the idea that you will be a Leader. All five groups will be going out."

"Is that safe?" asked Sulwyn, but Daijiro just raised an eyebrow. "Leaving the Empire without at least one of its strongest guards?"

Daijiro shot up swiftly, sitting cross-legged in front of her. He bent so close to her; his breath breezed over her skin, eliciting a shiver out of her. He smelled like the same sweet rain and burnt wood, but this time, there was a hint of mint. She moved back a bit.

"Are you showing concern for the Empire?" he asked wickedly, but Sulwyn just shoved him back.

"There are innocent people that live here. The best place to attack is within the Empire before escaping outward."

"Nero is powerful." Galahad stood from his chair and moved across the room. "He wouldn't leave the Empire unguarded." And with that, he took his leave, closing the door.

Sulwyn stared after him, confused at his sudden departure. Until she turned her eyes on Daijiro, but he put his hands up in surrender.

"Galahad has gone through a lot these last few weeks. You should be patient with him."

"Are you his advocate now?" she snapped. Galahad was keeping things from her, and though she decided to be patient, everything changed now that she realised not only had they been sharing things, Daijiro knew whatever was deeply affecting Galahad and she didn't.

Him?

Over her?

"What about you?" she huffed. "I've heard Galahad's story for the most part. What is yours? Where do you really stand..." she whispered the last part. She couldn't face any more betrayal. Not again. And just like

Galahad, her heart wanted to put trust in Daijiro, no matter how much of a tyrant he could be. She had seen it then, and he still did it now. Whenever he glanced at the scar on the side of her head that he created by accident, he carried regret.

He faced her properly, looking at her intently. The Velikat necklace of small delicate leaves that he always wore glinted a rainbow light from the fires around them. No doubt something given to him by someone special. "I guess it's only fair. I've already told Galahad..." He smiled, taking one of her hands and telling his tale.

ভ৹৵

Sulwyn had fallen back asleep only to wake late into the night. Her dreams were full to the brim with everything that had been on her mind. Most recently, Daijiro. She never expected him to have such a story. And now that she knew it, she realised that all that time ago, he really did understand what Caldwell had gone through or the terror of Artaxiad's revenge. She fully understood what it meant when Arsinone said his soul was broken.

And her nightmares... Full to the brim of Artaxiad's hazed green eyes. How many people had been damaged throughout Artaxiad's reign? How many more would she find like this, poisoned and black, unable to be free from the things that tormented them? Even with them dead, they left a scar on the world and on the people within it. And now more than ever, she was one of them.

X

Can You Look Surprised Without Eyebrows?

| SULWYN |

SULWYN tapped a finger impatiently on the wooden table, waiting for the other men.

She had been in bed for the last two days, and though she knew she needed that time to heal, she was restless. The only person who could visit her was Taru, but as he ended up having conversations with everything else instead of her, it quickly made her tired.

Arsinone had been given a day of rest as well, but even she was busy helping Eztli and Nori. With prisoners at large, the entire army was at work, and the amount of consumption tripled. Not to mention the chaos that was going on without Artaxiad. Nero had doubled patrols around the Empire in case of outside attacks. He sent word to pull all Néosan from their rotational duties across Vartugaul, leaving only five per major town. He put his number one priority on recapturing everyone who escaped from the Solus while trying to maintain a show of power.

Kione, she finally learned, had left the Empire altogether, insistent on tracking his sister, Diesirae. With him already being blamed once for Diesirae's radical group that attacked the Empire, he was the most in danger. But Sulwyn still reprimanded them all for letting him go alone. Kione was a bright soul and she never wanted to involve him in any of this. Had she known this would be the outcome, she would have never approached him when she had duties in the Solus. He would have stayed safe, being a rare Common One that was promoted to a Protector; the elite guards of the prison. It wouldn't be until everything had settled that he would learn about Diesirae.

He was supposed to stay away from all of this. But she knew it wouldn't last. He would learn somehow, and he would get involved some other way, alone. And that would be even worse. Even if he felt it was his duty and partially his fault that all of this had happened, Kione wasn't supposed to get involved this way. He wasn't supposed to be captured and tortured for his sister's mistake. He shouldn't be on the run looking for her. The last thing she wanted was for him to be tainted. She prayed they'd be reunited soon.

Galahad and Daijiro were needed to aid the Empire's forces, and so Sulwyn spent most of her time sleeping or exercising until finally, today, Nero summoned her to meet with the Leaders in Eques at the meeting room. She had even worn a dress to appropriate the situation, though it was the simplest one she could find of grey silks that reached her collarbone and exposed only her arms.

But everyone was late.

She continued to drum her fingers against the table. The last time she was here, both Pandora and Artaxiad were still alive, and they had yet to go to the fog town where part of Galahad's clan resided, hidden for years. The room was unchanged, the dark blue curtains still fluttering in the cooler air from the open windows. The room was as lavish as any other. She contemplated leaving and wandering, but the door finally opened. The first to join her was Galahad, who smiled lightly but avoided her gaze. Ever since he killed Artaxiad, he'd been different. Distant, but they hadn't had the chance to talk about it further. Even that time when she was in bed, he didn't mention it. And it was driving her insane. This awkward dance around each other made her more restless.

"How are you feeling?" he asked, taking a seat to her right. She had placed herself at the head of the table, where once upon a time, Artaxiad and Pandora had sat. She stilled at the memory but pushed the thoughts to the back.

"Better, clearer, but still confused..." she admitted. Her mind was full of so many thoughts she'd been having trouble sorting them out. With Nero here, she needed to step up her game to impress him as queen, and they were unsure if he knew she was Kintana or not but didn't want to broach the topic just in case.

"Take your time, Sulwyn. A lot has happened in a short amount of time. And with this new task at hand, we'll need to maintain our place." He reached forwards to brush her hand gently before pulling it back. He still looked tired, anxious even, but she had to leave it alone for now. She trusted he would talk to her soon, or so she tried to remind herself.

Daijiro entered next, and for once, he looked sullen. Quietly, he took his place to her left, nodding to Galahad and glancing at her. What was wrong with these two? But they all turned their attention to the door as multiple voices reached them. Finally, Nero stepped in, followed by two other men she had never seen before.

The first one was tall, easily over six feet and lithe. His brown eyes instantly found hers, piercing and deep set, more so because he was bald. He dressed a little like Caldwell did, with loose grey pants up to his knees and a sleeveless black tunic that exposed his thin arms and muscles. It took her a while to figure out why his face looked so out of place. Then she realised, he had no eyebrows. His face was a little gaunt as well, enhancing his sharp features.

Directly behind him was a vastly muscular man. His violet tunic and pants seemed small for him; the only thing fitting were the large white boots. He was shorter than all the other Leaders, with straight grey hair tied back into a long ponytail that reached the middle of his back. In contrast to the other man, who had a light golden tan, this man had deep russet skin with dark orange eyes and scars everywhere. Along the side of his neck, she could see numerous marks that definitely signified torture at some point in his life.

Sulwyn was happy she didn't get Kione involved in this. These men wanted to be here. Worked to get where they were and had the scars to prove it. At least, that's what she presumed. But three out of five Leaders turned out to be people who never actually wanted to get this far and ended up doing it anyway. Would they be different? Or were they Artaxiad's men through and through?

The bald man took his seat next to Galahad, the other taking his next to Daijiro, while Nero sat at the end opposite Sulwyn. Silence rested upon them, long enough that she was even more uncomfortable than before, but she kept it in. Galahad's gaze weighed on her before he spoke.

"My queen, this is the first time you have met," Galahad said, his back stiffening at the formality. "This is Eurus, the Leader of Uferor Vier." He gestured to the bald man who tipped his head in her direction.

"The honour is mine." His voice was rough, as if he made it a habit to speak as little as possible. He stared at her unabashedly, but Sulwyn nodded her head, staring back.

"And this is Tarak, the Leader of Uferor Fimm." He waved his hand to the other man who, despite his size, got up quickly and bowed, placing a fist over his heart.

"I am sorry it has taken us this long to introduce ourselves." His voice was exactly as she thought it would be, deep and gravelly, and could possibly travel across leagues of land without raising the volume.

"The days since my arrival have been busy for all of us, I'm sure. The pleasure is mine." She, too, stood and bowed. This flustered him, but he stayed bent all the same.

Nero watched her carefully before he finally spoke, just as Sulwyn and Tarak sat back down. "I have called you together to explain what it is I want you to do. If our queen agrees, that is." Sulwyn was sure he was forcing himself to add that last part. Regardless of what she said, she figured he'd find a way to conduct his plan one way or another.

He looked at her straight in the eyes, and against her better judgement, she looked away. She had a hard time looking at him, his similarity too much for her to bear at most times. And today was one of those days. She had woken up with a nightmare still fresh under her eyes. Raghnall's face atop the bodies in the lower dungeons stuck to the inside of her mind, all the while thinking about what it meant that his scar was not on his face. But there was also another nightmare that plagued her every night since Artaxiad died. His eyes were always the last thing she saw before she woke up. Daijiro kicked her leg, bringing her out of her mind and back to the problem at hand. Their eyes connected briefly, her hands tingling slightly.

"Despite our best efforts, many horses were taken when the prisoners escaped. It looks like the bells signifying their escape was delayed for quite some time, adding to this situation. But I have received word that there have been sightings of the four people responsible for the king's death," he continued. "As our queen will be new to leading an Uferor group, I will send her with Divi and Vier.

"I don't agree with that choice..." Galahad started, but Nero silenced him, holding up a hand.

"Sulwyn will be taking over Caldwell's group Uferor: En, who specialise in stealth. Based on what I've heard, I think she can adapt to this group. Divi is interrogation, which I believe will balance well with En, especially to cover for Sulwyn's inexperience."

She wanted to show him what inexperience looked like, but she held her tongue, clenching her jaw. She caught Daijiro and Galahad exchanging looks, both smirking for just a moment.

"Vier is speed. With Divi and En, I believe you will get faster results." He turned to face Galahad; his tone emotionless as ever. "Galahad, San has always been the balanced group. Having you with Fimm, the group of strength, is our best bet. I don't intend for you to stay separate the whole time either. You will reconvene back here to report in a week's time. I don't expect them to make it easy. If you see a lead, take it. If not, come back, and we will revisit and plan again. Besides, we may need you back once word makes its way across Vartugaul."

"There were four people," started Sulwyn, "but we're separating? Do you have word that they have split up?" Nero's unwavering gaze met hers. She found it strange that Ildri would leave any of them yet. Either his sources were off, or he was planning something. They all turned to look between her and Nero.

"A woman with blond hair and a tall man were spotted together. No one else was with them," he said. "In another town nearby, they have noticed two suspicious people coming and going, but as they have no idea who we're looking for, we don't have proof. The first set matches the description given by the Validus who found you that night."

She didn't like his tone; he was still suspicious of them. She needed to pull it away any way she could.

"If you want us to take them by surprise, wouldn't it be better to send each group individually? Or as was done with the fog town, pick the people most suited to the task and create a smaller, more convenient group?"

"This is why I said with your agreeance, my queen." He nodded, leaning back in the chair. "I had considered that, but there is the off–chance that you will meet other prisoners. And it's best if we have the full force of the Uferor at the ready."

Sulwyn followed suit, leaning back. She couldn't fault his logic, and again, she was reminded of Raghnall. Did he truly hate Raghnall? If it were her, she would go out of her way to make sure they didn't have anything in common. Despite how much Nero detested him, he only proved to be more similar with each moment she interacted with him. But he was the enemy, and she needed to fool him.

"I agree with your strategy, but I am unfamiliar with areas near the Empire. I trust you'll give that knowledge to the others. Besides that, when do we leave?" she asked, standing now.

"Tonight, with the cover of incoming rain. Luckily for you, it's not acid this time."

�✦�

A knock sounded at the door, but before she could turn to reach it, the door opened, and Eurus stepped through and into her room without invitation. While it surprised her, she wouldn't show it.

"Eurus, correct? What brings you here?" It was near time to depart, and though they were all to meet at the Empire gates, he had come here. She eyed him wearily but maintained civility.

But he just stared at her, his eyes hollowed with not a trace of warmth in them. A shiver went through her, but she hid that too, raising an eyebrow. Would that be offensive since he had none?

"Speed. That is what Vier specialises in," he stated, and Sulwyn was more confused than before. "If possible, I'd like to get this assignment over with quickly."

Was he insinuating that she would slow them down? How she wished these people knew! But Sulwyn continued to hold her tongue and instead smiled. "I would like nothing more. Please be patient with me." She inclined her head politely, but he continued to watch her as he walked backwards, closing the door with a snap and leaving her to stare after him. What was the point of that?

Shaking off the warning bells he had left her with, she finished placing the daggers in their proper spots in her belt. She was glad for this again. She had been trapped, tortured and bedridden. She needed out, needed freedom. But she was afraid.

With both Artaxiad and Pandora gone, it was only a matter of time before someone really started to realise what was happening. And she was sure it would be Nero. Until then, she would use this chance to get to know everyone in the Uferor so that she could stand against them when the time came.

Sulwyn glanced at the full-length mirror to her side. She was happy for something other than dresses. She laced the black calf-high boots over loose deep brown pants, adjusting them as she stood. As queen, she was given something else to her attire. Over her crimson tunic, she draped a long, black and red embroidered jacket that went mid thigh in the front and flowed out to her ankles in the back. It was thick, meant to prevent the brunt of hits or weapons, as well as prepare her for the cold that was soon to come in the next few weeks.

Sulwyn stared at the brown leather belt in her hands. The belt Raghnall had made her once she was able to handle every blade she held in it. It was worn but still strong. Just like the ring she carried. She groaned in frustration, passing a hand roughly through her hair. It would do nothing for her to ruminate right now.

She wrapped her belt twice around her waist, then secured the buttons on the double-breasted fold, hiding the belt underneath. She folded the sleeves up to her elbows for better movement before finally tying the sides of her long hair back, leaving it loose with some of it up and away from her face and the rest hanging unrestrained.

And then she stared.

These grey eyes so much like Pandora's, but darker.

This violet-tinted black hair was the same shade as Artaxiad's. Wavy like it too. And their skin was almost the same olive tone. Though hers was a bit darker from the sun.

Little bits of her features, like her lips and eye shape. Her face and body shape. All these things had a likeness to both. There was no doubt to anyone that she was their daughter. And now, she would always be reminded of their dead faces.

Sulwyn took a deep breath. She could do nothing about who she was born to, but she could destroy what they created. And right now, she needed to find Ildri and her group and make sure they escaped before the Empire found out. She wished Galahad were with her as well but figured it would be best this way for now.

It was late evening when Sulwyn made her way to the front of the Empire astride Ki. Divi and Fimm were already there, preparing their horses or sharing items for their journey. As she got closer, she also spotted Demir standing with the rest of what she presumed was En.

She found herself looking at the forest in the direction of where Caldwell was buried, though his body had been dug up and burned the night of Pandora's death. She hoped they left the bodies of the family she failed alone. But she never got the chance to check. For now, she could only wish for strength to deal with what Caldwell had left behind. Demir came up to her as she slid off Ki and walked towards them.

Instantly, they all bowed, holding a fist to their chests. She waved them off, watching them fall back into line. She looked at the four men, including Demir, and noted they were all similar in stature. The perfect weight and height to maintain secrecy and stealth. Stealth happened to be something she was decent at when she wasn't blowing her cover because she got curious and involved.

"In an unconventional way, I am now the Leader of Uferor En. Before we begin, I want to let you know that despite his flaws, I had come to minimally respect Caldwell, and I trust you will do the same for me. I want you to teach me how he led this group so that I can follow suit, but with one rule." She looked at each one individually as they hung onto her words. At least they seemed well–behaved. "I don't want unnecessary casualties."

Demir stepped forwards. "My queen… Caldwell already enforced that, so not much will need to change."

Sulwyn's hands grew cold when a tingle passed through her chest. Caldwell had tried. No matter what he had turned into and ultimately had done to her, he ensured that the rest of them wouldn't become like him. She nodded, dismissing them to continue preparing for departure.

Soon, sweet rain, burnt wood and now mint wafted around her, and she turned to see Daijiro coming up from behind. "Why do you always smell so nice?" she blurted out to his surprise.

That same heat made its way up her neck, but he just laughed at her. For once, he was dressed heavily in a thick sleeveless leather jacket over his golden yellow tunic and leather armour over his forearms and calves.

He even carried a weapon, an elegant walnut brown bow with red arrows across his back. Though his clothes remained true to his style underneath, a black sash tied around his waist, draped over a belt of small daggers. His blond and white hair blended in perfectly with each other. It was only now that she noticed how long his hair had gotten since they left the fog town, brushing the top of his shoulders.

"Off to a good start, are we? I wanted to give you something." He lifted a sheathed sword off his back and handed it to her. Carefully, she took it, feeling the weight of it in her hands.

"Galahad makes clothes or has them outsourced. I can't make weapons, but I know people who can…" He trailed off, gesturing for her to unsheathe it.

She pulled the blade out, watching as the bright silver caught in the torchlight; rainbow flecks dancing around them. It was the same metal used to make his necklace but with swirls of purple embedded into it. The hilt itself was pure matted black, a contrast to the sparkle of the blade.

"How did you get the Velikat metal?" she whispered.

"I shared the insight with a few trusted sources and there's a scarce amount left. If I need something, they make it from that metal and only for me."

She nodded. "This… It's beautiful." Unable to say more, he nodded too, his red eyes reflected in the silver of the blade. He touched her arm lightly before going back to his own group just as San and Vier arrived.

Still marveling at the sword, Sulwyn noticed the sheath could fit two ways and decided to carry it on her back. Slinging the strap across her shoulder and over her chest, the sword rested neatly between her shoulder blades diagonally.

She noticed Eurus watching her but dismissed it as Galahad slid off his horse and beckoned them all over, dressed as heavily as Daijiro, his sword at his side and his clothes full of green. "Sulwyn, are you ready?" he asked softly, looking at her with so many unspoken questions. But all she could do was nod. Ready or not, she had no choice.

"We need to find them…" she whispered, the intent clear between them. He brushed her shoulder before addressing the rest of the Leaders.

"You've been given your town; both are approximately two to three days away. If our targets are there, they already had a head start and there is a chance they may move on. Each team has a relay horse. Make sure to use them to report to each other between towns in case there is anything out of the ordinary. The clock is ticking. People will start to take a stand once word has spread about the death of both the king and queen and the prison break of the Solus." He spoke clearly, all men listening to him without interruption. Whatever had been happening to him didn't show now, and for once, he seemed like the same man that showed authority way back in Antac on their first mission together.

"It's been a while since we've had something this big," started Daijiro, rubbing a hand over his face and through his hair. "Actually, I don't think we've faced something bigger."

"They will pay for dishonouring the Empire," boomed Tarak, looking the same, with leather armour like Daijiro, but strapped to his belt were two large copper gauntlets with spiked knuckles. She had never actually seen anyone use gauntlets as a permanent weapon. She glanced at Eurus more closely. He, too, wore the same thing from earlier with leather armour, and carried by his side was a dark red spear. Having lost her own spear many years ago, she respected the choice.

"Try not to break the town this time." Daijiro smirked, earning a scowl from Tarak.

"That was one time," he huffed.

"One time more than anyone else." Daijiro shrugged.

Galahad shook his head. "Let's not loiter any longer." He dismissed them all. The other Leaders called for their teams to prepare to take off, all of them getting onto their horses. No carriages were being brought this time. They needed all the speed they could get.

"Sulwyn," called Galahad, reaching for her wrist, holding it gently. "Be careful. I don't think we'll find what Nero is looking for, but we might find other obstacles."

Sulwyn looked at him, his eyes warm but his expression stern. "I won't do anything I shouldn't…"

"I know, and Daijiro is with you. But just… keep your guard up." His eyes moved towards Eurus for a fraction of a second. He whispered, "You are the queen. You are Sulwyn. Nothing more can be shown." Understanding dawned on her.

She needed to look out for Eurus.

XI

Madness Rules Madness
| SULWYN |

"WHERE are we going?" Sulwyn called as they quickly passed through the new barriers and guards surrounding the Empire. San and Fimm had already started riding more north as they turned off southeast.

"Macil," answered Eurus, coming closer to her right.

This would be another new town. She had been through the Tranquillum Forest that created the border of Antiqua and Guāngcǎi, but never crossed over Antiqua, not until Raghnall had brought her to the Empire. She was quickly learning that Antiqua's towns were far larger and more populated despite the fact that Guāngcǎi had more small villages and towns.

The benefits of living near the Empire, or at least for the towns that provided necessities for them, showed. The difference was vast, and she was sure she would see it in this town as she did in Antac, back when she went on a mission with Galahad and Caldwell all that time ago.

They travelled in silence for the rest of the night, rain joining them halfway through as they galloped straight across the land for several hours until they stopped to rest before continuing in the morning. To her understanding, Macil was three days away, while Synd, the town Galahad was assigned, was two. If the rumours were true, she would come across someone from the Pain Cells. She wasn't sure if she wanted it to be true or not, not with Eurus here. But she would figure something out.

⚜

The sun started its descent to the west when they finally saw the outskirts of Macil. Daijiro held up a fist and they all slowed their pace. As they trotted closer, they could hear a garble of sounds. It wasn't until they could see the town clearly, their symbolic flag—a diamond with a small circle on the top—blowing softly, did they realise the town was screaming.

"Ki! Go faster!" yelled Sulwyn, ignoring Daijiro's warning and throwing caution to the wind. She looked to her side to see the rest of En following behind her, Demir's face full of determination.

As they got closer to the border, Sulwyn could see smoke rising in various places. She spotted the bare minimum of five Néosan running about the town—the informants for Nero. But five people wouldn't be enough to deal with what the Solus held.

Sulwyn crossed the gate with no one to check her in, only to have Ki take control and slide to the left, galloping behind one of the buildings. They were under attack, arrows raining down over the entrance of the town. The men of En followed right behind her, joining her in the cover of a large building.

She watched Divi split off towards the side of the town, disappearing behind trees as Vier did the same in the opposite direction.

"Ki, I need you to find safety," demanded Sulwyn, sliding off and unsheathing the sword Daijiro had given her. Ki stomped in protest, but she slapped his hind legs to get him going. He neighed loudly, taking off back out of the town and out of sight.

"I don't know about you," started Demir, "but I think you need to re-evaluate the meaning of *stealth*."

"Oh, shut up. You followed me, didn't you?" Sulwyn snapped as a hail of arrows pinged against the metal rooftops above her. "Go be stealthy then and help me figure out what's happening in this town." She looked at the rest of the Validus turn to Demir apprehensively. But eventually, they split up, taking to the shadows to cover more ground.

Sulwyn wasn't expecting the town to be under attack, and yet at the same time, she wasn't surprised. But she needed to move too. They had seen her hide here, whoever they were. She looked around quickly and saw a large fire to her left. Though she heard screams, she couldn't see any people. They must be further in.

This town was clean, just like Antac, the brick buildings a little old but well-kept, the cobblestone in pristine condition. It wasn't like the towns she was used to seeing in Guāngcǎi where everything was falling apart; the people using what they could find to create stores and homes. The people themselves struggled to keep what they had.

But right now, *these* people needed her more.

She slid back behind the rough brick building she was using for cover and ran. She met no one on her way, the sky growing darker with each scream that rent the air, pressing her to go faster. But the yells only grew louder.

Minutes passed as she continued, still meeting no one, not even the others she had come with. Dread filled her every step.

Finally, she reached what looked like the centre of the town and in the middle were hundreds of townspeople, all chained and on their knees, trapped within a circle of fire encroaching on them. The flames ate at the grass around them, burning quickly.

But the people orchestrating it weren't anyone from the Pain Cells. Instead, they were prisoners she recognised from the outside cells of the Solus. They continued to chain more folk from the town, tossing them to the already too-large group. Limiting the space away from the fire. Why were they doing this?

"You are the forsaken!" yelled one of the escapees, a woman with dark blond hair and sharp features. "We believed in the High City all this time while you carried on, feeding the Empire, clothing them!" she called, starting to flick rags dipped in oil into the crowd. The others in her group continued their assault on the people, pushing them into the circle. Forcing them to cross through the fire.

"There was no other choice!" a man called from somewhere in the middle, a woman clinging on to him for dear life. This was not something Sulwyn could condone. Screw stealth. But Galahad's warning kept her back.

Sulwyn hesitated, and in that moment, a spear launched itself from the sky and embedded itself straight into the guilty woman's chest. In the far distance stood Eurus, his bald head catching the firelight before he hid in the shadows. He wasn't joking when he said he wanted this to be over fast.

But that woman wasn't the only threat.

Once her body hit the ground, the other escapees who had climbed the roofs started to jump down and surround the townspeople facing Eurus, the unknown threat. Sulwyn counted fifteen of them in total, but she couldn't be sure that there weren't others hiding elsewhere.

"The Empire is here to silence us!" called a man holding up his bow and arrow.

"Let it be known! Artaxiad is DEAD! Pandora is DEAD!" another man roared to the sky, his voice echoing. Sulwyn watched the people in the circle whisper quickly, heads turning despite the danger they were in.

"What do you mean? I thought it was just the queen?" someone bravely asked, and another escapee, a woman, turned to look at them.

"They are both dead. Their inexperienced daughter is queen. This is our chance to retaliate!"

"It's not retaliation if you kill people just like you," started Daijiro, casually looking at his nails. Divi had spread out, holding their own weapons towards the circle of prisoners. The people within the ring of fire were quiet, huddling as much as possible.

"Oh, the king's mad dog is here!" yelled one of the men, and the others jeered. Daijiro grinned wildly.

"Is that what they call me?" He relished in it, nodding to his group. Each member hit fast and slashed at the ankles of the person closest to them. Four people fell to their knees. Soon after, the four men of Eurus's group, Vier, and Eurus himself, joined the onslaught, taking spots in between Daijiro's men.

Nine to ten.

"Are you the only ones here?" Daijiro called, placing his arms behind his back and pacing as if having a normal conversation over tea. The woman closest to him spit on the ground. His eyes darkened, but he continued.

Sulwyn noticed movement up and behind Daijiro. A man with more arrows started to crawl across the top of the building. Others appeared on adjacent roofs. She looked around to see members of En hidden in the shadows, one across each new person. She watched a Validus pull out a small dagger and quickly whip it across the sky, stabbing an escapee on the roof. When Sulwyn looked back, the Validus was gone.

She was right. Stealth meant assassination in Caldwell's books. The group was meant to have fewer casualties. One by one, the enemy men and women on the rooftops were dropping; all the while, the ring of fire was burning ever closer to the townsfolk.

A man with short black hair and light brown skin stepped forwards, going to his fallen comrade and pulling the spear out. He tossed it to the ground, turning to face Daijiro. "The king and queen are gone. Their daughter is a mere placeholder, probably a shell that carries their ideals. You can all leave if you want to. There's no one to stop us now," he yelled at Daijiro, the others nodding all the while the fire edged closer. Until finally, it started to touch the people within it.

Screams rent the air as people started to pile atop each other, panicking and kicking others closer to the high walls of fire to save themselves. Daijiro turned on the man. "This is what happens when madness rules madness!" he yelled, signalling to his group. Divi stepped out of formation and instead dispersed around, looking for water.

"There's a well here!" yelled a Validus a few feet away, and soon, they were hauling buckets. She knew that wouldn't be enough. She needed to try and get these people to safety. There was nothing left but to have her be a distraction and hope that one of the others would start rescuing the townspeople.

Sulwyn stepped out of the shadows, all eyes turning on her.

"Well, if it isn't the new queen herself!" yelled the man. She only then realised how stupid it was to show herself so easily. Why hadn't she thought to hide her face? But that was something Kintana did, and she didn't want anyone to know. Sulwyn raised her sword, holding it at the ready.

"These people do not deserve this," she started but turned. Without warning, the flames erupted upward. They all turned to watch as the flames gently pulled away from the people and climbed high into the sky, wrapping the townsfolk in a tall tunnel of embers.

"What the hell..." the man murmured.

Sulwyn looked at Daijiro, his hands balled into fists in front of him. She had never seen him concentrate so hard. His gaze was unfocused, filled with the reflection of fire as if it sat in his eyes, glowing briefly. He started to whisper things she couldn't hear when the fire burst apart into tiny flecks of glowing cinders, making the night seem darker.

For just that moment, every single person, enemy or not, stared at Daijiro. But then it ended, and their attention snapped to Sulwyn instead. The man pointed his own sword at her, nodding to his people.

Quickly, they ran towards the captives, each picking a hostage from the crowd. Daijiro had yet to recover from whatever it was he had just done, standing perfectly still, his eyes glazed and unfocused. Eurus and the rest of Vier, Divi and En all emerged, creating a new circle around herself, the enemies, and the hostages.

More screams erupted, some crying over those who had been eaten by the flames, others yelling for those with a knife held to their neck. Sulwyn stood straight, dropping the sword to the ground, her hands up.

"Don't do this," she started, seeing the thin scars that traced his body, seeing the hate and the anger in his eyes. Eyes that wanted justice. But the man's smile grew wide.

"Or what? Your parents are dead. The Empire will fall. And it's our chance to take back what was stolen from us!" he yelled, turning to the townspeople. "Look at her! Look at how entitled she is, wearing clothes we could never have. Carrying weapons that we can't touch! Who benefits from the rule of the Empire? Us?" Sulwyn could see the words sink in, casting doubt into the town's eyes. Watched as they looked at her with as much fear as they held towards the Empire.

"They are *dead*! Vartugaul can be ours once again! And anyone who stands in our way will perish!" He nodded, and one of the woman escapees pushed a hostage his way. He grabbed the older man, pulling his arm back until he cried out.

"You supplied the Empire; you are in the wrong," he growled, then snapped the man's neck and dropped him to the floor. A woman from the middle screamed. Sulwyn watched her collapse in tears.

"How are you any different?" Sulwyn argued, holding her hand up to stop En from coming forwards. She looked at Eurus and shook her head. Though he glared at her, he kept Vier in their positions.

"Artaxiad and Pandora were in the same place you are now, once upon a time," Sulwyn explained, inching her way forwards without notice. The man scowled, pointing his sword towards her neck.

"What do you know about it? You've been in isolation your whole life until you made your way to the Empire and reaped their sows."

"Call off your people. These are innocent lives at stake," she continued, keeping her hands up. "I can't change what's happened to you or the other people from the Solus. But you doing this makes you no better than who you hated this entire time."

He shrugged. "Fight me for them. If you win, I'll let them go and come quietly. But if you lose, well, we're just going to continue."

"I will not fight with lives on the line," she snarled, thinking of the family she let down in her battle with Caldwell. Seeing the same tears in the woman's eyes, her children and husband dead before she followed their fate.

"Did you hear that?" he goaded the townspeople. "She's not willing to fight for you despite her words. You know why? Because she is their blood, the queen. And nothing will change."

A deep gasp sounded from Daijiro as he looked around wildly until he found Sulwyn. He looked petrified, staring at his hands before, all too soon, his eyes turned to the men and women holding the townspeople.

"You have three seconds," he called, his voice a little strained, but Sulwyn didn't think anyone else noticed it. He held up his hands, palms facing out. The man paled, as did the other escapees. They all knew what Daijiro could do, even if they didn't know what he was.

"Three."

They looked to their leader, a tic in the man's jaw.

"Two."

"Do it!" roared the man, and before Daijiro got a hold of them, each prisoner slit the throat of their hostage.

Daijiro immediately made two fists and instantly crushed the bones of each person who had killed their captive, his face livid as the screams of terror rose around them once more, their cries full of pain at their dead.

"Looks like you've lost your touch, mad dog," jeered the man, but stepped back quickly at Sulwyn's movement.

"I warned you," she hissed, stomping on the hilt of her sword and flipping it back into her grip. The man ran towards her, slashing widely until he froze in his steps, paralysed. Daijiro spun to face them, walking before the man while slowly forming a fist as the escapee struggled to move or breathe.

"Do. Not. Touch. My. Queen." Daijiro grabbed her sword and stabbed the man in the chest.

XII

It's Not My Blood

| SULWYN |

"THAT was a mess," said Eurus, but Sulwyn only glared at him.

They had burned the bodies of all the dead on the outskirts of town and rounded up the remaining prisoners to take back to the Solus. The townspeople remained afraid of them as they did when faced with anyone from the Empire. Except, Sulwyn noticed the unrest and the way they looked at her. The word would spread faster now, how the new queen herself was out terrorizing the people. Even if Artaxiad and Pandora were dead, the reign hadn't ended.

Now they remained on the outskirts to rest for the night before going back to the Empire with their report. Eurus, Daijiro and Sulwyn all sat around the fire as the other Validus continued to make camp.

"That was *messy*," repeated Eurus, and Sulwyn rounded on him.

"I'm sorry it wasn't up to your expectations. What would you have done differently?"

"Let the fire burn, take the people back and let them all pay for their crimes in the Solus." He looked at her with zero emotion. She couldn't get a proper read on him at all. Was it due to the lack of eyebrows? She wasn't sure, but she knew with certainty he was not on her side.

"That would have made their crimes higher and led to needless death," she seethed, but he only shrugged, cleaning his spear.

"Eurus isn't normally one for confrontation," Daijiro said, eyeing her in warning. "He likes to get in and out. This is new for him. But I also agree that was messy."

She stood, annoyed. But they were right. She had messed up. Sulwyn had acted on instinct and that could have gotten them all killed. She had been so focused on finding Ildri and the others that she forgot she needed to act like she belonged to the Empire.

"I apologise," she started. Eurus looked up at her, mild shock in his eyes. "I am new to the aspect of missions, let alone being a Leader. I haven't had training, and I shouldn't have acted on my own. My nerves got the better of me. There has been a lot of death recently…"

Eurus stared at her. She had managed to catch him off guard, if only for a moment. "We all lost the king and former queen. I meant no disrespect." He nodded politely, standing and bowing to her. She watched him walk off, collecting a bag of fruits from his horse's pack before retreating into one of the tents.

Sulwyn clenched her fist in frustration, but Daijiro came next to her. "Take a walk with me…" he muttered before calling out to the other Validus. "We're going to go back into town to question them."

One of the Validus from Divi ran up to him. "Do you need us to follow?"

"That town has seen enough for one day. We won't get much from them if we maintain hostility. We're more than enough." He winked, and the man blushed lightly, saluting and going back to prepare dinner.

"Take it easy on him." Sulwyn chuckled, following him towards the town. "He'll fall in love with you at that rate."

He returned the laugh. "I can't imagine anyone falling in love with me. I don't even do it that much. But enough to make someone happy from time to time is a little fun." He winked at her too, the pull washing over her, but she only smirked. They walked back slowly towards the town, Sulwyn waiting until they were far enough from the camp to speak again.

"What happened with the fire?" she whispered, and he looked at her with that uneasy fear. A fear that seemed more like a haunt than actual fear. She narrowed her gaze. "I'm not your father, Daijiro, and your strength doesn't scare me. Not anymore, and not with who you've become or gone back to being. Eztli explained everything you did when we first came back from the fog town when I was in a coma, and I saw what you did with the flaming arrow when Diesirae attacked us before that. There's more you haven't said. And if I'm going to trust you, you're going to need to divulge a little more."

He stopped, looking at her like he'd never seen her. "I..." He closed his mouth, unsure and looking around carefully. But the camp was far behind, and only the low perimeter of the town walls loomed in front of them. It was odd to see him like this.

"Some Velikat had contracts with powerful animals or creatures..." he started, looking at his hands. "My mother only mentioned it once when I was younger, so I don't know much, but in her death, it would move onto the next heir automatically, which was me. But she never mentioned it again for fear of my father learning. It never really showed up until recently, so I don't have much control over it. I don't even know what I *can* do with it. I feel like I've been blocked my whole life, stunted somehow. Until I met you," he explained softly, eyes narrowed.

She could feel a stronger flutter from her heart this time at his words, that same vulnerability she'd seen before shining in his eyes. "Your contract is with fire?" she asked, a little confused at the mechanics of it all, and under the impression there was more than he was letting on.

"It's with a phoenix." He held out his hand, and a tiny ball of flame formed in the centre of his palm. He held out his hand to her, and she gave him hers, palm up. He dropped the ball of light onto her hand. It stopped just a few inches from touching her skin, the heat strong despite its size. But it stayed still and glowing until he pointed at it, and it went out.

৩৩

Nero looked at her skeptically. "I decided to keep you as a Leader because our king had the idea of it. But I no longer feel that you are up to the task."

They had sought out Nero as soon as they returned, the Validus going back to Eques as the three Leaders went to Valens to give their report.

Nero remained in the same room she had met with him the first time. Though his bedroom lay elsewhere in the castle, he made this room his own office of sorts, with various bits of furniture moved in since they left. Though, she didn't know why he didn't choose somewhere larger; it was fairly tight in this room.

"With all due respect," Daijiro began, "a lot has befallen our new queen and sending three groups became more chaotic than good." He glanced at Eurus, who tilted his head a bit.

Sulwyn stood between them, the object of Nero's scrutiny. "I admit, it could have gone smoother. But the end result would have been the same." She stepped forwards, looking at Nero steadily. "None of the people from the Pain Cells were in that town, and no one else had recognised their description."

He eyed her carefully, and Sulwyn could see the distrust in his gaze. "Eurus, Daijiro, you are dismissed." He kept his eyes on Sulwyn, his hands folded behind his back. Eurus bowed, taking his leave first, but Daijiro lingered. Nero glanced at him, eyeing him up and down. Daijiro finally bowed, leaving and closing the door behind him.

Sulwyn maintained her stance, standing tall and staring at Nero's hazel eyes. "As a Leader, you acted recklessly. As a queen, even more so," he started, pacing around her. "Innocent people were killed because of your actions."

"Innocent people are killed all the time regardless of my actions," she retorted. "They had already started their assault by the time we arrived. Being stealthier or more powerful wouldn't have made a difference. They are angry and will lash out at those who had freedom for the same things they were locked up for."

"Are you saying that the people living in towns have the same rights as murderers from a prison?"

"Not all of those people in the Solus were murderers. Some were there for treason in the Empire's eyes or less. The point of this is that we were late. We were too many steps behind to avoid casualties. And it will continue to be so, especially if we stay so concentrated in groups. You didn't have the Néosan move out until days after the breakout. They stole horses and had a head start, all of them. Not just the Pain Cell prisoners."

But Nero stopped pacing, coming closer to her, his eyes never leaving hers. "You treat me like a fool, *Kintana*," he hissed. Hearing someone call her "Kintana" sent a thrumming wave of adrenaline through her, but she remained impassive.

"I know what you are capable of. You could have acted differently had you wanted to. I also think that it was foolish to let you roam free so quickly despite Artaxiad's wishes. I knew my brother. I know his ideals. And I know there is more to this story than what meets the eye."

"If you know so much, then how can you be blind?" spat Sulwyn. She knew he suspected her, knew it was a long shot that he wouldn't know who she really was despite how he acted. But she needed to be wary of what would happen if he could pin their deaths on her.

"Until I can truly figure out how to deal with you, I cannot overstep my boundaries. You are the queen, and the late king's wish must be respected. I am giving you another chance. Once the prince returns, I am sending you to another place. I will leave the Pain Cell scum to Vier and Fimm. Something I should have done originally, though I thought you would do better." He stepped back from her, going to sit behind his desk. "Before I left to come here, there were disturbances. Reports of human-like creatures terrorizing the borders of Guāngcǎi. As queen, it's time you demonstrate your duties to your people."

"You all need to be extra careful," Sulwyn said just as she entered the kitchens. It seemed like forever since she last saw Eztli, Nori and Arsinone in a proper mindset. They turned just as she walked through the doors and towards the counter they were working at.

Arsinone ran up to her, hesitating for just a moment. Sulwyn stooped down. "I'm so sorry, Arsinone. To all of you. For everything I did. Regardless of if I remember it or not, I was responsible." She hugged Arsinone, looking at Eztli and Nori.

"Ya aren' at fault, sweetness," Eztli stated, glancing at the other cooks in the kitchen. All of them were too focused on whatever project it was they were working on. Nori followed her gaze.

"They are preparing a large dinner for Nero's arrival. It's been years since he's been here," she whispered.

"They just want to throw dinners and parties for any reason..." Sulwyn replied, releasing Arsinone.

Her uneven eyes narrowed. "I know what you want to ask," she started immediately, and then she spoke into her mind instead.

"When Artaxiad had used those drugs on you, your soul was screaming. It never stopped. I heard it if I was close. That's why the Seers went in search of Taru. You fought every day until the hold on you grew weaker."

"What are they doing?" asked Eztli, shaking her head. "Even if ya do that, ya can't just stand there starin' at each other. Yer making it obvious."

"Then let me eat," Sulwyn said, smiling at Eztli as she dashed past her to go through bowls of food to pick.

"You can continue..." Sulwyn added, but the thread in her mind that connected to Arsinone was oddly thin.

"You've noticed it. It looks like your Seer descendants are adamant on protecting your mind. But I need you to know something else..." Arsinone walked forwards, gripping Sulwyn's hand tightly. *"The voices feeding your obedience... it wasn't only Artaxiad's. There was another voice. It was hazy like a cloud of bees, but it was thick like honey. And it wasn't demanding. It was coaxing and calm, and it pulled at your desires."*

It was late into the night when Sulwyn heard a soft knock on her outer door. She woke instantly, sitting up, her room dark save for one candle she left to burn. The knock sounded again, softer this time.

Sulwyn got off the bed and donned a plum robe. Carefully she walked out into the sitting area and towards the door. She could see a shadow shift under as if hesitating to knock again before it moved away altogether. She rushed to the door, pulling it open and peering out into the halls of Eques.

There stood Galahad, his face covered in blood and dirt, eyes weary.

"I'm sorry, it's late..." he whispered, turning to leave, but Sulwyn reached forwards, grabbing his wrist and pulling him in. He tensed at her touch but she continued anyway, closing the door and leading him towards the bathing room.

"They don't have elaborate plumbing in Eques, so I can't draw you a bath. The water I have in the sink is cold now, but it's better than nothing," she started, motioning him to sit on the stool near the basin. She didn't like the look in his eyes. She had never seen him look more defeated than he did now.

Sulwyn dipped a clean towel into the porcelain sink, shivering at the sudden change of warm, dry air to cold wetness. Squeezing it out, she turned to Galahad, but he held her hand. "It's not my blood." His eyes pierced hers in some kind of warning, waiting for her reaction.

"I didn't think it was," she answered, moving past his hand and wiping the sides of his face and neck. The situation was reversed. Though, he didn't have as many wounds as she did when he found her in the caves after Diesirae and her people had taken her as a sacrifice. He was just as blood covered, if not more distraught. She rinsed out the towel a few times, wiping his face over and over, his neck, and then his hands. She could do nothing for his clothes but tried to dust them off a bit.

"That's enough, Sulwyn, thank you." He spoke softly, touching her wrist to stop her. It took everything in her not to explode with questions about what he'd obviously done that he regretted so much.

"Are you okay? After Artaxiad..." she started, but she didn't know how to continue. He looked at her with so many emotions flitting in his eyes, yet stayed silent.

"What's done is done. We have too many unknown threats to focus on that any longer." Sulwyn just nodded. He wasn't ready to talk about what had happened. She would continue to wait.

"Did you find them?" she asked instead, pulling forwards another stool tucked behind the door. The sole torchlight danced over his face, darkening his expression further. She tightened her robe around her, trying to suppress another shiver.

"No... And I didn't think we would. Ildri shifted all of them away from the Empire. Nero is using logic, assuming they could only get so far because they should be on horse, choosing to ignore that she is a Devinal despite what others saw. Even if there were eyewitnesses that reported to the Néosan, I think Ildri planted it on purpose to lead us away from their trail," Galahad explained, but Sulwyn just smiled.

"It's very Raghnall of them." And then Raghnall's face atop a pile of dead flashed in her mind again, and she looked up at Galahad, grabbing his shoulders.

He started a bit, leaning back in reflex, but she ignored it. "I know it was some time ago. But do you remember when you found me in the lower dungeons searching for Raghnall?" He looked at her a little oddly, ghosts of his past in his expression from when he lived there as a child, but nodded all the same.

"Did you look at Raghnall's face?" she whispered, her heart pounding in her chest.

He was quiet, thinking. "I did... It was badly beaten."

"I know, but... how did his face *look*?"

He furrowed. "It looked like when I first met him, but bruised. I don't understand what you're fishing for."

"Was there a scar across his face and neck?" she demanded, and he just stared at her.

"Should there be? He didn't have one when I saw him in person, and I don't think there was one in the dungeons, but he was a bit dirty..."

Sulwyn's hands and feet grew cold. The entire time since she had arrived at the Empire, something had been wrong. And upon seeing his body, there was always a nagging in the back of her mind that there was something so glaringly obvious that she was missing, but for the life of her, she couldn't figure it out.

"Raghnall was burned the night he saved me," Sulwyn said, moving back and pulling the robe and the nightgown up to reveal the large burn she had on her inner left calf. Galahad looked down at her, touching the burn lightly.

"I've seen your burn before…" he responded, confusion on his face.

"When Pandora and Artaxiad left to finally overthrow the High City, they left me behind in their burning house," she started, remembering the time Raghnall told her the same story. "He and a friend of ours named Wilkson had been tracking them for days, but at the last moment, they split up. Wilkson went after them while Raghnall went into the house only to discover me." She looked at the silver ring, fiddling with it.

"As he tried to escape, one of the wooden beams fell, but it was on fire and ended up burning us both. It got my calf, but Raghnall caught the brunt of it, and it burned the left side of his neck and face." She pointed along her skin to demonstrate.

"No one ever listed a burn as large as that, if at all, in his descriptions…" Galahad said, puzzled.

"That's the point." She smirked. "Raghnall always said that would be the easiest way to mark him. Everyone knows his name, but his description was too bland to stand out, and he wanted it to stay that way. So, he had Wilkson develop a cream that he could apply once a week, and it would hide his scar. Wilkson is the Devinal I mentioned before, far more powerful than any I had met before Gwydion." Comprehension dawned across Galahad's face at her words. "I don't know what it means yet, but there was no scar, Galahad."

XIII

Join The Festivities

"**J**UST straight to the point, aren't you?" Daijiro asked. Sulwyn stood next to him and Galahad as Nero came to a stop in front of them. She watched as Néosan and Captains ran in and out of Eques, crossing the training grounds that were otherwise empty from actual training at this moment. The grass had been compacted down even further with all the activity, trying to keep up with the demands to round up everyone from the Solus.

"This isn't a game, All-Command. How you made it that far is a mystery to me. But more proof towards the fact that something is not right here," Nero said, his voice never loud or soft, just the same tone, over and over. Sulwyn wondered what it would take to get him to show more emotion.

"My true reason for coming back to the Empire was to gain permission to investigate these human creatures with the aid of an Uferor group. But as we are spread so thin, I'll have to settle for you three and three others of your choosing. You leave in the hour." Nero bowed shortly to Sulwyn, only staring at the other two before he turned on his heel and left.

"Want to drag the Validus from our fog town expedition?" suggested Daijiro.

❧

For this journey, they readied one of the larger carriages full of food, weapons and sleeping gear. It would take over a week to get to where they were directed, but Sulwyn was simply happy to be leaving Antiqua and going back over to Guāngcǎi. This was also her chance to find a way to contact Wilkson, even if she had to rough him up for answers.

It was also easier to assemble their team since it consisted of Validus from En, Divi and San, and none from Vier or Fimm, who had been assigned elsewhere immediately. Sulwyn had to put faith in the fact that even though Ildri and the others had been locked away for over twenty years, their instinct to survive and hide would still be strong, able to evade the Uferor. She was sure there would come a time when she would need their help and had to believe that they had found some-where safe for now.

For eight days they travelled, stopping for the nights and waking early with few stops throughout the day. Focused on getting there as quickly as they could, they barely spoke. It wasn't until the tenth afternoon that they all had a meeting. The other three Validus began to set up camp before the sun set. Ki had gone off near a stream, keeping himself away from other horses as they, too, drank and ate. They sat in a circle near Demir, who had collected wood, creating a fire pit next to them.

"He's sending us towards a Slave Base…" said Galahad, slowly looking over their map.

"I didn't think they would care if anything was disturbing slaves," she spat, but Daijiro just shook his head.

"Not the Slave Base exactly… There's a town near it. That's where we're going. They aid in feeding the Néosan and slaves alike. Send food to them every so often. I've never been sent to a Slave Base, let alone near it. You?" He looked at Galahad, but he shook his head as well.

"The Slave Bases are overseen by Nero and Gwydion." He looked at Sulwyn. "There are four of them. One is in Uhuru. They collect sand for glass. One at the base of Mortui Gemma where they mine crystal and ice. The one we're going towards mines Neuore and delivers it to Antac to make weapons and armour. And the last is near Malumagri, and they collect poison and chemicals from the border of that tainted land."

Malumagri.

Sulwyn had only seen it from a far distance. Dark purple and green clouds hovered over the area. Trees looked malnourished and dead, but she was never allowed near it, and it wasn't only her.

No one went there.

It was deemed uninhabitable, and even Artaxiad kept his people away from it. Anyone who ventured into the jungles too far never came back. She had no idea that they had a Slave Base at the border.

She sat back. "Well, he briefed you both on his reasoning for this mission. Let's hear it." She didn't miss the look that passed between them. Daijiro spread the map out further for all of them to see.

It was a worn map and didn't depict all of Vartugaul but a closer version of Antiqua and Guāngcǎi. "According to Nero, he's been getting reports of people that aren't quite 'people' from towns in this area." He pointed to a few smaller towns that all surrounded the Slave Base they were going towards.

"The first town to report the incident as well as have the most sightings is this one." He pointed to Wallasyn, one of the largest towns in the area. "Which is where we're going."

"And the threat?" she asked, looking at the towns around Wallasyn. The only pattern she could see was that they were all near the Slave Base.

"Human but not human?" started Daijiro, shrugging. She looked to Galahad, but he was at a loss for words.

"The reports he gave us to read all said that they showed up at night, so the details aren't clear. They had the shape of humans, so people thought that's what they were. But they walk with an unbalanced gait and just wander. This specific one ignored everyone except one man."

"Which caused this investigation in the first place?" she assumed, watching the sun finally go down, and the fire cast them all into a light glow as Demir tended the flame.

"The person was killed. Someone nearby said the creature launched itself at the man, biting and hitting him until he died. No one wanted to go near it, some tried to scare it off, but it didn't work. Then it just stopped and stumbled off into the surrounding forest."

"Food is ready!" called one of the Validus, breaking up their meeting.

Unease crawled its way through her, agitation making it impossible to sit still. Sulwyn stood, looking around for some sort of excuse to breathe. "I'm going to fetch some water…" She waved off Daijiro and Galahad, aware that they were staring at her. But she needed space.

She made her way through the thin thicket of trees over to where Ki was resting. He nuzzled her lightly before continuing his small path of destruction of eaten grass. Sulwyn stooped down, filling her canteen, but her focus was blurred.

Something about this whole mission felt forced, and she wondered vaguely if it were another attempt to remove her from Valens so that Nero could investigate without her presence. Before she left, she warned Eztli, Nori and Arsinone to stay vigilant around him, and if they had the chance, to observe him and his intentions.

Sulwyn looked down at her canteen, the water overflowing. With a sigh, she stood and twisted the cap. Until a high-pitched scream rent the sky, and she dropped the canteen onto the ground, watching as the water flowed out around it. A flare of pain shot up through her veins and into her heart and soul, paralysing her as the screaming continued.

She looked around wildly, but Ki wasn't reacting, and neither were the other horses. Birds chirped, going about their business. A scream like that would echo through the skies. It was only then she realised, the screaming wasn't around her, but *in* her, and the pain felt real. Real enough to make her collapse hard, her knees flaring and teeth biting her tongue. Sulwyn flopped over holding her head as if it would explode.

Was this related to her visions? To the Seers? But nothing about this was familiar, and soon, the pain in her veins deepened. Like shards of ice were digging into her, piercing the nerves of her arms and legs. Until a voice spoke, distracting her ever so slightly from the ongoing screams.

"Tricky, tricky girl!" the voice sang shrilly. It was girly but gravelly. Something about the way it connected within her mind was familiar, but she could barely focus on it, only able to keep herself from screaming as well. She rolled into the river, freezing water in her face, burning up her nose and choking her. She tried to hold her breath and move, but she couldn't with the screeching and the fire and ice going through her.

"The puppet has sent you to plaaay! And play you will with our puppets. We have a treat for you, tricky girl!" cooed the voice, but every time it spoke, it sent a new bead of pain through her.

"Sulwyn?" asked a deep voice that she could barely hear over the water and the screams and the cackling.

Soon, she was being pulled out of the river and onto her back. Sulwyn hacked water out of her lungs, soaking her clothes further, taking deep, ragged breaths. And then it all stopped.

The screaming, the pain and the taunting. All of it pulled away, leaving her free and in silence. She looked up to see Galahad's eyes over hers, his face pale and covered in sweat. He looked how she felt. Sulwyn moved back.

"What happened to you?" she demanded, but he was perplexed.

"Me? What about you? We suddenly heard screaming and laughing and realised it was you. The others went to check the perimeter." He moved to touch her forehead, but she pulled back.

"Laughing?" The cackling of the woman's voice still resonated in her head. Did she also laugh along with her? But she glared at Galahad instead. "You are hiding something from me, Galahad." She coughed. Sweat crawled down the skin of her back despite the cold water. She knew how she looked. So why did he look the same?

Galahad remained silent, staring at her with apprehension and something like fear. But she wouldn't back down. Not now, not when they were this far in it together. She had been patient. She needed answers. And she knew he could tell that's what she wanted.

"I felt it," he started, and she stared, leaning back against Ki's legs. He looked at her carefully, kneeling next to her. Some of the colour returned to his face, tinting his cheeks. "I have been recently reminded that some in my clan... When they have a strong bond with someone, be it in a positive or negative light, they can share emotions or physical feelings with another person." He avoided her gaze, looking at her boots instead. "It's not something I wanted to tell you. I didn't think it was pertinent, nor did I want to use it as a means to make you feel a certain way."

"Are you saying you've bonded with me?" Sulwyn asked curiously. He still refused to look at her, so she inched forwards, intently keeping her eyes on him.

"I believe so..." he muttered; the tips of his ears flushed as well.

"What does it mean if I can't feel your emotions or physical feelings?"

He looked up at her then, taking her in. "You aren't part of my clan. It's unprecedented that I share this bond with you. Though, it only seems to be pain and nothing else. You won't or shouldn't be able to feel mine. It's one way in this case."

"That's a little unfair. My pain is my own. I don't want you to bear it..." she muttered, her own face growing hot. But she looked back up at him. "Did you hear it?"

The confusion in his eyes gave her the answer. "I don't understand..."

"A voice, someone's voice, spoke to me. But before that, when the pain started, all I could hear was screaming." She shivered, the echo still in her mind.

"I didn't hear anything." But his eyes widened in alarm, looking around the forest as if the cause were nearby. "We shouldn't linger here longer than we need to. We'll keep our stay shorter tonight." Galahad stood, holding out his hand for her to stand.

She gripped it tightly, the warmth giving her comfort from the cold deep inside her. But she didn't let go, and he turned to look at her. "Did you feel it then?" she whispered. He looked at her with a deep sadness, knowing she referred to what Artaxiad had done to her.

"Yes, I did. And it made everything so much worse," he said darkly, and the warmth was shattered by a chill that ran through her at the darkness in his eyes.

৩৹৶

"This…" started Sulwyn, but she couldn't continue.

"Life is full of surprises." Daijiro chuckled.

They both turned to Galahad, but he was at a loss for words.

They reached the border of Wallasyn at dusk, and just like any other town, they had the low brick walls and assigned flag (two dots to the left of a triangle) blowing in the wind. But it was as if she had gone back into the past when she first laid her eyes on the ballroom in Valens during the Waning Summer Gala.

Though men stood guard at the front gate, within it, past the walls, was a huge festival. The entire town was celebrating! Music and cheers and warm, sweet smells flowed towards them. She glanced at Demir and the other two Validus from the fog town. They all seemed around the same age which was probably why they were all so close.

Sibril was taller than Demir, his blond hair and green eyes standing out against his dark brown skin. He seemed like he needed a little more training. Elian, on the other hand, was shorter than the two, and always seemed just a step behind them. But she didn't think he cared. Half the time he fiddled with his long red hair that he kept in ties, his dark grey eyes warmer in colour than her own. She really hoped they were better than the time they went to the fog town. And oddly enough, she did want to get to know them even though she practically ignored them the last time. She knew neither of them had seen anything like this before, nor did they realise it was allowed. And instantly, Sulwyn was apprehensive. But the look on their faces made her keep her words to herself. But soon, Galahad brushed it off and signalled them forwards.

"Regardless of what is transpiring, this is the town we were sent to investigate," Galahad started as they trotted forwards. "And if we want to get back to the Empire before anything else happens, we need to continue."

"Welcome!" said a man brightly once they reached the gate. He checked over the carriage and documents of travel signed by Nero. "Oh! He's sent the Uferor instead?" His smile never faded but his red hair looked dry and brittle. "That means he's at the Empire now. It's been a while since he's left Guāngcǎi, hasn't it?"

"Are you on good terms with Nero?" asked Galahad as the others got off their horses, moving to tie them outside, but the man looked at them, waving them off.

"No, no! Please stay here! Our town is fairly large. Come and enjoy the festivities!"

"What are we celebrating?" Daijiro asked, sliding off his horse.

"What? Why, the Empire, of course! Many from the Empire come here to rest and enjoy themselves," the man explained, and he ushered them all in. Soon, other townspeople came forwards and took the reins of their horses and led them all through the side streets. But Ki stood his ground, refusing to move when someone else took his reins.

"Leave him be..." Sulwyn said, politely taking the reins from another man. For a moment, he looked remarkably puzzled, but then he was smiling again and waving her forwards.

As they followed, Sulwyn started to spot the same form of entertainment from the Gala in this town. Acts of all kinds fluttered through the streets, tents lighting up, lanterns being lit across the cobblestone paths. Sweet and savory smells wafted over patrons and entertainment alike. Some danced, and others performed intense feats like swallowing fire or balancing on one hand over a rope. And then she saw them—masked people flitting between others, dancing and engaging with guests.

"Daijiro..." she whispered, nudging him. He turned to look at her, but she caught her words. He was looking at her the same way he had all those weeks ago when they first danced together at the Gala, his eyes aflame with many unspoken words, yet soft and intimate. Before everything had come crashing down around her that night.

She took a deep breath, searching for that familiar smell of burnt wood, sweet rain and now mint, which she came to realise wasn't one of the original scents—but it wasn't there. He gave her a curious smirk, waiting.

"Do you remember… at the Gala," she started, but his smile deepened, as did the soft intimacy in his eyes. Sulwyn pushed on. "Two people interrupted us, like them." She pointed subtly behind him, and he turned to spot a multitude of people in masks and elaborate dresses.

His gaze narrowed, annoyance at the memory. "What of it?"

"Did the lady prick your hand?" And as she said it, something stirred in her. Like worry or doubt in the pit of her stomach.

He looked at her, eyes narrowed. "No…"

She scowled, silence coming over her as she tried to think about that night. Daijiro continued to stare at her, but she didn't want to say anything until she knew what she was getting at, so she waved him off.

On the night of the Gala, nothing about herself felt right. And she never had the chance to look back and think about it until this moment. But as she thought about it now, most of it came to her in a blur and that in itself was strange. She couldn't say she never forgot details, but to have a hazy memory of events that had only transpired a little over a month ago was not something she did. Everything else had recovered after Artaxiad's torture, but these memories evaded her.

The entire night was chaos since she stepped through the entrance doors of Valens ballroom. She could recall Gwydion leading her down the steps and dancing with her. But her emotions thereafter were odd, strange, even in her eyes. Her behaviour was wrong, and it wasn't until Daijiro and Galahad showed up that it melted back into normalcy. But then she was pricked by something on the hand. And once she knew Caldwell and the family had been dug up and learned that Arsinone had been taken, the mess of her emotions returned.

Sulwyn looked at her fingers and the back of her hand, thinking hard. Gwydion had provided that aspect of entertainment on Artaxiad's behalf. Gwydion had egged her on during his speech with Caldwell, her emotions rampant until she faced Pandora. And it was Gwydion who created the poison that Artaxiad copied to use on her to bend her will.

"Sulwyn?"

She stopped, looking at Galahad, concern etched all over his face. They had long since passed most of the festivities and reached beyond the centre of town to the edges near a large inn.

"Sorry…" she muttered. Galahad and Daijiro exchanged looks. And this time, her temper flared. "Why do you both keep doing that?"

"Doing what, Cailín?" Daijiro asked, but he stepped back as she advanced. The other Validus watched. Even the happy man who escorted them seemed a little weary.

"Do not patronise me," she began, all the annoyance flaring at once. But she couldn't speak freely, not here.

"Well, you all had a long journey!" started the man, clapping his hands together. "Why don't you get settled in your rooms and join the rest of us in the festivities? Not many other places have the privilege to set this up."

"How *are* you able to do this?" rounded Sulwyn, taking her frustration out on the man.

He was startled but unfazed. "A few years ago, the proposition was made to make this town a getaway for the Privileged. We are funded by the Empire. Did you not know of it?"

"No, I'm new to the rules and ways of the Empire," Sulwyn said, realising they might not know anything about what had happened at the Empire recently. But given the reverence they held for the Empire, she figured it would be better that they didn't know she was currently queen.

He gestured for them to enter the large inn. It was bright and spacious, full of patrons talking and eating while soft music accompanied them. It wasn't like any inn she had been to before, and she could see traces of the Empire everywhere, from the heavy crimson curtains to the elaborate wooden tables and chairs. It was strange that they would dedicate a town to the Privileged outside of Antiqua and in Guāngcǎi, but they were lavish to a fault. It didn't surprise her.

Soon, each of them was guided to a different room along the fifth floor reserved only for them. She removed her belt and sword, tossing both onto the small bed. But before she could even sit, a knock sounded on her door. Demir, Sibril and Elian stood outside her room, all apprehensive but their intent clear.

"Yes, you can go. It's late, and the journey was long. Be ready first thing tomorrow morning." She waved them off and they bowed quickly, thanking her and hurrying to enjoy the night.

"What a generous queen you are…" Daijiro mused from his own room diagonally across from hers. He had just opened the door, propping himself against the doorframe.

"Please, I don't want the people here to know if they don't already…" she said, exhausted. "Where is Galahad?"

Daijiro pushed off the frame and came in front of her door. "Conversing with the innkeeper about who is currently staying here. Official duties and all." He smirked, looking at her carefully.

"What?"

"We aren't patronising you," he replied, his tone serious. Daijiro raised his hand to her hair, tugging at a particularly wavy piece. She was suddenly very aware of their proximity and instead looked at him to continue. "We are worried, Sulwyn. Is that such a terrible thing?" he asked quietly.

She had been so caught up in everything around her she hadn't stopped once to think that she would be worrying others, let alone worry for herself.

"No. It's not. But I didn't ask you to, either of you. This is the life I chose," she said, unsure of what she was trying to say.

"It was a life you were *forced* into regardless of your choice. None of us wanted it to be this way," he said softly, absentmindedly twirling the piece of her hair before dropping it and stepping closer. "Whether you like it or not, you've got a bunch of idiots willing to follow and worry over you. Accept it." And with that, he leaned forwards and pulled her into an embrace.

XIV

Jealousy, Fear & Despair
| SULWYN |

WARMTH enveloped her, easing her mind of all the questions and thoughts that had been smashing against each other. That had been tormenting her since she escaped Artaxiad, and he had been killed.

That familiar scent wafted around her, and though she thought to push him away, she decided to return the embrace. His back stiffened at her movement as her own arms wrapped around him tightly.

And they stood.

Just like that.

Soft music tinkled through her bedroom window from the fair.

Finally, a question made its way onto her lips.

"There's a new smell…" she said quietly. His head moved as if to look down at her.

"What do you smell?" His voice was muffled and somehow deeper.

"Rain as if it were sugar-coated." She felt his intake of breath but continued. "Of burnt wood when a fire has gone out completely on its own and…"

"And?" She noticed his note of hesitance.

"There's a new one… It started recently. Like fresh mint." He pushed her away immediately, holding her at arm's length and looking at her with a mix of alarm and confusion. His hands gripped her shoulders tightly but not enough to hurt. Sulwyn was about to speak when they heard footfalls coming up the stairs. Without a word, Daijiro let go and returned to his room, closing the door softly.

"Oh! Good!" said the man from before, smiling as bright as ever. "The prince is asking for you and the All-Command."

"We'll be right down," Sulwyn replied, her heart beating erratically. She fanned her face with her hands, taking deep breaths before she closed her own door and walked towards Daijiro's.

She knocked twice and was prepared to bang on it when it swung open, and maddened red eyes met hers. "Are you okay?" she asked, confusion more than anything rising in her.

"Lead the way, Cailín," he said gruffly, gesturing for her to go first as he closed his door, maintaining a space away from her all the way down. Once they reached the bottom of the stairs, his crooked smile and lax self were back.

"Where to?" he asked Galahad calmly, but Galahad looked between them, a brow raised. Without breaking eye contact with either of them, he pulled out a small pouch of coins, opened it and retrieved a few.

"They've given us tokens for the festival. It can be used for food or entertainment, and they insist that we enjoy ourselves. But we should be discreet," he said, dropping coins into Sulwyn's palm.

They looked just like the coins marked by Artaxiad and Pandora's sigil of an "A" and "P" back-to-back, but they were smaller and made from zinc instead of copper. They wouldn't be worth anything even if someone collected them and melted them down.

But Sulwyn beckoned Galahad closer. "The attack happened in there—" Galahad placed his hand over her mouth, warning in his eyes. Daijiro looked at them, but reached for the bag and pulled out a pile of coins.

"I'll be going now." He turned to walk through the main hall and straight out the door of the inn.

"Please enjoy yourselves!" called the man. "The festivities go well into the night, but they do close!"

ꙮ

"Don't tell me this place isn't suspicious!" hissed Sulwyn as soon as they exited the inn. She spotted an outside bar and seating area around the side of the building where patrons could enjoy the last bit of summer air. Galahad stood momentarily, looking towards the centre of activity, but turned in the opposite direction. Sulwyn followed him, looking around them carefully. There was something strange about the large town that she couldn't place.

"I agree…" he started, looking to the east. Sulwyn looked too, noting the low mountains that bordered the town separating them in that direction. She could see a worn path that led towards the frontmost mountain. "I don't think it's safe for you to be out for too long," he continued, looking back at her, but Sulwyn just stared.

"Safe? Nothing is safe, not really. Why would here be any different?" Her annoyance rising. First Daijiro and now Galahad. Galahad, who was keeping things from her.

"Sulwyn, we just got you back. And just before that, you were in a coma. You need to slow down."

"You sound like Eztli. And I'll tell you what I told her. The Empire doesn't sleep. It doesn't rest, and it won't stop even with Artaxiad and Pandora dead. Nero is a factor, Gwydion is a factor, and the millions of people who follow their rule are a threat. Rest or not, coma or not. They will keep coming," she huffed, her gaze fierce, but she stepped closer. "The last time you lied to me, I almost got sacrificed. And though that wasn't your fault, we would have had a better chance were we together. So, whatever it is you and Daijiro are hiding from me, I need you to come clean. We're not in the Empire." She waved around her. "No one around us is listening!"

Galahad sighed, rubbing his face in frustration, hesitation in every movement he made until finally, he spoke. "I'm not in control of my power, Sulwyn. At all." He stared at her, but she just waited for him to continue. "Ever since I parted with you the first time, I've been losing control. There is rage in me that does not feel like my own. And it rises *so* quickly."

He sounded defeated, looking up to the night sky. The multicoloured stars reflected in his tricoloured eyes.

"But I had a hold on it. Even after we came back from the fog town. I did. Until Artaxiad took you." His eyes held hers, and she could see the wrath within them. "Whatever little control I had snapped after that. And it's spiraled since. I've stayed away from everyone. But it's not enough, even Taru is concerned, and he thinks…" He paused. Sulwyn could see a hint of black making its way to the whites of his eyes.

"There isn't anyone around Galahad," she assured him, taking his hand in hers.

"He thinks I've been tampered with."

Sulwyn treaded carefully. "Is that possible? Was it Tiergan?"

"I don't know, and I don't think so. But I don't think I could ask him either. He's probably dead by now. The only choice I have is Nero. But if I do that, I'll be admitting something is wrong. And I can't have anyone realise what is happening. It's better if they associate me with Artaxiad's and Pandora's insanity than know it's due to my clan."

"I'll find a way," Sulwyn said, but stopped when he frowned. "What?"

"Daijiro said Gwydion told him it would only get harder from now on."

"I don't understand…" she started, but another warning thrummed through her.

"He told Daijiro to tell *me* that it would get harder."

Sulwyn let go of his hand and placed her palms on either side of his face. "Whatever it is, you will face. I will be here. So don't be afraid. But we need to figure out what is happening here, right now, before we can go back. Okay? One thing at a time. We've made a huge mess." She smiled.

Galahad's eyes never left Sulwyn's as he raised his hands to hold hers, his face leaning into her palm and the black in his eyes receding. He nodded once, breathing deeply. Until his stomach rumbled loudly.

Pink tinged his cheeks, but Sulwyn snorted. "We might as well enjoy the night while we investigate." She took his hand in hers and pulled him forwards.

ҩ҃ҩ

"This is the furthest thing from discreet..." Sulwyn stated.

She and Galahad made their way back to the centre of all the hustle and bustle, quickly finding large chicken-and-potato skewers that caught their eye, before walking to the entertainment. But they paused when they spotted a large crowd, and on closer inspection, found Daijiro in the middle. Sulwyn could smell his unique scent from where she was standing and knew he was alluring the people around him. But he was being reckless.

"Well, let's try this one, shall we?" he called to the small crowd of people around him as they left one stall to another. The man seemed taken with Daijiro instantly but carried on anyway.

"Try your luck with this one! All you need to do is shatter the glass," he said, handing Daijiro three white balls. Sulwyn and Galahad stepped closer, and she caught Daijiro's eye, but he ignored them both and took the balls.

He chuckled, looking at the glass. "These are pretty weighted. What's my prize if I win?" Sulwyn could feel the pull too, though not directed towards her.

"Anything you want, good sir, within reason, o' course." The man with a tall hat and a scruffy jacket smiled. Sulwyn looked around to see other stalls with similar owners, each a unique game with food or small trinkets for prizes. But as she looked on, the crowd began to grow.

"Daijiro..." warned Galahad.

"Care to join us? There are many things to do." Daijiro's eyes slid down to Sulwyn and Galahad's interlaced hands. "Though, I feel like maybe you've made a choice."

"Daijiro," Sulwyn started, never letting go of Galahad and staring him down. How was she going to deal with them both? Now that she understood a little more of what Galahad was going through, she realised what he meant. His hand was tense in hers, holding it tightly. She glanced at him, seeing a tic in his jaw. Daijiro was drawing too much attention, but if Galahad got angry, it would get worse.

Daijiro looked at her in defiance, turning his back to her and facing the thick glass a few feet away from them. But before he could throw one, Sulwyn stomped on his foot, grabbed a ball and whipped it as hard as she could.

His eyes blazed as he looked at her, but they both turned back to the glass when they heard a crack. She had hit low on the surface, cracking a starburst pattern, but it didn't go any further.

"Not good enough!" teased the game leader. Sulwyn scoffed just as Daijiro took the next ball and chucked it at the glass. His mark was far higher than hers, cracking the glass with deep lightening–like streaks. Daijiro looked over at her, smirking just a little.

But Galahad reached forwards, taking the last ball from Daijiro, and flung it at the glass. They all watched it strike dead centre before it cracked and shattered into thousands of pieces.

"Who's not being discreet now?" called Daijiro over a ton of cheers. Sulwyn looked over at the game leader, his smile like ice before she looked at Galahad, who was furious.

"Look at that! We have a winner!" yelled the man, his icy smile growing. Once the cheers died down, the crowd began to disperse, and Sulwyn could feel the pulling waves easing back. Sulwyn pulled Galahad next to her, feeling his tension ease a little. Daijiro stepped right up to the game leader, looking down as if to choose a prize, but he beckoned the man forwards. He stepped down from his tall stool. "You can take anything you like. Even though you didn't land the finishing blow, you did pay for it!" he said brightly.

"Is that so?" Daijiro asked dangerously. Sulwyn looked at him carefully; he was clearly in a mood, and that could be good or bad. "What if I just want to talk? Does that count?" he asked, and the man nodded, though confused. Galahad and Sulwyn stepped closer, both pretending to look at the trinkets for offer but listening carefully.

"We were recommended to come to this town for its festivities," started Daijiro, waving around them. "Working in the Empire is a little taxing."

"Oh, I wouldn't doubt it. There's a Néosan base just a little west of us. They come all the time. Though recently, the rotation was pulled." He frowned, unsure.

"Empire business, you know what it's like," Daijiro continued, picking up a small, ornate mirror and looking at it. "I talked to a few of them actually, they raved about your town, but they also mentioned something about a fight that happened recently." He set down the mirror and picked up a small glass bear.

"Fight?" The man looked even more confused but smiled again. "Oh, that was such a small thing." He chuckled. "A man thought he saw someone attacking someone else. But it turns out they were just fighting over a prize!"

"Really?" Daijiro beamed, picking up the same tone as the man. He put down the bear and stood straight, looking at him carefully. "I definitely need to spread the word to the Néosan when they come back. They were upset that they might have to do extra work on their time off."

"Oh no, no need to worry there. We are always up and running, save for a few hours at night and during the day. We're always ready to accommodate!" He saluted, his smile brighter still. It wasn't until that moment did Sulwyn realise something was on his arm. She moved to say something, but Daijiro grabbed her hand quickly and pulled it gently behind him.

"What's that you got there?" He pointed to the man's arm. He looked bewildered, looking down at his limb. Sulwyn got a better glimpse of it, but she couldn't believe what she saw. His arm looked like tree bark. But the man only smiled wider now.

"It's a gift," he said, then abruptly started calling out to other patrons. "Come test your strength against our glass! Can you shatter it in one try?"

૭∘ર⚬

"I told you to be discreet!" Galahad hissed once he closed the door.

Immediately after Daijiro had questioned the man, Galahad pulled Daijiro back with him and made them all return to the inn. They had all gone to Sulwyn's room, as it was conveniently the largest.

Daijiro glared at Galahad. "You were the one that shattered the damn thing. If you weren't so delicate, I wouldn't have to do things my way."

"Daijiro," warned Sulwyn, but he ignored her again.

"While you two were strolling along, I was actually doing what we sought to do. Need I remind you that interrogation is my specialty, and contrary to your belief—" He shot a glare at Sulwyn. "—I can do it peacefully."

"Why are you directing that at me?" she asked aghast, but he avoided her eyes.

"Fine. I concede. What have you learned?" Galahad said, turning to face anything but Daijiro or Sulwyn. She watched his fists clench.

He was quiet for a moment. "They don't know anything," he started, and Galahad turned to face him. "They all responded like that man. I talked to five other people who seemed at the centre of the fair. The ones with the most traffic passing them. And all of them had the same skin condition on various parts. This man had it on his arm. Another guy had it on his hands. A woman had it along her neck." He started pacing.

"And they all said the same thing?" Sulwyn asked. "That it was a gift?"

He looked up at her, and for a moment, she thought he was going to disregard her again, but he nodded. "Or that they were lucky. And no one knows anything about that report. Normally, I'd assume that the Néosan got their information wrong. But the people here aren't adding up. And sure, they seem fine, but once you start questioning them, it turns into what you saw."

"There isn't anything more we can do now, not until it's light and we've had rest," Galahad replied, his expression unclear. He turned to face Sulwyn knowingly. "You deserve to have a moment to yourself. As long as you stay hidden, you should be fine, but I don't think I can join you tonight." He smiled sadly. Sulwyn could see the tremor in him, and it pained her to witness his struggle.

He walked towards her, placing a hand on her shoulder. "I'm okay. It's best if I sleep. It's harder if I'm tired. Please go explore. But don't come back too late." He touched her cheek lightly before turning and leaving out her door.

Sulwyn had no idea what she could do for him, but if investigating anything more helped lessen his burden, she would try. She turned to grab her belt and sword, but she felt Daijiro's eyes on her.

Sulwyn felt self-conscious, something she normally didn't have an issue with. But since he left her earlier, there was a tension they had never shared before, on top of the fact that he had blatantly been ignoring her. She squared her shoulders and continued to walk towards the bed.

Quickly, she wrapped the weapon belt back around her waist and slung the sword over her shoulder, extremely aware of the fact that he had given her said sword atop all the other pressure filling the room. If he was going to act this way with her, then two could play this game. She adjusted her hair, pulling it out from under the sword on her back and turned to leave. But he had moved in front of her.

"I'm sorry," he started, reaching for her wrist and holding it gently.

"For which part?" she muttered, unsure of why she was so quiet.

"I could make you a list..." The corners of her lips tugged up, wanting to smile, but she pushed it down.

"Let me go," she spoke quietly again. He wasn't stopping her, but she said it anyway.

"I know what you're going to do."

"Then stop me, join me or leave me be." He had drawn even closer to her. She could feel his breath near her forehead, every scent enveloping her but not swaying her in any way. Something she noticed he stopped doing to her for a while, save for lifting the mood in Valens.

"I don't think it's good for anyone in this inn if I tried to stop you." His other hand reached for a stray lock of hair once again, closer to her neck. "I also don't know if I should join you since I've made such a name for myself tonight."

Sulwyn had been keeping her eyes ahead of her and over his shoulder, looking at the clock behind him that read half past midnight. But she soon made the mistake of looking up at him and into his eyes. Her breath caught in her throat, his gaze engulfing her with so much heat.

"But I could never leave you be," he whispered, the hand on her wrist moving behind her waist, pulling her closer until his lips were a hair's breadth away from hers.

Her door burst open. "Have you enjoyed the festivities yet?" Demir called cheerfully as he waltzed in with Sibril and Elian, a faint smell of liquor on them. Sulwyn stepped back from Daijiro, her face burning with annoyance and heat.

"Daijiro, no!" She moved forwards, but she was too late. He launched himself at Demir, taking his half-drunken tankard and dumping it on Demir's head, irritation in his eyes. Sulwyn just pulled him off Demir, pushing him aside and stooping down. The other two had already staggered away towards their own rooms, leaving Demir to Daijiro's mercy.

"Hey." She slapped Demir's face, earning an unfocused gaze. "Hey!" Another slap, and he sat up quickly. Looking first at Daijiro in horror and then at Sulwyn in despair before he prostrated himself.

"My queen, I am so sorry!" He kept his head on the floor, his hair blending into the dark brown rug.

"What do you have to say for yourself?" She spoke as if reprimanding a child.

"I should have known that you would need your privacy as well. I didn't mean to disturb you—" But Sulwyn just cleared her throat loudly.

"Not that," she said, ignoring the fact that Daijiro just roared with laughter behind her. "You're on a mission, Demir. Go to sleep and sober up for tomorrow." She patted him on the head. "And don't mention I'm the queen, please." He nodded vigorously to the floor, getting up quickly and bowing before staggering off.

XV

The Voice Keeps Yelling At Me

| SULWYN |

SULWYN left the room shortly after on her own, unable to face Daijiro. She decided to continue as she would on any other mission, just as she had done in the past: explore at night.

But skulking around this town was harder when everyone was awake and still so active. She passed by many people, and though there were fewer out than when they first arrived, the events didn't look like they would end any time soon. The game leader at the glass stall said they close for a few hours at night and during the day. She assumed it was a shift change and adjusting and cleaning the stalls. But nothing was happening yet, and it was already an hour past midnight.

Sulwyn wrapped the cloak around her, tossing the hood over her head for good measure, but no one looked her way. All too preoccupied with the stalls of fun or food. All mingling or dancing or interacting with the talents strewn throughout the town.

Where did these people live? Because now that she was walking on her own, she realised there were no houses. There didn't seem to be anywhere to stay besides that large inn. And though the inn could accommodate more than she knew, it didn't seem enough for workers and guests alike. And unlike other villages or towns, they didn't have shops or workhouses that she could see. It was as if the town was a festival itself and nothing else.

Lost in thought, she almost walked into a group of people, but pulled away at the last moment. However, all three turned and stared at her, smiling widely like the inn–and gamekeeper.

"Are you enjoying it?" a lady asked, her smile wider. Sulwyn looked her over. The woman dressed simply enough, not a Privileged, but someone who didn't struggle. Sulwyn stopped at her leg. Along the calf was that same blotch of skin, like tree bark peeking out from under her skirt. But how could it be bark?

"I am, thank you!" Sulwyn started, smiling brightly. "Can I ask, how did you get that mark?" She gestured to the woman's leg, but the woman kept her warm brown eyes piercing into Sulwyn's grey ones.

"We're gifted," she said, matter-of-fact.

"Do you want to see if you can receive the gift?" the man next to her spoke. He, too, had it on his chest, some of it poking out onto the base of his neck. The pounding rush of blood to her head throbbed angrily. Warnings all around her, telling her to turn back. But if she could solve this now, she could help Galahad.

"Okay!" she said happily, smiling as widely as they did.

"Perfect!" said the woman, but they made no effort to move. All three of them, the woman and the two men, remained still, staring at her. Sulwyn shifted unsurely. Abruptly, a bell rang out, and everyone sighed in unison.

"Come back later!" the lady instructed, and she and the two men turned away from Sulwyn and made their way towards the inn.

Sulwyn stared. The patrons stopped whatever *they* were doing and also made their way to the inn. As they began to clear out, the workers, too, all went in the same direction. She threw caution to the wind and slowly started to follow them.

As they walked, no one spoke much to each other. Not about their day or how anything else was going. Sulwyn couldn't imagine that no one had anything to say. But after a long bit of walking, they finally made it back near the inn.

While the guests went inside, the workers turned and continued towards the path Sulwyn and Galahad had gone earlier. She moved to follow but was stopped by the innkeeper, as if he appeared out of nowhere.

"Hey! It's getting really late! It's time for a break, so how about you come in and get a good night's rest for tomorrow?" He smiled brightly. He was looking at her, but his eyes were vacant, cloudy even.

"You're right," Sulwyn replied, keeping the same tone they all seemed to be using. "I'll enjoy myself in the morning. Have a good night!" she called and turned towards the inn. She looked back to see the faint outlines of the workers in the distance.

She wasn't entirely sure, but she had a feeling they were going towards the mountain path she had seen earlier. And she was going to follow them.

Sulwyn did as she was told and made her way quietly back to her room. None of the other guests seemed to pass by this floor. A lot of them didn't even go to their rooms. Instead, they flooded the main hall and other areas of the inn. But it worked for her either way.

No one was outside.

Sulwyn closed the door to her room softly. She stood still for just a moment, listening just in case, but nothing came. She dashed over to the other side of the simple room, past the bed and wardrobe, and pulled back the velvet cream curtains. She unlocked the window and hefted it up. It was stiff and creaky, as if it hadn't been opened in forever. After a few painfully slow moments, she had it open wide enough for her to fit through, throwing a leg over the ledge and straddling the windowsill.

Sulwyn looked down; they were five floors up, but as luck would have it, there was a smaller roof a level down from her that covered the back entrance. She looked out into the distance, seeing the faint outlines of the mountains in the moonlight. Though, she could not see any more people.

She shifted her other leg over, kneeling on the ledge and turning so that her back faced the outside. Sulwyn brought the other knee up and gripped the edge of the windowsill tightly before she dropped herself down and dangled for just a moment. She let go and fell onto the roof a little ungracefully, but with minimal sound. Looking around carefully, she continued her way down.

She did the same thing over the ledge of the roof, making sure to step onto the wooden gate that wrapped around the back of the inn. Balancing, she let go of the roof and jumped down to the ground. Perfect. No one was around, and she had yet to be spotted.

So, she ran.

Sulwyn made it to the edge of the worn pathway. Everyone had travelled this way, completely out of sight, with no sound carrying on the wind. It couldn't have been more than ten minutes since the innkeeper stopped her. How did they all leave so quickly?

But she continued, stepping onto the sandy path and walking among the small stone peaks. In front of her, she could see a larger mountain rising with many other smaller ones surrounding it. As she walked closer, a clicking sound reached her ears, like the hundreds of clocks Artaxiad used to collect in his office. Deeper in sound, like a larger, heavier set of metal gears. She was surprised she hadn't heard it before.

Darkness enveloped her path, even though the moon was still high in the night sky. The mountains cast shadows over her, and still, she saw no one. Sulwyn looked back to the town, marvelling that it seemed so far away. But then she was struck with a sense of déjà vu. This path altered her sense of time like the tunnel she had gone through back in the fog town. Though she knew she couldn't have walked for hours to that pit, it seemed like she had.

There was magic here.

But all too soon, that flare of icy needles flowed through her veins again, followed by the screaming of despair and ruin.

"Clever girl. Stupid girl," sang the voice in her head, and she finally placed the familiarity. This wasn't like Ildri, who cast her voice to Sulwyn at the Solus. It was like Arsinone, where her voice was in the soul. Sulwyn did

her best to keep her thoughts hidden, just in case, but the voice cackled, becoming increasingly disembodied as it coated itself in the multitude of screaming.

"Cocky girl. Vile girl! Get out!" the woman screeched, and all the other screams turned to wails of "get out" over and over again until bile burned her throat from the pounding in her head. But the voices wouldn't leave her alone. The dark mountaintops waved at her, the path even darker than before. Cold sweat forced a shiver out of her. She was too disoriented. How would she make it back? She needed to end this, but she only had one really bad idea.

Everything was blurring while she looked around for a large rock, eventually spotting one over a slope of sand up the path. Stumbling over to it, the pain throbbed like a pulse, the voices still banging around in her head and resonating in her soul. Their pain and confusion fueled her decision. She picked up the rock and slammed it against the side of her head, knocking herself out.

ॐ

| GALAHAD |

Galahad tossed the sheets over him. Pain like sharp glass coursed through his body, tearing at each vein and muscle. His shirt stuck to his skin in a cold sweat. He looked around wildly, his hands balled into fists. It was well into the night, silence greeting him. The festival was over, but he knew Sulwyn had gone and done everything she shouldn't have.

He tumbled out of bed, rocking forwards as a wave of nausea passed through him. Sulwyn mentioned something about screaming when they were by the river. The paleness of her face when he first got her out of the water...

It was worse for her, and he needed to remember that.

Galahad dragged himself forwards towards the door, opening it with unsteady hands. He slid across the wall to the door next to his, to her room.

He knocked once but knew it wouldn't matter. He turned the knob; it was locked. Cursing loudly, he tried to centre himself before taking a deep breath and kicking at the door hard. It rattled in the doorframe but did not budge. He tried again and again until finally the knob broke, and the door swung open. A cool breeze filled the room, sweeping the curtains back and blowing them gently to reveal the open window.

A tremor of annoyance and fear barreled through him. He turned back to face Daijiro's door just as it opened.

"I don't think that's how you should enter a lady's room," he started, but faltered when Galahad dropped to his knees.

A moment of blackness entered his vision, pulsing in his head. The other pain had eased, leaving his body altogether, only the dull ache in his mind, but soon that, too, started to pass.

"Where did she go?" Galahad asked, kneeling on the wooden floor. But when Daijiro didn't answer, he looked up to see his hardened stare.

"She went to lessen your burden," he spat, but helped him up all the same.

"I expected her to explore and investigate, but not alone. Why didn't you go with her?" Galahad let go of his arm, stepping back. He'd been paranoid ever since he let Artaxiad take her. Regretted that he let her cover for him, let herself be taken to protect him. That he didn't just up-turn the Empire and take her back immediately. Regretted that he ever left her side the first time.

"Before you turn your rage on me, need I remind you that she's not a child?"

"That doesn't mean you should have let her go on her own."

"It's neither of our places to tell her where she should or shouldn't go. And you should know she'll do what she likes regardless." Daijiro's tone was harsh, and Galahad didn't understand where this stance of his even came from. He watched him step into her room, taking in her means of escape.

"We're five floors up, impressive," Daijiro said from within. Galahad went to follow him, looking around before ultimately going towards the window.

"This will be faster," Galahad replied, letting himself down from the windowsill and dropping onto the lower roof.

Daijiro quickly followed him, both landing softly on the ground. "That wasn't as impressive as I thought. There were many ways down." Daijiro dusted the sand off his hands. Galahad just stared at him as he shrugged. "Where to, prince?"

He looked around. The area was desolate and quiet. There was something eerie about the place. Even the inn seemed too still, given the number of people that must be in there. He knew Sulwyn was too practised to leave a trace behind, but he figured she would go east, considering the festival had nothing to offer now.

Galahad beckoned Daijiro to follow, and they both took off towards the mountain path. But just as they started to walk through it, a bell resonated around them. They both turned to face the inn, seeing lights and flames instantly illuminate the festival grounds in the distance. But the silence still stretched. Galahad frowned, turning at the sound of shuffling feet.

๛

|SULWYN|

Sulwyn rounded the corner, the side of her face tickling from the blood that trailed down her cheek. "Move!" she hissed, pushing them both forwards, her expression not the least bit surprised that they were there.

"What—" Daijiro began, but Sulwyn just pushed him harder.

"No questions, just go!" And she took his hand in hers, pulling him along. She looked at Galahad's bewildered expression but grabbed his hand too.

Her idiotic plan worked enough to let her escape the voices. But it left her exposed. She was lucky that the bell resonated when it did, stirring her. Because the rumbling she had woken up to had reached them.

"What is that?" Galahad asked, but she let him go and ran.

"I don't think we should be found here. Come on!" she urged, taking off in front of them. All three continued to run until Sulwyn deviated from the path and instead of going towards the inn, went straight for the boarding forest. Galahad and Daijiro followed her, all taking cover behind the trees. Just as a horde of the same workers from before came out of the path and towards the inn.

"Those are the same people. What time is it?" whispered Sulwyn.

"Nearly two…" Galahad answered quietly.

"That's not enough rest." She stooped down, pulling out a small rag from the pouch around her leg and dabbing her head. They both turned to her; one slightly amused, the other highly not. "It wasn't the worst plan!" Sulwyn snapped, beckoning Galahad to sit. She looked at Daijiro and gestured for him to sit as well.

"Why did you go alone?" Galahad reprimanded.

"I have been doing this longer than you seem to believe," Sulwyn replied hotly. "I don't need guidance."

"That's not what I'm getting at," he argued, but they all stopped, turning to face the inn. Sulwyn crouched forwards, creeping her way closer to the copse of trees for a better look.

All the guests from before, and some that she hadn't seen, came out from the inn to resume the festivities. The hairs on her arms and neck raised with a shiver. There was nothing normal about this town. She flopped back down, dropping the rag, but Daijiro picked it up again.

He pulled out a small canteen from within his black sash and poured it on the rag. Slowly, he dabbed the dried blood on her head, the cool water dulling the throb. But she couldn't look at him. She reached forwards and he let her take the rag back, leaning and sitting against the tree instead.

"There's someone here similar to Arsinone…" Sulwyn started, looking pointedly at Galahad. He had been looking back and forth between them.

"The screams I heard a few days back. I heard them as I neared the mountains."

"What screams?" Daijiro asked haphazardly.

"Disembodied screams of torture? I don't know. Whatever it is, it's painful, as Galahad can attest to." She shrugged. "But besides that, there's magic here. I didn't feel it the way I did in the Empire or in the fog town at first. But when I woke up, I could feel that thin, syrupy air for just a moment when the bell rang."

"Are you saying Gwydion is here? Isn't that a little reckless of him?" asked Daijiro, but something unreadable flitted in his eyes. She knew he was still angry at Gwydion's escape. Could see the urge to invoke his revenge on him.

"No," started Galahad, "Gwydion is smarter than that. If Nero has this town marked, he wouldn't linger."

"Unless they are on the same side?" suggested Sulwyn, Nero reminding her of everything else she needed to reevaluate. Daijiro looked between them both.

"I don't think he'd be on the same side, but they share a common enemy, which could be worse..." Galahad looked at her.

"What? Me?" Sulwyn asked, and to be honest, she hadn't even considered herself an enemy, at least not to Vartugaul. But she was an enemy of the Empire, and if Nero was looking for ways to get her out, then letting Gwydion carry out his plans would be in his best interest as long as it didn't threaten what the Empire had established. Was that why he was ignoring her claims that Gwydion is a Devinal?

"Sulwyn," called Galahad, and she focused on him. Exhaustion pulled at her and she would be no help if she was tired.

"I'm going, I'm going." She stood to see the last few patrons leaving the inn.

XVI

Sweet Rain, Burnt Wood And...

"WHAT do you smell?" Daijiro asked, trapping Demir between him and his inn door.

The sun had just risen over the horizon and the festival was still going. But not everyone in the inn had the same behaviour as the ones they saw last night. When he went down earlier, some people had just checked in, a few from the Empire that Daijiro recognised in passing.

"I don't understand, sir..." Demir said, but he wouldn't look him in the eyes.

"Just shut up and answer," he said deeply, and watched Demir relax.

"Wet dirt."

Daijiro shoved him back into his room. "Where are Elian and Sibril?" He intended to try them as well.

"I think they went to get breakfast, sir." Demir's attitude snapped back to him once Daijiro stopped trying to appease him. "And I honestly don't think you should act this way just because of last night," he mumbled, but froze when Daijiro held out his palm to him.

"I don't even have to stop you myself; your fear did that on its own." He smirked wickedly, earning an embarrassed glare from Demir. "Go get breakfast and tell the others to find me."

"What about you?" he asked, moving slowly past Daijiro and out of the room.

"Don't mind me," he snapped, and took off towards Galahad's room.

He knocked once before letting himself in. Galahad was already awake and in the middle of stretching. He looked over in mild confusion.

"What do you smell?" demanded Daijiro, walking closer, and though he knew Galahad was more aware than Demir, he hoped he would still get an answer. But Galahad only stared at him.

"What?"

"Why does everyone have problems answering questions?"

"Because you're probably asking too unexpectedly for anyone to register your insanity." He narrowed his eyes, taking off his nightshirt and rummaging in his pack to find a fresh tunic.

"Just. Answer," he gritted.

Galahad faced him, inhaling deeply. "Fresh rain and wood. You're a candle. Happy?"

Daijiro cursed and left the room.

How could he let things get so far? Never did he imagine this was possible. He appreciated Sulwyn and thanked her for taking him off his path and bringing him back to his original one. Respected her. And he'd be lying if he said he wasn't attracted to her, but it wasn't just her appearance that got him. It was her soul. Everything about her made him want to be better, something he had forsaken ages ago. He hadn't even realised how much he wanted to be free from his bloodlust and how far down the hole he had travelled. But it didn't matter how many people he asked. He knew the answer would be the same. Hell, he was even a little surprised that Galahad had pinpointed the scent as closely as he did. But no one would smell it the way she did, with mint of all things.

"Shit…" he muttered halfway down the stairs, banging the wall with a fist.

❧

| SULWYN |

Sun streamed through the open curtains and onto her face. She rolled over, trying to avoid it, but the smell of food made her eyes open.

On the small table in front of her sat a tray loaded with a plate of eggs and fruit, and a glass of juice. She decided right there that when she won Vartugaul back, she would ensure that everyone could wake up to breakfast like this.

Sulwyn sat up, sliding over to the edge of the bed. Who had brought her breakfast? She really hoped it wasn't that innkeeper. Thinking of him in her room while she slept left a bad taste in her mouth that had nothing to do with the morning.

She chewed some mint and washed up quickly, ate the food and changed back into her day gear. Just as she wrapped the belt around her waist, there was a knock. She wasn't sure who she was expecting and berated her heart for beating so quickly. But berated herself more for feeling let down when Demir entered.

"Morning my… Lady?" he said unsurely. But she waved for him to continue. "Everyone is down in the main hall. We're ready when you are." He saluted. "What happened to your head?" For a fraction of a second, his expression was smug, like his normal self.

"I tripped. Did you get the alcohol stains out?" she teased, and watched his face blanch before straightening it.

"Please forgive my rudeness." He bowed deeply, but she just grabbed her sword and ushered him forwards, closing the door behind her.

Sulwyn followed him down the five flights of stairs and towards the main hall. The rest of them were sitting at a table, all ready to get to the bottom of what was going on. Like herself, the others had removed the leather pads of protection, reduced to their more casual wear, or in the case of the Validus, their uniforms.

"Did you three learn anything useful last night?" Sulwyn asked, pulling up a chair and sitting across from them. Daijiro stifled a laugh, but he'd gone back to avoiding her eyes.

"We did actually," said Demir, indulgently nudging the other two.

"Yes! There is something very odd about this place. We wanted to show you this morning," Elian added. Sulwyn had grown to enjoy his presence as much as she could, but she blamed that in part for the fact that he reminded her a bit of Kione's boyish face.

"Well, if you're all ready, let's get to it so we can get out of here sooner," Daijiro urged, standing abruptly and making his way through the hall and out the door alone for the second time.

"What's wrong with him today?" Sulwyn asked, standing with Galahad.

"He's been going around asking everyone what they smell." He just shrugged. Sulwyn stiffened, remembering the night before, but brushed it off.

They all left the inn, another innkeeper waving them out, and followed the Validus. The Uferor went back towards the festival, which looked far less glamourous in the day than it did in the night. Though the people continued the same way, the festival itself had a worn-down quality to it. The workers and guests alike looked strained in the new daylight, but they still laughed, played, and ate.

It was strange that they had so much food. Even if they were funded by the Empire, where did they get it from? Was some of the Empire's haul allocated to it, and weren't they supposed to supply the Slave Base with food?

Sulwyn stopped, staring at the man who had just walked in front of her. His face was hidden behind a mask, but the eyes were icy blue, the same colour and shape as the man she had danced with at the Gala.

"Wait!" she called. He caught her eye and quickly leapt away, dashing into the crowd.

"Sulwyn!" Galahad shouted, following her before the rest of them joined.

She needed to ask him; she *would* ask him. But he was nimble, and soon, the festival goers crowded her, getting in her way even though she tried to push past them. Based on their reaction, Sulwyn was sure that there was something far more sinister going on here. Someone was controlling them, and then she stopped running, remembering that shrill voice.

"The puppet has sent you to plaaay. And play you will with our puppets."

This had Gwydion written all over it.

How? How was he a part of this?

She had no idea, but she would figure it out. She needed to. These people were trapped here. Even though she lost the man in the mask, she was closer to the crowd. Though they spoke to her about the wonder of the festival, it was all the same, all of them vacant, all of them strained. Only Empire guests seemed unaffected, doing as they would anywhere else. The others were being controlled somehow and whatever it was, was far stronger than whatever Artaxiad had used on her. But who was the puppet that sent them? Was the voice referring to Nero?

"Hey!" Galahad said with a heavy breath, pushing his way to her. "Are you okay?" He looked at her with concern, but it annoyed her instead.

"I'm fine, Galahad. Really. You need to stop thinking that I can't manage myself!" Now that they stopped running after the man, the people started to spread out, continuing their way. She looked around, far past the stalls and the entertainment. Whoever was behind this needed to be around them. Even if they couldn't see them, she was sure there was a perimeter if her theory was correct.

"Lady, Sir," Sibril said, his light brown skin covered in sweat and his blond hair sticking to his face. "If you continue straight, you'll get to what we were talking about. We didn't investigate it much last night; it was too dark. But, well… Come on…"

Sulwyn went forwards, aware that Galahad was watching her carefully, but she didn't have time for that now. The more she looked at the people, the more she noticed that they were wasting away.

"Galahad…" she mumbled, and he bent near her. "I've been wondering about where they are getting the food, but have you noticed? Most of them aren't actually eating it…" She pointed to some of the people near them, holding tin bowls of food, but not a single person made an effort to touch it.

"Here!" called Demir, but the crowd around them slowly started to follow.

"They obviously don't want us here," Sulwyn said hurriedly. She lost sight of Daijiro, but Galahad was behind her. "They must have let these three get away with it because they were wasted."

"They got drunk?" he asked incredulously.

Sulwyn made a face and dashed through the crowd. Finally, they passed behind the last stalls and reached an open road of space. Daijiro came up from the rear and turned to face the crowd.

"They aren't fully aware of us right now," he called back to her, his arms out, waiting to stop them if necessary. "Elian, Sibril."

Both Validus flanked Daijiro, standing at the ready. Sulwyn looked at the crowd. The untainted ones went about their business, noticing nothing, but others slowly turned at them, moving in their direction.

"Sulwyn…" Galahad started, his tone strange. She looked over her shoulder and realised that behind all the stalls and festivals and decorations and lights, there was a town. But it looked abandoned.

Store after store lined the dirty street they stood on, bordering the entire festival. The windows were coated in fine dust and sand, the signs tattered and weather–worn. Looking far on either side, she could see small wooden cabins, what must be homes in the same state.

"I don't understand…" She walked closer to a store in front of her. It looked like it sold fine dresses at some point, a sewist. Sulwyn brought her hand to the window, rubbing the outside dirt away as much as she could before looking in.

The store was trashed, fabrics and clothes were strewn everywhere. Cases broken; mannequins upturned. Until one turned and looked at her.

An unnerving jolt spread through her chest as she jumped back, but soon the door opened, and a worn-looking, brown hand dragged her in.

"Sulwyn!" yelled Galahad, but the door slammed shut, muffling his voice as more hands pulled her in.

What she thought were mannequins turned out to be people, but they weren't people. Not anymore. Dark, wooden-looking arms grabbed her waist and clutched her throat. They pinned her arms to her side and soon hoisted her up and carried her to the back of the small store.

Sulwyn tried to look out of the window, blurred, dirty images dancing by until darkness swallowed her as they descended.

XVII

Two Leaves & One Tree

| SULWYN |

SULWYN couldn't see anything.

But a cool, damp air filled her lungs, and she knew she was underground once again. Hands covered her mouth, gripping her wrists until they stung. But she refused to move. There was no way she would find out what was happening if she didn't let them take her. This time she hadn't been knocked out, dragged to a cave and almost sacrificed. This time was different. This time, she was conscious.

Or at least she was until the screaming started again.

It was stronger, more concentrated this time. Knives scraped at her veins and nerves. But if she was feeling the pain, so was Galahad, and she needed to try and suppress that somehow. She had no idea how his clan worked and what made a connection so deep. But they would need him out there, and if he lost control, they wouldn't solve anything.

Sulwyn took deep breaths, trying to ease the flow of pain. She didn't know what part or why it seemed to cause a ghost pain for him, but if she could shut out Arsinone, then she could shut down his bond. And if she could do both, she could do it to this person.

Because whoever they were, they were related to Taru and Arsinone. She was sure of it. Something about it had a similar nudge.

"You're stupid. But strong. Very strong. I can feel you resisting," sing-songed the voice in her soul. The pain, the screaming, everything made her brain

want to erupt and her old scars burn. She was briefly distracted by the steps evening out as they carried her. Wherever they were going, they were reaching the end. And soon, a new sound joined, but this time it was outside of her mind, a real sound.

The loud mechanical ticking resonated around her, and soon, all the strange humans screamed too. A heavy, metal-screeching door dragged open on the floor, and then she was tossed onto the ground as the ticking stopped.

Sulwyn looked around, eyes hungry for the few candlelights around her. Instantly, she realised where they were—inside of the mountain. And all around her were these wooden-looking humans, all staring at her with blank eyes. Once she started to breathe normally, a wretched smell reached her nose. Bile burned up her throat, vomit threatening to follow at the stench and grotesque state of these people.

They were rotting.

Held together by the strange, bark-looking skin and sinew that grew onto them. They had to be people from the festival. People hoarded for whatever reason.

Cackling echoed around her and Sulwyn stood, drawing her sword. "Face me!" Her voice echoed back. How had they hollowed it out like this? But she needn't have asked. If Gwydion were a part of this, something like that would be easy.

"So brave. So stupid. So rash," said the voice now echoing around her. It was higher this time, scathing and condescending. But she had yet to come before her.

"I said face me," demanded Sulwyn, watching the rotting humans come closer, waiting.

"I was told you were spoiled," said the voice, and soon, she came out from behind the creatures.

Sulwyn stared. She was prepared for something similar but not so identical. The short woman looked at her with uneven eyes, the right grey, the left purple. But aside from her eyes, she looked exactly like Taru.

"Who are you?"

The woman smiled widely, her teeth sharp and stained. "You've seen my brother!" she sang. Sulwyn remained silent, gripping the sword tighter. "I don't need you to confirm it. He's read your soul. I can tell." She cackled, stepping closer. "Where my twin can read the history of a soul, I can control it."

Sulwyn stilled, a shiver creeping over her. This meant the entire town was under her control. But if that were true, that couldn't be enough. If they were twins, then their powers must be similar.

"This isn't your doing alone," Sulwyn started, and the woman frowned. "Even if you can control a soul, there is obviously something wrong with these people. They've been poisoned, and you only aided it." That was the only thing that made sense. It had to be.

"Clever, clever, clever, *clever*, cle–ver. CLEVER," the woman snapped. "It doesn't matter if I can't do it on my own. The point is that it is done. Do you like them? They're DrvaMørk. And they are *mine*," she seethed, pulling one forwards, gripping its arm and biting down hard. Dark, brown-ish blood filled her mouth and flowed over its skin and onto the ground.

The DrvaMørk screamed, and when it did, so did the others. And Sulwyn finally realised where all the screaming in her mind came from. It was from them. From these humans who had been stripped of their lives and tested on to become whatever it was they were now.

"Why?" snarled Sulwyn, the hilt cutting into her palm from holding it so tightly.

"Why not?" She sneered, the DrvaMørk doing nothing to defend itself. She could see a shadow of the person it used to be—*he* used to be. His skin stretched across his bones, sinew exposed with cuts and bruises where the wood-like skin didn't grow. Pus oozing from old bite marks and metal cuffs where chains used to be attached, skin scarred and infected. Evidence that they once fought against what had been done to them.

"How did you even manage this?" Sulwyn asked, trying and failing to rein in her anger. She needed to learn as much as possible before she made her move.

The woman shrugged. "Malumagri, trial and error, me and magic."

Sulwyn barely managed to guard herself as one of the DrvaMørk ran towards her. Not only were they strong, but they were fast. Surprising, considering how wasted away they were. But she got all she needed to know.

Sulwyn moved forwards and slashed the knees of the closest creature. It fell pitifully to the ground. "Why are you hiding in this mountain? With an army like this, you could take over."

"Failed!" she spat, kicking the one that had fallen. "They are failed ones. And so, we hide them. Use their energy for the festivities!"

"Did you like the festivities?" they all asked her at once, voices ragged and dry. She pulled back, unable to fight at such proximity. Sulwyn sheathed the sword and grabbed two short daggers from her waist, stabbing the DrvaMørk in the neck one by one.

They were already dead at this point. There was no way they could be cured. Not after they had gotten this far.

"SAVE ME."

Sulwyn faltered, turning to a young woman behind her. She appeared newer, less tainted. Could she be saved? But once she spoke, so did the others.

"SAVE ME!"

"SAVE US!"

"WHERE IS MY CHILD?"

"WHY HAVE YOU DONE THIS?"

"HELP US, OUR QUEEN!"

"Stop this!" Sulwyn yelled, looking for the woman, but she had walked back towards an open area. She could see the large wheel with seven handles sticking out parallel to the ground. At least thirty people could stand at each one.

"You..." Sulwyn began. "You drain them for energy?"

"That's what I said. I said we use them for the *festivities*. To feed the better ones." She smiled brightly, hopping on her heels.

"How are you *so* different from Taru?" But that was the wrong thing to say because the woman now screeched in anger.

"Don't you *dare* compare us! He's a fool! He's a FOOL!" she shrieked. "Everything has a story," she mocked, giggling. "Everything has a soul meant for good. Every soul can be fixed! NO! He can't fix them anymore!" she sang. "He's given up. He ran away. I control them now. I can lead them!" Soon, the screaming started, both in Sulwyn's head and around her.

She watched the DrvaMørk fall to their knees, screaming in agony.

"Stop it!" cried Sulwyn, her own pain and anger filling her. How could they do this? Haggard men and women surrounded her, but soon, she spotted a few children.

"Enough!" yelled the woman, and a bunch of them stood and walked over to the giant wheel. Mindlessly, they took their post and pushed, turning the large wheel, and as they did so, Sulwyn watched their bodies slacken as the energy in them depleted, flowing up the long metal pipe and out of the mountain as if she could see it.

She didn't understand much about magic or whatever tainted disaster was happening here. But they seemed to be pumping it into the air. Casting it over the festival. It's no wonder people began to sound like that gamekeeper. She was tainting *them all*.

"If I kill you, then this ends," Sulwyn said, and she ran towards the woman who looked so much like Taru. But once she bared her pointed, blood-covered teeth, Sulwyn could no longer see him in her.

"Bad girl!" She spat, looking at one of the DrvaMørk near her. He came towards Sulwyn fast, and before she could evade, kicked her calf hard.

A crack rent the air and Sulwyn screamed. A scratching of sharp knives travelled up her bones, jarring her nerves. Her leg was broken. It had to be. She couldn't imagine feeling this pain if it wasn't. She unsheathed the sword, stabbing it into the ground to stop herself from collapsing.

"He said you were strong. Oh, so strong," the woman mocked.

"What is your name?" Sulwyn asked in between pants, forcing herself to stand and not give into the nausea rolling through her.

"My name? Why, how kind of you to ask!" She smiled brightly, her teeth oozing blood from her tongue. "You can call me Tiamat, dear Kintana." She bowed and Sulwyn used that moment to dart forwards and try to stab her in the chest, but she missed and caught her shoulder instead.

The woman screeched, immediately reaching for something in the pocket of her worn, white dress. Sulwyn recognised it. A small bottle of light-yellow liquid. She had only seen it once before with Wilkson, but knew Tiamat was going to use it incorrectly.

"Stop!" Sulwyn yelled, but she was too late to grab the bottle. Tiamat threw it at her own feet, shattering the glass. The temperature dropped dramatically around them, darkness swallowing Sulwyn, silence pressing on her and a light tingle flowing within her until her legs smacked onto hard ground, and she roared in pain.

Sulwyn squinted around her, trying to see through the blinding sun, eyes watering from the light and the pain. She was outside in an open field of grass and sand, a thicket of trees off to her left. Tiamat lay on the ground in front of her, breathing heavily, blood seeping into the fabric on her chest. Sulwyn had gotten in range of the magic and shifted with Tiamat to another place entirely... Where, she had no idea, but the smell of pine and sweetness surrounded her.

"I didn't think I'd see you so soon." A wave of calm washed over her, the voice honeyed and light. But it was soon replaced with a deep chill. Sulwyn turned to see Gwydion in his full glory. Not like she had seen him the first time, with modest, short brown hair, a kind face, and glasses.

No, before her stood Gwydion as his Devinal self with sweeping dark grey and blue folds of fabric more suited to Guāngcǎi. His violet eyes pierced hers, his long blue-black hair tied high into a ponytail enhancing his sinister stare.

"I see you tagged along. I told her not to use that so close to anyone else, but you can't teach intelligence." He continued to speak as if she weren't folded over in pain in the sand and he was not the cause of the chaos that had befallen. Gwydion stooped down in front of her, touching her leg lightly, but she pulled away.

"Refusing my help won't get you anywhere. You've come this far. You might as well serve a purpose." Before Sulwyn could so much as pull a blade to his throat, he back-handed her face hard, whispering intangible words, and knocked her out.

❧

The image of Eztli's wide eyes in fear startled her awake. Memories of what she had done under Artaxiad's will flooded her. But he had no idea what he was doing, and this time, she was trapped with the man that had invented that poison.

Sulwyn awoke, arms and legs strapped across a steel table, candlelight flooding the room, and the first person to greet her was Diesirae.

"Is this where you're hiding then?" asked Sulwyn nonchalantly. No one could save her now, and she berated herself just a little for not taking more caution like Galahad had advised. Maybe she wouldn't have been caught by the same person twice. But she couldn't give up now.

"Waiting. Not hiding," she said, folding her arms across her chest and leaning against the wall. "You know, you are revered as the great Kintana, even if everyone thinks you're dead. But you seem to get yourself caught quite often."

Sulwyn scoffed. "I'm surrounded by insanity. A cannibalistic old lady, a blood-drinking, sacrificial idiot—"

Diesirae was in front of her in a second. "Do not insult our trials."

"I'll insult what deserves it. If blood gave people the power you so claimed, then many before you would have done it and succeeded. And Artaxiad would never have been in power." Sulwyn spit at her, relishing how it landed on Diesirae's face.

But Diesirae just smiled wickedly, wiping it off. "You will get what is coming to you, Kintana. People believe you to be on their side. But they will see. They will learn that Kintana only abandoned them. Left them to rot as she gallivanted in the Empire as princess and now queen."

"Don't ruin it for her," Gwydion said from somewhere above her head. She hadn't heard him come in wherever it was they were. She couldn't even sense the sun. But for all she knew, he had layers of barriers over them. Hiding him from everyone, they could be in plain sight, and no one would be the wiser.

"I didn't intend to use this on you, not now at least, but Nero wasn't in my calculations as of yet. It seems he has a bit of hunger for power after all," he continued, and Sulwyn could see his shadow over her passing back and forth from behind, busying himself with something. "To my understanding, Artaxiad had his fun with failed versions of my creation. You're lucky nothing worse didn't befall you." He lifted his hand to her face, showing her a small syringe of clear liquid. A faint buzzing flitted in her mind, but she disregarded it.

"Are the DrvaMørk your pincushions? Creating a better world, are you? Controlling the innocent and turning them into that? Tell me how Tiamat fits into this with her control over souls," Sulwyn said, proud that her voice came out strong despite the panic beating in her. If Gwydion only needed this one vile of poison, then the version Artaxiad used on her was primitive in comparison.

"It doesn't really matter," he spoke, the smell of pine shifting in the air as he passed. Sulwyn's eyes narrowed, trying to look at him and failing. "Tiamat has limited control, but with some assistance from me, we are potentially unlimited. But as you saw, there is still a lot of trial and error. However, that was regarding mass amounts. In concentrated doses…Well, let's say you aren't my first study. Actually, you should have witnessed my first study by now and the unexpected, lasting effects." She could hear the smirk in his voice until a cool needle pricked her neck, "I imagine it won't take long for them to find you once we start…"

His laugh warbled around her until everything was white.

XVIII

Don't Let The Mud Hide Your Light

"YOU'RE up, Star," said a voice in front of her. Star looked down at her hands, dried blood coating her palms, chunks of it under her nails, but she didn't know if it was hers or not.

She stood, her back and legs protesting at the sudden movement. Her one leg was still stiff, but she didn't really know why. Healing from something or another. Just another day. How many days had it been? Forever? But what was time here? She didn't really have a concept of days.

Fight, eat and sleep. How many fights happened? She didn't remember a single one but somehow knew that they were happening. Who was she fighting? And what for? Star looked down at her hands once again. A black ring on her right hand and a worn silver ring on her left. These must have importance. She wouldn't let them take it, though she didn't remember if they tried.

"Star," said the voice, a woman. She looked up at her and glared.

"I'm coming," she retorted, watching the woman tut in annoyance. When could she fight her?

Why was she fighting?

Star followed the dark brown woman, with long hair and one side shaved, out of her cell and into the hall. The walk was not far, and they were not underground. Soon, she could see light flooding from the small tunnel opening. She was vaguely reminded of another time, a sadder time.

A man with white-blond hair and scars all down his arms flooded her mind and she faltered.

"If you don't fight, we won't feed you." The woman sneered.

"I could just eat you if I had to. Or drain your blood for power," Star said savagely. Why she said that, she had no idea, but the woman paled. Hastily, she reached into the pocket of her blowing orange pants, taking out a small syringe of clear liquid.

"Punishment. If you don't accept this, it doesn't matter if you win or not. I will personally have you starved."

"A puppet will always remain a puppet," Star replied, and the woman marched towards her.

"I swear to you," the woman hissed into her ear, "that I will end you one day." And she plunged the needle into her neck.

A familiar sensation flowed through Star, like a large yawn that had just escaped. Calmness ebbed within her, but a pinched sort of nagging began to form in the pit of her stomach.

"Go," demanded the woman, and Star walked forwards and out of the tunnel of light.

Squinting against the sun, she saw a small crowd of people around her, nothing more than a hundred or so, all sitting in a small, roughly made pit. She didn't recognise any of their faces. But instead of cheering or jeering, they were weary and on edge. Hisses and whispers whipped around her, but she couldn't understand why.

She looked down at herself. A belt of various unique daggers hung at her waist and wrapped around her twice. A tattered, padded jacket hung over her, trailing behind her ankles, and though she thought she should toss it, she kept it anyway. She reached behind her reflectively, but her hand came up empty. Something was missing.

But she stopped. A young man was now in front of her. He was unceremoniously tossed out of his tunnel, a sword thrown near his feet. She only had daggers. Why did he get a sword?

"You grace us with your presence… This isn't your first dance," said another voice somewhere beside her. She turned to see a tall man with short brown hair, brown eyes, and glasses. He was modestly dressed in browns and white. But his voice suggested he was more than he appeared. He looked at her with a hint of surprise as if this was the first time he saw her. Though, she had no idea what she had done to garner that expression.

"It won't be my last," she started, turning away, but called back to the man. "What has he done?"

The man narrowed his eyes, casting a glance at the woman who escorted her. "It seems we've neared our time with you," he confessed, but her confusion grew.

Star turned back to the young man. "Name yourself." She had seen his face before, but she couldn't place it right now. Her head was fuzzy, like cotton was stuffed inside.

"Kai…" he called back, and though his eyes darted around, unsure and nervous, his hand gripped the hilt of his sword with confidence. She smiled.

"Kai, I hope you're up for this." Then she charged towards him, aiming to kill.

The man's eyes widened but pulled back quickly. She was vaguely aware of the growing hisses and whispers of the crowd. Knew that something was wrong yet again. But the itch deep in her soul figured that if she killed this man, it would end.

But it wouldn't.

It would never end.

Then Kai was in front of her. "I hope *you* are up for this, Kintana," he whispered, and in her hesitation, he slashed her arm. She dropped the dagger she was holding, gripping her limb instead. The cut burned but it wasn't deep.

"Gwydion…" she heard the woman call.

"They came faster than I thought they would, to be honest." The man, Gwydion, shrugged. "It won't work on her again after this. She's stronger than her parents. Artaxiad ruined any chance I had. But the damage is done and word will spread." He smiled wickedly, stepping forwards and into the crowd.

"As you are all aware, the woman before you is none other than the great Kintana." The crowds hissing became stronger now, fear rippling through them. "And as you can see, she is not your friend."

"Stop," she gasped, dropping to her knees. The dread rose as the glass in her mind shattered. She let it happen again. Let them deceive her and control her again. She forced the memories to come to her, prodding the haze that was just beneath the surface, clouding her once more.

"This woman bears the symbol of the Empire." He pointed to her back, and she remembered that this jacket had been given to her. Forgot that it had the "A&P" sigil of Artaxiad and Pandora on the collar behind her neck.

"Kintana and Queen Sulwyn are one and the same. The Star, as you've seen her here, has fallen to the Empire's ways. Did you not hear how she slaughtered innocent men and women in this very circle? Only a few days have passed since we brought you proof, and she has killed seven people since."

"Seven?!" She gasped, unable to remember any of that. Her thoughts stopped on that metal table. Kai stood close to her, his eyes on Gwydion. Her memories were jumbled. "Who are you?" she whispered, hoping it didn't carry over the angry hordes of voices.

"A man with a message for you," he uttered, and tossed his sword to the ground, kneeling next to her. "Trust your instincts. And don't fear the unknown, Sulwyn."

Sulwyn's eyes widened, the haze vanishing in an instant. She knew exactly who she was looking at. This was Kai, Wilkson's son. The boy she somewhat grew up with. He smiled coyly but put his hands to his lips. "I contacted Galahad. They should be here soon."

"No!" she started, still kneeling. "Where is he?" she asked haphazardly, hand outstretched. And though she was referring to Wilkson, when Kai turned to look at her, his eyes hid something else.

"Kai? Is that your name?" Gwydion asked, but a whistling interrupted him just as an arrow ripped through his shoulder. A suppressed grunt escaped him. But Gwydion's eyes were fierce, scanning the frantic crowd.

"Leave, Kai." Sulwyn stood and stretched her injured arm. Her now-healed broken leg was stiff and slow. Gwydion must have mended it. But his magic was heavy and thick like mud. Kai saluted before dashing off into the confused crowd.

All eyes were on her and Gwydion, failing to notice a man with blond and white hair stalk past them. Diesirae ran to Gwydion's side, pulling out her own curved blade, but Gwydion just snapped the arrow and pushed it out of his shoulder.

"It takes more than that to harm me," Gwydion announced, but he frowned.

"I'm just the distraction," called Daijiro, shrugging and nocking another arrow. He stood poised in between the panicking people.

"How?" growled Gwydion, showing a surprising amount of irritation.

"You said it. As a Velyūn, I have some right to magic even if I wasn't born a Devinal. I can't hold it well, but I can sure as hell see it," Daijiro goaded.

But the people around them started to whisper about Devinal, Gwydion's game turning on him. "This is ridiculous," he called, the illusion fading, his eyes vivid purple and hair flowing down around him alongside his robes. He lifted the magic right before these people's eyes, which meant he planned to kill them all.

"Don't step beyond you, Daijiro," started Gwydion, holding his hand to the sky. "It's strikingly like your father."

"What did you say?" Daijiro hissed, his hand loosening its hold on the bow and arrow.

Gwydion mumbled words as if he were hissing them, and soon, a small formation of electric clouds formed above them. "Diesirae."

She whistled, and two horses came forwards immediately. One of them had Sulwyn's sword tied to it. She ran towards it despite her body's protest.

"Stay back, Kintana, unless you wish to be struck!" Diesirae yelled, jumping onto her horse, but Daijiro's gaze was strong, making eye contact with the black and white steed Diesirae rode upon. The horse galloped towards him instead, disbelief in Diesirae's eyes. Daijiro grabbed the sheath with Sulwyn's sword off the side of the saddle. With a wave of his hand, the horse bucked Diesirae off, but the other was out of reach and at Gwydion's side.

Diesirae rolled forwards and ran towards Gwydion just as he brought his hand down. Lightning struck in multiple places, slashing through many of the people he had gathered there that day. He quickly jumped onto the horse, Diesirae hurdling up behind him, and they took off.

But there was fury in Daijiro's eyes. Rage Sulwyn hadn't seen in a long time. He motioned the stolen horse forwards and jumped on before galloping towards her. She grabbed his forearm, scrambling, but he pulled her up with ease. Bringing her up behind him.

Sulwyn looked around quickly, but Kai was gone, and the people around them were left in distraught piles of sorrow, blood, and death. She saw the glares they gave her, but Daijiro spurred the horse forwards, and they took off after Gwydion. He handed her the sword and sheath, and she swung it over her back.

Daijiro rode fast, Sulwyn gripping his waist tightly as they followed behind, closing the distance between them and Gwydion, leaving angry cries in their wake.

"Daijiro. Please," she begged, and he tensed under her.

"You've been gone for three days." Voice wavering in concentration, trying to keep the horse from disobeying, its allegiance clearly with Gwydion. "We managed to get into the mountain, but by the time we got there, you were gone. I figured you were somehow shifted elsewhere. Galahad and I left immediately, leaving the other three to figure out how to deal with what you left behind."

"What do you mean?"

"I don't know what those things are, but the ones in the mountain started acting up right after you left. We shut them in, so hopefully, that was good enough. We decided to head to the nearest village first, but we came across that man, Kai. It seems like he's been looking for you."

"He's Wilkson's son."

"Who?"

But Sulwyn waved him off; Gwydion had sped up, and she could see why. In the distance, there was a fire growing rapidly. Sulwyn could also see the remnants of a translucent indigo barrier surrounding the circumference, holes pierced through with fire, disintegrating into nothing.

"He's gone overboard…" cursed Daijiro just as Gwydion came to a stop, dismounting his horse.

Daijiro and Sulwyn stopped a few feet from him, but Gwydion made no moves to approach them in any way. Instead, he looked a little exasperated, and a hint of something like unease passed through his eyes as he looked at the fire.

"You let him run wild," started Gwydion, turning to face Daijiro, but Daijiro lunged at him. Diesirae tried to block his attack but was frozen in place when Daijiro held a palm forwards. Instantly, he made a fist, and Sulwyn could hear the bones crack and watched her shoulder sag forwards.

Diesirae grunted, eyes wide at the agony she refused to show, but Gwydion advanced, throwing another barrier over them both. This seemed to weaken Daijiro's hold, but it didn't keep it out, and Sulwyn could see the confusion in Gwydion's eyes even if he tried to hide it.

"We've done what's needed. This was only a temporary base anyway." He reached for Diesirae's uninjured arm, and like Ildri, his eyes turned white, and he was gone, taking Diesirae with him.

Daijiro roared, fists pounding the sand, but before he could fully act on his anger, the barrier in the distance finally shattered, and the fire erupted higher.

"Is it Galahad?" Sulwyn asked quietly, the heat of the flames stinging her eyes, ash falling and sticking to her clothes.

He pointed ahead. "I shouldn't have let him go alone... He's not the same..." he whispered.

Sulwyn looked where he had pointed, the flames coating the old brick building, pieces falling apart. She squinted and saw a large shadow of a thing coming from the fires. She realised that it was walking.

Realised that it was Galahad.

But it also *wasn't* Galahad. His eyes were black, and his brown hair hung loosely over his taut, impassive face. His forearms and hands were coated in what she thought was black ash, but upon closer inspection, it was his skin, nails long and sharp. And the shadow she originally saw was shaped like wispy black wings, just like a demon from the Lost World. But as soon as he stepped out from the inferno, they vanished into smoke, rising alongside the fire.

"Daijiro..." Sulwyn said, unable to manage anything else, her hand to her mouth. But as she got over the initial shock, she noticed that he was carrying someone.

Daijiro moved closer and in front of Sulwyn, as if guarding her from Galahad, who finally noticed them and walked closer. But Sulwyn sensed nothing of Galahad in this person's mannerism until he made eye contact with her and faltered.

"Sulwyn..." he choked, but she collected herself, hiding her fear and walking towards him.

"Are you okay?" she asked gently, gesturing to the fire, but Daijiro didn't have the same sort of caution she did and rounded on him.

"I trusted to leave you here and be discreet as you so often harped on about!" he hissed, pointing at the crumbling building in the background. Something exploded within, making them turn back and watch.

"I did what I set out to do. Look for Sulwyn, and you would look for her at that gathering. I didn't find her. There was no other purpose for that place. So, I burned it," Galahad answered emotionlessly.

His tone struck Sulwyn. So heartless and cold, and then they heard the pitiful sounds of screaming and chaos erupting from the flames.

Though Sulwyn couldn't remember it, the tension she had originally felt when Raghnall told her he heard her cries in that inflamed house, sent chills through her. Just like this.

"There were people in there?" she asked in disbelief. He turned to her. A crease marked his brow, but his expression stayed the same.

"People who work for and with Gwydion. It's no one's loss."

"Who is she then?" asked Daijiro, pointing to the woman across his arms. Sulwyn finally directed attention to her, noting her pale and wasted figure. She had long, limp black hair and what was once a soft face. And she looked strikingly like Nori if she were older…

"Prisoner…" Sulwyn said, and Galahad nodded.

"The only one there." Galahad moved to one of the horses, looking for something to cover the woman.

"Daijiro," Sulwyn said, looking at him pointedly.

"He isn't yours to fix," Daijiro snapped, but she placed a hand on his arm, stopping him.

"You aren't mine to fix, either, but we've all helped each other," she whispered to him. His eyes blazed, taking her in, but soon, he backed down, pulling away gently.

Daijiro marched over to Galahad, taking the woman from him while Sulwyn approached slowly. "Galahad…" she started, and he glanced at her.

His body remained tense, looking at her but not really seeing her. She didn't know what to say to him, how to reel him back in, and out of the extent of his power. She could see the fear growing in his eyes, but it was constantly being smothered by what he could be if he let it go.

Gently, she took his hands in hers, shivering at how cold they were despite the fire and the sun. Noting that not only did the skin darken and the nails sharpen, but his hands themselves became more dignified, elongated even. His tunic was dirty and tattered at the edges. He looked just as bad as she did. They all did.

She let go of one of his hands and turned him so she could see his back. The tunic was whole, with no rips going through it. The wings must have been a phantom illusion from his power, but she wondered if it would become a reality.

Sulwyn knew he was watching her, but the tension in him started to recede. She stood right in front of him now, taking back the other hand and holding them both in hers. She looked past him for an instant, seeing Daijiro crouched beside the woman covered in a blanket from one of the horses. He looked up at her, and her breath caught in her chest, but she looked away and up at Galahad.

"Do you remember..." she started, "during the month when you were helping me train to fight Caldwell? You insisted that we have at least one day of rest." She studied him carefully, watching his response. And though his face remained impassive, his pure black eyes wavered. "Because we had to stay in the Empire, you took me to the pond that sourced the rivers in your bedroom. And we did nothing. Nothing that entire day besides lounging around in nature and talking and talking." She smiled, and his hands gripped hers tighter.

"You told me about some of your travels after we had first met. That one story about the goldflies that wouldn't leave you alone once you stepped into the field of sweet flowers. Do you remember? They stuck to you even at night, making it impossible to sleep for their buzzing and glowing." She watched him close his eyes, his shoulders sagging. "About your mother who tried to stop you from jumping in a pile of mud to rid them and then how you cried after because you thought you killed them all. But slowly, they emerged from the mud and shook it off. Flying away into the evening, looking like stars." She finished just as his eyes opened, and the black began to recede. The flames reflected in the blue, purple and red of his eyes.

He pulled his hands from hers, the ashen black fading and the nails shrinking back, his hands normal and warm. He pulled her forwards into a strong embrace.

"I'm sorry..." he cried, his hands clutching the back of her jacket tightly.

XIX

Ashes, Ashes, We All Burn

| SULWYN |

DAIJIRO was convinced that Gwydion had manipulated the horses using magic, so he couldn't control both horses and hold the woman at the same time. Now that Galahad was calm, they decided to entrust her to him, helping him get her on Gwydion's horse and he behind her. Sulwyn mounted Diesirae's; Daijiro behind her.

"Galahad can fill you in," Daijiro started, falling silent as they took off. He wrapped one arm around Sulwyn, who tried her best not to feel the tension that remained around them.

Galahad glanced at her, looking at them thoughtfully for a second before speaking. "You were gone for three days."

"I know," called Sulwyn, proceeding to tell him what Daijiro had said. "How did you meet Kai?"

"He found us. I think he's been tracking you," Galahad said with a note of suspicion. "He told us that it was time for you to come back and showed us that bracelet you said Raghnall gives people. The one with the circle in the square? So, we took a chance on him."

"He's Wilkson's son." Galahad turned to her in confusion, but she pressed on. "Wilkson has one son and one daughter. Neither are Devinal, which he is happy for. But if Kai was looking for me, then Wilkson is finally ready to talk," she gritted, annoyed. "Kai was probably using a guide from Wilkson. It's weak magic, but because I have a close bond with them, it works."

"Well, without Kai, we wouldn't have found you," Daijiro said.

"You told Gwydion you can see magic?"

"I can, but not from a distance or anything. I feel it more than anything, like at Valens. We followed Kai and then I felt the place that's now burning down." She knew he must have glared at Galahad.

"Where are we?" Sulwyn asked. There was nothing to mark where they were, just open terrain and mountains in the distance. Were those the same mountains from Wallasyn?

"They are," started Galahad, and he smirked a little at her. She accepted defeat long ago during the time she spent in the Empire with him. He still always knew what she was thinking. "This base of his was a little southwest from Wallasyn, a day away. Close enough to control those creatures, it seems."

"DrvaMørk," Sulwyn replied.

"Excuse me?" Daijiro veered their horse, but Sulwyn pinched the hand holding her waist.

"Concentrate," she demanded, and he just pinched her back. "DrvaMørk are trafficked humans. People they stole from that town, using the festival as bait. Tested on with..." Sulwyn stopped. There was a theory that had been growing in the back of her mind, but she didn't know if she should say it. She just needed time alone to think and hoped she would get it soon.

"Cailín..." whispered Daijiro, and she relaxed for just a moment.

"Bear with me." She took a deep breath. "Taru has a sister." Galahad looked at her in confusion again. "They're twins, and where his power can read souls, hers can control them."

"Taru can read a soul? Read it how?" asked Daijiro, and the horse started to veer again before going back on track. Sulwyn glanced at Galahad, his eyes closed for a moment, apprehension on his face.

"He can read the history of a soul…" Galahad trailed off. A tingle of foreboding ran through her. Both horses deviated for a fraction of a second. Sulwyn could feel Daijiro sit straighter, his arm around her waist pulling her closer.

"Her name is Tiamat," continued Sulwyn, "and undoubtedly, she is nothing like Taru. She's insane and Gwydion has her on his side for whatever reason. DrvaMørk are something they created together. Failed experiments to control people. With her ability and Gwydion's poison, they created that."

"But why?" Galahad asked, but they all stopped talking when he looked down. The woman sighed a breath.

"We can kill her if she speaks. Just continue," Daijiro growled, his hold even tighter. She could tell now; he was panicking, and she didn't understand why.

"He said what Artaxiad used on me were failed versions of what he has been trying to achieve…" Her mind was noisy, the theory growing stronger. If she was right, then this involved them both.

"Sulwyn?" Galahad asked.

Her mind raced back to their conversation, her eyes refocusing to find his worried ones. "Tiamat shifted using a travel vial, but I got in the way of the spell and ended up coming back to Gwydion's base. He took me and…"

Her horse drifted again and Daijiro's breath was warm near her ear. "What did he do?" he asked lowly, a shiver flowing across her skin from top to bottom. The foreboding grew deeper.

"Artaxiad had four different syringes of poison, a drug, if you will, that he would constantly use on me, but Gwydion had only one. One small, clear liquid syringe that he injected and… I have no memory…" Her speech faltered, remembering that he said she killed seven people. She didn't want to believe that was true. That she would have zero recollection of what she had done; but if it were true, then there were enough witnesses to turn the tides against her now. At first, she hadn't realised what Gwydion and Diesirae kept hinting at, but once she escaped, it was obvious. The goal was to tarnish her name as Kintana.

Gwydion had revealed what Artaxiad and Pandora wanted to hide for fear of revolution, but he warped its truth. Soon, word would spread that the great Kintana was nothing more than the Empire's blood through and through.

ॐ

It was twilight by the time they arrived at Wallasyn, and unlike the first time she laid eyes upon it, it was dark, silent and still. The horses abruptly stopped just outside the town, shifting nervously and trying to buck them off. Sulwyn looked back at Daijiro, beads of sweat upon his brow.

"I can't hold them anymore anyway..." he said roughly, sliding off. Sulwyn dismounted quickly, and as soon as she did, the horse neighed and ran.

Sulwyn moved to Galahad, helping him take the woman down as he, too, climbed off. Daijiro bent down, holding his knees, with a deep sigh before he let go—the other horse taking off as well.

Galahad hefted the woman with his knee and held her carefully across his arms, leading the way forwards. Sulwyn looked at him warily, his expression laxer though his eyes were creased with worry. She turned to Daijiro, who was exhausted from the effort of having to control Gwydion's horses. But he looked back at her, shaking his head and waving her off.

As they crossed the entrance to Wallasyn, the stillness pressed on them. There were no patrons or workers. But Sulwyn wasn't yet sure if that was because they were shut down for a moment or if it stopped permanently. But the effects, regardless, were creepy.

There were no firelights or sounds around them. Everything appeared even more abandoned than it had during the morning before she was taken. But she couldn't shake the feeling that they were being watched. And that feeling only grew as they approached the inn.

Once the building loomed before them, they could hear a few intangible sounds of people still awake in the main hall. When they stepped through the doors, Sulwyn hesitated.

There weren't many patrons, new arrivals complaining and confused by the welcome they received or lack thereof. The innkeeper from before looked up at them and smiled, but it was forced and cold. Or at least it appeared to Sulwyn as such.

Galahad kept walking, avoiding contact with anyone they passed. They all continued towards the halls and up the stairs. As soon as they reached the fifth floor, a door somewhere near the end of the hall flung open, and Elian stepped out, his face pale.

"Finally…" He sighed and put a hand to his face.

"What's wrong?" asked Galahad, but Elian just shook his head.

"Nothing, but now that you're back, I'm assuming we can leave soon. Demir and Sibril are at the mountain for their shift. Who's that?" He pointed to the woman, but Galahad only shrugged.

"Prepare what you can. I want us to leave soon, if possible," Galahad said, and though Elian looked like he needed five days of sleep, he saluted and took off back into his room.

"Keep her in my room," Daijiro said, and Sulwyn could see the unspoken words pass between him and Galahad. Knowing that it might be safer to keep her with him than with Galahad.

Galahad turned and they all went to Daijiro's room. In the corner, there was a small couch where he carefully placed the woman, wrapping the blanket securely around her.

"Is she going to survive?" asked Sulwyn, afraid that this woman may be on the brink of death. Daijiro stepped closer to her, a strange expression crossing his face. He reached out carefully, placing a hand on her forehead, but after a few seconds, removed it completely as if stung.

"She's a Devinal," Daijiro answered, holding his hand carefully. "She's protected her mind completely. But I guess that means she's alive."

Sulwyn just watched Daijiro take a few steps back, annoyance and something else unreadable crossing his face.

"We'll leave her here for now. If Gwydion didn't stop me from taking her, I assume she was disposable in his eyes," Galahad said stiffly, turning to exit the room. He had become distant again. "Take a few hours to rest," he started, looking mainly at Sulwyn. "We will reconvene shortly and decide what to do once the sun rises." He brushed Sulwyn's hand, taking his leave, weariness etched on his face. She remembered then; the time Galahad used his ability as clan prince to punish other members for joining Diesirae as well as his uncle, back in the fog town. How drained he became from that. She couldn't imagine now how much energy that aggressive transformation cost.

She turned to Daijiro, who for once, wasn't looking at her and was looking at the woman's still form. "You should rest too …" Sulwyn whispered. He glanced at her carefully, but before he could say anything, she walked out of the room.

❧❧

Sulwyn knew she should be sleeping, but she needed to think.

To finally sit and figure out exactly what was happening and if her theory was plausible. But sitting never worked for her, so she started to pace all around the room, throwing open the window to let fresh air in and clear her mind.

Everything became chaotic once Gwydion entered the picture and that was a fact. Then, aided by Zalika's influence, they had turned the whole Empire upside down in just a few weeks. Though she hadn't actually cared to wonder what happened to Zalika, she did want to know where she had gone, and would have to get to the bottom of that once they returned.

But the one thing that was clear to her was that Pandora began to blame Gwydion for treason because of Diesirae, fearing that they would rise together against them as they did to the High King so many years ago. But Gwydion had been with the Empire for thirteen years, gaining trust with all the Privileged in the Empire. So why would he waste that on treason? Was Pandora going mad, or did she know even more?

Sulwyn figured it must be the latter because Pandora seemed to keep a lot of secrets, revealing that she knew Raghnall was tracking her and that there were more enemies besides Artaxiad. She was cryptic with what she said, and this confirmed Sulwyn's suspicions. Pandora knew Gwydion was a Devinal, and for whatever reason, he could no longer be trusted. Or maybe she never trusted him and kept him under watch all these years.

If Sulwyn broached her theory further in this direction, then it made sense; Pandora knew Raghnall was following them from the beginning, which in turn meant she knew that there would be a chance Raghnall and Sulwyn would come for their heads.

But this didn't happen, and instead, Raghnall betrayed her to the Empire, killed by Pandora no less. But the body Sulwyn saw had no scar, and after figuring out how many days it had been before she saw his body in the lower dungeons, it was a day over a week. Meaning the cream from Wilkson would have worn off, and the scar should have been there.

She would check that one off her mental list and come back to it, the nagging in the pit of her stomach still there.

She paused.

A rustling outside her window. She strained to hear more but heard nothing, so she continued pacing.

Tiergan.

Tiergan purposely led them to Antac just so he could lead them all to the fog town. Though his intentions were unclear to Sulwyn, the fact remained that he had baited Caldwell, and in turn, baited Artaxiad to taunt Galahad about his clan. But unbeknownst to any of them, Diesirae was there practicing psychotic rituals for her own gain. Or *were they* rituals? Kione said blood drinking for power never existed in his tribe, and that blood was sacred and blessed at birth, and for the Sacred Weapon.

Sulwyn sat, crossing her legs in the centre of the black rug. When she was in the cave with the self-proclaimed group of revolutionists, some of them mentioned that they drank each other's blood mixed with the sacrifices. And when she spoke to Diesirae on the metal table, she mentioned trials.

What trials?

At first, she thought this was Diesirae's personal agenda and Gwydion just let her be, but what if that was part of whatever they had been testing? Aside from that, it was obvious that Gwydion trusted Diesirae. The fact that he needed her to get to Raghnall confirmed this. Another point she was going to go back to.

Though Tiergan was of no consequence, it seemed like seeing him caused Galahad to lose even more control. And once they returned from that town and Pandora learned of Gwydion's involvement, that was when everything started to snowball.

Due to Zalika's involvement with her own Velyūn ability to bring out jealousy, Pandora acted irrationally, but towards Gwydion, not Artaxiad. And it wasn't only Pandora.

Though Sulwyn had decided to act on her vision and use the argument between Gwydion and Pandora as coverage to kill her, she knew she was not herself, and after meeting Gwydion again, this made more sense to her.

Ever since she spent the first few minutes with Gwydion at the beginning of the Gala, she felt different; and when she confronted those Privileged who were harassing Kione, she knew she was acting just like her parents. And she couldn't stop it. Not until Kione distracted her long enough to bring her back to herself.

Sulwyn looked at the back of her hand, remembering again that masked man who pricked her hand while they danced. Knew it was the same man she had seen at this festival here in Wallasyn. Someone had injected her with something, and she was sure it heightened her desire to kill Pandora.

Desire.

She was driven by it, and Gwydion fueled it further when he mocked Caldwell and used Arsinone as leverage. That was the first time she had been exposed to whatever it was he had created; she was sure of it.

It was also desire that Artaxiad acted on. Wanting to become even more powerful, even if it meant having a child with her. He had mentioned desire to Daijiro before escaping the Solus. This would match Nero's growing suspicion as well. Artaxiad had lost his mind, and she was sure it wasn't all due to Pandora's death.

Whatever Gwydion was doing, he was trying to control people, and not just individually. Thanks to Tiamat and even some words from himself, the mass creation of whatever this drug was, was still failing. But individual doses seemed to be working just fine.

Sulwyn flopped back, lying on the musty rug and staring at the dark ceiling. Heat tingled through her chest and up her neck. Another fever, another vision. But she continued her thought process.

Gwydion believed she had built immunity during Artaxiad's attempts with his makeshift versions of Gwydion's creations. If that was the case, then at least something came out of that.

Had he used it on Artaxiad and Pandora? Sulwyn breathed out heavily. She didn't have enough evidence for that thought, so she moved it to the side.

Whether she killed seven people or not in the last few days, her name was sullied in Gwydion's favour. If he could turn everyone against Kintana, then he had eyes off him to continue what he was doing while Nero kept an eye on her in the Empire.

But that was beside the point.

Because there were three things she theorised and needed to solve.

Gwydion warned Daijiro that it would only get harder for Galahad. And Taru was under the belief that Galahad had been tampered with, though he had no memories of such a thing happening. Sulwyn closed her eyes, dread seeping deep in her heart; Gwydion purposely told her she wasn't the first to be tested on and that she had even witnessed it without realising it.

Sulwyn was sure it was Galahad.

At some time in his past, probably around the time Gwydion first came to the Empire, he had done something to him. But because Galahad had been repressing everything about himself, it never manifested until now. Now, he was emotionally exploding because of her, his clan, and the imbalance of his power. Because of fear.

That was her first theory.

Her second was that Gwydion, with the aid of Diesirae, had gotten to Raghnall. This was the only thing that made sense to her. And maybe it was naive of her to assume that Raghnall would never fall so low, but she had hope that she knew him well. This only doubled when she met those from the Pain Cells. Could see they still revered him even after they learned of what he'd done. He betrayed her for coins and status? Nothing about his reasoning added up.

But if Raghnall could get caught in Gwydion's poison, it left her with little hope of being able to defeat him. If Raghnall couldn't fight it, who could? Even if she had immunity, he was still a Devinal with many at his feet. And she could never get Wilkson to fight him. He wasn't a fighter, and as a Zalman, he'd lived in hiding since the fall of the High City. She would never ask him to sacrifice himself, leaving his family behind.

But there was something she was still missing. Something she was denying because it couldn't be true. How could it be true?

But he had no scar.

And if he had no scar, that meant that wasn't his body.

And if that wasn't his body, where was it?

There wasn't anyone who knew the High City better than Raghnall.

That bastard.

Sulwyn sat up, a cry of pain escaping her lips before she could silence it. The fever was almost at its peak, burning through her in waves of tiny needles. She hated her visions now; they came in a flash with barely any warning and immense agony. She vaguely thought of Galahad. She didn't ask him if he had felt her pain or if she had managed to block it off or not. But she tried to consciously keep that in mind as agony rolled through her.

Sulwyn heard muffled footsteps, but she couldn't keep the vision out any longer, and in one wave of hot anguish, it flowed over her.

This vision was already different than her last. Instead of watching the scene, it was through her own eyes. The room was dark but familiar, even if it was blurred.

Blurred from what? She lifted a hand to her cheek; tears. Someone was in front of her, but before she could figure out who, their hand reached forwards and slammed her back against the wall, fingers tightly wrapping around her throat. The grip was strong, nails digging into her skin, tearing and stinging.

She gasped, trying and failing to move the hand that was around her throat, pushing at their chest and kicking. Clouds moved past the night sky, the moon illuminating the ashen black forearm through the window. Sulwyn struggled harder now, clawing at the hand and looking up into pure black eyes that were full of loathing and anger. But crying with so much despair.

"Hey!" a male voice called to her, shaking her shoulders.

Sulwyn wheezed, scurrying back to create as much distance as she could while holding her neck. She breathed deeply, panic threatening to rise. The lingering sensation of strong fingers still jammed against her windpipe. Her face was damp, tears littering her cheeks before she started to cry from the black eyes in her vision.

Someone knelt before her, taking her hands in his own. She looked up to see Galahad's tricoloured eyes. So beautiful and so lost until they shifted to black, and all she could feel was his hands around her throat again.

She pushed his shoulder, sliding back to make even more space. She knew the image was only in her mind, but she couldn't shake the terror that tremored through her. And instead, hatred erupted towards Gwydion for doing this to him. For tainting a power respected by his clan and making it dark and murky and black. For putting him through more than he deserved. And yet still, she couldn't look at him for too long, even though his eyes were wide with concern and shock.

"Did you feel anything?" she managed to whisper, but he shook his head. "Did you feel anything in the last three days?"

He looked at her oddly but answered, "At first. I felt it when you were taken into that mountain, but soon it stopped completely. Only a sliver of it passed through until there was nothing. You've shut me out."

"Good." He tensed at her answer. "I don't want to burden you with more, that's all," she added quickly. She could see the hurt in his eyes. Knew that having a bond like that with her meant something more to him. But if it wasn't a true bond like those from the Kurome clan, then she didn't want it. Not if it only caused suffering.

A loud bang and Galahad was shoved back. Her door opened wide, bouncing off the wall. Daijiro stood before them with his hand out and wrath in his eyes.

"What have you done?" His voice low.

"Stop," Sulwyn demanded, glaring at him. "He's done nothing wrong..." But she raised her hand to her neck in error, the ghost of the feeling still there.

"Lies," snarled Daijiro, stepping forwards and bending to pick up Galahad by the collar of his shirt.

Galahad kept his fists clenched but made no move to retaliate, and like a memory so long ago, Sulwyn found herself standing, pointing two daggers in between them both. One at Daijiro's neck and the other at Galahad's stomach.

They both looked at her, aware she was still crying, but she couldn't stop because she knew that eventually, her vision would come to pass, and what would happen after would be up to her.

"Stop..." she whispered, the vision's exhaustion taking over, and she slumped back onto the ground.

XX

Would You Have Hid & Watched?

| SULWYN |

"SHE'S done enough…" said a quiet voice around her, but she couldn't place it. It was low, angry and worried.

"If we don't include her, she'll wreak havoc on us," said the other voice, but it held humour and endearment and had a jumpy edge to it. Her cloudiness ebbed away, soft down and warm sheets surrounding her.

"Daijiro…" Galahad started, but silence spread between them.

"I'd rather you talk about me in another room," Sulwyn said, sitting up and looking around her. The sun had risen but not too high in the sky. Good, she wasn't out long. At least her recovery was shorter too. She lifted the covers off her, the filth of three, no four days, itching her skin. She needed to wash up before anything else.

"Sulwyn… How are you feeling?" Galahad asked, and though apprehension rose in her from her vision, she smothered it as much as she could.

She turned to him, smiling. "I'm fine. But I would like to bathe…" She trailed off. She noted that they were both clean and ready to move on, and right then, that was the only thing she could focus on.

Galahad moved to reach for her hand, but hers twitched away, and his own fell back. He looked at her in a way she could not read, and just turned, taking Daijiro with him.

Sulwyn relished having a bath, and though Wallasyn didn't have the same system as they did in Valens to draw warm water directly through pipes, it was clean and cool against her sore skin. Though she shouldn't be used to the scars and the cuts and the abuse she put her body through, she also welcomed it. For now, it meant she was still alive and could still fight. Regardless of her enemy and their intentions towards her. But she never finished concluding her last theory, and for that, she needed Daijiro.

She stepped out of the cold tub water, drying off and finding a maroon tunic and fresh, cotton brown pants. She donned her clothes, and ran her fingers through her damp hair before staring at the intricate jacket she had gotten from the Empire, symbolising her status to other Empire personnel as queen.

Though it was tattered at the hems, and a bit on the cuffs, somehow it was more suited to her than before. But she turned it around and looked at the small sigil of the A and P back-to-back. She would need to burn and char it so it would blend into the black fabric. But for now, she put it back on and secured her weapons belt underneath before buttoning the front of the jacket.

Sulwyn laced her boots, tied her hair back into a braid, and picked up her sword, slinging it across her back. She was stalling. Double-checking her hair, tightening her boots, counting the daggers. But that tingle of nerves only grew, forming in the pit of her stomach and crawling in her jaw, knowing that what she was about to ask would allude Daijiro a little more to her suspicions.

She realised it when she caught Galahad's reaction too late when she mentioned Taru. He had kept Taru's abilities from Daijiro for a reason. And that would raise his interest even more. But she needed to confirm something to be able to better understand Gwydion.

Sulwyn picked up her pack to attach to Ki, all the while taking deep breaths. They intended to leave once they dealt with the DrvaMørk.

She stepped up to the door and opened it to see Daijiro was already there, hand raised to knock. His eyes widened a little in surprise, but he stepped back, and she walked into the hall. Her nerves were numbing at this point, but it was now or never.

"Ready?" he asked, but she could see the questioning stare in his eyes.

"I am. And I think the sooner we can leave, the better. Something doesn't sit right with this place since Tiamat left," Sulwyn warned, unable to bring her question to the surface. "Where is Galahad?"

"He and Elian went to get the horses and the carriage; everything is prepared for our departure..." He spoke a little formally, avoiding her eyes. They stood silent for a breath until he asked, "Are you okay?" She could hear the worry laced with a kind of panic in his voice.

She looked at him carefully, his red eyes unwavering to her grey ones. "I've noticed something about you," she started, and he tilted his head a little. "You panic when I hesitate." She watched him narrow his eyes, but she continued. "Or when I'm hurt or unsure of myself. *You panic*. Why?"

He bit his lip and clenched his jaw, considering her; stalling. She could see he didn't want to answer and she was about to move on to her other question when he reached forwards and brushed her cheek gently with the tips of his fingers. "I found solace in you," he whispered in a voice that was anything but confident.

A hollowness in her stomach unrelated to the nerves formed, and her own eyes narrowed. She was a source of comfort for him? Like a pillar to lean against and nothing more? Why did that strike her so hard?

Sulwyn leaned out of his touch, but he brought his other hand gently to the side of her neck. "Not like that," he whispered, and she stared, waiting for him to explain, unsure of her own reaction. "After I learned, quickly I might add, that you were not someone to underestimate, I found comfort in you. At first. You reminded me of something I had lost so very long ago." His voice was low and deep, and with or without him realising it, that soft pull was all around her. Not to allure her, but to comfort her. There was nothing swaying her mind at all. It just gently brushed against her.

"I panic when you are unsure because I rely on your strength. To keep me from being what I don't want to be anymore. To remind me that I am better than I thought. If you are unsure, you, Kintana..." He stepped closer. "Sulwyn... Then the world is black to me. Everything about you is light whether you see it or not, even on your darkest days. I want to achieve your goals with you. I want to make my own goals next to you and with Galahad. Both of you have shown me everything I've forgotten. But I am still learning. So, when you waver, so do I." He leaned down and kissed her softly despite the heat that radiated from his lips.

The way sweet rain smelled because of him had changed the expectations of her love for real rain. All her memories of doused-out fires in her time camping and running with Raghnall had changed to the charred burnt smell of wood Daijiro created. And the mint that she didn't understand; it was fresh. It made her want to keep it in a pocket so that she could always hold the smell in her hands. Though gentle and tamed, his kiss made her feel the fire she knew he could create. It burned through her in a way she wanted to hold onto, even distracting her nerves for just a bit.

But she needed to ruin this moment and ask her question.

Sulwyn pulled back gently, watching his eyes widen in fear of retaliation, but she just pulled his head forwards and leaned her forehead to his. "Thank you. Daijiro. For accepting me as I am. And for pushing me to do better. For being my equal. For trusting that I know my strengths and my weaknesses no matter how much trouble I get in. For seeing me the way that you do and holding me to such a regard of importance. For understanding me. For letting me learn and see the true you."

She watched him close his eyes, holding the sides of her neck gently, making her forget the fear she had earlier from her vision. But she needed to continue.

"Right now... This isn't the time," she started, watching his eyes open and seeing the fire that flared in them, his breath hot over her face.

"I need to ask you something, and I need you to trust me and not look too deeply into it."

He leaned back but didn't make space between them, waiting for her to continue. She was hyperaware of their proximity to each other, mixed conflict and guilt swimming through her that she didn't want to face right now. She took a deep breath, but he was patient, moving his hands away from her neck and to her shoulders.

"I need you to explain how these smells work," she started, but the response she got wasn't what she expected. He looked nervous for once, unsure. And then she remembered his reaction to the first time she said she smelled mint.

"It's not a real smell," he explained, not looking at her directly. "It's an illusion. Meant to distract and allure when a Velyūn uses their given ability, whatever it may be. Though that isn't always the case... Like my situation with you..." He trailed off. She wanted to know what he meant regarding her, but her fear was being confirmed. "I've met two other Velyūn and couldn't smell either of them. I assume half-breeds can't smell other half-breeds. But I could smell my mother's allure and she mine, though rarely due to my upbringing. You said you smelled bitterness and sun when you encountered Zalika," he continued, and she just made a face of annoyance. "That was her allure at work. The thing is, most people don't properly notice it, not the way you do, or even Galahad. It's something in the background of their consciousness. But it's not a real smell. It's stimulated and controlled by us."

And all she could think of was pine and honey.

Pine and honey wafted over her subtly in the background whenever Gwydion was around, or even when he wasn't, but traces of him were.

His goal was to control people on a massive scale, using whatever means necessary to achieve it, to replicate it because, as Daijiro said, the power is not in the blood. It cannot be used, but it may be possible to recreate it.

She looked up at Daijiro's white and blond hair, thinking vaguely of Zalika's deep red and white hair and then of Gwydion's blue and black hair.

And she knew.

She knew with unwavering certainty that one of those colours was meant to be white and that Gwydion was using his Devinal magic to hide the fact that he, too, was a Velyūn.

Sulwyn stepped back from him, her hands growing cold, but she could not tell him. Would not tell him. She just hoped beyond hope that maybe now that she was aware of it, it wouldn't work the same way. Hoped that it wouldn't work on Galahad any further since he'd been so exposed to both Daijiro and Zalika. And that Daijiro would never draw the connection until the time was absolutely necessary.

But Daijiro was looking at her closely. She knew he suspected her, would question her, and if he really wanted to, he could get it out of her, though she trusted he wouldn't do that. Daijiro stepped closer, and with every step, she took one back until she was against the door of her room.

"What are you hiding?" he asked, eyes flashing. But soon, she could hear footsteps running up the stairs, and she took that moment to push past him.

"Trust me…" she muttered, walking to the stairs to stop and stare at Galahad looking up at her.

"Are you ready?" he asked, looking between her and Daijiro. His eyes narrowed, but Sulwyn just smiled, trying to calm herself.

"Ready. I want to get back to the Empire soon," she stated, steering Galahad around by the shoulders and running down the stairs.

But as soon as they made it down the stairs and through the doors to the main hall, Sulwyn knew everything was wrong. Galahad froze, looking at the emptiness and stillness of the open area. They all glanced around carefully, slowly walking through.

"There were people. They were *just* here as I made my way up to you… I don't—" he stuttered, but then the bell rang out, stopping all three of them in their tracks.

Sulwyn looked around. Everything was left as if the people had just vanished. Food and drink littered the tables. A washcloth hung against the bar, candles flickering in all their metal brackets. Playing cards and wooden chips cast about the counters.

And then they heard screaming.

She was the first to react, running past Galahad towards the entrance and hearing him call her to wait, but she opened the door and ducked.

A DrvaMørk swung fast at her head, its fist crashing into the wooden door. It smashed back against the wall and splintered, breaking off the hinges and hanging open. She rolled forwards, escaping its next move just as Daijiro and Galahad stepped out, pushing it back.

But too soon, they had their own DrvaMørk to deal with, unable to walk more than a foot away from the inn's entrance. Sulwyn scanned the area quickly, evading another one that came at her with a large piece of metal.

There were hundreds of them, and unlike the workers or patrons who had only just begun their slow transformation, these were the ones she had seen in the mountain. The ones so far gone, she didn't think there was any saving them, even if they pleaded and cried for mercy. Which they did.

They were all wailing and moaning as they attacked the "gifted" and visitors alike. Sulwyn noted some of the people that wore clothes from the Empire, Privileged, and they, too, were running around trying to escape. Until they spotted her.

"It's their daughter!" yelled one woman, turning around and coming straight to her for protection. Others finally noticed her, Galahad and Daijiro as well, and they began to run towards them too.

But Sulwyn didn't want to save them.

She recognised many that were from the Gala, that goaded and slandered Caldwell's death, that mocked Kione. It might not be a good idea, but she didn't want to help them.

So, she didn't.

Instead, she watched as the DrvaMørk made their way to them, pummelling them once they caught up. Hitting them with inhuman strength, their souls tainted and dark and wild. Soon, other Privileged realised that she was only watching and they began to curse her as they ran back to the stables for their private carriages.

Demir rounded a corner from the road, steering their own carriage through the carnage, with Sibril and Elian bringing up the rear along with their horses. Ki was just behind them on his own, weaving between the DrvaMørk. But three of them grabbed him and pulled him down to the ground.

"No!" roared Sulwyn, and she crouched low, avoiding another, and took off running towards him. But Ki would not stay down. He bit the DrvaMørk nearest to him, a cruel shriek piercing her ears as it called the attention of the others.

Sulwyn slashed their legs, her sword catching on the thicker parts of bark as she went along, but she ripped it out, watching them fall to the ground until she stopped next to Ki. There was only time for a short bend over her knees to catch her breath before more arrived.

She stabbed one near Ki's head and another near his back leg, allowing the horse to get up and buck behind him, taking two down under his hooves and stomping wildly for good measure.

"Sulwyn!" called Galahad, and she turned to him. "We can't let them leave this town!" But she could see convulsions roll through him every so often as he tried so hard to hold back. The fear of his eyes and his hand over her throat paralysed her for just a moment, letting a DrvaMørk catch her, gripping her arms hard and pulling back.

Sulwyn screamed, but Ki tackled the thing, forcing it to let go, just as another one tried to ram a small knife into her. She barely missed the brunt of it, cutting her arm instead, the sting of the air burning the now-bleeding wound.

There was no way they could take them all, not while trying to protect themselves and the patrons who were innocent. She turned to see the other Validus fighting to protect their carriage as other Privileged gathered around them. But they were making it harder for Demir and the others to fight.

Soon, the horde overwhelmed the Validus. Elian was tackled down, Demir and Sibril trying to reach him. Sulwyn mounted Ki and galloped back towards them, spotting Daijiro far off to the left with his own mass of bodies.

She rode past him, holding her arm out. With barely a glance, he grabbed her forearm and she pulled him up. Once seated, he put his daggers back and nocked arrows instead. She patted Ki to steady as they weaved through the thicket of DrvaMørk, making their way back to the Validus and Galahad. She somehow strayed so far from them.

Daijiro aimed for the head, shooting arrow after arrow straight at them, hitting each one perfectly, even when Ki lost a bit of footing, until he ran out of arrows.

Sulwyn pulled the reins, stopping Ki right in front of the other Validus.

Daijiro held his hands forwards, holding the DrvaMørk back from killing Elian, but his hold didn't seem as strong as it normally did. She turned to him, but he only grumbled. "Their will is joined. It's harder for me to hold them like this. They're like one large consciousness."

Soon, the carriage was knocked over, and in it, the woman Galahad had saved fell out of the back, still unconscious, limp over the entrance. Sulwyn ran towards her just before another DrvaMørk came to take her. But finally, a tension rent the air, stronger than the presence she was used to. Sulwyn found Daijiro's eyes, and they both looked at Galahad, who'd finally lost control.

Her eyes found Galahad's, his expression apologetic as the black swallowed the tricolours of his eyes. But his expression was still his own. Sulwyn could see he was fighting. Fighting to keep his own humanity and not let his power consume him. And if he could keep doing that, it was enough for her.

The rest of them created a perimeter, Elian free from the DrvaMørk as they stood around the surviving patrons who hid behind the carriages and horses. The unconscious woman was safe for now, and Galahad was cutting through the masses with his black blade that shone with brownish-looking blood.

But even that was not enough.

Even though they took some down, more kept popping up.

Until finally, they were completely surrounded by DrvaMørk.

Sulwyn looked around her, unable to see how they could escape. If she could lead them somewhere, anywhere, they might have a chance. But behind her were the mountains and the forest, and in front of them was the rest of the town and the entrance, and they couldn't let them out. She figured the forest would be their best bet if they could separate them and take them out one by one. But a sudden pressure in the air interrupted her planning.

Without warning, a chill and a strange drop in temperature surrounded them. She looked around past the large encroachment of DrvaMørk to the open road before the festival stalls. A large puff of yellow mist exploded behind the DrvaMørk, and Sulwyn could see a crouched figure stand as another, who had fallen, got up.

"To think I'd have to assist you, Kintana." Diesirae smirked as the yellow mist cleared. Gwydion must have had many of those spells at the ready instead of doing it himself. But the fact that he wasn't there didn't surprise her. He had shifted them, and according to Daijiro, shifting cost the user a lot depending on how far the distance was and who they were carrying. Using vials of magic was the safer choice. Though, now that she thought about it, Daijiro seemed to want to say more at the time, but he stopped himself. She vaguely wondered if he could shift to another location too. But Daijiro wasn't a Devinal. And that didn't really matter at this time.

"This is your mess," called Sulwyn, holding the hilt of her sword between both hands. The DrvaMørk turned to see the new arrivals, and upon seeing Tiamat, they all wailed towards her, encroaching on them and trying to get to her.

"We are not saving you," Diesirae said, but Sulwyn just scoffed.

"I'm aware of that. You just don't want your mess getting out onto the rest of Vartugaul until you're ready." She watched Diesirae's eyes widen, a hint of weariness in them that Sulwyn had caught on to what was really going on. There were a lot of holes she needed to fill, but for now, Sulwyn only smirked. "Carry on, then."

Sulwyn sheathed her sword just as Tiamat bared her pointed teeth.

"I'd let you rot, stupid girl!" she hissed, but since she had come, the DrvaMørk stayed exactly as they were.

"Tiamat. Do as you were instructed," demanded Diesirae, and Sulwyn could see she, too, detested her.

"But they are mine!" Tiamat whined, which was in great contrast to the fact that she looked like an old woman.

"Are you defying me?" Diesirae asked, but Tiamat just sneered.

"No, I'd never talk back to the great Ubusuku," she mocked, and instantly, all the DrvaMørk started to scream. But the screaming resonated through Sulwyn, rocks jabbing her skin as she fell to her knees. Tiamat's cackling echoed around and mixed with the shrieks of these creatures. Sulwyn would not scream in front of her. Not like the DrvaMørk, and for now, she would thank the fact that Gwydion wasn't ready to let the rest of the world know he planned to do this to them in some way or another.

Soon the DrvaMørk stilled, falling dead to the ground as brownish blood oozed from their mouths. The screaming inside her mind continued until it abruptly stopped. Galahad had taken Tiamat down, his ashen hands tightening around her throat.

Sulwyn reached up and brushed the skin against her neck, the ghost of his hands on her, his face twisted in vindictive hunger while he stared down Tiamat. Diesirae moved slowly, looking on in disbelief and possibly with a tinge of fear, but soon, she was held in place by Daijiro, his palm facing her.

"No," Sulwyn croaked, looking at Galahad's crouched form. His shoulders twitched, but his hand was still, straining not to crush her neck then and there.

She didn't want him to kill like this, to feed into it like this. Not when he didn't have control. Sulwyn knew what it felt like to act on thoughts she didn't even remember having, hurting those around her. And though Tiamat was an enemy, she was also Taru's sister. Part of something that seemed to have a lot of history.

Sulwyn couldn't explain it to herself, maybe searching for justification, but she knew they represented some kind of balance. And if they killed Tiamat without understanding it, they would regret it later. Taru was the light, and Tiamat the darkness. They must be important.

So, she ran towards Galahad, unsheathed her sword and pointed it at the back of his neck.

"Oh, oh! Oh! My brother has read your soul, all of it. You bared it *all* to him!" jeered Tiamat. "Just a child, just a child! I could control you *so* easily if you let me. I could free you from your bonds. Just give me some of your blood." She purred, then snapped the air with her pointed teeth. Galahad shoved her further into the ground, his hold tightening.

"Galahad," called Sulwyn, inching the sword closer to the back of his neck so that the point rested on the bone of his spine. He stilled again, neither of them moving. Diesirae tried to struggle against Daijiro's hold, Sulwyn noticing that her shoulder had already been healed.

"Galahad…" Her words were soft, but this time she pushed the blade further, drawing just a drop of blood. He removed his hold on Tiamat and stood, turning to face her. Sulwyn barely had a second to catch the movement, adjusting her sword and continuing to point it at the nape of his neck.

"Take Tiamat and leave, Diesirae. Our fight isn't now, no matter how much I want to kill you," Sulwyn said, her eyes never leaving Galahad's black ones. She knew Daijiro was ready to hold Tiamat if necessary. And slowly, he allowed Diesirae to move as she drew another vial of yellow from an inner pocket at the chest. Diesirae dragged Tiamat back with her, away from them all before they disappeared with a sudden drop in temperature and a puff of pale-yellow mist.

"Demir," called Sulwyn, and he answered. "Get the guests back inside. They need time to pack so they can return to the Empire and burn all the dead, even the DrvaMørk. One of you can stay behind with them as an escort. Decide between the three of you."

They saluted her, but she didn't miss the whispers that rose around her. That she was not suited to be queen. That she purposely let some of the Empire people die. That she wasn't ready to lead and that Nero was right. But she ignored them. Keeping her hand steady, the sword was still pointed at Galahad's neck; his eyes were still black, and his hands were still corrupted with ashen skin. She held out hope that he had a little more control than when he destroyed Gwydion's base since the shadow wings never appeared.

Soon, it was just her, Galahad and Daijiro left, surrounded by dead DrvaMørk. The smell of rotting blood and flesh rising around them.

"I had a vision last night." Her voice shook, and she watched his eyes waver under her steel tone. The moment she pointed her sword at him, she had decided what she would do if the time came. Daijiro walked closer to them, standing somewhere to her left, but she continued, "You try to kill me."

Galahad shook his head, eyes wide with disbelief, until she watched them fade yet again to their tricoloured glory.

"How?" he rasped, looking at her in fear.

"Exactly the way you planned to kill Tiamat just now." She lowered her sword, lifting it behind her and sheathing it. But she knew neither of them missed the shaking in her hands.

"I will *burn* you," Daijiro threatened, the bloodlust in his eyes, but Sulwyn looked at him, silencing him with a hardened glare.

Galahad stepped closer to her, and there was anger in his eyes. "This is your fault," he seethed, cold dropping into her chest at his words.

"Had you not been born, they *never* would have taken me!" His fists clenched, but he continued. "Had you never existed, my family could still be alive! They wouldn't have targeted me. To have someone as your equal. To destroy you!" He stepped even closer, but Sulwyn held her ground. Her heart breaking with every word he spoke. "And it didn't even matter, Sulwyn. It didn't *matter*. Because you came here anyway. They wanted to keep you, to taint you as they did to so many others. My clan died for no reason!" His voice cracked as he yelled, but Sulwyn still stood her ground. She could see Daijiro from the corner of her eye, pacing.

"They would have killed your clan regardless, as they did Daijiro's and countless others," she retorted, but then he shoved her hard in the chest, forcing her to take a few steps back.

"No! The only reason they found us was because they found Tiergan! If they were not looking for someone to counter you, they would never have acted on his lead! Never would have been able to find us," he cried, and she could see he berated himself for everything he was saying.

"And would you have stayed there? Hidden in your clan while they took over and lay waste to everyone else? Even if I hadn't been born, the events that followed the downfall of the High City would still have happened. Lay blame where it belongs," growled Sulwyn, trying to keep the tears from falling, his face blurring a little.

"I've killed Artaxiad, and I still can't find peace, Sulwyn." He sounded hollow and strained. "The only thing I'm left with is this power that consumes me when it shouldn't and now the knowledge that I might kill you in the future." He looked down, the fight taken out of him, leaving only despair in his shoulders.

"I can defend myself. I will kill you if I need to, Galahad," Sulwyn said coldly, seeing his eyes reflect how she felt deep inside as she turned away from him and walked back to Ki.

With every step she took, sharp pain like glass slid in and out of her heart with every beat. Even though she knew it was only anger that drove his words, they had to come from somewhere. And she would accept his blame if it helped.

Had she not been born, then he may not have been a target, and knowing that alone hurt her more.

XXI

Return What Is Mine

| SULWYN |

THE journey home was painful. Sibril had stayed behind, staying a day to escort the Privileged back to the Empire, but the next several days home were a nightmare.

Sulwyn refused to talk to anyone besides Ki, which resulted in Galahad only talking when necessary and Daijiro not talking at all. Demir and Elian tried to keep the mood up, but even they eventually gave up. Most of the ride home was silent.

The only other person who could be more silent than them was the woman who lay unconscious in their carriage. Every day, Sulwyn would talk to her for just a little bit to see if anything would happen, but to no avail. Sometimes, she would spot Daijiro standing near her when they were resting; the carriage door open to give her fresh air.

Even though Sulwyn wanted to talk to both of them, she couldn't make herself do it. Instead, a wedge came between all of them.

When they finally made it back to the Empire, it was exactly as they had left it, in high security with Validus and Néosan alike patrolling all areas of entrance around the high black walls. Going through security quickly, they made their way to Valens.

As soon as she was in range, she called for Arsinone, and in turn, for Eztli and Nori to meet them in the stables.

"You're back!" Arsinone said brightly, hugging Sulwyn around the waist. But she faltered once she saw everyone else's expressions. Sulwyn turned to face Demir and Elian. "You both are dismissed," she said casually and saw their look of relief when she let them go, taking the carriage with them.

But before they left, Galahad brought the woman out, holding her carefully.

Sulwyn looked at Nori before beckoning her closer. "Nori… We think this woman is a Devinal," she whispered. Nori just nodded, moving closer to Galahad as he knelt and placed the woman on the hay-strewn floor.

Nori took in the woman's face, her hands hesitating to touch her, and instantly, tears began to flow.

"Are ya okay?" Eztli asked, looking at her and the woman at her feet. But Nori just broke down in hysterical tears, kneeling and bracing against the woman.

Galahad and Daijiro both looked at Sulwyn, who only acknowledged their glances. She hadn't told them about her thoughts on the woman, not wanting to make the wrong connection. But she seemed right.

"Where did you find her?" whispered Nori between tears.

"She was being held captive at Gwydion's base," Galahad answered, his voice unused. Arsinone looked between all of them, but Sulwyn pointedly avoided her gaze.

"Nori, be careful. It seems like she's sealed her mind or something," started Sulwyn, but Nori just nodded.

"I know. I could see it when I looked at her. Hold on…" Nori said, and she knelt further, bringing her forehead to the woman's. As soon as she touched her head to hers, she gasped, and the woman under her began to stir.

Slowly, she opened her eyes. They were swirled in opaque blues until they faded away and left light green irises. Blinking the sleep and daylight away, the woman started, sitting up shakily and squinting from all the lights until her eyes found Nori.

"Oh, the goddess…" the woman whispered, her voice cracked and hoarse. Nori smiled wildly, throwing herself around her.

"So is anyone gonna explain…" started Eztli, but Arsinone answered.

"They're sisters."

♋

They had all made their way back to Galahad's room in Valens, unable to report to Nero as he was dealing with prisoners who were returned to the Solus. While they waited, they decided to hear the woman's story after offering to place her in bed. However, she wanted to sit up with them, and instead they took residence in the sitting area.

Nori fussed over her, excited to have her back and saddened by what she had been through. The scars around her wrist, neck and ankles didn't go unnoticed by any of them, and once they cleaned and changed her, they all noticed a patch of black vine-like marks going around the side of her neck. Once they got her food and water, she was ready to speak.

"My name is Riko…" She looked up, though every time she did, her stare lingered on Daijiro. "As you know, I am Nori's older sister. My time in captivity is full of holes, but I will do my best to answer you."

Sulwyn spoke first, unable to take the silence that had seeped between her, Galahad and Daijiro much longer. "You seemed to be the only prisoner at this location…" Sulwyn mused, and Riko just nodded, holding a cup of hot tea in between her hands.

"After our parents were killed, Nori and I travelled alone. But we were soon found and taken to the Empire. Nori stayed here while I was given to Gwydion. I found out later that he captured me to learn more about Devinal magic. It seems his teaching at the time was inadequate in his eyes, though he seemed far beyond any I had ever met." Her voice was softer with food and drink, but the hoarse taint of captivity still lingered on most of her words.

"Did you see him often?" asked Sulwyn.

"No. Eventually, I sealed off my mind with a magic not even he could touch. Only blood could release it. I didn't know if I would ever see my sister again, but even if I never woke, I did it. It was better than helping him."

"Did he learn a lot from you?" Sulwyn whispered, and she could see her hands clench the cup tighter.

"Each Devinal is different with how they use and hold magic. Because of this, many of my own understandings and unique abilities didn't work for him, and this upset him. But he did learn a few distinctive things from me. Like perfecting the ability to disguise and using the elements... but..." She hesitated, thinking hard. Sulwyn waited patiently. If there was any weakness to be had, she would accept it. "He could never control fire. In fact, I think he fears it," she finished, and Sulwyn frowned.

"Why fire of all things?" Sulwyn asked, but Daijiro answered, his eyes never leaving Riko's.

"Fire is alive. And if you don't earn its allegiance, it will betray you instead."

Sulwyn caught the small smile that passed over Riko's lips at his words, her eyes looking at him differently than the rest of them, even Nori.

"Exactly..."

"Was there anything else about him that seemed different to you?" asked Sulwyn, earning a look from Daijiro and Galahad. Sulwyn couldn't step further without alluding them to her growing theories, so she'd have to take what she could get.

Riko frowned, thinking deeper. "No... Though he seems to lack any kind of empathy as a person, in terms of ability, he is a real Devinal." Sulwyn stood quickly, walking over to her.

"Thank you, Riko. Please get some rest and feel free to stay here. I will ensure your safety." She touched her shoulder, noticing again the black on her neck. Sulwyn was about to ask, but Riko subtly shook her head, glancing at Nori.

"Later," she whispered and turned her attention to the room. "This is a nice change from a cell..."

By the time they could meet with Nero, the Privileged had returned. And not only did they quickly spread rumours of how Sulwyn had treated them as queen, but another rumor had finally made its way to the Empire.

Kintana and Sulwyn were one and the same.

"This… Is this how you do things?" Nero asked sternly.

The three of them had been summoned to his office, but Sulwyn could see the elation in his eyes despite his tone. At this rate, her tarnished name would aid in him getting her out. But if she continued to act as she always had, the people could say nothing against Artaxiad's final rule. Or so she hoped, because now everyone was questioning why Pandora and Artaxiad said Kintana was dead, while others assumed they meant metaphorically.

"I did what was necessary," she started, but he held up a hand.

"You destroyed a town meant for the enjoyment of our people here," he said, but Sulwyn would not stand for it.

"We investigated the town on your instruction, and in turn, destroyed a town for the safety of *our* people! If you would stop ignoring the fact that Gwydion is a threat, you wouldn't have this issue. Regardless of how I oversaw the situation, those elitists can tell you what attacked them. 'Cause it sure as hell wasn't me," she ground out, her temper flaring.

She was tired.

Tired of being the centre of blame.

Tired of hiding.

Tired of this corrupted place.

The days of silence took its toll on her. If they wanted to blame her for this too, then go ahead. What else was there for her to lose? She'd make the Empire fall one day anyway.

"Forgive me, my *queen*," he mocked, but Galahad stepped forwards.

"Gwydion took her and used her for his own vendetta," Galahad explained, his tone impassive.

"As I have heard. It seems like Kintana has destroyed her name, killing seven innocent people. If anything, he helped reveal the truth."

"I have no recollection of that!" cried Sulwyn, feeling Daijiro's and Galahad's stares. She never had the chance to tell them, didn't want to.

"Regardless, if you've forgotten, it doesn't look like they have. I look forwards to how you will handle this next." He gave her an odd look, and it unsettled her. He was going to do something soon; she was sure of it. As of now, he dismissed them all, carrying on with his other duties.

Sulwyn turned and stormed out of his office, marching down the hall until finally, she screamed, depleting every ounce of air in her lungs until the muscles in her chest pulled like they would rip. All the servants around were beyond startled, dropping anything they were holding. A hand touched her shoulder, but she grabbed it and spun, twirling the person around and bringing their arm with her, his arm pressed up between his shoulder blades.

"Sulwyn…" Galahad said tightly, trying to shift her hold. She let go, continuing her way, but soon, she was held in place. She turned, able to fight Daijiro's hold even if it was a struggle, and faced them.

"Seven?" asked Daijiro, dropping his hand to his side, the hold gone.

"Do *not* start with me," she roared at them. "How dare you." Her hurt was showing at them both, and she couldn't stop it. "How dare you show me concern after all this time. Especially *you*." She pointed at Galahad, but he returned her stare in kind.

"I was angry, Sulwyn, and I am sorry. You know I meant none of it," he said, but he faltered under her glare.

"You thought about that at least once down the line to have said it to me. Do not lie to me. I accept your blame, but do not use me as a means to hide from your own battles. *I* meant what I said," she seethed and continued walking, leaving them behind.

She needed to find Arsinone, but Arsinone found her first. She smiled brightly, taking Sulwyn's hand in hers and leading her through Valens.

Slowly, they walked out the back and through the stables right into the forest.

"I know they disrupted his grave…" started Arsinone, "but I found his axes, and we buried them instead exactly as you had it. The family next to him were untouched." Soon, they were at Caldwell's grave.

Her lip trembled in a way that it hadn't done since she was a child. Sulwyn closed her eyes and fell to the ground. The smells of earth and leaves wafted around her, calming her ever so slightly until she could bring herself to ask Arsinone.

"I need you to read my soul freely and find the last week…" She took deep breaths.

Arsinone smiled sadly. "Are you sure?"

"I need to know who they were, Arsinone." Sulwyn turned to her, but the girl held out her hand, palm up.

"Gee-Gee has been teaching me. I can get the answers you are looking for better if you give me a drop of blood." She sat next to Sulwyn, crossing her legs.

Sulwyn took one of her smaller daggers and pricked a finger, watching the blood pool over it and drip onto Arsinone's hand. Just like Taru, her eyes shut, but unlike Taru, she reached forwards and touched Sulwyn's chest.

She stayed as still and quiet as she could, letting the sounds of nature pass over her, soothing her and bringing her guard back down so that Arsinone could find her way better. Soon, Arsinone reached forwards with the hand that held her blood and touched Sulwyn's forehead.

Unlike before, when Arsinone showed fuzzy thoughts, the memories were clear, and she found herself overhead of her body on the metal table. "This is where you last remember?" asked Arsinone quietly.

"Yes…" whispered Sulwyn, her own eyes closed.

"I can't get anything from you when you are asleep, so let's move forwards…" she started, and soon, she could see the cell in front of her, the one she only started to remember the day she escaped.

Diesirae stepped in front of it, opening it carefully and beckoning her out with demands. They watched as if they were another person altogether, following after Sulwyn and Diesirae into the light at the end. But just before she got there, Sulwyn stopped and refused to move.

"I'm not fighting anyone." She gasped, already struggling to stay put, much to Diesirae's surprise.

"You will do as you are told," she hissed, kneeing her in the stomach and injecting her in the neck with the same clear liquid.

Sulwyn fell to the ground, but she refused to move. "Kill me if you want. But I think your master would be mad at you... woof, woof." That one earned her a kick to her back. Soon, a shadow crossed over her, and Gwydion was before her.

"Damn Artaxiad..." cursed Gwydion, and soon he was muttering words and directing them to Diesirae. As if there was a blur over their eyes, Diesirae shortened and took on Sulwyn's appearance.

"We'll have to continue this with you. It's her name we want to tarnish anyway," Gwydion said, a tic of annoyance in his jaw.

Sulwyn and Arsinone sifted through the rest of her memories until she got to the point where she faced Kai. Arsinone released her hold over Sulwyn, instantly collapsing onto the soft patch of grass and falling asleep.

Relief flooded Sulwyn, though it was bittersweet.

Even though she still had no recollection of her own during those three days, she had defied Gwydion at the last moment each time, no matter how they tried. If Gwydion was right, then she really did have to thank Artaxiad for his insanity. It saved her.

But they still managed to get what they had planned. If word had spread here, then it had already started to spread across Vartugaul. She would lose the name she had made for herself eventually. They would think her just like them, selling out for the luxury and ease they provided.

But that was fine.

Just like no one knew Raghnall had a scar, few knew her face as Sulwyn. They associated Kintana with a scarf around her face and a spear she had lost long ago. She could work with that if need be.

ॐ

| DAIJIRO |

Daijiro left Galahad alone to his thoughts when Sulwyn marched off in anger. Though he didn't agree with what had transpired between them, he hadn't helped the situation either and somehow lost his nerve to talk to her. He was irritated. Even though he knew she was suffering. But she hadn't told them about the seven kills she may or may not have caused.

Why did she hide it from them?

What else was she hiding?

He kept asking himself this question after their interaction on the stairs in the inn at Wallasyn. She had realised something and wasn't alluding to it.

Why?

Were they not trustworthy?

Daijiro knew he was difficult to deal with, and their time spent together hadn't been long. But he thought they were doing all right. Was sure he was even being a bit nicer to her little companions. He sighed for the umpteenth time, rubbing his face aggressively, and after wandering for a while, made his way back to Galahad's strange garden room, even though the plant life was long dead save for some vines.

Upon entering, he noticed that everyone was asleep and only then realised it was late into the evening. He walked in slowly, checking to see if Sulwyn had come there or not, but when he couldn't find her, he started to step back, until a voice called to him.

"Wait…" And Riko walked forwards, illuminated slightly by the one candle they had left alight. She pressed her finger to her lips and led Daijiro out of the room.

"What?" he snapped, and though she looked at him a little apprehensively, she gestured for him to lead the way. "I don't know what it is you want. Why should I lead?" But every time he responded to her as he would anyone else, a heavy guilt sat deep in his chest. Something he hadn't felt in a long time until he had hit the side of Sulwyn's head while interrogating Galahad's stupid uncle.

But since the moment he laid eyes on Riko, he knew she looked familiar. And it wasn't because of Nori. He was trying to ignore it, when she gestured again for him to lead, assuming she had something to say.

Daijiro wasn't sure exactly where to go, but he figured anywhere outside of Valens was a good start. So, he led her to the surrounding forest behind the stables, where the remaining horses were already fast asleep in the now-set sun.

Once they reached the forest, she continued to lead the way, walking among the trees and grass curiously. He wasn't sure how she was kept captive before she sealed off her mind, but she must have missed nature at some point, especially since she was a Devinal. Soon, she stopped, finding a small clearing where the crescent moon could shine brightly over them.

She looked over at him cautiously. "I heard about your family…" she started, and Daijiro's eyes widened. "I am so sorry for your loss…"

He considered her for a moment, knowing there was something stirring in him from seeing her, trying to piece it together himself and failing, building frustration instead.

"If you know me, then say it," he demanded, his patience waning. It was only at times like these did he realise how much he hadn't grown. The only people he could really tolerate were Sulwyn and Galahad, and the little mind reader.

Riko smiled sadly, and something about it looked familiar. He watched her walk between the tall grass, breathing in the open air. After just a few days, a bit of colour returned to her skin, light golden like Nori's. Her long black hair went well past her waist, and her eyes were bright green and narrow in shape like his own.

"The fact that you don't remember me is not your fault…" she said quietly, coming to a stop in front of him. He frowned, his hand twitching just to get the information from her directly. But he couldn't bring himself to do it. "We first met when we were ten…" she continued, and Daijiro's hands and feet tingled to ice. What was she talking about? He did not remember her at all. Nothing about what she said sounded familiar. But after years of interrogating and torturing, he knew she wasn't lying either. She smiled again and slowly lowered to the ground, sitting cross-legged and beckoning him to do the same. He sat reluctantly.

"Nori was not with me then. My mother liked to travel sometimes, and I would go with her. Our father, who was not a Devinal, would stay with Nori when we left as she was too young then."

Still, Daijiro had no idea what she was talking about, but old fear started to crawl within him.

"One day, we met your mother, Selia, and she brought us home with her. Since then, we played as children every day and visited frequently for two years in a small house lent to use nearby."

"What are you talking about?" Panic rising, and with it, his urge to destroy. But Riko reached forwards and touched his hand, and something like electricity ran through him from her finger. He flinched, but she gently grabbed it again, holding it tightly.

"My mother would leave and go back home from time to time, but I would stay with you at your home."

But that couldn't be true. Daijiro had no memory of this, and neither did his mother. Hell, even if his mother kept it from him, his father wouldn't have, and besides that, how did they stay with him there?

"I think I was meant to find you again. The fact that it was you and your companions that found me leads me to believe so."

Daijiro stood now, eyes wide. "I do not know you. Nor what you are saying. How can you say that two years of my life are *missing!* I remember when I was ten, and you and your mother were not there," he hissed, but she, too, stood.

She looked downcast, and that pinch of guilt rolled through him, but why should he feel anything towards her? He was done with this.

Daijiro turned to leave, but she reached out her warm fingers, gently grabbing his wrist. That same electricity flowed up his arm, and in rare panic, he hurriedly tried to hold her in place. But when she spoke again, he stopped everything. "Would you be upset if I gave your memories back?"

"If you have something of mine, then I would obviously want it. You're insinuating two years of my life—" He was caught off guard when she pulled him down quickly and kissed him fiercely, her eyes closing.

That same electric sting flowed through him as he watched tears fall from her closed eyes, until finally, images and sounds started to fill his mind. It wasn't like what he experienced with Arsinone. Instead, it was like missing pieces of a puzzle were being returned and refitted, pulling out makeshift ones that were never meant to be there.

Soon, the memories he had of himself alone filled in, and she was there, younger and healthier. A happier time. Memories that weren't ever there before filled in too, with his mother and what must have been hers laughing together, carefree and happy. He didn't know when he'd ever seen his mother like that. Thought he'd never seen her like that.

But soon, that happiness began to ebb when a fear he hadn't had in a long time started to creep through. The fear he associated with his father, Tamesis. Until one memory played out fully.

They were twelve now. It had been nearly two years since he had met Riko. They were playing outside until the last bit of sun faded when they heard a scream from his house that paralysed them both. Daijiro grabbed Riko's hand and pulled her back to his home.

Just before they went in, they peeped in through the windows and saw Tamesis in a raging fit, alone with Riko's mother. His own mother was not there, out for the evening with her sister, unaware that Riko's mother was coming back that night.

Riko's mother had been bound to a chair as Tamesis began to beat her, drunk with madness and lust. Her eyes were unfocused, drugged, and unable to react with magic. Before Tamesis could do any more, Riko left Daijiro's side and entered the house, fueled by her own anger.

But Riko was still young, unable to control her magic, and though she managed to make him stumble, it wasn't enough.

Daijiro charged in, using Riko's distraction to free her mother from her bindings. But Tamesis grabbed his shoulder and shoved him to the floor.

Riko tried again, but Tamesis lashed out at her, knocking her into a small table and cutting her head on the corner. "Stupid children, getting in my way," he barked, going back to the woman.

Daijiro, flooded with fear, hesitated, but soon he pulled a dagger from out of his boot and launched himself at Tamesis, stabbing him in his knee and forcing him to fall onto the ground. Tamesis grabbed his throat, squeezing tight and shoving Daijiro back against the floor. But all he could hear was Riko's scream, and soon fire erupted from within him, forcing Tamesis off and back, burning his face and his hand, his clothes catching fire.

Tamesis howled, running outside and diving into the river that ran through their village. But he didn't have time to wait. He moved to help Riko untie her mother and immediately, she pulled Daijiro into a strong hug.

"I'm sorry. This was not your fault. I want you to know that," she started, and Daijiro's heart dropped, knowing this was goodbye.

"One day, these will be returned to you, and if that happens, it means my daughter has found you again and is safe. Until then, Daijiro..." He tried to push her away, not caring about how he looked, crying, knowing what they were going to do. But soon, she pressed her forehead to his, and he froze, his last memory, Riko's tear-streamed face.

XXII

What's Done Is Done

| DAIJIRO |

"DAIJIRO..." whispered a voice, and though he imagined grey ones, green eyes looked down at him.

He took a deep breath, sitting up wildly, holding his palm out but soon relaxed when he saw Riko sitting next to him in exactly the same spot she had been before.

"I'm sorry. It was reckless of me to give you all of them at once... It could have killed you, but I believed you would be okay." She shrugged as she stood, and he just stared at her incredulously, his body shaking from the violation, pinches of electricity passing through him, easing with each moment.

It took him a little longer to clear his vision, his eyes blurring each time he blinked, fragments of the memories he had just gotten back passing through his mind. Riko moved to touch his hand again, but he pulled away, forcing himself to stand and put space between them.

"Just... wait," he demanded, running his hands through his hair. Cold sweat coating him. His chest was tight from his short breaths. Unbalanced, he wanted to brace himself, trying to calm down slowly. But his anger flared, and he finally held his palm forwards and paralysed her.

Her eyes widened, fear in them, but he didn't release his hold until he walked up to her only a few inches between. He paused, looking down at her, before he wrapped a hand behind her neck and pulled her forwards to return the kiss she had given him with just as much ferocity.

She froze as he pulled away, and soon, he wrapped his arms around her. Feeling the nostalgia. Remembering that there was a time in his past when he and his mother had been happy, at least for a moment.

"Why did you take our memories?" he asked after some time, creating space between them again. They stood awkwardly apart in the centre of their small clearing.

"We thought we had put you in danger. We didn't realise that doing that wouldn't have mattered as your village was attacked regardless. She did it to protect you, as Devinal are hunted, alas..." She trailed off.

"You should have left it. My village was old, and the Empire was growing. It was a matter of time before they would attack either way. It would have brought my mother peace to know there was a time she could laugh like that."

"You were her happiness," she said.

"Don't speak like you know what we went through," he spat, seeing her flinch. "What you saw was nothing compared to the years to follow." He breathed heavily. "You removed yourself from the entire village..."

"Magic is a lot of things. My mother wished it, so once it left you, it left everyone. She healed your unconscious father as well."

"That sounds selfish to me..." he said bitterly, but he could see why she looked at him the way she did. "That was a long time ago, Riko..."

"You may have forgotten, Daijiro. But I remembered every day, even when I'd sealed my mind... I cannot change how I feel, what I have felt since I met you. What I grew up with and what helped me get through what I have been through," she said a little haphazardly.

Daijiro turned his back to her, looking to the sky. "Ten is a very young age. I wasn't who I am now. And neither are you." She nodded, her head low. But he wanted to confirm. He wanted to know, and after some more silence, he asked calmly, "What do you smell?"

She looked at him a little oddly but inhaled deeply. "Sugary rain," she started, and he held his breath. "Hmm, and old wood?" She shrugged, confused by his question. His power was mostly dormant when she lived with him, so he knew she had never experienced his before.

Daijiro closed his eyes, his answer set in stone for him at this point.

"We've been missing for a while. Your sister will lose her mind if you are gone for too long."

Silence spread between them once again. And though Daijiro was slightly elated that something that had always been missing was returned to him, it was a heavy burden. Lost in thought, he didn't realise they had made it back to the edge of the stables.

Daijiro held up a hand, signalling for Riko to stop and crouch with him. They were hidden behind the stables and the few sleeping horses that hadn't been stolen. Few candles illuminated the area, casting them in deep shadows.

"Are you sure?" whispered one Néosan. Daijiro peeked to the side to see the man nodding, their faces pale. "How did he find out?"

"One of the Validus on the night confirmed it. And another saw her the same night as the Gala go into that room long before. He's gathering us all slowly now to avoid her notice."

Daijiro's blood froze.

He knew that there were no witnesses that night. They ensured it, and made sure that what anyone saw was what they wanted them to. Someone was lying, fabricating it. But it didn't matter.

They had been caught.

"Their daughter is to be executed publicly for the murder of King Artaxiad and Queen Pandora."

❧

| SULWYN |

As Sulwyn made her way back into Valens, she knew something had been set into motion. But for whatever reason, no one was acting on it, and she couldn't find out further because Arsinone was still asleep in her arms. However, once she entered Valens Muros, Sulwyn was on high alert.

Avoiding the main halls, she walked quickly and stealthily back to Galahad's room, only to run into Daijiro and Riko down the hall near the door. Taken aback by the odd combination of people, she stopped walking when his eyes found hers.

Her heart stuttered.

Nero found out.

Nero knew what she had done.

And even if he had faked it or not, it didn't matter. They needed to leave immediately.

"Riko, take Arsinone back to Eztli and prepare to leave," Sulwyn instructed, her voice low.

Riko was bewildered. "We haven't even said anything..." But Sulwyn watched her turn to Daijiro just as he cast his gaze away from Sulwyn. She could see the look Riko gave him, but she didn't have time for that now. They were all in danger.

"Where is Galahad?" she hissed, but Daijiro shook his head.

"I don't know... but I'll find him. Just ready everything you need, and I'll get whatever you have at Eques." He hurried, brushing her shoulder and running off.

She ran into the room just as Nori and Eztli were stirred awake by Riko, and Arsinone was placed on the bed. Sulwyn went about lighting enough candles to see before she pressed on. "Nero knows. We all need to leave. Pack what you need. If you have anything elsewhere that isn't as important, leave it behind."

"Everything we use or own is in this room now," said Eztli, the sleep gone from her eyes immediately.

"What's wrong with Arsinone?" Nori asked, touching her cheeks.

"She should wake soon, but pack a bag for her as well," said Sulwyn, and she proceeded to find whatever she had left in the room.

Half an hour passed, and they were all ready when Arsinone sat up abruptly. "What about Gee-Gee?!" She gasped, looking directly at Sulwyn.

Sulwyn crossed over to her on the bed. "Daijiro went to Eques. He will know," she whispered, hearing from the open window voices raised, grouping, and moving closer to Valens.

Soon enough, Daijiro entered the room with Galahad in tow. "Taru took off with Hana, don't worry about him," Galahad said. Arsinone nodded, getting off the bed.

Daijiro tossed Sulwyn a bag full of clothes and supplies she always kept together. She grabbed extra weapons lying around and filled the spaces in her belt. She didn't have the choice to be meticulous right now.

"I've secured enough horses and sent them to walk a discreet path through the forest behind this room," said Daijiro, looking at them all.

"It will take some time for them to get into this room by force. By then, we should be far enough," Galahad finished, stepping past the sitting area and over the recently filled stream. It would evaporate again, and this room would turn fully to dust. But that didn't matter anymore.

Galahad cut past the ivy that covered the old wooden door leading outside, and after throwing his shoulder against it a few times, it opened. Sulwyn ran forwards with the girls, Daijiro trailing after her. Galahad turned, closing the door and pressing his hand against it. Sulwyn watched through the window as the vines regrew, hiding the door once again.

She turned, looking around. She had only been here once during that day of rest when she was training to fight Caldwell. It was a small hidden garden with touches of Galahad all over it. She looked over at him briefly, and his small smile confirmed her thoughts.

"It's hidden by the trees behind Valens and the tall trees in the area from above. You can only see it from the bedroom windows. But once they know it's here, they can figure out how to get in from the forest side."

"By then, we'll be gone," Daijiro said, and they all entered the back forest, ripping through trees and bushes.

And they never stopped running.

They kept going and going until the alarm rang out across the Empire. It sounded like a distant thing. For now, they were safe.

Sulwyn slowed to a jog, hearing the crunch of twigs in the near distance. She paused, crouching low as the others stopped behind her, looking around, but soon Ki emerged alongside Taru and Hana, the other horses flitting just behind, between the trees.

Arsinone ran to Taru, hugging him closely as they all turned to Sulwyn, Galahad and Daijiro.

"Where are we going from here?" asked Taru, still holding Arsinone and patting her head. "The trees are anxiously waiting for them to enter the forest. We have some time to decide."

"We're splitting up," Sulwyn said after a moment to a barrage of protests, but she held up her hand, silencing them.

She stood straighter, taller as she spoke. "They are after me. Nero has been waiting from the start to pin their deaths on me. And whether he has proof or not, our leaving sealed our fate. But I wasn't going to stay there and wait to find out what he knew."

She could see the looks they gave her now. Even Daijiro and Galahad looked at her a little differently. Her demeanour changed. As if she were on another long escape with Raghnall. And it was thrilling.

Being in the Empire, being careful of how she acted and who she could trust or talk to had been draining. And finally, she had an out. She wanted to relish in it, but she also had many lives at stake at the cost of her friendship, and she wouldn't let them die for her.

"Daijiro, do you know where Kione is hiding?" Sulwyn asked.

He raised an eyebrow. "I do. He checks in every so often. Last I heard, he went to Illa. It's west from here. He's staying for a while because it's already so hard to get to. No one will look for him there right now."

"That's a dangerous location..." said Galahad, and they all looked at him. "It's near the border of Mortui Gemma, and a day or so travel from there is the Slave Base I mentioned before."

"No one will be looking too closely at the Slave Base when they're looking for me. I'll make sure to leave a trail in the opposite direction," she countered. "You need to get to him and let him know. And then travel together. He can keep you all safe."

"What do ya mean…?" asked Eztli, reprimanding Sulwyn with wide eyes.

"Eztli. You can't come with me. None of you can," she said softly to the girls and Riko. "And we all can't travel together. It stands out too much."

"Taru can take care of you until you get to Kione," Galahad added gently. Taru nodded, remaining quiet for once.

"You need to change from your maid uniforms to the clothes you brought. Quickly. We shouldn't stay here any longer…" Sulwyn said with a note of finality.

༄

Daijiro had managed to secure four horses. Soon, everyone had changed and gotten familiar with their steed. Taru and Arsinone would ride with Hana. Eztli and Nori would have one horse and Riko her own. While Daijiro and Galahad took the horses they used most often, and Sulwyn had Ki.

Sulwyn looked at them all, unsaid words lumped in her throat, choking her and bringing tears to her eyes. She looked at anything but them, staring into the sky, the light of the moon shining through the trees. She hoped beyond hope this wouldn't be the last time she saw them.

"Where will you go?" asked Taru, but Sulwyn shook her head.

"In case this goes wrong, I don't want to tell you. But I'm going back towards Guāngcǎi." Taru reached for her hands, holding them tightly; they were warm but gentle. He nodded with one last pat before moving to the side for the others.

Arsinone hugged her tightly around the waist, Eztli hugging her around the shoulders. "Please be safe, sweetness." Eztli tightened her hold.

"Don't give Taru and Kione a tough time. And remember to be inconspicuous," Sulwyn said into Eztli's neck. She hugged them longer than she meant to, but soon, she was letting go and turning to Nori.

"Please keep them safe... I'm glad you have your sister with you. Though I'm sorry you didn't have much time to recover more." She turned her last words to Riko. But Riko's eyes softened.

"We can't always get the luxury of healing. I'm only glad to be free." She smiled and hugged Sulwyn gently. Nori hugged her tightly as well until Riko took Sulwyn's hand and looked at the black ring.

"You are all wearing one?" she asked, looking at each of their hands.

"Kione has one too," said Nori.

"I can work with this," she muttered and beckoned them all to give her their hands with the black ring on them. "When we get to this Kione, I'll do the same. It's not much, but it's something..." She held her hands over their rings and muttered the same language of words Nori did. Unlike Nori, her magic was like the wind, gentle and calm. But at the last moment, Sulwyn flinched as if something pricked her. It burned for a second before fading. Sulwyn glanced around but there was no reaction from anyone else. She looked at Riko, their gaze connecting, her eyebrows furrowed.

"I'll be fine..." Riko muttered, touching the black veins at the side of her neck. "Next time we meet, I will explain..."

Though the veins looked the same, Sulwyn was sure they were just a bit darker, but she couldn't be sure if that was because Riko was pale, and they only had torchlight to illuminate their path. She wished she had time for an explanation. However, there was no choice but to trust her right now.

Sulwyn had asked Arsinone to read her and trusted that Arsinone's judgement was right. Riko's soul was not a happy one, but with Nori by her side, it was healing and untouched by Gwydion.

"What did ya do?" asked Eztli, looking at her ring and seeing no difference.

"The next time one of us is close to another, it will heat slightly." She smiled. "It's not much, but since we are splitting up, it could help find each other."

"Do we have a meeting point?" Galahad asked, looking at Taru and Sulwyn. They looked at each other, Taru shrugging before she spoke.

"Antac," Sulwyn answered, and though she was unsure why, it made sense.

"That's a bit risky…" Daijiro started.

"By the time we all get back there, the Empire should be looking for us in Guāngcǎi."

"I agree," Galahad said, and they turned to look at him. "There is someone there who I think will help us." He shrugged.

"Time?" asked Riko.

"Let's go there in a month's time. If you don't see the other party by the fifth day, leave and come back again in another ten days," Sulwyn explained, a system that Raghnall and Wilkson had used to meet each other.

Soon, Sulwyn was waving away Eztli, Nori, Arsinone, Taru, and Riko. The five of them took off at a trot towards the west, already at an advantage because they could use the forest as cover. Sulwyn could also go the same way, the longer way, and use the Tranquilium forest around Antiqua to curve back around the Guāngcǎi, but she wanted the Empire on her tail for a bit. She would ride in the open, out of the small forest that was south of the Empire, and into the open terrain straight towards Macil and cross the border. But instead of going southeast back to Wallasyn, she was going up north a little to the west past Paraga, her home.

The forest grew quieter since the others left. The sound of hooves thudding on dirt, getting farther and farther away. Uneasiness settled in her heart. Maybe this had been a bad decision. She turned to Daijiro and Galahad, trying to maintain the authority she had used over the others. "Maybe you both should go with them," she started, but was instantly rebuffed.

"You can't go alone. What would be the point of that?" Galahad asked, moving closer to her.

"I'm willing to bet I know my way around Guāngcǎi better than both of you. I don't need the assistance. They do," she insisted, fear rising in her. She had sent three young girls, a woman who had been in captivity for years, and a well-meaning but old man on their own.

"They will be fine," Galahad assured her, raising his hands to grip her shoulders. He bent down, levelling with her, reassuring. "Taru isn't what he looks like. And if what you say is true about Tiamat, then you can understand that."

But Sulwyn's eyes were wide. "I didn't get a chance to tell him!"

"I'm sure he knows…" Galahad said darkly, and Sulwyn had to believe he was right. Because since they had returned, Taru had been quiet and vigilant. Something that just didn't suit her original idea of him.

"You can't get rid of us that easily." Daijiro's gaze was intense. "Even if you don't want to share the same space with us right now. We're all each other has…" He trailed off, a sad smile across his lips.

"Fine," she conceded, knowing that what they said was true. And once the others found Kione, they would be okay. Plus, Galahad was just as much a target as she was if Nero truly knew the truth. She mounted Ki, holding his reins tightly and patted him gently before she turned to them both as they followed suit.

"But you follow my rule." She spurred Ki into motion as the three of them took off at a trot.

"Spoken like a true queen." She could hear the smirk in Daijiro's tone, but she would not engage. For now, she needed to focus on making sure their trio left witnesses for the Empire to follow.

XXIII

What Does Trust Mean To You?
|SULWYN|

THE journey this time was awkward.

Each day they rode in silence, only speaking to look at the map and adjust their course. At night, they would eat in exhaustion and two would sleep while the other would watch. They made sure to pass by the outskirts of Macil, hoping someone would spot their movement before continuing.

Their intended destination was a town called Pliflyn, a week from the Empire itself, a day's ride from the border of Antiqua into Guāngcǎi, where they would veer off towards Paraga in secret. She wanted them to think she was going past Wallasyn, far east to the mountains.

They also rode past the watchtowers of the Empire in the distance and passed a few of the small Néosan bases outside its vicinity to ensure they were seen, so that when they followed, they would follow them and *only* them. They made sure to make it as inconspicuous as possible so that Nero wouldn't suspect them. But she figured at this point he wouldn't care. He just wanted it known that she was the Empire's enemy, murderer of their king and queen.

She wasn't even sure if it worked or not, but she could only hope. Instead, all these days and nights gave her even more time to think about the things she had been putting off.

Was Raghnall alive?

Ever since she theorised the body she had seen was not Raghnall's, this was all she could conclude. Could it be true? It was all she could think of, and it ached her. She also didn't want to let herself believe it in case she was just trying to force what she thought she saw. But the thought he may be alive made her heart swell with relief and worry at the same time. Because if he was alive, why hadn't he contacted her himself? It had been over half a year since she was left in the Empire. And all this time had passed, and it was only recently that Wilkson had sent Kai to find her.

The days had started to grow shorter after the Summer Waning Gala, the nights becoming cooler that she severely considered sleeping in the tents at night. Something she had been avoiding because she didn't want to be alone with either Galahad or Daijiro right now.

Her head was pounding.

"Sulwyn..." whispered Galahad, and she flinched, looking up to see the fire had died down. She had spaced out on duty.

"I'm sorry," she said, moving to stand, but he placed a hand on her shoulder and sat next to her.

"Please talk to me..." he pleaded as he did every night with her when they switched shifts. And every night, she brushed him off and bid him good night.

She was still angry with him. Angry with herself. But it wavered with each passing day that they travelled. Missing their conversations as she punished them all by not talking. Making it awkward instead, and she knew that that could get them in trouble now that they needed to travel and trust each other more. She sighed, finally looking him in the eyes.

"I'm sorry my existence has caused you so much trouble..." she said spitefully, but he shook his head, laughing bitterly.

"I should have never said that to you. But I shouldn't have lied either." He turned to face her properly. "Those are thoughts I had, but when I was younger. When I was first taken and woke up in the Solus, I was terrified and angry, and I wanted *so* much to destroy them all. I turned the blame to you instead, and at first, that helped. But soon, I knew that it wasn't your fault either." He took her hands in his, his face taut and eyes full of regret. "When you told me what you saw in your vision..." he started, swallowing, unable to hold her gaze. "That same fear grew in me. Has been growing in me. And just like before, I looked for someone to blame and ended up turning it on you."

"I know..." Sulwyn said quietly, the tension escaping her at his words and leaving her tired instead. She needed to tell him.

"We need each other now. Regardless of what is happening with me, our priority is saving Vartugaul," he said softly.

"Your priority should be yourself, first and foremost. If you aren't there, I can't do this alone..." she murmured. "I saw it the last time, you were fighting it. And I know I don't understand how difficult that is, but you were given this power for a reason. You are connected to the First Children! If they didn't think you remained worthy, I'm sure they could do something about your power. They stripped people of your clan of it! There's no way they can't do that to you if need be. And the fact that they haven't intervened means they know, just as I do and just as you do deep down. You will conquer it."

"But that's not the problem," he started, looking at her with a sense of panic. "It rises faster than it should. My mind and body can't keep up with the strength of it. I'm supposed to grow together with it. And maybe that is my fault for trying to suppress it—"

Sulwyn held up her hand "It's not your fault... Galahad... There are a few things I've come to realise. And though I am not one hundred percent sure if I'm right or not, I think the chances are high that I am close to the truth." Sulwyn held his hands in turn, looking at him seriously. "Taru believes you were tampered with..." She watched him nod slowly, eyebrows furrowed. "I agree... and I think it was Gwydion." His hands tightened within hers, eyes narrowed, jaw set. She needed to do this carefully. "For whatever reason, I think Gwydion is trying to… control us, control everyone."

"How?" Galahad gritted out, his jaw still clenched.

"Artaxiad drugged me, but so did Gwydion. Fortunately, because of Artaxiad, it looks like I built immunity to Gwydion's version as well. I didn't kill seven people…" She took a deep breath and Galahad's tension faded, his eyes worried instead.

"But he used magic to make Diesirae look like me and she killed those innocent people instead. Acting as Kintana and dragging my name through the mud. Slandering all I worked for and revealing that Kintana and Sulwyn are one and the same. She made those people, who believed in me, think that I killed them in their last few moments, and I'll never forgive that… But that's beside the point. Gwydion alluded you were his first test. I think he may have wanted to see the limitations he would have by trying it on the most extreme kind of human. And I don't think he got the result he intended because it's never left you. Your powers seemed to grow off it, absorb it instead, accelerating somehow. And instead of controlling you, it's left you *out* of control. If that makes sense." She held up his hands, holding them gently.

"But you can't let him win this. These are *your* powers. Not his. Don't let him think he owns you with his failed test because that is how he's been acting. Confident that you will lose control completely and probably hopes you will take us all down, removing all obstacles in his path for his twisted sense of domination." Sulwyn touched her lips to his hands, kissing them gently before she let go and wrapped her arms around him.

"Please trust in yourself and in me," she whispered.

He nodded, holding her tightly. "Sulwyn… If that time ever comes…" His voice wavered.

But she pulled away, gripping his shoulders tightly and looking him straight in the eyes. "If I ever think you are a threat that cannot be stopped, then I will consider it. But don't let it come to that. We have one enemy, and it will not be you."

He took her hands, leading her to stand with him. "It's your turn to sleep." He smiled, and Sulwyn was glad that they finally managed to make peace. She could see the resolve in his eyes and that put confidence in them both.

"In the tent," he called, just as she was about to go towards Ki. "It's cooler at night now. You know that." He smirked, sitting back down. Curse their stupid brotherhood. She knew he wanted her to reconcile with Daijiro as well.

"Fine, fine..." she huffed and turned towards the tent instead.

Sulwyn crouched, carefully opening the soft fabric flap before crawling over the down blankets and cotton rugs for padding. Slowly, she shuffled over to where Galahad had been sleeping, lying down and covering herself, only now noticing the chill as the warmth spread through her.

"Are you better now?" whispered Daijiro, his voice low and heavy with sleep.

"Were you listening?" she asked, turning to face him though it was too dark to see more than just the outlines of his face now that the fire was out.

"I happened to wake while you were speaking. Figured I might as well listen so you wouldn't have to explain it twice." Humour laced his voice, but dread began to creep over her skin at what she had yet to say about Gwydion.

She let Daijiro go with the flow of their silent feud after her fight with Galahad because she found it easier to avoid him when he wasn't talking to her. But now that they were travelling together, she debated whether she should tell him her suspicion or wait until she could confirm it. But how else was she going to confirm it if she didn't have a Velyūn to do it?

But Daijiro wasn't the only one she knew.

"Can I ask you a question?" she whispered, and he moved closer to her. The heat from his upper body warmed her further.

"You mean a second question?" he teased, but she just shoved his chest. He grabbed her hand quickly, trapping it in his, holding it to his heart. The dread rose more, cancelling any sort of thrill she could have felt otherwise.

"What happened to Zalika?" Once the words were out, she wasn't sure if she should have asked at all. She felt his chest stutter, holding his breath.

"Why? I didn't think she was of any concern to you." He was wary, and she needed to keep in mind that there wasn't anyone better at getting information than he. Which meant he would know if she was searching.

"She was a storm at one point and then she was gone," she started, making sure to sound annoyed. "I didn't even realise she disappeared when I was taken by Artaxiad."

Daijiro was quiet, his thumb rubbing the back of her hand absentmindedly. "Gone."

"Did you kill her?" she mocked.

"Would you have liked that better?" His tone dark.

"A little, but no..."

Daijiro scoffed. "She disappeared the same time Zander did. No one knows where, or how, or why. And until we see Gwydion again, preferably not trying to get you back from his grasp, we can ask him." He placed her hand back down to her side, turning his back to her. "Sleep, Cailín, we are almost there."

Sulwyn was a little abashed at his dismissal, but the dread had risen more. She could tell he was starting to suspect, and she didn't know what would happen once he started to question her.

They could see Pliflyn in the distance as they fell into a trot. The terrain was rocky and full of scattered trees. Their town was near a large, healthy body of water, so environment naturally took over most of the space. The trees here were different. In Antiqua, they grew wide with tons of branches and thick leaves, with large spaces in between. Here, they grew thinner and taller and more condensed, the branches starting higher.

It had been a long time since she visited Pliflyn since it counted as a major town. When she travelled with Raghnall, they made a point to avoid the larger towns and opted to stay in the small villages. But now that the rotation was cut back, she hoped it would be easier to travel without too much notice.

"You both stand out a lot…" Sulwyn said as an afterthought, looking them over.

"What about you? You're wearing the coat of the Empire!" Daijiro replied indignantly.

"I've already burned the sigil off a few nights ago. And we're both lying if this looks like it's up to the Empire's standards after all it's been through…" She lifted her arms, showing them her alterations.

She had cut the sleeves up to the elbows and trimmed the back hem just a bit, enhancing the tatters that already showed. Though the embroidery was still there, it suited her more than ever now. Sulwyn smirked at Galahad's subtle nod of approval.

"Look, both of you may have travelled a lot for your missions and assignments and interrogations." She shot a glare at Daijiro. "But you haven't travelled like a common person in years. You both look well–off."

"You aren't wrong…" Galahad mused, busying himself with his pack. Though they had cloaks with hoods to cover their heads, the weather was still too mild for it during the day. Wearing it any time before evening unless it got colder would draw attention.

"For starters, you can't wear green anymore…" she said quietly, knowing it would sadden him. They both watched him nod slowly, eyes sullen.

"It's funny that in the Empire I managed to make everyone accept it, but I can't now that I'm free of it." He trailed off, silence falling over them all.

They made one quick stop before they exited the cover of trees and reached the large town. Galahad switched his current green tunic for a black one, folding the other neatly and hiding it at the bottom of his pack with the others. She was glad he had brought more than just the green ones.

"Daijiro, are you from Guāngcǎi?" she asked, noticing that Daijiro didn't bother to change much. He had donned a simple black silk robe that hung delicately over his shoulders and switched out the flat shoes he normally wore for boots like theirs before they left the Empire.

He looked up at her, a subtle sadness in his eyes. "Yes, far and deep within."

She could only nod; she always thought his form of dress was different from most she had seen, but since she had crossed over to Guāngcǎi for the first time in a while for Wallasyn, she realised he fit in a little more. At least in terms of his clothes. Because he and Zalika and even Gwydion, when he wasn't hiding his appearance, stood out in a way no other person did. Even more than Galahad and his clan. How was no one else putting this together?

But she was distracted, putting these thoughts at the back for now. Sulwyn could no longer hide her face; it had become a signature for Kintana, and since she didn't know if the rumours had made their way here or not, she didn't want to risk being associated with the name. Instead, she braided her hair back, leaving her face wholly exposed, hoping to blend in with other travellers. There were many women with long, dark hair and grey eyes. She would have to trust that doing this was enough, just like how Raghnall used to hide in plain sight.

ꙮ

It was past noon by the time they reached the gates of Pliflyn. There was a townsperson at the entrance instead of a Néosan who let them through after a brief inspection and asking the intention of their visit.

Though it had been years since she had last been there, it looked the same. Unlike Antiqua and Wallasyn, which was an abomination from the start, the majority of Guāngcǎi continued building small huts and stores. Because they had fewer people despite having more land, they were more spread out and less showy. They also had heavier rotations than Antiqua since they lived farther from the Empire's eye. For them, these people didn't matter. They brought nothing to the Empire aside from pleasure in dictating those they found unworthy. They were towns meant for living and surviving, and that was all. Their export was minimal, most of it coming from the Slave Bases and select areas of farming. Though not dirty, they were impoverished.

"We don't want to stay long..." whispered Galahad.

Sulwyn noticed that everyone glanced at them once they began walking throughout the town. And though they kept their heads down, looking only once, she knew the townsfolk were suspicious. Which meant some of the news from the Empire had trickled its way over. And with the Néosan pulled, they would be even more wary.

"We should gather information on how much news has travelled this far," Sulwyn said, quietly leading them to the butcher and the grocer. She had warned them before to be careful with how many coins they showed. Though it was the only way to purchase anything, if you had too much, you would stand out, and they would know you came from the Empire.

Artaxiad and Pandora had abolished all trading unless it was to the Empire for imports, implementing a copper coin to be used as the only currency. They all had the sigil made with a special black dye so that no one could copy it, recreate it or melt it down. But no one had enough to do something like that anyway.

"Do you want to come back here after you visit your home?" asked Galahad, gathering their purchases. Daijiro and Sulwyn took some each and proceeded back to where their horses were tied.

"Yes... but we're going to make another detour before then..." she said, saying nothing else.

By the time they would return to this town, she was sure the rumours would grow. But they had done what they sought to do, and that was lead the Empire on another trail for as long as possible.

Once packed and ready to leave, they took off out of town from the other end. It was a three-day ride towards Paraga from Pliflyn, but they were going to go past Paraga to her home, a place she hadn't been to in years.

XXIV

Someone Should Cut The Grass

"**P**ERFECT. We'll only have to wait an hour or so!" Sulwyn wiggled happily. But Daijiro and Galahad just stared at her in confusion. They had ridden past Paraga with a short break to a large, isolated forest of old blue and green trees going towards the coast.

"Wait for what?" Galahad asked, but Daijiro huffed and folded his arms. "This Wilkson guy…"

Sulwyn smirked. "I said it. He's a genius. But he won't fight Gwydion, so don't ask." She plopped onto the long grass overlooking a vast, still body of clear water. "Also, don't touch the water, no matter how refreshing it looks. It's not real," she said darkly.

Galahad and Daijiro turned to each other before taking their horses far back and tying them to the surrounding trees. Sulwyn didn't worry about Ki. He had already approached the water, and with a flick of his head, dismissed it completely. The two men sat on either side of her, both looking at her intently.

"The water isn't real, but if you walk into it, you'll be pulled into an illusion that lasts about a week. By the time you're out, you'll be too weak to fight us off. That's if we find you in time."

"What about from your side, where your home is?" asked Galahad, his eyes wide in fascination.

"It doesn't activate on our side. Only this side of the forest. Behind our home is a cliff. There is only one way to get through, and we're waiting for it." She pointed up towards the darkening sky. "It's good the seasons are changing. Night comes faster, and so do the stars."

"Stars?" Daijiro said, looking up as well.

"It's a trend between us, can't you tell?" she said coyly. He looked at her sharply, red eyes dark with the setting sun. But she turned back to the stars, catching herself. She really needed to give some thought to her own feelings. "The stars reflect onto the still water. The path is where the stars don't show up, depending on where the clouds are."

"Then someone could easily follow you and follow the way you walk even if they don't understand," Galahad said pointedly, glancing at her as well. What kind of mood was this? What had she trapped herself between? She tried her best to hide the growing conflict in her mind.

"What if there are no clouds?" asked Daijiro.

Sulwyn shrugged. "Fortunately, there are always clouds. He did mention there was a fail-safe in case that happened, but I don't know what it is."

"Sounds a bit irresponsible and flawed but it's still very creative..." Daijiro said quietly, still looking at the stars.

"He's the best. I should probably tell you both... He's King Zelimir's last son." She anticipated their reaction as they both looked at her. Daijiro's brows furrowed in a slightly confused manner while Galahad's mouth was agape in plain surprise.

"There are still Zalman left?" asked Galahad, astounded.

"Well, considering that he's got children, more may come one day." Daijiro shrugged. "How has he lasted this long?"

"No one knew he was a Devinal. They thought he perished when the High City fell, but he was with Raghnall most of the time," Sulwyn explained quietly. This was the safest place. She wondered if she could tell them about her thoughts on Raghnall.

"I don't know much about Devinal magic, but if he's as powerful as this, then it's not surprising," Galahad said.

"I don't think it's so much power as it is intelligence," Sulwyn began. "He's a coward, but he has strength when it matters. Though he was roped into a lot of things thanks to Raghnall and me. Hell, he probably faked his death to hide once the High City fell."

Sulwyn stood swiftly, just as the stars started to reflect on the still illusionary water. "Of course!" she exclaimed. Both Galahad and Daijiro went from confusion to concern.

"Sulwyn?" Galahad asked tentatively, but she turned to face them both.

"I think Raghnall is alive," she said bluntly. There was no point in explaining it. When it came down to it, this was the main idea. She just needed to figure out if it was true or not, and if it was, did he really betray her?

"Excuse me?" Daijiro said, but Galahad remained quiet. He turned to him. "You don't seem surprised…"

"We had a prior discussion back in Eques, but Sulwyn, you weren't sure if he had the scar or not."

"Kai had a message for me. 'Trust my instincts and don't fear the unknown.' If he didn't betray me and he's alive, then that message came from him." She knew it sounded far-fetched, but when Kai said those words, she could only hear Raghnall in them.

"Sulwyn…" Galahad said softly, "please, don't look at me like that. It's not like that, I swear. I don't doubt you, but you may be reaching because of your time in need."

Sulwyn clenched her jaw so hard her teeth hurt. "I know better than to let my emotions alter how I see logic." But even as she said it, she knew that wasn't exactly true either. She could see Daijiro smirk, but quickly turned away.

"Forget it. I'll do what I set out to do with or without you," Sulwyn said, and she turned, looking at the water. The sky had darkened significantly, and the dark clouds were perfect. She walked along the edge, searching for the path that was void of any reflection, locating it a few feet away from where they had been sitting. "Ki!" she called, and he trotted towards her.

Daijiro and Galahad untied their horses and followed her carefully. "Daijiro, you might want to make sure the horses don't try to touch the water…"

"Already doing that," he said lightly, and they continued to follow her carefully.

She stepped forwards, knowing it wasn't water, but still surprised that her foot just stood right on top of it. It had been ages since she last did this, her heart trying to break out of her chest from nerves alone. Raghnall had set this up when she was younger and still untrained. Though he was confident no one could find them through all the trees that preluded their small house, he did it anyway.

The path was winding. It moved backwards quite a bit, to and from the edge of the water, then to the left and to the right and in a circle, until finally, they neared the other side where all the lush blue and green trees grew, hiding the home further still.

The smell was the same, and the land was too. Once she stepped off the water and onto the grass, nostalgia hit her in waves. Her world was dizzying for just a moment. Only less than a year ago, she was still travelling with Raghnall, going around and making trouble. Never did she think she'd come back here, without him of all things, and with people she'd met from the Empire.

Sulwyn fell to her knees, overwhelmed by all her theories and all her emotions towards those she had met in the Empire and at what she had done.

At how much has happened.

Towards Galahad and Daijiro.

How much had changed?

How much did *she* change?

"Hey…" Galahad kneeling next to her. "It's disorienting, I know…" he whispered, his voice calming. She knew she didn't suffer the same way he had, but she also knew no one else would understand it better than him either.

"You haven't even seen the house yet," Daijiro said, reaching forwards and touching her shoulder. She choked out a laugh, punching his leg. Ki nudged her head with his muzzle, and she just laughed more.

Sulwyn didn't even remember the last time she laughed, and now it just rolled within her.

"We've broken her," muttered Daijiro, taking her hands in his and pulling her to stand, but she just kept laughing anyway.

So much had changed, and not all for the bad.

She took a deep breath, stifling her laughter and crying. "Okay, let's go home…"

ু৹৹৻ুু

If she thought she felt nostalgic before, it was nothing compared to when they finally parted through the last set of branches and viewed the land before them.

Raghnall was a crafty person and built their home from the ground up with some assistance from Wilkson. It had taken about a year to finish, and during that time, she stayed in the care of Wilkson and his wife, Amalthea.

"This is really…" Galahad started.

"Warm?" she suggested, unable to stop the few tears that escaped her. It was exactly as they had left it two years ago. Though the many flowers, shrubs and grass grew an alarming amount, she could still see the coloured stone walkway to the door from where they now stood.

The house itself was a mix of brick and wood, with only one floor and a few cellars hidden underground. It was wide and of good height to make the place spacious even though it was a single level. Along with the grass needing a trim, the windows needed cleaning, and it looked like the bucket to the well had fallen into it. Regardless of its slightly neglected state, all she could see was her home. A rush of longing for what she could consider a simpler time flowed through her, tingling her fingertips and catching her breath.

But they wouldn't be here long enough to make these changes, and she knew it was a bad idea to show signs of a visit even if it was near impossible to find her here. At least not now. Not when she needed to learn the truth of Raghnall. Only then could she feel like she was truly coming home. So, until then, they would rest here for a day or two while she dug around.

"Well, let's go in…" she whispered unintentionally. The other two followed her quietly through the tall grass and onto the coloured path.

Littered all around were traces of Sulwyn's childhood straight through her training. There was an odd mix of strange decorations, wooden and steel swords, a stray arrow or two and various other things mixed into the wild tangle of nature.

All three of them looked around, and she knew they could feel what she did.

Why she could never believe that Raghnall had truly betrayed her.

There was love everywhere.

And when she stepped up to the threshold of flat pebbles, found the spare key under the stone frog and opened the door, thoughts of betrayal became a whisper to her. She lit the inside torch by the door, and it illuminated the space before them.

Tendrils of dust reflected off the firelight. It had seeped its way through, making the air thick and coating the furniture. The house was an orderly mess. In every corner, there was something to be found, and whether it was used every day or not used for many years, it didn't matter. Everything there had a purpose, and Raghnall found a way to make it fit.

"Well, we can't light the fireplace until we clean it…" Galahad said, already looking at every angle of the house.

"This looks very like you…" Daijiro gave her a smirk.

Sulwyn smiled. "It feels like me…" Her voice was small and quiet. She had missed this place more than she had realised. And not because it was an actual home, away from the camping and rationing, away from the chase and the eyes of everyone. But because it reminded her of who she really was.

Just Sulwyn.

"Even if our stay here is short, we can't stay in this dust..." Galahad mused, his tone light, and she knew he was trying to bring her back to the here and now.

"It is rather dusty. Let's do this quickly so we can eat!" She took a deep breath and coughed. Daijiro and Galahad laughed at her before they both started lighting candles and torches around the home. Throwing the windows open and taking the cushions and carpets out to dust.

Sulwyn skulked about, pacing back and forth in front of the fireplace. Raghnall was bad at magic, but she had learned a few things to help with the house, and one of them was cleaning the fireplace. But the words escaped her. Either she would set the house on fire, or she would succeed.

She moved to sit right in front of it, still fishing for a poem in her mind until she froze.

The fireplace had been cleaned recently.

Her heart banged against her chest, shaking her as she sat on the dusty pillow, her ears drowning from the beating and rushing of blood to her head. Sulwyn was surer than anything that no one could find this place on their own, not even by accident.

This could only mean two things in her mind. Either Wilkson came by, which he did every so often to renew the illusionary water, or Raghnall had really betrayed her. Or, if she really let herself think it, three things: Raghnall himself had been here.

But since she told Daijiro and Galahad her final theory that Raghnall was alive, she started to lose hope that it was true. Because it was ludicrous and far-fetched. And even if Wilkson had managed to help him fake his death, why?

What reason did Raghnall have to get her into the Empire that he had to go so far as to fake his death and not divulge the plan?

"Sulwyn?" Galahad asked softly. He had knelt next to her without her realising it. She really needed to get her mind back into focus. She was on the run again. Sulwyn turned to him, worry and a bit of curiosity in his eyes. The look he gave her these days more than not.

This was her problem; she wouldn't burden him further.

Sulwyn smirked. "I remembered the spell to clean this." She pointed to the empty fireplace grate. "There should be some wood in the shed by the side of the house."

"Already got it, Cailín," said Daijiro from the threshold. His eyes darted to the hearth and then to hers with suspicion. She hated that he was so perceptive. More perceptive than either her or Galahad. Something she'd never have thought he could be when she first met him. But if he had any thoughts, he kept them to himself.

Galahad got up to take some of the firewood from him, and within moments, the house was wrapped in warm firelight. Using the new illumination, they continued to tidy up a little more, make dinner and then sit in the small kitchen at the old wooden table.

The kitchen was like anywhere else in the house, full to the brim of unique things alongside necessities. Sulwyn gazed around the little space. The utensils for cooking were old and battered and nothing like the ones she saw at the Empire. An odd mix of pots and pans, all aged and made from various materials, but well taken care of. The swirls in black and purple spread across the yellow walls, giving it a whimsical feel. And there were tiny trinkets Sulwyn would collect from all of their travels to decorate the windowsill, cabinets, shelves, or plates. There were so many things, it overwhelmed her. But it was home.

"How are you feeling?" asked Galahad, looking around the kitchen before he got up and investigated the cupboards. Daijiro and Sulwyn watched him find mugs, collecting other things as he went along.

"Unreal..." started Sulwyn, watching as he lit the stove and filled the iron kettle with water from the sink. They had managed to fix the well, and thankfully, it hadn't dried up, nor was it tainted.

"I can imagine..." he said quietly.

"Have either of you..." she began, but somehow, both men stiffened at the question.

"No, I've never gone back," Galahad answered solemnly.

She glanced at Daijiro, a faraway look in his eyes. "I burned it down."

"The entire village?" she asked, eyes wide.

He turned to her, his eyes dark and dangerous, terrifying even. "Once I killed Tamesis, I returned to a village of rot. Everyone had been killed and left behind. There was nothing left but to burn it all."

Galahad set a mug in front of each of them. It was steaming and full of hot tea with bits of flowers in it. Sulwyn turned to look at him and Daijiro. Taking in both of these men that she never thought she would meet nor form any kind of bond with. She wanted to give them everything they had lost. "It's messy. Full of mystery, probably some traps, stray weapons and various other things I couldn't explain. But you're both welcome here. As a home away from home." She smiled, and she knew by the way they looked at her that that meant more to them than they could ever explain.

XXV

The Place She Never Called Home

| SULWYN |

"SHE'S keeping something from me." Daijiro's voice low and rough. Galahad and he remained at the wooden table even after Sulwyn bid them good night, telling them they could sleep wherever they wanted.

"She's hiding things from both of us…" Galahad said with a sigh, "and I don't blame her."

"She tells you more," he complained, and he knew it was childish even as he said it. "It's frustrating."

"Because you want to know or because it's me she's telling and not you?" asked Galahad slyly.

Daijiro glared at him. "Because I don't need protecting. And that is why she's hiding it. That is why she hides things from you, why she isn't being fully open. You can see it in her eyes when she thinks no one is looking." Daijiro stood, itchy agitation rising in him.

He understood why she kept things from Galahad. He was a mess and a danger to all of them right now. But he thought he'd proven that he could be trusted.

A chair scraped the wood floor, and Daijiro turned to see Galahad standing too.

"Don't wake her. I know you want to confront her, but she deserves to rest, and this is a rest she's needed for a long time in a place that brings her peace and comfort. She doesn't ask questions unless she must.

Sulwyn has given her trust. She brought us here, didn't she? We should wait until she comes to us," Galahad warned, placing his empty mug quietly on the wooden table and beckoning Daijiro to follow him. "But you're right," continued Galahad as he followed him through the kitchen, through the hall, passing various doors, past the sitting room where the fire crackled merrily and out the front door. "She hides things from us to protect us. Because Sulwyn is convinced she needs to bear the burden for everyone. Believes it's her duty to take Vartugaul back because it was her parents that made it fall."

Something deep inside him squirmed. Galahad knew her well. It was obvious how close they had grown towards each other. But Daijiro listened to him carefully, knowing his words were correct. Even if it bothered him. "I don't have patience like you. Or at least like you used to."

Galahad laughed bitterly. "Why does everyone always assume I had patience? I was simply better at masking it." He turned to face Daijiro as they stopped in front of the house in the middle of the tall grass, his eyes pure black.

Daijiro watched carefully, wondering if this was him losing control again, but realised that wasn't the case. Galahad carried himself as he normally did and soon stood in a stance, ready to fight hand to hand.

"If we want to help her, we need to better ourselves. I don't want her vision coming true," said Galahad solemnly. "But she was right. These are my powers, and I need to rein them in."

Daijiro smirked, the agitation slipping away for excitement instead. "And you think I'm the best choice for that?" But he fell into his own stance that mirrored Galahad's; their feet shoulder-width apart, one foot in the back and one in the front. Both hands up and waiting.

"For now, I'll have to make do with what I have," he jeered, and Daijiro could sense the edge of competition from him.

"Neither of you can be trusted on your own!" called Sulwyn, and they both turned to stare at her. She was sitting on a stump, wrapped in a blanket next to the stone steps illuminated by the fires from inside the house.

"Shouldn't you be resting?" Daijiro replied, but the elation in the pit of his stomach at the sight of her caught him off guard. It did every time he caught her stare when he wasn't expecting it. And more so tonight with her hair loose around her and her demeanour relaxed and not guarded.

"I should be. But with the amount of rage and drive to fight emitting from both of you, it's kind of hard. Plus, I want to watch." Her grin was wide and wicked. Another drop of elation seeped into his soul.

Daijiro laughed, looking at Galahad, who was also smiling for once. "I think the queen wants a battle."

Sulwyn shrugged. "I'm tired of everyone watching *me* fight. Let me watch for once." She pulled the blanket closer around her and waved them to continue.

Daijiro focused on Galahad, and they both resumed their stances. He had learned to fight from his mother a long time ago, but only the basics. She used to train him in secret, because just like many, she believed a time would come when he would need to know how to defend himself. It's why her parents taught her. But as he got older, Tamesis tried to instill fear into him. To stop him from growing his own strength. And none of it even mattered because in the end, his mother was right, and he needed to fight for himself.

And that was how he gave into his bloodlust, falling off his path.

After he left his village to train, it turned into a mission of revenge. Killing Néosan and any other Empire personnel became easy to him. To the point where it couldn't even be considered fighting for defence or survival, but for justification and control.

And to make a point.

When he presented a hundred severed heads at the Empire's door, a few at Pandora's feet for extra measure, his path was covered in blood. And instead of fixing it, he ended up drowning in it.

"Daijiro," Galahad warned from afar, bringing him back to what was in front of him. He looked up. They were currently locked in a scuffle of arms, beads of sweat forming over Galahad's forehead, his expression taut.

But if Galahad was going to get a hold of his power, he needed a bigger threat.

"We've only been locking arms for a few minutes, and you're already losing control?" He pushed Galahad back, creating space between them. Galahad was a good fighter. Though he didn't think Galahad was better than him, he was a challenge. And because of this, he needed to cause trouble.

Daijiro held up his palm and touched the energy of Galahad's body in front of him. He took hold of it and squeezed his palm into a fist, feeling the tendrils of strength. The effect was immediate. Galahad's body froze mid attack and strained.

"Daijiro…" warned Sulwyn, and he just nodded.

"I can take whatever you give, but you won't rise to the fight if I don't bring it," he said, and though his voice was even, he could feel Galahad's essence and will pushing his own power away like the pressure from two negative ends of a magnet. And soon, Galahad was breaking free.

He charged forwards, moving to grab Daijiro's arm and put him in a lock, but Daijiro slipped through him and pushed him back again. Now, Daijiro faced Sulwyn and could see the worry in her eyes. Distracted, Galahad struck him hard in the jaw with his fist.

Daijiro recoiled a bit, the hit more than he was used to from Galahad. So, his power amplified his physical prowess? He'd just have to try harder. Daijiro held out his palm again and brought pressure to his lungs.

Galahad choked, unable to breathe as he fell to his knees. But that still wouldn't be enough. He brought his other palm forwards and skimmed the light tingle of nerves that flowed throughout Galahad's entire body, and then he pinched them.

Galahad grunted, holding his voice back, or maybe he was unable to yell since he couldn't breathe properly.

"Daijiro!" Sulwyn shouted. From the corners of his eyes, he watched the blanket fall to the ground as she stood, but he didn't release his hold on the prince. Galahad's hands were changing to that ashen black. He watched as it crawled from his nails to his knuckles and past his wrists.

Soon, the hold broke like a taut band, and Galahad's palm smashed Daijiro's face.

He hadn't even seen when he stood, and it was his fault for letting his own guard down. Galahad doubled over, catching his breath. Just like his hands, his bare feet had the same ashy-black colour crawling its way up and past his ankles under his pants.

The familiar burn and tingle made its way from the bridge of Daijiro's nose, and blood dripped down onto his lip. He could hear Sulwyn curse, but her voice seemed so far away. Galahad's faded too, even though he could see him struggle against his own power. Daijiro thought he had grown in this short time with them. But as the image of his father holding his mother's detached head grew increasingly vivid, he realised he needed to grow too.

Because every time Daijiro spilled his own blood, all he could see was his mother's.

All he could see was Tamesis, laughing at his triumph until he turned and saw Daijiro. His eyes were wide in rage and terror.

Her head fell to the ground with a heavy thump.

Her body twitched and crashed to the floor.

And her bleeding eyes stared at him as her head rolled towards his feet.

The cold ice that ran through him melted. The fire that hid in his veins flared, and his power gripped every part of Tamesis's body.

All he could do was let the anticipation rise in him as he let Tamesis go. Run out of the house he had grown up in for the last fifteen years. The home that was now destroyed like his heart. Watch him think he had a chance to survive after what he had done to his village.

All he could ever feel when his blood flowed freely was the elation he had when he finally killed Tamesis.

Galahad tackled him to the ground just as Sulwyn made her way over. Daijiro gasped, unaware that he'd stopped breathing. For the first time in a long time, his bloodlust worked against him. Instead of losing control, he froze.

Maybe he *was* growing.

"Looks like I'm not the only one that needs to bring themselves under control..." Galahad huffed between breaths, and though his nails were sharp against the skin of Daijiro's neck, and his hands and feet were black like death, he had finally managed some ounce of control. Daijiro knew it as soon as he saw some of the colour peek through the black in his eyes. And seeing this brought him out of his own trance.

Daijiro pushed Galahad off him, a slight throb of pain in his neck as the long nails scraped against it. But something had happened to them both tonight. And in his eyes, he considered it a win, regardless of how small.

ৡৢ

| SULWYN |

The sun peeked over the horizon, but Sulwyn was already awake. Watching Galahad and Daijiro both confront their weaknesses last night had given her the confidence to do so as well. No matter how small it was.

Sulwyn opened her eyes fully, seeing the familiar ceiling of polished deep oak over her. She turned onto her side, the air slightly chilled but her bed warm. Her room stayed the same since she was younger. Always collecting small rocks or stones that had a special shape to them. Lining her windowsill or the shelves of her bookcases. Lining the door and window frame. Tiny jars filled with coloured sand from various places they'd been to. Small, metal trinkets that Raghnall would bend and shape with spare iron from when he made weapons.

A tear tickled her cheek as it rolled and fell onto her sheets and into the bed. Joining countless others from when she was younger and would cry about everything. Joining all the hidden questions she never asked Raghnall about Pandora and Artaxiad, about why everything had gotten so messed up.

Sulwyn sat up, the sheets falling off her torso, a shiver running through her. She sat still, absorbing everything around her. Listening to the creaks of the old wood. She could sense Daijiro and Galahad's energies somewhere in the house and hoped they were still asleep. Because what she really came back to do was something she wanted to do alone.

Raghnall hadn't picked this place on a whim.

He picked this place because he knew it was close to somewhere Artaxiad and Pandora would never go again.

Raghnall picked this place because only an hour's ride away to the west was the house he found her in.

Sulwyn stood and carefully walked over to her small closet. Finally, she had her own clothes back. She spent some time reveling in something familiar before getting dressed. Once finished, she walked out of her room wearing a chestnut brown tunic with too-long sleeves and loose, black pants. Quietly, she padded down the hall, passing by the rooms Galahad and Daijiro had chosen to sleep in. She stepped quickly into the kitchen to grab the little pack of food she had created before joining them outside last night.

She knew where every loose floorboard was in this house. If there was anywhere she could truly be a shadow, it was here. And she knew neither of them would wake, not until she was where she needed to go. But because she knew they would worry, she wrote a quick note and pinned it to the inside of the front door, then opened it.

Cool air passed over her face, waking her up just a little more, her hands hidden in the sleeves. The mist was low over the tall grass, making it seem shorter than it really was. She always loved summer. It was easier to travel in. But she had an appreciation for the crisp air that followed the harvest season.

Sulwyn walked over to the stables that she had shut the night before in anticipation of the chill. Soon, Ki was welcoming her, nuzzling the side of her neck but poised and ready to go. Though she tried to keep her nerves down, she was sure Ki could feel them. As soon as she settled herself onto the saddle, he was off towards the trees.

Once she passed through the forest, the illusionary water ceased to exist from her side. Instead, it looked like a field of yellow and green grass, damp and slightly bent by the morning dew. Ki seemed mildly shocked at the new terrain but continued forwards regardless, back the way they came before turning west.

Sulwyn only knew the vague direction of the house. Just like the Empire, Raghnall had never allowed her to go this way. And Sulwyn never felt the urge to do so. The only thought she had when she ever looked west before leaving their home was hate and revulsion. Now, she felt those things and more. Now, she was full of confusion towards Pandora and fear from Artaxiad. Something she had never admitted to the others yet.

While she tried not to remember her nightmares, on days when she was more exhausted or stressed, he interfered.

Nightmares of his face looming near hers and of her turning into what he was trying to create. Of the blood of everyone she had come to love coating her, dead by her hands. Despair from what he was trying to do. And if she hadn't broken free, or if Eztli and the girls, or Galahad and Daijiro hadn't been there, he may have succeeded. What if he had? What would have become of her? What exactly would he have done *to* her...

Ki slowed to a trot, bringing her out of her thoughts. Her hands wound deeply into his mane, and though not enough to hurt him, he had tensed, shaking his head to get her attention.

"I'm sorry, Ki... Please continue. We're looking for an old house..." She patted his neck, and he took off again through the forest.

Raghnall had only talked about the area a handful of times. But from what she could remember, he'd gone over a large hill to reach their house, hidden all around by trees into a pit of land. She figured they must be going in the right direction when the ground started to incline. Once the trees parted, they were faced with a hill of indigo and teal grass that rippled gently with the breeze. Ki hesitated briefly before he pressed on, and together, they trotted up the hill.

Soon, they crested over the top as they stood and looked down to a burned two-storey house tucked in the corner of the pit of grassland.

XXVI

Poisoned, Tainted Heart

| DAIJIRO |

SULWYN dismounted her horse as soon as they made their way down the hill.

The land looked untouched, with no traces of human to be found. Ki roamed the area as she trudged through the thigh-high grass. The wetness soaked through her pants, sending a deep chill to her bones stronger than the one she had when she first laid eyes on the house.

For something that had been set on fire and abandoned, the house was still standing save for one half where the fire had burned through. Raghnall suspected the house could still be here if left alone since it was raining that night, enough to put out the fire. But he was never sure, and they never really cared to wonder. Sulwyn was glad for it. Because this way, she could have a thorough look at the place.

She came to a halt right where the entrance of the house was. But instead of going in, she let Raghnall's old story fill her mind.

"It was dark. I was too late…" Raghnall started one day as they sat in front of *the fireplace. Sulwyn always knew Raghnall wasn't her father, but she never found it in her to ask how he had come to have her until today. Now, she sat between his crossed legs as they drank warm ginger tea.*

"Wilkson and I were on a tracking mission, but we heard crying from the house. I knew…" he faltered, but Sulwyn looked back at him. His eyes seemed sad, and she hated making him feel that way.

"I have something to tell you, but I'll tell you after this story, okay?" Raghnall said, holding her tightly. "I sent Wilkson away to carry out our mission, and I went into the house instead. You see, it was on fire. But as luck would have it, the fire was far in the left corner."

Sulwyn looked at the left part of the house. It was charred and broken, a huge hole through the roof exposing the beams of the second floor and letting nature run through it fully. The fire had spread towards the centre of the structure. Some parts of the roof caved in, but otherwise remained standing.

"There was an open window far to the right, and I went straight through it, landing in a kitchen!"

"Through it? That wasn't smart. What if you landed on something sharp... like knives!" But Raghnall only laughed, eyes crinkled like he had no care in the world.

"I know well enough not to land on knives, silly child. But you are right. I'll be careful next time I roll into any open windows." He smiled softly at her and continued. *"The cries were louder now that I was inside, and I traced them up to the second floor. By then, the fire hadn't made its way too far. Once I located the room, I found you, all wrapped up in a wooden crib crying your eyes out. I was going to escape out the window, but it was too high for me to maintain your safety."*

"You went back into the house? Is that why we have burns?" She turned around to face him, pounding his chest with her small fist. And though she couldn't see his burn right now, she touched his cheek and neck where she knew it was.

"Yes, but that was the only way. It wasn't until I was halfway down the stairs did a wooden beam collapse onto us. But it all worked out in the end, didn't it? I managed to escape, and here you are!" He smiled brightly, but she knew something was wrong. Knew there was more to say. And so, she stared him down until he would say everything.

"You are rather perceptive, Sulwyn, especially for a six-year-old..." he said softly, and he turned her to face him properly. *"I'm going to tell you about your parents..."*

Her chest constricted at the memory as she looked on for the first time at the house Raghnall had saved her from, the place that started their whole journey together. It wasn't only Galahad and Daijiro that needed to work things out. If she was going to win this battle, she needed to find out exactly who she was fighting.

Sulwyn stepped forwards, turning to the right and locating the same open window. Though the windows were now broken and the sill tarnished, it held her weight as she crawled inside.

If she thought her house was dusty, it was nothing in comparison to this place. Not only did dust coat the stone oven and the floor, but so did black and grey ash, as well as whatever nature and the wind had swept in. Mice and other small animals scurried out of her way as she landed on the rough stone floor.

Inside, she could see where parts of the ceiling had crashed onto the ground. As she walked out of the kitchen, she found that most of the hall and what would possibly be a sitting area were barred off by broken walls and more wooden beams. She only stopped for a moment to look around the area. The house was relatively empty.

If there were any personal effects, they must have taken it with them, but somehow Sulwyn thought this house was more of a temporary living situation than anything else. Somewhere to stay until it was time for them to leave and take down the High City. But even as she thought it, it made no sense to her.

Pandora said she left her to rid herself of her weakness. If Sulwyn was a weakness for her, why did she even bother carrying her to term? She could have found ways to end her pregnancy even later on. Or could have killed her herself. But she saw why Raghnall found it strange for the fire to start in the corner of the house. And now that she knew Pandora was aware of Raghnall following her, it was hard for her to deny that Pandora knew more than anyone realised.

Silently, Sulwyn walked through the house, sidestepping many fallen beams and stones, her boots creating deep footsteps in the ash and dust.

She found the stairs, most of it fallen through. The wood was rotten from moisture and insects; the rest burned around the bottom. She stepped on the outside of the stairs, assessing the sturdiness with her leg and pushing. It seemed well enough, at least for now. She used the handrail for guidance as she pulled up and around the caved-in floor until she reached the top.

Just as she reached the last outer step, a loud crack echoed around the house. Part of the railing gave way and dropped down onto the first floor with a muffled crash. Mice shrieked and scurried away to somewhere unknown as she got her footing and stood on the second floor.

There were three doors, only one fully open while the rest hung off their hinges but still in the doorframe. She would go to these first, her hands numb at the sheer thought of going to the open one.

Slowly, she opened the door nearest to her right. The creak buzzed in her ears as the door came to a rest against the wall. Light flooded the room, part of the wall broken and exposing the outside sky. It was a small bathing room, modest and nothing like what Pandora and Artaxiad were used to back at the Empire. But like the rest of the house, it was empty save for a hairbrush and one tattered cotton towel. Vines had crawled their way from the first floor and into the gaping hole, breaking through the narrow window and latching onto the walls and stone tub.

Sulwyn left this room and went to the next. As soon as she pushed the door open, it unlatched from the hinge and collapsed onto the floor. Coughing, dust and ash created a plume of white particles dancing in the streams of sun, burning her eyes and throat. Waving the dust away, Sulwyn found a small bed made for two in the centre of the room. There was a desk and wardrobe to one side, and on the opposite side of the bed near a window was a small cradle.

It was becoming difficult to breathe, only shallow breaths coming through.

The numbness of nerves travelled to her feet, but she stepped onto the door and into the room regardless.

There wasn't much for her to look at. The same vines made their way through this room as well. The sun streamed through the dirty windowpanes. She was sure Galahad and Daijiro would be awake by now, but she wanted this time alone.

She rifled through the small wardrobe, only rotted clothes and moths to be found. Sulwyn turned to the desk to see a few pencils tucked into the corner and a small stack of unmarked books. She picked each up, the first a small, thin volume about the High City, though the words had since faded from neglect. Another about water and how to filter it from tainted lakes. And another about the lore of what happened from the Lost World to now. These were books she had seen before. But as she flipped the pages of the one in her hands, a sheaf of paper fluttered out and landed on the floor.

Placing the book back onto the desk, Sulwyn picked up the paper that she quickly realised was a piece of canvas used for drawing or painting. Flipping it over, she saw three people in their adolescence.

She let out a gasp at what greeted her eyes. An audible click sounded from her teeth, her jaw clenching so hard it burned. Muscles tightened as she tried not to crush the canvas then and there.

Pure panic filled her to the brim.

Here in this once vibrantly painted portrait of Pandora and Artaxiad as teenagers, there was no mistaking it: between them both stood Gwydion in his plain, grey clothes. But instead of the brown eyes and short brown hair—or even blue and black hair she had seen when he revealed himself—here he stood, with his natural violet eyes. Until Sulwyn peered even closer and saw his hair, long and to his chin, indigo and white slicked-back waves.

A Velyūn trait.

Waves upon waves of dread and dizziness spread through her. She knew the rest of what she was looking for was in this house. She was almost there.

But this picture!

This picture changed everything.

Pandora and Artaxiad had met Gwydion long before Sulwyn was born; this picture was proof there was some kind of relationship cultivated between the three in their youth. It meant Gwydion had been with them far longer than she could have ever guessed.

But why? Why was that kept hidden? Why wasn't Gwydion in the Empire from the start? No one talked about him. No one seemed to even know him until he first came to the Empire based on what she learned from all those balls and classes. But everyone revered him. All his achievements with the Empire are listed after he joined the Diarchy at the time, a few years after Artaxiad's Ascendancy.

Sulwyn sat on the floor, ignoring the dust and ash that tickled her nose, the portrait crumpled in her fist, her head spinning, and nausea rising. Pandora's last breath was spent warning her against Artaxiad and Gwydion. Pandora knew he was a Devinal. The answer was here.

She stood, the room blackening around her, briefly throwing her off-balance. But she leaned against the desk, then pushed off and stormed out of the room and into the one she had been dreading.

Because as soon as she walked into that room, her chest weighed like a pile of stones, and her body was stiff like lead.

The room was untouched.

The fire never reached this far.

The walls were a faded yellow, once bright like the sun, the paint chipping and peeling. Across the centre of the walls, wrapping across the room, were little paintings of cows and chickens. In one corner was a small wardrobe next to a rocking chair. And in the other stood a wooden crib with a handmade toy that hung above with little stars and moons.

Sulwyn couldn't do anything but place her hand over her chest.

She couldn't feel anything.

Not the ice of her hands or the lead of her limbs. She just stood there and stared around a room that was obviously prepared in anticipation of a child.

As she stared at the crib, she noticed a small bulge in the corner of the rotted blankets. Carefully, she walked over, the picture still crumpled in her other hand. Resting on the moulded mattress was a small doll. It had dark red hair and grey eyes, her purple dress coated in dust, and the paint on her skin flaked. Sulwyn brushed it gently before lifting the blanket and the bedding to reveal a worn leather journal.

In the distance, she could hear a neigh from Ki. He must hear them in the forest now, trying to find their way to where she was. But it didn't matter to her. Nothing but the journal mattered. Slowly and carefully, Sulwyn unwrapped the leather that bound the book together. The sheets were dry but not brittle.

She breathed slowly now, the spine cracking as she opened it to see a single letter "P" scratched in the bottom corner of the page. Sulwyn flipped another page and quickly saw day-to-day entries dating back a few years before her birth. Most were simple, trivial things about planning as a group. But then they started to get longer about the next year to follow.

> *Artaxiad has agreed to leave Gwydion out of the rebellion. As he needs to leave so often to go about his own business, it's probably best for stability purposes. The people have chosen Artaxiad over anyone else anyway. And though Gwydion first introduced them to us, it is a little odd that they DON'T TALK about him anymore... but I digress. This time next year, we will be at the top.*

Sulwyn skipped over more of the same things until the writing began to look a little distressed:

> *Even though he's been gone for a few months, I FEEL HIS VOICE IN ME. The buzzing that HAUNTS MY DREAMS. Artaxiad doesn't think anything of it besides the stress of pregnancy.*
>
> *I think the noise is lost to him. Too far gone. And Artaxiad doesn't know what I do. He doesn't know how I battle, how I challenge THE VOICE IN ME. But my HATE has grown so much more than it used to be. My unborn child... AM I POISONING HER?*

She sat back onto the floor once again, the picture and the doll clutched against her chest as she flipped to the next page.

He has come back. It's HARDER *when he is here.* SO MUCH HARDER *to fight. Artaxiad is* TOO FAR *gone. His will was always* WEAKER. *And now Artaxiad is cursing the child,* OUR CHILD? *Says she will be a* BURDEN TO OUR GOAL. *The goal we have* WAITED *so many years to achieve. To save everyone who has been treated like vile scum as we have.* SHE WILL BE A BURDEN. THIS FILTHY CHILD.

The anger ate her from the inside alongside the burning of tears in her eyes, head pounding with every word she read as everything she ever knew began to crumble. But still, she kept reading. She needed to know.

SHAME. I BRING SHAME TO OUR CAUSE. *To our hopes and achievements.* I BARE A WHORE WHO CAN ONLY TAKE A NAME. *Who cannot lead. Who will* BRING WEAKNESS *upon our name.* I HATE HER. I HATE MYSELF *for bearing her.* I HATE WHAT WE'VE BECOME.

She turned the page once more to what looked like the last entry, the words quick and messy, written in haste the night she was born.

In these last few months, THE BUZZING AND THE VOICE *were nothing but an echo to me. But tonight, as I hold you for the first and last time,* IT IS BLARING. AND IT IS PAINFUL. *I managed to get Artaxiad to agree to at least let me birth you. To let me meet you, though, I did not tell him this part. I only said it would be safer if I bore you now and be rid of you.* SET OUR PAST AFLAME AND START ANEW. *But I will* NEVER BEAR A CHILD AGAIN. *And he will do me that favour because I know what he is, and I know he will do this least I tell Artaxiad the truth.* MY SOUL HAS BEEN TAINTED LONG AGO, *and even if I did keep you, it would only* END IN ANGER AND DEATH. *One day we will meet, and I will no longer know these feelings. But we will meet because the* STEEL *is strong, and you can face the challenge I could not win against. And...if I become an obstacle... it is in your right to* END IT________

"NO!" Sulwyn shrieked, whipping the journal against the wall. In that moment, she heard movement below her.

"Sulwyn?" called Galahad, his voice far away and underwater to her. Soon, she could hear them both making their way up, presumably around the stairs. But she didn't want to face them now. She couldn't face them now. Not when her tears wouldn't stop, and the anger wanted out. Not when she just needed to think. To hit. To do anything to ignore this cavern of emptiness inside her.

"Cailín?" Daijiro called, and just as he stepped in front of the doorway, Sulwyn crushed the portrait and stuffed it into her boot. Instantly, his eyes narrowed, but she couldn't let him see it.

"What was that?" he asked just as Galahad came into the room as well.

"Leave me alone," she barked.

Agitation bubbled under her skin like an itch. And that was only the tip of it. Nothing could have prepared her for this. She wanted to scream for days until her throat ripped. She wanted to run until her feet were broken and bleeding. She just wanted to sit and become nothing.

Because at one point in her life, her wretched mother wanted her.

Because at one point, her vile father wanted her.

And because this was all done by Gwydion, a Velyūn with the ability to somehow poison a mind.

To make their ambition real.

To make their desire real.

And though he wasn't there with her now, all she could smell was pine and honey, and she wanted to vomit.

The floor was spinning under her as she tucked herself into a ball of a human and cried.

XXVII

"SULWYN…" whispered Galahad, and she watched him crouch next to her just as Daijiro went and picked up the journal she had flung against the wall. Some pages had ripped from the binding, the paper askew, but the spine held.

She remained quiet, listening to him ruffle through the pages. Silence spread over them all as Daijiro sat cross-legged next to her and handed Galahad the journal to read. Softly, Daijiro stroked the top of her head, moving some of her hair off her face. But Sulwyn didn't move.

She couldn't.

She needed to push past this, and she needed to think.

But no matter how hard she tried, acid rose in her and burned her insides. All she could see was this room and the doll in her hand. The doll was like all the dolls Pandora had in her room. Her blood coated Sulwyn's hands.

But the queen wanting her once upon a time didn't stop her from being the tyrant she was. It didn't end the crimes she had committed and the families and people she murdered or helped destroy. Pandora was right; she was tainted, and she would have brought her down with her. And because she knew that, this made it worse.

Because it meant she saved Sulwyn.

She knew Raghnall was coming and lit the fire at the opposite end of the house. Pandora had a sliver of hope that Raghnall would save her and raise her so that one day they would face each other again and Pandora would die by her hand. But Pandora had forsaken everything about herself. Did she even remember the words she wrote in this journal?

"Buzzing sound?" Galahad asked aloud.

Sulwyn sat up quickly and snatched the journal back, forgetting that Daijiro had looked at it first. Slowly, she turned to him, and she could see the suspicion in his eyes. But it faltered when he took her in. Saw his tension ease; for him to do that, she must have looked terrible.

Sulwyn stood, her footing uneven and her breathing shallow while the walls, crib and wardrobe spun around.

"Sulwyn, you need to breathe," said Galahad quietly. He reached to touch her shoulders, but she moved back quickly.

"No." She pointed to him, her eyes wide and her mind reeling. She couldn't stay here. She needed to leave. To move. With Kai showing up, she knew Wilkson was back home. She needed to go to Wilkson now. "NO!" She pointed at Daijiro instead as he, too, tried to move forwards.

"Stay away. Just. Stay away," she choked, clutching the journal and the doll to her chest.

"This doesn't take away what they've done, Sulwyn..." Galahad started, and she knew he was trying to reason with her. But she didn't want to reason. She wanted to be irrational and let herself drown in this. She didn't want to hear any of it. Not right now. Not yet.

Run.

She needed to run.

Sulwyn threw the book and the doll back at Galahad, who swiftly caught it. But in that moment, she leapt out the broken window.

"Sulwyn!" Galahad shouted just as she tucked and rolled her landing. A shock and tingle travelled through her feet and ankles, but she shook it off and ignored the lingering twinge.

Then she ran.

Ki neighed and trotted after her, but she disregarded him and kept going.

She ran across the wet grass and crawled her way back up the hill so she could just run and run, crashing through the trees of the forest. Until finally, she was out of breath and her scream rent the air.

ଶୁଣ

Though her throat wasn't bleeding, it felt raw. And though her feet could not be cut because of the boots, her ankles stung. But the smell of the dirt and sand that wafted up her nose drowned the smell of pine and honey that her mind so cruelly created. Soon, she could hear the patter of rain on leaves. And then, they landed on her skin; cool and numbing.

She had no idea how long she had been lying on the grass, but she was happy that they hadn't come after her. She needed to breathe the fresh air and remove herself from that house of ash and dust and hate and faded expectation.

Now, her mind was clear, and though it was still hard to breathe, she could finally think.

Gwydion was a Devinal and a Velyūn. Though she was unsure of what exactly his allure was, it seemed to connect with ambition or desire. If he knew Pandora and Artaxiad from when they were teenagers, then he's had a lot of time to use his influence on them. And to be honest, she knew nothing about how they were raised and what they may have gone through in their lives. But something must have made them want to take over the High City. And though it was wrong and the worst thing to happen to Vartugaul since before the Zalman clan brought peace, it was their goal, taken and heightened.

Just like how she had nothing but pure desire to kill Pandora. And though that was her intention, her emotions had been blinded by it until she finally got hold of herself. Just like Artaxiad's lust for power manifested into something much worse towards her.

Gwydion had to be the true source behind the fall of the High City, and he used Artaxiad as a catalyst so that he could stay out of the public eye and continue what he was doing all along. Trying to recreate his power as a Velyūn into a poison that could control the masses, not just the people he interacted with and had a hold over.

And if Gwydion could do something as large as this, then alluring Raghnall would be simple.

Sulwyn haphazardly sat up just as the rain grew heavier, seeping into her hair and clothes. If Gwydion could heighten desire, then why was Raghnall's request for money and status? Sulwyn was sure that those were not things Raghnall would have desired. Not enough to make him act on betraying her. But as she thought harder, she finally, finally figured it out.

Gwydion needed Diesirae to assist him somehow to get to Raghnall.

And if that was the case, that meant they never really got Raghnall.

Raghnall got them.

Sulwyn laughed.

And laughed and laughed until she was crying all over again. She rolled around on the wet ground, the grass and sand sticking to her. But she didn't care. She flopped flat onto her back, looking towards the leafy sky, the rain dripping into her eyes as she took one deep breath. She knew there were a lot of grey areas, but one thing was strikingly clear to her.

She would kill Gwydion.

ᔆ∘ᕬ

| GALAHAD |

Galahad looked down at the journal and the doll.

Pandora never meant to abandon Sulwyn and put her trust in Raghnall despite him being the enemy. "She was right…" he started, and Daijiro looked up at him. "Raghnall didn't betray her. Not in the way we all thought."

Daijiro walked to the window, looking out as the rain began to fall. "She's going to do something stupid." He turned back to Galahad before walking out of the room.

"Where are you going?" he asked, taking one last glance around the room; a room that displayed nothing of what he was used to while growing up in the Empire.

Galahad followed Daijiro into the middle room, his boots crunching against the door on the ground. Daijiro flipped through books on a desk before he opened the drawer.

"What are you looking for?" Galahad asked, but he could sense the tension rising in Daijiro.

"She found something else," Daijiro replied darkly, slamming the drawer in the desk before turning to a closet of rotting clothes.

"If she's found something else, then it won't be here," Galahad said sharply. "We've given her enough time. But I agree she's going to do something reckless. We should leave." He made to leave the room.

Daijiro followed and snatched the journal and doll from Galahad before he could stop him. Silently, he tucked them away into his sash, gesturing for the other to lead the way.

After crashing through what remained of the stairs and dodging wooden beams that waited until that second to fall, they made their way carefully out of the house.

Galahad spotted Ki at the top of one of the sloping hills in the far distance pacing back and forth as if waiting for them to see him before he took off. Quickly, Galahad mounted his horse, and Daijiro followed suit. By the time they had galloped up the hill, Ki was far gone, but a path of bent branches and hoof-stomped grass led the way.

"I need to find a horse like hers…" Daijiro sighed, staying close behind Galahad as they rode into the forest.

"Can't you just… control them the same way you do people?" Galahad asked curiously. He still didn't really understand how Daijiro's ability worked, and didn't think it was something he ever could.

"Animals are different from humans," Daijiro muttered. "They are, for the most part, innocent. To control them is unfair." Galahad turned back to look at him for a second, seeing the seriousness in his eyes. "They've done me no wrong. And there would be no bond. I see no reason to do that to them unless I need to. Like Gwydion's horses."

At Gwydion's name, Daijiro's eyes grew menacing, and he remained silent. Galahad looked ahead, seeing the trail that Ki had left. Daijiro realised something he didn't, and whatever it was, was putting him in a dangerous mood. Galahad was the last person who could help him, or Sulwyn, if things got too far. At least, not the way he was now.

He had seen the suffering in her eyes. Read the words in that journal. If there was any time for him to gain some ounce of control over his power, it was now. When she needed him, when she needed them both. Because it looked like their threat was much bigger than any of them realised.

But first, he needed to get to Sulwyn and stop her from moving rashly.

Soon, they were out of the forest, steadily travelling east, past the forest that protected her home and closer to the coast. But Galahad wasn't as familiar with Guāngcǎi as he was with Antiqua. Daijiro rode up next to him, his eyes sharp as they both looked out into the distance. Though they could not see her, they found Ki's fresh tracks across the soft dirt. It lined the mid stone walls that blocked the ocean's high tide. Galahad was sure Ki stuck close to the soft land for this purpose.

"Do you know what's in this direction?" asked Galahad.

Daijiro looked around. "I'm fairly sure there's a town a day or so from here... Staultbrand. But I've never been."

"I've never heard of it..." Galahad said, but urged his horse faster, deciding that even if they saw her in the distance, he would keep his space for her sake and follow along.

৩৵৶

<h1 style="text-align:center">| SULWYN |</h1>

If anyone could help her now, it was Wilkson. Or at least, that's what she hoped for, hoping that he was where he should be, especially if Kai reported to him. Because if Gwydion had spread his reach as far as Raghnall, then it was possible he had gotten to Wilkson. She could only hope her trust in him was not wasted.

Sulwyn could see the outskirts of the town, but she needed to be careful here. She wasn't sure if word had spread, but she knew Nero would waste no time in sending everyone out as far as they could go. As they got closer to the town and rocky coast, Sulwyn reached into the saddlebag and pulled out a long, dark burgundy cloak. She was thankful for the chill today. It wouldn't stand out for her to wear this even with the hood on. She draped the cloak around her, covering the sand and dirt that coated her crusty clothes, and donned the hood over her head just as she reached the town gates.

It had been less than a year since she had been back here. The last time was just a few weeks prior to waking up in the lower dungeons of the Empire. Raghnall and Wilkson met up as usual while she sparred with Kai. But before that, it had been months since they met in his town. Usually, they met elsewhere to ensure they didn't bring any unwanted attention to his home.

Wilkson's wife, Amalthea, was strong in mind but had a body unable to keep up with it. After she gave birth to their second child, she had days where she needed to rest more than not. Instead, Wilkson took over their bar fully, with her aiding here and there. Sulwyn had no intention of bringing any harm to them. But if there was betrayal from Wilkson, she would make sure he paid for it.

The town guard let her pass, though he tried to see under her hood. And though no one here had seen her face, she wanted to keep it that way, even if it wasn't under the guise of Kintana.

Sulwyn dismounted from Ki, and instead of bringing him to the front stables for visitors, sent him back outside of the town walls. She knew Ki had left clues for Daijiro and Galahad to find her, and could sometimes even see them in the far distance during her times of rest. And though she was a little annoyed by it, she knew Ki had her best interest at heart.

He nuzzled her head before taking off, and Sulwyn moved forwards into the small town.

Eyes watched her. Though they could not see her face, she kept her eyes on all of theirs. The people always had an air of suspicion to them; she didn't see anything that looked as if they had received the latest news.

Good.

That would make this easier for her.

The sun was high noon, and the bar would be open and full of people on their lunches. Though the town was small, they lived near the coast and were allowed to sell fish to other towns in Guāngcǎi and export it to the Empire. All things considered, they were a prosperous place.

Sulwyn reached the centre of town, the stores and houses similar to Paraga, except the people were a little better off. At the entrance of the bar, there was only a sign with a castle on it. She pulled open the door, a bell tinkling as she entered.

The place was packed with people and chatter. Chairs scraping, laughs, and frustrated sighs depending on what was being discussed. The clang of utensils and pots. It was a small stone-worked building with two floors. One for the bar and dining area and the other for a few places to stay. A fire roared in the far end, making the place a little stuffy, but the smell and the coziness brought a wave of calm and nostalgia over her. If only a little. Because now that she was here, she didn't know how to continue.

She would be confirming or denying her theory on if Raghnall was alive. Unless of course, she was completely wrong, and Wilkson had nothing to do with anything and Raghnall was indeed dead. But she wouldn't think that yet. She needed to hold on to the fact that she would learn something here.

Sulwyn pulled her cloak tighter, keeping the shadows over her eyes so that only the bottom half of her face was exposed. No one gave her a second glance as she made her way through servants and guests alike, weaving between tables and chairs.

Finally, she made her way to the back where the worn wooden counter sat so that Wilkson could overlook the entire bar. If there was anything he made sure of, it was that he and others had a quick means of escape.

Her heart warmed for the first time since she left that burned-down house, when she spotted a round, robust man at the centre of the counter, pouring water into glasses for guests. Kai was there as well, helping him bring food out from the back that Amalthea made. Or if she wasn't up to it, her daughter Lelia helped alongside another woman she believed Lelia was in a relationship with.

Without a word, Sulwyn took a seat on the high barstool and rapped the wooden counter. Wilkson looked her over. "Just a second…" he grunted, handing Kai a tray of freshly cut mushrooms. "Give it to your mother… Make her find something to use them for."

He turned to Sulwyn. "What can I get ya?"

She looked up just enough to see his face. He had changed little, but she could see the deepening wrinkles around his eyes. His hands were stained with various dyes from the meals they prepared, his deep brown skin coated in many colours. He looked a little broader, but she wasn't sure if it was his wildly grown black beard making it seem that way. And of course, it looked like he decided to part with his scraggly hair and go bald.

Sulwyn clenched a fist between the folds of her cloak, lowering her voice slightly. "It's been a day, yeah? What's the strongest ya got?" she asked, her voice husker than she intended, but the effect was still the same. Wilkson knew her well, but he had never seen what she was like when she needed to deceive. She hoped her persona would hold, because it was her weakest one yet.

"Hmm." Wilkson turned around and looked at the wall of crystal, bottled drinks behind him. "We got a nice red rum, a shot of that should do you some good. Clear your throat a bit too." He glanced back at her, waiting.

"Hear ya got Midnight Star," Sulwyn said, and the shock on Wilkson's face almost made her break her feeble character.

"That is some extraordinarily strong stuff, missus. I'd have to suggest you book a room after that shot."

"Maybe I will, but I think more than one will be good." Sulwyn gave a mischievous smile to the wooden counter. Midnight Star was expensive and ridiculously strong. It was also hard to get, so Wilkson made sure to keep it hidden and out of sight. But word-of-mouth had spread the name far, and every so often, he got an idiot or two who wanted to try it.

Wilkson eyed her suspiciously, but soon, he was gone behind the wooden doors. Within minutes, he was back holding an ornate decanter with dark blue liquid inside. A few people around her stared in silence to watch as he pulled the lid off and reached for a small shot–glass.

"Shot's fifteen each. But I'll discount the room by thirty percent." He poured the shot just as the door to the bar opened, and a bell tinkled again.

Sulwyn glanced to her left to see two men enter the bar. And though they, too, were cloaked in black, hoods up, she would recognise their gaits anywhere. Sulwyn huffed, lifting her hood only a little to make eye contact with them. They both made their way to a table not too far away, taking seats that could face her.

Wilkson slid the shot over the bar, and without waiting for the peanuts to chase the burn, she took the shot straight. Some people around her gasped softly as she hit the shot–glass back onto the counter, hard.

It had been about nine years since she had this shot. When she was fifteen, Raghnall went to scout a base and left her there. Wilkson decided to let her try the shot as a joke, but she ended up taking two before she passed out. Raghnall struggled to be furious and impressed at the same time, but she was knocked out for the rest of the day.

The burn was the same, but somehow, she could now appreciate the taste a bit more. It was bitter at first, but there were hints of vanilla and sweetness after it made its way down her throat.

Sulwyn pulled a small pouch from within her cloak and tossed it at Wilkson. "Should be enough for two more and that room."

"Two more? Are you insane?" he exclaimed, but she knew he needed the money. Wilkson never cut costs when it came to his bar, but he also helped a lot of people around the town. She would have given it to him anyway, but at least this way, he thought he was earning it.

"Do you want me to take that back?" she asked, laughing slightly at his hesitation. She gestured for him to pour the next one.

As the second shot burned its way down, a light tingle floated and skittered across her mind. But as it did, the anger and confusion she had earlier melted away with it. Once she took the next shot, she was sure she would finally ease her heart. And though she didn't condone drinking to ease emotion, she needed this to clear hers. Because she was reckless and on the hunt to do something more stupid.

"Are you sure you want the last shot, missus?" Wilkson whispered, but as he did, Daijiro and Galahad stood from their corner and sat on either side of her.

"Glad you could make it…" she whispered, her smile crooked as the wave went through her. It was a much more pleasant experience than the first time. And though she never tried it again, she was rather good with all other alcohol. She sometimes wondered if it was because of those first shots so long ago that she built such a tolerance. "Do you know her?" Wilkson started. She could see he was a little worried about if she should take the shot and if Galahad and Daijiro were here to try to take advantage of her.

"We do," Daijiro replied, and Sulwyn could feel the pull even though it wasn't directed at her. "In fact, we've come to make sure she doesn't make rash decisions. Seems we're a bit too late."

Sulwyn reached over, her hand hidden under the wooden table, and placed her palm on his arm. Wilkson would feel it even if he didn't understand it. But she didn't want Daijiro to use his power on him.

Instantly, the pull was gone, but Daijiro grabbed her wrist, and she could feel the stiffness in his. She looked at him, and though his tone was playful, his eyes were murderous. Before she could stop him, he reached forwards into her boot and pulled out the crumpled canvas.

But before he could unfold it, Sulwyn reached for the shot and downed it quickly, knocking back her hood purposely, and before either of them could move, Wilkson muttered one word that froze all three of them from the waist down as if they were fused to the stool.

Taken aback, Daijiro tucked it into his sash. For now, Sulwyn had time. If he was going to find out the truth, she would rather it be away from this bar.

"Kai!" Wilkson called, and quickly, the wooden door swung forwards to reveal his son confused at the commanding tone in his father's voice. He demanded quietly, "Show these guests to the round room."

XXVIII

Three Shots Is Enough

| SULWYN |

"I should have realised. There isn't anyone stupid enough to take three shots of that stuff besides you and Raghnall…" Wilkson sighed, closing the door on Kai's retreating back.

Sulwyn looked around the small stone cellar. She had always hated this place. It was full to the brim with the smell of fermenting beans and cabbages, no windows and a strange ticking that to this day, she had no idea what it was.

Despite how much that annoyed her, seeing Wilkson in front of her with a guilty look on his face brought warmth to her heart. But only for a second.

"I'm giving you *one* minute, Wilkson," Sulwyn said as she tossed her cloak onto the ground, the alcohol burning in her veins. Galahad and Daijiro stood somewhere to her left, now fully bound by magic. Even though Kai confirmed he had met them, Wilkson didn't know anything about them, and until he felt safe, that was his house rule. But she would never be able to express how thankful she was that Daijiro was currently forced to stand still.

She glanced at them, her eyes falling on where he had tucked the portrait into his sash. He caught her eye, and his glare sent a wave of guilt over her. But he was not the current problem.

"Little one, I'm glad to see you're safe," started Wilkson, and hearing his relieved tone and the nickname he'd call her until she was old and dusty, almost shattered the anger that had started to rise. The same anger she had forced down from the burned house. One full of hate for being lied to and deceived.

"Thirty seconds," she grunted and watched as he cast her a nervous glance.

"It's complicated—" He was cut short when Sulwyn pulled one of the short daggers from her boot and flung it past Wilkson's head. It embedded itself into one of the fermenting barrels, but not deep enough to crack it.

"You're my family, Wilkson. If you've betrayed me too—" But she couldn't finish that sentence, her words caught in her throat as he strode forwards and brought her into a deep hug. His large arms and chest warmed her limbs and flooded her with longing.

"I haven't betrayed you, Sulwyn, we haven't betrayed you..." he whispered onto the top of her head. Tension filled her eyes and nose and mind, and she wanted to cry in frustration, but she couldn't anymore. She had shed her tears in that forest. Now, she was here for answers.

Sulwyn pulled away seeing the struggle in Wilkson's honey–gold eyes about what he should tell her. So, she would ask the questions instead.

"Is Raghnall alive?" she asked, her blood pounding in her ears.

Wilkson stared at her, then breathed out deeply. "I don't know."

She watched him closely. "What do you mean you 'don't know'? When was the last time you saw him?" The alcohol in her was starting to take its toll, and instead of maintaining any sort of calm, she was starting to panic again.

"Three weeks after you were given to the Empire."

Sulwyn plopped onto the ground, her knees giving way.

"Sulwyn..." whispered Galahad, concern in his voice, but she waved him off.

"Did he betray me or not?"

"No."

"So why aren't you telling me the whole story!" she cried, getting up again and taking a dagger from her other boot. This time, she stomped right up to him, shoving the blade at the base of his neck. And though they both knew she wouldn't use it, she had never pulled a weapon on him before.

"How much do you know?" he whispered, unfazed with the knife at his throat. He turned his head and blew in the direction of Galahad and Daijiro. Instantly, they lurched forwards a bit, the hold over them gone.

Galahad pulled Sulwyn away from Wilkson gently, taking her hand in his. Sulwyn dropped the dagger, her vision swaying. "Breathe, Sulwyn..." he whispered calmly, and she did just that.

What did she know? She gathered it all in her mind, leaning into Galahad for support "If Raghnall didn't betray me, then he gave me to the Empire on purpose."

Wilkson smiled a little. "Have you found the true enemy?"

"Yes," Sulwyn whispered. She looked at Galahad, and then at Daijiro, who had yet to move. Sulwyn let go of Galahad and stepped towards Daijiro, looking at him carefully as she stood right before him. "I'm sorry ..." she murmured, and his eyes widened. She reached into his sash and took the folded canvas. "Have you heard of Gwydion?" Sulwyn asked, turning back to face Wilkson. His eyes narrowed.

"He's a member of the Triarchy, isn't he? A scholar or something. Found him a few years after the Empire began to rise into power."

"Yes and no..." said Sulwyn, taking the picture and unfolding it. She held it up for him to see, his jaw dropping.

"Raghnall was right then... He always thought someone else was behind them. The day he saved you, there was a magic barrier around the hill. So, *he* was the Devinal." His voice was hushed, taking the picture carefully between his fingers. Galahad stepped closer to look at it as well before turning to Sulwyn, his eyes wide.

"They've known him from so long ago?" he asked, until finally, he grabbed the picture and peered closer.

"Show me the picture, Galahad," Daijiro demanded, and despite the sweet thrum of liquor in her veins, she could feel the hostility rise in the room. Galahad had yet to move, holding the piece of canvas tighter and staring him down. He glanced briefly to Sulwyn, and she knew he understood how careful they had to be with this situation. "Show it to me!" he yelled, holding out his palm, but Sulwyn reached forwards and placed her hand over his arm. She turned to Galahad, who wearily gave her the portrait. Facing Daijiro, she took a deep breath and held up the sheet of canvas.

Daijiro seized the picture, scoffing as he did so, his red eyes flashing as soon as he saw Gwydion in the picture. "Talking like he knew the traits of one. He is one himself. How did I not see it?" he hissed, and the corner of the portrait began to smoke. Sulwyn grabbed it out of his hand immediately before the fire that now danced across his palm could burn it.

"That is not magic..." Wilkson said apprehensively as the fire went out as quickly as it came.

Sulwyn turned to Wilkson and Galahad quickly. "Let me talk to him," she whispered, nodding her head at Galahad to get Wilkson out before Daijiro got worse.

Reluctantly, he gestured for Wilkson to follow him and they both left the cellar. Galahad's multicoloured eyes lingered on hers for a moment before closing the door. Sulwyn confronted Daijiro.

He stepped right up to her, heat radiating from his chest, his hands clenched. "Is this what you've been hiding?" he seethed, his expression wild.

"I hid it because of *this*. I knew exactly how you'd react!" she retorted, dizzying waves floating through her. Her eyes burned to sleep. Why did she take three shots?

"No, it's because I don't have your trust," he spat, taking the picture from her again. "He's a Velyūn, Sulwyn. A fucking Velyūn! And you didn't think you should tell me? Is it because I couldn't recognise him as one? Do you think I'm lesser now? How Zalika is to me, I am to him?" He jabbed her in the chest.

"That's not even a thought that crossed my mind!"

"Did you think I'd rejoice and join him? Or did you think I couldn't face him? Because he escaped the Solus under my guard?"

"Are you hearing yourself? Nothing you've said makes any sense!" But she took the picture back yet again, another corner now singed.

"Is that why you got closer to me? All to learn more about a Velyūn, to figure out if he was one or not?"

Sulwyn was affronted, trying to keep her own rage from growing. "I've gotten closer to you because I *care*, Daijiro. I asked you to trust me because I knew you'd become like this. You don't trust anyone! You are broken and jaded and think you don't deserve any form of happiness or care!" She leaned right against him. "Even as you're yelling at me, all I can smell is mint!" Somehow, this made him step back completely, his arms falling to his sides, all fight in him gone. "It doesn't matter what he is. We have one enemy. I didn't want to tell you because it would hurt you. Because you would find some way to blame yourself. But him being a Velyūn has nothing to do with who you are to *me*."

"And who is that, Sulwyn?" he asked bitterly. "As a Velyūn, I'm obviously under him. I couldn't even tell he was one. I can cancel out Zalika because she's below me. That means Gwydion could neutralise me if he dared try. All this time, I thought I could be of some use to you because I had a hold on him. I thought I had some leverage. But if he's been hiding his true self, then that means he let me."

"You don't know that. And you're not here for me to use you… You are more than your powers…"

These words stunned him into silence. He stared at her with un-wavering eyes as if he had never truly seen her. Until he stepped up to her again, pulling her into an embrace. The words seemed to have evaporated all the tension in him, leaving him breathless against her as if he had been running.

The waves of sweet rain, burnt wood and mint wafted stronger around her, mixing with the waves of alcohol in her system. And though she knew they weren't real scents, she couldn't stop herself from breathing them in.

"He doesn't smell like you…" she whispered into his chest, letting him hold her as tightly as he was. Trying to tame the shaking throughout his body, his panic subsided.

He breathed into her hair.

"What does he smell like?"

"Pine and honey… I've come to hate both."

Daijiro chuckled and sighed in defeat. "Mint is the smell my mother gave off and it seems I inherited it," he started, and though Sulwyn tried to pull away and look at him, he held her closer. "Velikat had one unique aroma and it could only be distinguished by someone that cared for them the way the other did. My mother loved me, and I her, so I could smell mint. Tamesis never could. You smell mint because I'm in love with you."

Sulwyn tried to pull away again, and this time, he let her. For the first time since she could remember, her mind was still. Absolutely silent. She had no idea how to respond or if she should. Though it didn't make sense, it was like her brain had cracked, unable to comprehend the thought.

So, she blinked.

A lot.

Daijiro's smile was wide and coy. "Timing is important. I know your priorities lie elsewhere right now." He took her hand gently, intertwining their fingers before he kissed hers. Then gently dropped her hand and stepped away, moving to open the cellar door. All anger from him, gone. Whether he was hiding it or not, she couldn't tell. But her mind was still reeling and the damn alcohol wasn't helping.

Wilkson and Galahad walked back in, looking at them both, and she was thankful the room was soundproof so that their conversation was not heard beyond the door. But Sulwyn still could only blink until a throb at the side of her head alerted her to the task at hand. She winced as the pounding started to the left of her eye.

"Ah, the side effect is strong in this drink," Wilkson said knowingly. "You didn't feel it last time because you passed out for the rest of the day." He laughed, smiling widely. Her anxiety was gone, and despite her headache, it was time to get some real answers.

"Just get me some water…" she groaned.

Wilkson walked back to the door and opened it. "Kai! Get this troublemaker some drink and food!" he yelled, and Sulwyn could only groan louder from the throbbing his yell brought out.

৩৽৵৻

After a few minutes of rest, eating and Sulwyn inhaling a jug of water and a plate of a sandwiches, they were all seated on the floor of the cellar.

"I'll tell you as much as I know. But you know Raghnall, when he plans, he tells you what he wants and that's it. You don't know the hassle he gave me this time." Wilkson sighed, leaning against a barrel.

Galahad, Sulwyn and Daijiro all sat across from him, each leaning on a different barrel with bated breath.

"A few months before you were taken to the Empire, someone had started to follow you both."

"Someone was following us?" she asked incredulously. She thought back and could not think of one instance when that was.

"You've already hit the problem…" Wilkson explained. "It took a few weeks for Raghnall to fully realise it too. The person seemed just a step behind each time until Raghnall made it easier for you both to be followed. When that happened, within a few months, someone contacted him."

"Someone?" she asked, but he shrugged.

"Raghnall didn't tell me who, only that he had met with them a few times after, and each time, he complained of something odd. There was a buzzing in his head that wouldn't leave him alone."

The three of them looked at each other, and Daijiro pulled out the journal. He handed it to Sulwyn, who located the page where Pandora talked of something similar and showed it to him.

"Oh yeah, that seems about the same... But he didn't go into detail. Instead, he said he was going to let them go ahead and do it."

"Do what?" asked Galahad, but Wilkson only shrugged again.

"I told ya. Raghnall is a man of few words once he gets a plan going. Next thing I knew, he was asking me to make something to clot blood faster. But each time I saw him—and no, Sulwyn, you weren't always there. I came to meet him a few times when you were in different towns— no, each time he came to meet me, he seemed a little different. Just a little more distracted than the last time. Until soon, it was more times than not."

Sulwyn thought back to the night before Raghnall brought her to the Empire. Though it had been over half a year, it seemed like yesterday. She and Raghnall were running from Néosan that were chasing them through a town. They travelled for hours through a stream before finding a safe spot to camp for the night. There were times he seemed like he wasn't even there and times when he was alert like his normal self. Especially when he had presented this worn silver ring to her. But then he was waking her in the middle of the night to run again until they were surrounded by Validus, with Raghnall's cold eyes the last thing she saw before he poisoned her and knocked her out.

The more she thought about it, the more she realised it was extremely similar to how she behaved under Artaxiad's poison. No, *Gwydion*'s poison.

However, if Raghnall got her into the Empire, it was for a purpose, and she was sure it was to figure out who the Devinal really was. Raghnall probably had a lot of theories, but unless she could find him, she wouldn't be able to confirm this. She needed him to be alive.

"The plan didn't go the way it was supposed to, did it?" she asked as she watched Wilkson pick nervously at his beard, a tell he couldn't be rid of.

"The plan went better than we expected, actually." His tone light. "He survived!"

Sulwyn just stared at him. "He did this assuming he was going to die?"

"He did it assuming you would live," he said solemnly.

"Fine, he's a sacrificial idiot, it sounds like," Daijiro replied. "How did he even get out of the Empire? I heard Pandora stabbed him and left him in the lower dungeons."

"That was another spell, wasn't it?" Sulwyn asked. "The body Artaxiad presented to the Empire wasn't his."

Wilkson passed her another sandwich without her asking. She gave him a sidelong glance and a smirk, she would not be drinking any more Midnight Star for a long time.

"He planned to get sent to the lower dungeons. No… more like hoped," said Wilkson shrugging.

"Because no one knew the High City better than he did…" Galahad added, looking over at Sulwyn.

She focused on Wilkson, eyes wide. "Are you telling me that Raghnall got you to make him a blood thickener in hopes that he would be taken and stabbed and miraculously sent to the lower dungeons? So that he could escape and leave the Empire before anyone realised?"

He shrugged. "That's pretty much it, yes."

"Is he stupid? Do you see how many flaws are in that plan?" exclaimed Sulwyn. "It's the Empire! For all he knew, they could have let someone from the Uferor deal with him, and he could have been taken elsewhere. Or killed on the spot, beheaded even."

"I tried to talk him out of it, Sulwyn, I did. But he wanted to go through with it. He needed to lure out the real threat."

"Are you saying he used Sulwyn as bait?" Galahad asked harshly with anger in his eyes.

"He trusted Sulwyn," said Daijiro sharply, looking at Galahad. "Gwydion being a Velyūn changes everything we thought we knew about him. Do you think Raghnall knows?"

Wilkson cut in. "He's a Velyūn? Those exist?"

But Sulwyn just pointed to Daijiro. "He's a Velyūn." Wilkson gaped, but Daijiro looked a little betrayed. She waved him off.

"Would he know?" continued Daijiro, but she just shook her head.

"I don't know. I didn't know based on what you looked like or your power. We know what you are by name, but I've never seen one before you, and I don't know if he has either. He might just be focused on the Devinal part. Which, in my opinion, isn't fair." She turned to Wilkson. "How is that possible?"

"Devinal are just born," Wilkson said. "There aren't any prerequisites. There wasn't anyone in my immediate family that was born one. It's just random, and this man seems to have drawn a lucky hand."

Sulwyn huffed in frustration. "We'll deal with him later then. I need to know exactly what happened to Raghnall."

But every time she asked what happened to him, Wilkson would give her a look that pained her to see. It was a look he showed when Kai was almost taken to the Empire during a collection before Raghnall stepped in, how he looked when her younger self had been gravely injured during a mission and ended up getting severely sick from an infection. It was eyes that shone with the ghost of witnessing the people he loved almost dying over and over. And her thoughts were confirmed when he spoke.

"The dagger he was stabbed with was poisoned," he said gravely. "I should have planned for that, but it slipped my mind. Everything was so chaotic. The dagger missed his heart probably because he shifted his body at the last second, but the poison spread far. By the time he had used the spell I had given him to turn someone freshly deceased into his likeness, he had already lost a lot of energy and blood."

Sulwyn clenched her hands together along with her teeth. Such a stupid, reckless plan. No wonder she was just the same.

"I was supposed to wait in the bordering forest until sunrise the next day, but I couldn't just leave even after time passed. He showed up just an hour after sunrise, blacking out." He reached forwards to take Sulwyn's hands in his. "I did what I could, but the poison had spread far from him walking such a distance, even with his blood slowed down. By the time he woke two weeks later, he was a shadow of himself. He'd lost partial mobility in his left side, mainly in his arm and leg."

"And you let him go?" she hissed, her eyes burning, but she knew the answer before he said it.

"You know I couldn't stop him. A week after he woke and was able to move properly, he took off. I haven't heard from or seen him since."

"You couldn't have gone far..." Galahad said, looking at him closely now, his eyes narrowed. "You both were in Antac, weren't you? The man who was lighting the town flames. Your stature fits."

Wilkson studied him closely. "That's a ridiculously small detail to remember. You're the prince, aren't you? I don't ask many questions, and if Sulwyn has brought you to my home, it means she trusts you. But I don't. I don't trust either of you." He turned to Daijiro. "You're both from reputable clans, but I can promise if you do anything bad by her, I won't stay quiet," he warned.

"Wilkson, if you were going to threaten them, it should have been when they were still bound, not now when we're basically sitting in a sharing circle," Sulwyn said, but she smiled a little at the sentiment.

"Don't think I couldn't do worse in less than a second," he warned all the same but turned back to Galahad. "But I digress. Yes, that was me... I heard the Uferor were coming, so I wanted to gather some information. But soon, I saw you both and realised the bastard's stupid plan worked."

"So, you were in Antac, and you didn't bother to let me know you were there?" she asked suspiciously.

"Raghnall planned the whole thing so that no one would know. At least if he survived. If he didn't, he hoped you would learn the truth regardless. He needed the enemy to think they had gotten to him and that he was dead. That would be the only way they would make any moves. While you are formidable in your own right, having both of you is a death sentence. And Raghnall didn't know who the Devinal was. I don't know who he met up with, but I never sensed a Devinal in the vicinity on the off times I was in the same town.

"I don't know any more than this, Sulwyn..." Wilkson said as he grunted to stand. The three of them followed suit, dusting off their pants. "I don't know if he's still alive or not, but a man like that wouldn't go down after surviving what he did. I think the only thing you can do next is find him."

Wilkson moved to leave the cellar, but Galahad held him back. "Did a man named Azhar help you in Antac?"

Sulwyn watched Wilkson raise an eyebrow but gave a small smirk. "You can trust Azhar. I'm assuming you've had a day. You can stay here the night before you go back home. That drink is going to knock you down soon anyway." He winked at Sulwyn. She grimaced just as the pounding headache started to come back.

XXIX

Exceptionally Reckless
|SULWYN|

"YOU should be sleeping..." Kai said just as Sulwyn walked down the stairs to see him and Wilkson closing for the night. She had just spent some time with Amalthea and Lelia. Like Wilkson, they reprimanded her and crushed her lungs with hugs.

It was late, past midnight, but Sulwyn couldn't sleep. Even though she was now relieved to know some of the truth, there was still too much for her to comprehend.

"When you end up like me, you don't tend to sleep a lot..." Sulwyn replied sadly, but she walked over to Kai and hugged him tightly. She didn't have a chance to take in his growth when he came to battle her. He looked exactly like his mother. Lighter brown skin, dark golden eyes and black curly hair that was made up of numerous tiny braids in a ponytail.

He had matured a lot since the last time she had seen him. And though they were only a few years apart, she always felt like she was the older one, even though he was.

"You can stay with us, and you wouldn't need to go through all of this." His voice muffled in the crook of her neck, holding her closely. "You're always welcome here."

"Just like me, the Empire doesn't sleep." She smiled up at him and waved him off before he was scolded.

"No, it doesn'," Wilkson said, slapping Kai on the back. "Go help your sister."

"Yeah, yeah." He turned back to Sulwyn. "There's always a bed for you here." He smiled brightly before disappearing behind the kitchen door. Her heart fluttered just a little, reminiscing at a time when they were younger and a little freer.

"Come," said Wilkson, beckoning her forwards. She followed him to the fireplace, its flame burning low, where he pulled down one of the candelabras. The fireplace moved back a few inches before sliding away to reveal a set of dark stone steps.

It had been a long time since Sulwyn had been down here, the temperature dropping with each step. Normally, Wilkson didn't allow too many people down at a time. He never liked others touching his stuff. It was the main reason she and Raghnall were seldom invited down.

As the ground leveled out, Wilkson lit the torches with barely a word, and the large room illuminated. It looked the same as it always did. Full to the brim with shelves upon shelves of herbs and flowers. Skins and teeth of various animals or wings of small insects. Also, along the walls were a multitude of books or journals with nonsensical trinkets shoved in between. Though the way down had been cold, this room was warm with pots and vials of boiling liquids. A mixed smell of damp paper and sugary things wafted around her with just a hint of something stale.

"Don't touch anythin'," he barked immediately, just as she raised her hand to a small green vial that was suspended over a tiny square patch of grass.

"I'm just looking!"

"That's what you always say, and then something is broken, and you're throwing up." He scoffed. "We won't be down here long. I wanted to give you a few things. Wait in that spot." He turned and bustled around.

Sulwyn made good on her word and kept her hands behind her back, watching him move through the room with practised ease and knowledge of where everything was. Soon, he was handing her a small pouch of shatterproof vials.

"You know what the yellow ones are. I only have these three on hand for now. Too much work. So, use them sparingly and carefully. The bag is indestructible as well." He took out the yellow vials like the one Tiamat had before she shifted.

"The red one is a poison, unidentifiable in any way. Use it carefully. Two drops are enough to get a good reaction without killing the person. Four if you want to. One vial should be enough. I don't know if you'll need it, but you can't be too sure." He moved them around, looking for another.

"The blue one is for messages. I only have one bottle, use it sparingly. Anything you write with it will appear in that notebook." He pointed to a large leather-bound journal that was laid open at the centre of one of his main desks. "Don't worry about the time. It'll only fade after I read it.

"This clear one is for if you get too cold and may have frostbite or hypothermia. Winter will be around soon. You'll have to drink the whole thing to get a favourable effect, so stay out of the cold. I've given you three. The same goes for this purple one, but it's for burns. Drink it all if you're really injured. Otherwise, you can soak a bandage in it and wrap the wound. Will heal you faster and better than that shoddy job Raghnall did on his neck and face and your leg," he grumbled.

"Hey, that's a mark that binds our meeting!" Sulwyn protested.

"Yeah, that's what he told you to make himself feel better about his shoddy job." But he cracked a smile. "This green one is for Raghnall if you *do* find him. It should help him out by the time he gets it. For health," he said wearily, and she knew they were both hoping he was indeed alive.

"Thank you, Wilkson... for everything, and for saving Raghnall." Sulwyn stepped forwards and hugged him. Trying to bottle this serenity in her memory to aid her in the journey ahead.

"You can thank me by staying alive and bonus points if you find that old fool. I know you're itching to leave, so get your mates and get going to your next stop. I won't ask you to tell me where. The less I know, the better… just in case." He squeezed her tightly before letting go.

⨎⨏

It was late and dark by the time they made it over the spellbound water and back to her home. While she wished she could stay with Wilkson longer, she knew that if she didn't push herself to leave, she might have stayed forever.

"Ki, I'm glad you've stuck around so far. I hope I'm living up to your expectations," she muttered as she rubbed him down for the night. He neighed softly, nudging her torso with his head before he looked up. She looked up as well to see Galahad coming towards her with a plate of meat and cheese they had brought back from Wilkson's bar. He couldn't give her much more because he had already rationed what he would need for the town for the next while. Sulwyn patted Ki once more, bidding him to sleep as she walked out of the stable to join Galahad on a patch of grass under the stars.

She knew Galahad glanced at her every so often as they ate in silence, until finally, he reached over and brushed her knee. The warmth of his hand flooded her, and even though the night was a bit chilly, it warmed her soul.

"I know I've been a bit distant this last month…" Galahad started, but she just shifted a bit closer and leaned against his shoulder.

"You don't have to explain yourself to me," she said quietly, looking at his hand over her knee. Just like the many scars on his back, she saw a few trace themselves into his hand. Knowing that each one bore a story from a past he did, and didn't, remember.

"I know, I know. But I want you to always know that I am here for you. Regardless of what I am going through. No matter what side I may show you…" He trailed off, and she knew he was thinking about her vision. A memory flashed in her mind at his mention. Of his eyes pure black and his nails digging into her neck. But as she turned to look at him now, with his stunning-coloured eyes warm and full of concern, she believed that she would be safe. Even if that vision happened, it wouldn't be the end.

Sulwyn sighed and leaned back against him. "The more I learn, the more I realise how everyone has been playing into his hand. Even Raghnall did, regardless of his plan, whatever it really was. He was put into action because of Gwydion. I'm afraid that it digs deeper than this. Deeper than just Pandora and Artaxiad, and maybe you." She looked down as he took her hand in his.

The warmth now travelled up her arm and to her chest, pleasant and a little electrifying, but she could feel a difference. His touch was calming and cautious. It made her feel like she could ask him to run, and he would. They would leave everything and everyone to find a different kind of peace. But when she thought of Daijiro's touch… it was everything else. It enveloped every nerve, cautious but wild. Protective but still equal. She knew he had her back, even if she didn't always like how he handled things. He would run with her too, but would also pull her back to the fight. And then they, too, would find a peace that worked for them.

She had yet to sort out her heart in that aspect, and though she knew neither Galahad nor Daijiro would make her feel anything she shouldn't, she didn't think they deserved to have her ignore them either. But even though she knew this, she couldn't make room for it. Not right now. She needed to sort through herself first before she could move on to someone else.

"Sulwyn…" whispered Galahad, and she closed her eyes, berating herself for how he could always read her. "We are behind whatever choices you make."

And though she could hear the bitter undertone in his words of the unspoken feelings between them all, she knew he also meant it towards their next step. She nodded, taking the time to listen to the whistle in the trees and grass as a cooler, sweet breeze passed over them. A faint hint of mint travelled towards her, and based on the slight twitch in Galahad's hand, he also realised Daijiro was somewhere nearby now.

She spoke a little louder. "Azhar is the barman at Antac, right? Did he say something to you for you to talk about him like that?"

"When we were leaving Antac after our mission with the criminals in tow, he told me to look out for you, and if I ever needed something, not to hesitate to ask for help."

Sulwyn's eyes narrowed in thought. "If he was helping Raghnall, then I think he might know more. Since we will end up going there anyway, I think we can take a detour first."

"Detour?"

"I want to go back to the last town Raghnall and I were at before I came to the Empire. He was meeting with someone there, and I think it was Diesirae, but I want to make sure. Raghnall wouldn't have been easy to catch, and I want to know if anyone saw their interaction."

"Why?" asked Daijiro, appearing behind them both.

Sulwyn could feel the tension in Galahad's hand but continued. "If Gwydion is a Velyūn, then he needs to be in proximity for his allure to work, no?"

"Usually," Daijiro drawled, choosing to stay somewhere behind them.

"Then if he wasn't there, they would have to rely on the drug he used on me. But Raghnall isn't easy to drug either. If there are any witnesses, I can figure out if both of them were there or not."

"I don't see how that would help," he pointed out, and Sulwyn tried to maintain some patience. Daijiro had been moody since they left Staultbrand, and she knew it was because of Gwydion.

"Because if it took both his allure and the poison to get to Raghnall, then there is hope for everyone else. His power and his drug aren't permanent if he can't always be around. But I need to know what it looked like to someone else. Someone not under the influence."

"You still don't fully trust that this was all his decision," Galahad said, holding her hand a little tighter.

"No..." she whispered. "Considering how far Gwydion has gone to infiltrate the Empire, it seems odd to me that he let Raghnall slip away like that."

"I don't think so," started Daijiro, and he finally moved to sit beside Galahad. "He's cocky. Like I said, everything changes now that I know what he is. I don't know much about Raghnall, but if he went as far as to let himself be taken and then possibly killed as well as involve you, he knew the stakes were high. That it would *take* that much before Gwydion let go. If he's a Devinal, there's a chance his power is more potent than mine. It may need to take hold in close proximity, but it's possible he can extend its reach."

Sulwyn remained quiet, pondering what he said. "That would make sense... All of this is a theory, but I told you back at Wallasyn that that masked man pricked me with something at the Gala. And that was sometime after I had had a moment with Gwydion. But if that's all it takes to just push someone, then I can't imagine what else he can do with more time," Sulwyn huffed, pulling Galahad down with her and laying atop the tall blue and green grass. He joined her without resistance as they looked up at the stars. She could now feel Daijiro's eyes on her, heat climbing her neck.

"Just lie on the grass, Daijiro," Galahad said, and somehow, his snarky tone made her laugh instead. She could hear Daijiro mutter something intelligible, and it just made her laugh more. And finally, one of the weights in her lifted.

Raghnall hadn't betrayed her, and there was a high chance he was still alive.

Sulwyn stood in front of her home, taking in every mismatched roof tile and broken pot. She looked at every bruise and scar the house had taken on when she was training. All the coloured stones of the pathway leading to the front door. She stood there for ten minutes straight, just as she had done inside, before she finally turned and walked towards Ki.

"You'll come back again," Galahad said, following her alongside Daijiro.

"I know. I just hope it's with Raghnall. It's been two years since we were here together. We spent the time travelling to smaller parts of Guāngcǎi and more within the borders of Antiqua." She mounted Ki, taking one last look at the house, and then they were off towards Pliflyn.

After a few days of travel, they could finally see the growing outline of Pliflyn by noon. But as they got closer, a dizzying sort of warning washed over Sulwyn, forcing her to pull on Ki's reins sharply.

Daijiro and Galahad both stopped, turning to look at her in alarm and confusion, but she just shook her head and pulled out her cloak. "It's been over two weeks since we left the Empire. I don't think this town will be as open as it was the last time. We might not be able to stay long." She threw the cloak over her, pulling the hood over her head, and urged them both to do the same.

As they neared the town, Sulwyn noticed that there wasn't anyone on guard at the front borders. And as she looked past the brick walls, she could scarcely see any activity along the streets or stores. Once they crossed into the town, the reaction was different from last time.

The few people she could see were tensed and huddled. They all shot furtive glares their way, even though all three of them kept their heads held high so that most of their faces could be seen. She slowed Ki down to a trot to line up with Galahad. "We have to get what we need quickly and leave."

"I agree," he mumbled, looking over at Daijiro and nodding. Galahad took the lead, and they rode through the town until they got to the inn's stables. Swiftly, they all dismounted, tying the reins to the post while Sulwyn left Ki untied to guard.

"If anything happens, he'll find me first and alert us. Let's split up," Sulwyn said, and before Daijiro or Galahad could protest, she made her way to the butcher for salted meats. She had a feeling they would need to ration for the next while until they made it back into Antiqua with the route they were taking.

She waited in line, looking vaguely around the small shop run by what looked like a father and son. By the time it was her turn to order, she could hear raised voices coming from somewhere outside down the street. She took a slow, deep breath, trying not to let her erratic heart get to her.

"Travelling, eh? What do you need? We're out of salted for the moment. Got smoked." Sulwyn looked up at him. He was a tall, lanky man with a bristling white mustache and pale skin.

"Three white fish and a pound of dried beef, smoked," Sulwyn said hoarsely, taking out five coins. This was as much as she could order without gaining any more suspicion. But her heart wouldn't stop pounding. Something was gnawing at her, warning her to be quick.

"That's a lot for one lady, buying for your father?" he asked lightly, writing the order and passing it to his son to get. He took the coins she had placed on the counter top and tapped each one against a metal block. She had seen some people do this to check for counterfeits. But she knew none could be made properly without the black dye.

"Yes, he's got a bad leg, so I do most of the errands."

"Good daughter he's got. Lot of work on you." His son came back with her purchases wrapped in brown paper and twine. He held them out for her to take but pulled them back and walked around the counter instead. She held out her food satchel for him as he dropped them in.

"I try my best, sir. Thank you for the food." She inclined her head and moved to go out of the store. But as she opened the door, it slammed shut, an arm above her holding it closed. Sulwyn feigned being startled and jumped back a bit. The man's son was next to her, his hand against the glass pane of the door.

"Some of Artaxiad's men came through here a day ago," said the son. She looked up at his face, her eyes hidden by the shadow of her hood. He was a young man with thick, blond hair and a recent black eye.

"They're looking for someone," the shop owner added, and he came up right next to her. Until finally, she spotted it just behind him against the wall next to a stack of baskets.

There was a drawing of her likeness pinned to a small board alongside Galahad's face. The waves of warning rushed through her, freezing her hands and feet as she read the listing:

SULWYN | KINTANA

The newly appointed queen, once princess and long-lost child
of King Artaxiad and Queen Pandora, is wanted for their murder
in attempts of treason of the highest kind. Wanted for the murder
of seven innocent civilians under the name **KINTANA**.
Wanted for the attack on Macil alongside escaped prisoners and
is being suspected of aiding and releasing the prisoners of the Solus.

Please note that **KINTANA** and **SULWYN**
are one and the same and should be treated with caution.
A bounty will be given to whoever presents the false queen **ALIVE**.

Next to hers, Galahad's read something similar:

GALAHAD

Prince **GALAHAD** is wanted for assisting
the false queen **SULWYN** in their acts of treason to
dethrone King Artaxiad and Queen Pandora, ending in murder.
Wanted for questioning on the deaths of Empire personnel
during a mission in Synd.

Do not approach alone. Proceed with extreme caution.

A bounty will be given to whoever presents the prince **ALIVE**.

Sulwyn's hood was ripped off her head, but before they could see her clearly, she kicked the man's knee and punched his son in the gut. Both stumbled to the ground as she yanked the door open and rushed out into the middle of the sandy road.

"Cailín, we need to leave," called Daijiro hurriedly, coming from another store a little down from the butcher shop.

"They can't really believe this—" But a hammer whizzed by her head and embedded itself into the ground behind her. The man from the butcher shop and his son stood outside the door glaring at her in terror, shock and disbelief balled into one.

Sulwyn looked around her and only now noticed the storefronts along the streets had the same notice posted in the corner. She read the bounty on her head. And it was high. Enough to get the person who turned her in, and their family, a life at the Empire for the rest of their generations. Signed by none other than Nero himself.

Soon, other people started to flood the road around them, coming out from various stores and trade workshops. Galahad came from around the side of another road just as a plate flew behind him, shattering on the ground.

"Kintana was Empire filth all along!" yelled one man.

"The Empire is lying to you!" Sulwyn exclaimed, but still, someone threw a bottle at her. "I share nothing with the Empire besides their blood. I didn't choose that!"

"You have been lying to us!" wailed a woman, ignoring her words, as another man threw a glass mug. Sulwyn caught it and turned to face them all.

"I have been wronged by the Empire just as you have!" cried Sulwyn, and somehow, she wasn't prepared for this. Not for the instant hate that she was receiving. She figured the Empire and Gwydion would turn the name Kintana against her, but she didn't think the resistance to it would be so little. She thought people would question it. Would remember Kintana in a good light despite what was being said. But all they could see was the blood of the Empire in her veins. And soon, they would all see what she truly looked like and there would be no denying that Artaxiad and Pandora were her parents. No one would be able to separate her from them.

Sulwyn whistled loudly, and Ki came parting a path of vengeance through the people who were now gathering closer and closer.

She pulled Galahad and Daijiro with her to follow behind Ki through the path he cleared. Ki was intimidating. A horse larger than what they normally saw with a ton of battle scars, no one wanted to get near him as his hooves pounded hard into the compacted sand. Deep prints left from his aggression.

"I wasn't expecting this to happen so quickly..." Galahad sputtered as they ran back to their horses, untying them quickly. Sulwyn threw her satchel into the saddlebag before she mounted Ki.

The townspeople came running towards them, screaming curses and hate towards her and Galahad—one person really getting to her.

"Traitors to Vartugaul! The Steel Warrior must be a traitor too!"

The voice echoed through her but Sulwyn clenched her teeth and spurred Ki forwards, followed by Galahad and Daijiro. Word would spread that they had been sighted there, but she was thankful it was now and not earlier when she was going home or to Wilkson.

Soon, they were out of sight of the town, and Sulwyn brought Ki back to a trot. "We're going to have to rest..." she called to the other two as she gently patted the horse.

"How quickly they turn," Daijiro muttered darkly as they continued slowly around the trees that bordered Antiqua and Guāngcǎi. "If we keep going this way, we'll be near a hidden village where the mind reader girl was found."

"Were you the one that took her?" asked Sulwyn severely.

A glint of guilt crossed his eyes. "We were sent there after a survivor reported what he found when he came to his village. You can imagine the Empire's thoughts on learning someone other than themselves laid waste to an entire village and on their own, no less. But they never had concrete proof it was her. Not that that would have really mattered if they didn't originally find her interesting. And your interference also helped."

Sulwyn turned Ki around and stopped Daijiro's horse from moving forwards. But he held up his hands in innocence. "If I had done any-thing to her or let anyone do anything to her, she would have told you.

If it helps, I made sure she wasn't harmed. She is still a child. I'm not *that* broken." There was a hint of malice in his growl as he said it, echoing her words from Wilkson's cellar.

Sulwyn eyed him with a bit of defiance and a little shame. "I'm sorry." She turned back around and continued forwards. "If there's anyone I feel sorry for, it's her. She's a child."

"No one gets to be children in this land anymore," Galahad said solemnly.

"I was younger than her, nine, when I had my first kill..." Sulwyn replied.

"You were younger than me, then. My first kills were when I came to the Empire."

"Am I the more innocent between the two of you?" Daijiro asked playfully. "Tamesis was my first kill."

"Your first kill was when you were fifteen?" Sulwyn exclaimed just as they reached a more condensed part of the growing forest. A bit further, and they could rest for a while.

"I think presenting one hundred Néosan heads to Pandora negates that..." replied Galahad darkly. Sulwyn turned in her seat to stare at Daijiro. That slight tremor of basic fear going through her, and then it was replaced by heartache at how far he must have fallen to do that.

He just sighed. "If you want to be accurate about it, I presented six at her feet. The other ninety-four were at the entrance of the Empire. Their bodies past that."

"They didn't consider that treason?" Sulwyn asked, unsettled.

"Pandora was too impressed with me to care. But I guess that shows you what type of people they really were."

Silence fell around them until they reached a spot near a clear river to rest at. By midday the next day, they had come across what was left of Arsinone and Taru's village. Though fires had been set to burn the bodies, Sulwyn could still see decomposing outlines of those that didn't get to burn fully or at all.

"Her power is terrifying in its own right," said Galahad, frowning at the burned houses. The village was a ghost town, not unlike others that had the same fate fall on them due to illness or punishment. But this was done to erase the bodies that had died due to Arsinone's unconscious attack. Sulwyn hoped that being with Taru would help her.

Ki stopped unexpectedly, getting Sulwyn's attention towards what he was doing. In the distance of the small village outskirts, she could see a lone figure on a horse. She looked over at Galahad and Daijiro sharing a glance. Someone was following them from their original laid-out trail, which meant they had predicted their path or at least hoped to. But they were still too far to see, and instead of rushing off, the three of them maintained their trot.

"Who do you think that is?" asked Sulwyn, veering towards the decision to do something exceptionally reckless.

Galahad squinted. "Validus or higher, probably. Unless it isn't someone from the Empire."

"At this point, it probably is," Daijiro retorted.

"We should apprehend them," Sulwyn said, looking to the north.

Daijiro smirked. "I agree with the fake queen. We ambush them. They think they know where we're headed. We can either leave the opposite way towards the lake, but it's a toxic one, or we can start crossing our way over the border now. There is a large cover of trees coming up. But they will still follow..."

"No, I meant now," said Sulwyn, and she patted Ki. Before Daijiro could stop her, she grabbed his extra bow off the side of his saddle, stealing a few arrows from his back. She spurred Ki forwards, and he took off at a run as she led him through the path she had been eyeing.

"Wait!" yelled Galahad.

Sulwyn and Ki ran straight through the edge of the trees, using as much coverage as she could to bring her closer. Normally, this idea would be ridiculous, but with Ki, she could do it. She followed the trail, seeing the dot of a person from between the thin tree trunks. She would work her way around and come from the attacker's side. As she got closer, she held her knees tighter, letting go of Ki's reins and nocking the bow. Just as they passed the edge of trees and rode into the opening, she let the arrow go.

She heard it whistle as it went, only now able to see who it was: Eurus.

Eurus turned to see her, noticing a little too late but still managing to dodge the arrow scraping past his ribs. She hadn't shot to kill, but now she wished she had. She couldn't be sure if Eurus was alone or not, but it didn't matter at this point.

She was going to bring the fight to him.

Sulwyn slung the bow over her, letting it rest over the sheath as she drew her sword. Something nudged her to save the four other arrows for later. She gripped the reins in one hand and spurred Ki faster.

Eurus's expression changed from shocked to concentrated in an instant. She had insulted him, coming alone. But soon, she heard the crush of hooves from behind her, and he smiled. Sulwyn turned; she miscalculated.

Tarak came storming out of the forest she had come from, thundering down the rocks and sand with his too large of a horse. It was the only one that could carry him. And while she was sure the breed wasn't the same as Ki or Hana, this horse was huge. Taking her attention off breeds, she stared at the two men in front of her. She didn't think the assailant would be alone, just not these two.

"You've made our job easier!" called Tarak, and she wondered vaguely if he thought of anything other than following Nero's or the Empire's rule. She didn't know much about him, but somehow, he didn't seem like he started out on their side.

Eurus, on the other hand, wanted nothing more than to take claim for catching her. She could see it as they both stalked closer in either direction. She sheathed the sword and pulled the bow over her, nocking it quickly as Ki maintained his pacing in a small circle, swaying his head threateningly and keeping his eyes on both as well. She had to put her trust in Daijiro and Galahad, but until then, she would need to learn what the world was saying.

"Have I?" she shouted, keeping her arms steady, the bow taut. "I could shoot both of you right now, perfectly in the head, and no one would know."

Eurus scoffed. "You think too highly of yourself, mock queen."

"I didn't ask to be queen," she spat, but reeled herself back in. "You know who I am now. What I said wasn't a bluff."

"Where are the others?" asked Eurus, ignoring her taunts.

"What others? I work alone," she countered, noticing as they edged closer to her small perimeter.

"We know the traitor prince and some maids are with you," said Tarak, but Sulwyn kept thinking about Galahad's wanted poster.

"What happened in Synd?" she called, watching his hairless brows furrow slightly.

"If you are referring to the Néosan that died by the prince's hand, I did not witness it. I was with you," he replied with a shrug.

"Galahad has killed many of the Néosan before. Why does it matter now?"

"Those are the Empire's people," stated Eurus, inching closer and closer to her. They were just a few feet apart. Too far for their horses to try and bother Ki, but close enough that if they wanted to, they could engage her in a fight. "None of them should have ever been killed. The king was too lenient with him."

"Did you ever stop to think that maybe he wasn't the problem?"

"What do you know about the Corrupted Prince?" he asked, his tone oddly proud. But Sulwyn was taken aback. She had never heard anyone refer to him that way. She watched Eurus lift a corner of his lips. She vaguely wondered if this was as close to smiling as he could get.

"That is a new name for you, isn't it? The Corrupted Prince?" he continued as Tarak maintained his pace from left to right. If they wanted to talk instead of engage, that was fine by her. "We know all about you now, Kintana. And you are not in your element here. Galahad has been part of the Uferor for ten years now. What do you think he's done in that time? How do you think he's maintained his position? It isn't by title alone." Eurus jumped off his horse now, circling her.

Ki stomped restlessly, but she shushed him, refusing to cast her glance elsewhere in case they noticed her looking. Daijiro and Galahad should be around now, but she didn't want them to intervene, not yet. And she hoped they knew that.

"What Galahad has or hasn't done isn't any different from what you both have done."

"Perhaps, mock queen, but I know what you stand for." He took a few steps closer. A trickle of sweat formed between her shoulder blades. She knew she couldn't stall them for much longer and she was worried for Ki. She didn't like the way Eurus was eyeing him.

Sulwyn jumped off the horse and slapped his hind leg. Ki whipped his head towards her, affronted, she was sure, but she didn't trust that Eurus wouldn't go after him. "Go, now," she demanded, and with a defiant huff, Ki galloped away.

A strange smile widened across Eurus's face as he watched the horse leave. But before he could raise his spear, Sulwyn grabbed her arrow and shoved it straight at his neck, closing the space between them and holding the arrowhead right against his skin. A small bead of blood pooled along the point.

"You harm my horse, and I will destroy you," she snarled. She regretted ever wondering what it would look like if he smiled. It was wide and thin and nothing short of creepy. Tarak turned away from them and widened his circle, pacing around them slowly and watching for Daijiro and Galahad.

"I'm only playing." But nothing about what he said had an ounce of playfulness. His eyes were dark and Sulwyn knew he wanted to get this over with so he could take her head back to Nero. He gripped the arrowhead tightly, blood streaming gently down his palm as he pushed it down and away. Sulwyn instantly made space between them and unsheathed her sword. "It is my honour, Kintana." He bowed to her before standing straight, his spear pointed towards her. "I've seen you fight countless times before from a distance when you didn't realise anyone from the Empire was there, and when your guardian wasn't with you."

The unease grew in her at his words. She had never realised someone was watching her. Meaning he was stealthier than she could have imagined. She tightened her grip on the hilt.

"You look surprised. I don't think you truly understood the Empire during the time you fought from town to town. But this brings me back to my point, Kintana. You, who fight against the Empire, have sided with the very core of it. The Corrupted Prince couldn't have led the entire Uferor if he had only pretty words and a calm demeanour. How do you think he got that far? He trained personally with Artaxiad for two years before he became the Leader of San, and then the Leader of all of us. What do you think he's done? Better yet, what do you think he *hasn't?*"

Galahad had trained with Artaxiad? This was the first time she heard of it. She had only heard the parts after he had gotten out of the Solus and a little after he had gotten out of the lower dungeons. But she had never really stopped to think about how he had managed to make his way to the Uferor besides the battles that took place for Leaders. She didn't know what else he would have had to do. She didn't really know anything. The ghost of Galahad's ashen hands tightened on her throat, but she shook it away. This wasn't the time for that.

"Did the king train him before his battles for Leader?" she asked, and Eurus's smile grew even more sinister.

"He did. And Galahad killed each prospect with relative ease. But if you've ever seen Galahad fight, Artaxiad's style is in him. To a T."

She didn't think she'd ever seen Eurus so elated. This was more than admiration. Was he fascinated with Galahad? Enamoured?

Sulwyn clenched her teeth. How much did he really know about Galahad? "Everyone has to learn from someone. As he was adopted, it's only right that Artaxiad trained him."

"How accepting," Eurus said, just as Tarak finally dismounted and crashed down behind her.

"What is the point of telling me this? It's nothing I haven't figured out before. If you are trying to get me to distrust Galahad, you'll have to try harder."

"I want you to keep in mind who you're travelling with on your journey, Kintana. Is he a faithful friend? Or the true enemy? You came and overturned all his rights as the next heir." And though she never really thought about how Galahad had made it to become the Leader of all the Uferor, she realised that Eurus had no idea what he was talking about either if he still thought Galahad was interested or even had the chance to become the next king.

"My enemy is the Empire," announced Sulwyn, and she knew this was a declaration, but she didn't care. "My enemy will always be the Empire. And anyone who is part of it or defends it is my enemy as well. If you know me now as Kintana, you will heed my warning." She pointed the sword towards Eurus, keeping an eye on Tarak behind her, who had yet to do much more than stand guard before them.

"And in terms of the 'Corrupted Prince' as you've called him," she continued, finally smelling mint, "there isn't anything you can tell me that would change my mind on where he stands. I may not know everything about him, but you know nothing at all. And I will not tolerate words against him." But before she could make her move, she was frozen in place, her eyes finding Daijiro's red ones as he stepped out of the trees.

A Demon Before Them

| SULWYN |

EURUS turned to the side to see Daijiro walking towards them. Sulwyn was paralysed just before she prepared to charge, the weight of the sword pulling at her wrist. But try as she might, she could not break Daijiro's hold over her.

Cold dread travelled through her veins as she caught his eyes, malice and bloodlust trapped within the reds of his iris. And in that moment, the only thing she could think about was that Daijiro didn't have a posting like her and Galahad. Though she brushed it off at the time as just missing from the ones she saw, she now wondered if it was because he wasn't wanted like they were. Tarak had even asked for her, the "traitor prince", and the girls.

If he was working with the Empire this whole time instead... It was Daijiro who had alerted her to Nero's plan first. Before anyone else could learn more, they left. But was that the point? Had this all been an elaborate game?

"Now, princess, we can't have you injuring the Leaders of our Uferor," he drawled, and Eurus lowered his spear, satisfaction in his eyes.

Tarak laughed, the boom of it vibrating her chest. "You owe me, Eurus. I told you, mad dog or not, he belongs to the king. He was out on a mission and caught wind of the chaos as he always does."

"To the land, to be exact. Unfortunately, there is no king right now," Daijiro said, and she looked at his fist clenched tightly by his side and noticed the strained muscles in his jaw. It took serious concentration to keep her this still, but she was so shocked she hadn't even been trying to escape.

"You're a liar," she hissed, the panic rising higher in her chest as she choked on her words and her heart beat painfully against her ribs. She would make him work for his hold.

Though his eyes were fierce, his voice was calm. "I've never lied to you, Sulwyn." But as she forced against his own will, she could see the struggle in his eyes. "But I don't always speak full truths."

He turned away from her and looked at Eurus. "You took your time. I expected to find you earlier. Is it just Fimm and Vier over the border or did Nero send them all?" he asked casually, but she could see the beads of sweat along his neck. His hold on her was different this time, stronger and tighter. Every time she fought against it, her sight blackened and her head felt as if it were being squeezed through a tube. Stars bursting in front of her eyes with every attempt she made. He glanced at her for a mere second as if to say something, but continued to look at Eurus.

"San went more north towards Pliflyn. En have gone past Wallasyn," Eurus answered, rubbing the back of his head. "She's going to pass out like that. Haven't you told her that it's impossible to break out of your hold?"

"Some need to learn that lesson for themselves," Daijiro noted, and he turned to Tarak. "There are others in hiding that we need to bring back with us some towns away from here. Threats to the Empire. We'll need more personnel to help. There's a Devinal among them."

"No..." whispered Sulwyn. Daijiro's glare ran deep into her soul. When he looked at her like this, it was far worse than any fear she had of him. It was desolate and cold. And she realised now... she couldn't smell anything.

"Only been here for ten minutes and you're already so demanding," Tarak boomed, but he mounted his too-large horse and took off back the way he had come.

"I can't hold her forever. How long will it take Tarak to get to them?" Daijiro asked, walking towards Sulwyn and taking the sword he had given her. She had to hand it to Daijiro, she had gotten cocky, thinking she could easily break his hold. But if he really wanted to, this was it. No matter how much she struggled, she couldn't break it. Instead, it was giving her a pounding migraine, and the inside of her nose tingled like it was going to bleed. But her panic bubbled over to anger. If he was going to bring the Empire to Wilkson, she would kill them all before they got there.

"What did you do with Galahad?" Sulwyn demanded.

"Galahad?" he asked, but Eurus stepped past Daijiro and aimed a punch to her gut instead.

Winded, she gagged, just as the hold over her loosened momentarily. It was in place before she could look up, but Eurus grabbed her by the neck and squeezed. She wondered how many he killed by doing this.

His teeth clenched as he came far too close to her. "You're in no position to demand, mock queen."

Without meaning to, her vision of Galahad's ashen arm and nails on her neck ran through her for the second time since this confrontation started. His eyes as black as night, the fear that flooded her nerves stopped her from struggling against Eurus's and Daijiro's holds.

But his hold was no longer there.

Eurus leapt back before Sulwyn's sword could stab through him.

"I never said you could *touch* her," Daijiro seethed as confusion and tiny dots of light passed through Sulwyn's mind.

"What are you doing?" barked Eurus, holding his spear across his chest in defence.

Daijiro shook his head, twirling the sword in his hand. "I wanted to get more from you. No, let me correct that. I wanted you to *willingly* tell me more. It would have been easier that way. But it looks like you've given me no choice but to do this *my* way. If you just. Hadn't. Touched her…

we could still be civil." Daijiro shrugged, then held out his palm to Eurus, forcing his mouth shut before twisting his fingers up.

She knew by now what that movement signified. It targeted nerves, and though Eurus couldn't yell in any way, she could see his eyes water, his face growing red and veins bulging in his neck.

But she was not done here. Sulwyn stood and marched straight to Daijiro, completely disregarding Eurus in immovable pain. Daijiro faced her with a look of alarm and darted towards Eurus, tapping him on the forehead. Eurus crumpled to the ground, unconscious.

Before she could get a breath out, let alone a word, Daijiro dropped to his knees, hands up, and tossed her sword at her feet. "Before you yell at me, this was Galahad's idea."

"Why don't you have a bounty out for your head?" Sulwyn tried to bring some sort of calm after what he said. But she couldn't. Daijiro was like Galahad, better even, at showing the face of the Empire. And though she knew she shouldn't be surprised, it was still jarring.

"You heard Tarak. We think Nero doesn't know that I've gone with you. I was supposed to be going on another mission to locate Kione," he said hurriedly, but Sulwyn raised an eyebrow.

"Why have I never heard this before?"

"It wasn't pertinent."

"Why would you be looking for Kione and why would Nero care?"

Daijiro's eyes lost the malice as soon as she advanced on him; instead, it was pleading. "He's trying to retrace the last trail. Kione is the only person anyone has seen and can put blame to. He hopes it will help him find Diesirae. You raced off! We made this plan very quickly with what little information we had. It was a long shot. They would believe me, and we only thought of it because there is no posting of me."

"You told them about Wilkson." She clenched her fists, her nails digging hard into her palms.

"I didn't technically tell them about him. Everyone knows there are Devinal here and there, but no one can ever really find them."

"That's not the point!" she yelled, her heart erratic. Slowly, Daijiro began to stand, keeping his hands up and open. "What have you done to Galahad?"

"I told you this was his plan."

"Where is he?" she demanded. Waves of panic, the fear of betrayal as well as the terror of her vision, rose in her. Instead of easing away, they were escalating. Clawing at her from the inside, there were too many emotions in her that she had no other way of expressing besides hysteria.

"He should be tracking Tarak back to their base. For a mission like this, they would have set up a temporary camp not too far. That's what Galahad wanted to find." He started to lower his arms.

"Stop." She glared at him as he stepped closer, but he continued.

"Galahad didn't want to act in case they would harm you, so we did this instead of my plan. He wanted to be cautious first," he started, his eyes still pleading. "He knows Eurus and Tarak better than you or me. I haven't been in the Uferor long. If we made any moves towards you, Eurus would have killed you."

"Again. Again, I am being underestimated! Did neither of you think I couldn't hold my own against him?" she shouted in frustration. "Raghnall couldn't tell me about his plans, using me as bait. Now, you both are doing the same thing! I am a lot of things, Daijiro. But I am done with Galahad or anyone else who keeps treating me like glass. Fighting against the people of the Empire is what I chose to do, what I was raised to do. I've been doing this longer than both of you. You both have the title of the Empire at your feet, and I know it wasn't originally by choice, but the result is the same. The battles you both have faced after receiving your titles are different. You have the king's name to back you up. My fight and your fight are different. They always will be. And I have earned my name, regardless of if it is now tarnished! Why doesn't anyone trust me? Despite everything, even the people won't stand with me."

"You aren't wrong. And no one is saying that. But you should be able to understand this, Sulwyn. Your emotions are disoriented. What is wrong with you?" he asked carefully, and she could see the concern in his eyes, something so fragile and deep looking. She wondered if that's how he looked when he was younger. But this was what she was trying to avoid. She wanted to deal with the Empire first, and then see to her feelings later. But after this, she realised she needed to address them before they added to the stress growing inside of her, distracting her from her purpose.

"As soon as you paralysed me, I couldn't smell the mint," she whispered, unsure of what she should say. "Then I saw your eyes, your face so full of hate. And the fact that you didn't have a posting. I doubted you faster than I could trust you… And—" Daijiro gently grabbed her hand and pulled her against him. His warmth seeped into her cold heart.

"Galahad warned me that if we went through with this plan, you might not react well. He's realised that you don't take well to being betrayed, fake or not. He also knows that your trust is hard to earn, but once given, it's hard to give back. You can beat him up when we catch up."

Heat tingled up her neck. No matter how or when, Galahad always had a way of reading her. In that instant, she realised how deeply she'd come to care for them both.

"You never heard it, but when I told Galahad my tale, I swore on my mother I wouldn't betray either of you… So long as I don't get bored." He chuckled. Sulwyn huffed, hearing the smirk in his words. She wrapped her arms around his waist, the heat radiating off him, burning through the panic and fear that had consumed her. "If I need to with concentrated effort, I can control whether you 'smell' the allure or not. I had to remove all of them. Though they don't know what I am, they would be able to recognise a faint scent eventually. And the anger I gave off wasn't directed to you. It was towards Eurus because I know a tad of what he's capable of. That's why we're going to take him for a bit."

Sulwyn pulled back from him and whistled for Ki. Instantly, he came crashing out of the trees to gallop around her. "Tie Eurus to him, make sure he has no way of hurting Ki."

Daijiro stared at her, but now that she had finally found a moment of calm, the warning of the "Corrupted Prince" rang through her. "Quickly and let's go on your horse and get to Galahad."

Sulwyn turned in the saddle, looking behind her as Ki followed along with Eurus strapped and unconscious on his back. Daijiro assured her that he should be out for the next hour while they continued the plan.

She turned back to the front, leaning past Daijiro to see the tall mounds of rock and dirt that signified the border between Antiqua and Guāngcǎi. Something she never truly understood. The Empire ruled over all Vartugaul. Why were there still different continents? Even before, during the High City times, they were separate. But that was something she would have to question later, because once they climbed past the mounds and down the hills, Sulwyn could smell fresh smoke from the camp's fire.

As they made their way through the trees, Sulwyn pulled a leg up and turned to sit side–saddle for just a moment before jumping onto the ground and running. Daijiro did not protest, and instead tossed her sword in the air.

She caught it, slinging it against her back and taking the bow instead, nocking an arrow just as Daijiro followed suit and jumped off the horse. Ki caught up behind him and grabbed the reins of Daijiro's horse. Both standing still and waiting.

Daijiro and Sulwyn crouched low, swiftly running between the trees and bushes of the forest floor until they could finally see a large clearing in the middle of the bordering continents. Galahad was in the centre, his hands up and in the air as Tarak and his Validus surrounded him.

"We have nothing against you, Galahad," a Validus said, "but Nero's orders are to bring you in alive for questioning. He just wants to get to the bottom of all of this." Sulwyn signalled to Daijiro, and they split.

She made her way around to see the front of Galahad while Daijiro went towards the back. Right now, the only threat was Uferor Fimm. Eurus had been telling the truth about where En and San had gone, though she was unsure of where Vier was. Sulwyn wondered how much trust they actually held towards Daijiro and Galahad to be like this. Even Fimm, who was surprised to face Galahad in this situation, was startled.

Tarak stood closest to him, his gauntlets donned over his large fists, but he held no stance. Instead, he looked at Galahad as if he were ashamed of him. "You're a lot of things, but I didn't think you would be a traitor."

"I'm only a traitor if you aren't on my side," Galahad said, and Sulwyn was sure that he was maintaining a hold over his power.

"We are on the side of the Empire. They have made our lives better," said another Validus. Galahad turned to him, his hands still raised. But he was still armed, his sword on his waist.

"Our lives?" he asked, and she could hear the tremor in his voice. "The lives of the Empire do not outweigh the lives of an entire land."

"The land is toxic!" Tarak said. "Artaxiad made it better for those of us who had suffered enough at the High City's hands. When they cut my family's resources to aid themselves, we struggled before Artaxiad's Ascendancy."

"Who told you that?" asked Galahad, now looking at Tarak.

"We all learned it in the Empire," he said unabashedly. "The High City wanted more power for themselves while ignoring the riots and the strife that continued to grow near the last few years of the High City's reigns. Who do you think tried to stop that and saved us?" He knocked his gauntlets together.

"Who do you think *started* those riots?" countered Galahad, and Sulwyn realised he was trying to get them to their side. Tarak faltered.

"Why are you trying to go against the Empire when they helped you?" said one of the Validus, and Sulwyn's heart dropped. "Wasn't that enough for you to pledge loyalty to their side? They saved you!"

Sulwyn spotted Daijiro across the way, seeing him shake his head as she considered moving forwards. But Daijiro couldn't see what she did. Blackness was starting to creep its way into Galahad's eyes.

"Saved me?" His voice was hollow. Sulwyn realised that no one in the Empire knew his truth. And he never had the opportunity to tell it.

"The Empire destroyed me," Galahad said emotionlessly, and within a second, his hands were ashen black just like his eyes. But still, Daijiro shook his head for Sulwyn to stay still. Instead, she nocked her bow and took aim at Tarak, waiting.

But soon, she was distracted by the same ashy colour of his arms that crawled their way up his neck and under his jaw, until finally, it looked like real ash was falling off his body and collecting into the shadow demon wings she had seen that time ago in the fire.

"What..." Tarak was stunned, his eyes wide in confusion and a little fear. The other men moved back from Galahad, who had yet to make any moves. He watched them all with eyes blacker than night.

"The Empire killed my clan," he started, vengeance rising in his voice. And yet she could see Galahad in front of her. Not controlled by his power or his anger, but channelling it instead. "Just like they killed Daijiro's clan. Just like they started those riots to make people turn against the High City."

"That's a lie!" yelled one Validus, honour clearly in his blood that now spilled before them. Galahad had unsheathed his sword just as the man charged. But he was not fast enough, and now he lay at Galahad's feet, his chest bleeding freely.

"Kintana has poisoned you," spat Tarak, disbelief in his face, hate in his eyes.

"Kintana has freed me," Galahad countered, and Sulwyn tried to think about how Artaxiad stood or what he looked like when he carried a sword. And for the life of her, she could not see his stance anywhere in Galahad.

His stance was regal, it always had been. Angular and calculated and never rash unless he wasn't in control. But he was, and there was a deep sadness as he looked at Tarak and then past him to see her; a minor jolt passed through her as their eyes connected.

"Tarak. I don't want to be your enemy," continued Galahad while the other Validus encroached on him. But they hesitated as they took in the illusion of a demon standing before them.

"Your clan is legendary. Even I know of them, though not much clearly. I've never heard of what you are showing us now," Tarak confessed. "Even I can't believe that the Empire could take them down. But here you are, claiming that it was done. If that is the truth, then why are you here? Why did you stay in the Empire?"

"They destroyed his family, a mere ten-year-old, so they could use him to fight me," Sulwyn said, revealing herself and keeping her arrow aimed at Tarak's head. The Validus stood between them, the four of them trying and failing to decide what to do next. But she agreed with them as they gave Galahad more attention. She would, too, if that was her enemy.

She looked Galahad in the eyes and smiled ever so slightly at his valiant effort. His eyes widened and he lowered his sword, taking a deep breath. But instead of releasing his power, he relished it.

"The Empire is a lie," Galahad said. "The High City may not have been perfect, but it didn't stand atop the people. It stood with them. We only want to bring that back."

"What happened to Eurus?" Tarak asked. Sulwyn noticed his stance had slackened just a bit.

"Tied to a horse," Daijiro replied, stepping out from the trees, his arrow also aimed.

"Galahad is one thing, but I can't see how the king's mad dog is a traitor too," Tarak said, putting his hands down in defeat. "I can't fight all three of you."

"I was never the king's. You heard the prince. My family was murdered as well. But unlike Galahad, I don't care if you decide to come to our side or not. I'd rather kill you now and not worry about you stabbing us later," Daijiro said harshly.

"One woman came and ruined our lives," a Validus replied, but Sulwyn shot the arrow, purposely missing by a hair's breadth and watching the projectile hit a tree.

"One woman brought the Empire down because its foundation was rotten," corrected Sulwyn. "Peace breeds peace. Hate creates death and poison. And that is what the Empire is."

Galahad breathed out deeply, the ashen smoke fading, the black receding and his tricoloured eyes on hers as he spoke to the rest. "War breeds war, and that is what is coming to the Empire regardless of the means. It took one person to start the revolution against the High City. Why would now be any different?"

Sulwyn smirked at Galahad, her eyes never leaving his. "Tarak, unlike Eurus, I think you have the potential to help lead a better world. Everything the Empire has taught you is a lie. The side you are on uses the death of others to stay afloat." She turned to look at him now, Tarak's dark orange eyes on her grey ones. "Aren't you tired of fighting to live instead of just living?"

XXXI

Half Hearted, Half Truths

| SULWYN |

"I haven't been here in a while..." Sulwyn said, forcing open a stone door hidden by vines and leaves in the middle of the vast forest. The door itself was slanted into a rock; a safe house lay behind it created by Wilkson. He'd also tagged it so that only certain people could open it, her being one of them. It had taken them two days to get to it, and she was starting to worry about making it to Antac in time. This safe house had them backtrack and go more south in the direction of Uhuru. But the little village she last visited with Raghnall was still in her plans since they needed to pass by it anyway.

The safe house itself was less of a house and more of a large, round cave with one illusionary window to let in some light. It did have a real sink with water from a well that flowed into it when it rained. Since it had rained recently, it had quite a bit, some spilling over into a drain going back into the ground. There was enough in the safe house storage for someone to live comfortably for about three weeks. Though she wasn't sure if it had been stocked recently. In a corner, there was a small table with a few chairs, and a cot lay off to another side.

Daijiro and Galahad pushed Eurus and the three Validus into the safe house and onto their knees while Tarak walked in on his own, though his arms were bound tightly behind his back. They had blindfolded them all on the way there, only removing them when she knew no one could figure out where they were.

She could see the change in Tarak's eyes and hoped that he would eventually make the right decision. But Eurus and the other Validus were Empire men straight through. And though Daijiro wanted to kill them, she figured it would be best to have less heads on her growing wanted list.

Sulwyn pulled the cloth out of Eurus's mouth only to have him spit on her. She shoved the cloth back in, pulling her hand away quickly as he tried to bite her, but Daijiro kicked him in the head.

"Are you sure you don't want to kill him?" Daijiro purred. Sulwyn rolled her eyes.

"No, but you can take your time getting whatever information you want out of him," she said darkly, and relished in the fact that Eurus grew at least two shades paler. Sulwyn knew what it meant to leave him to Daijiro's way of doing things. She wondered if Eurus would have feared Galahad if he had seen him the way the others had. But Tarak did not say anything to Eurus by the time he woke up. He remained quiet and attentive even when he was blindfolded. She left Ki in charge of his horse's reins because Tarak couldn't fit with anyone else, let alone on any other horse but his.

"You have a day, Daijiro, then we leave," Sulwyn muttered. She turned away from the Empire's men and carefully took out the blue vial and a small notebook from the pouch. She moved to the table and dipped a quill into the vial. Though the liquid looked like it was a deep blue, once it went into the quill it became almost translucent.

She didn't know what to say, trying to keep it as short and discreet as possible, until she decided what to write:

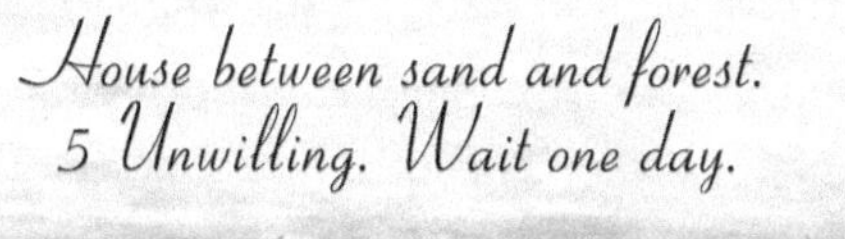

"That's not as cryptic as I thought it would be..." Daijiro mused, looking over her shoulder.

She looked past him to see Eurus listening. "It won't last long. It's good enough."

"That was more cryptic." He rested his chin on her head, but she ignored him despite the flutter in her heart When she finished, she tucked the notebook into a chest pocket and carefully corked the lid of the vial.

"Wait for me before you start," Sulwyn instructed before she turned to Galahad. Without word, he followed her outside of the safe house and back into the forest.

Sulwyn walked a fair bit away to ensure no one could hear them before she sat against a small boulder and looked at Galahad intently.

"I apologise," Galahad said instantly, still standing. She raised an eyebrow and smiled when he remembered she didn't like people standing over her. He took a seat on the leaf–strewn ground in front of her and took her hands in his.

"Daijiro said it was your plan." Now that she was calm, she could see where he was coming from. But it still annoyed her. And she was done with monologues in her head. She needed them to talk.

"I didn't want to use you as bait. But I thought you could hold your own while we figured out a plan. Eurus is dangerous, and the only way I could think to intervene was to send Daijiro out since we hoped he wasn't suspected yet. As for Tarak, he's always been soft-hearted, and though he came from a family that supported the Empire, I wanted to give him the chance to make his own choice. But I didn't want to waste time trying to find their camp among this forest. It's too large and we have limited time before we need to meet back with the others."

"I know..." Her voice quieter than she wanted, annoyed with herself more than anything. "But you need to stop trying to protect me." She looked up at him and could see the unease in his eyes. "Artaxiad taking me was not your fault. It wasn't anyone's. It was the result of Gwydion's allure, or at least, I think it was. Just like actual poison, I now believe that Artaxiad and Pandora were slowly driven mad from years of his influence. Artaxiad became so blinded that it manifested into insanity. Him taking me would have happened either way and neither of us could have predicted that at the time."

He held her hands tighter now. "You have nightmares…"

Sulwyn glanced at a tiny yellow bug near her boot. Watched it scuttle around in search for something. She knew she wouldn't be able to keep the nightmares hidden.

"If I'm being honest, I'd be more worried if I didn't." She squeezed his hand back.

"Do you want to tell me about them?"

She remained silent, watching the bug disappear behind brambles. She didn't want to talk about it. She didn't want to think of it. While she was aware that people of all kinds had been subjected to many types of assault, the fact that it came from her own blood, that he wanted to rape her and create an heir—everything about that disgusted her. Enraged her. It terrified her. And even though she watched as Galahad stabbed him, she couldn't get his leer out of her mind. Of the way he would brush her skin or try to restrain any other desire. She couldn't shake the pain that burned through her when she was whipped, someone who looked almost like her, beating her.

"No."

"Okay… That's okay. But know you can if you ever want to." He tightened his hold on her hand, tracing her scars gently along her arm with the other. But he was fiddling, clearly nervous. Something she rarely saw from him. Then he was looking at anything but her as he spoke. "I should be honest with you, Sulwyn. I have been undermining you without realising it. Using my own need to protect you as a means to cover the guilt I feel. And though I never meant to belittle your skill or experience, it's happened because of my own inexperience and my feelings of failure towards you."

"I'm not your responsibility," she started, and he looked at her. "I am no one's responsibility but my own. And if that gets me killed one day, then it was my choice."

"Sulwyn." He narrowed his eyes.

This was something she never told anyone, not even Raghnall. "I don't see myself surviving this to the end, Galahad. I came to terms with that a long time ago. I just want to see Vartugaul reach peace before then, but if I do fail, I hope I've helped create enough movement that the rest of you can see to it instead."

"Do you understand what you're saying? Is that how you've been living your life thus far?" he asked, letting go of her hands and standing. She stood with him, watching the blackness at the edges of his eyes.

"It is."

Galahad laughed in disbelief. "I am honestly disappointed in you. I thought you valued life more than that."

Sulwyn was affronted. "I never said I didn't."

But his glare cut through her. "Is that why you're so reckless? That you think you can throw yourself at any and all danger as long as you've made it 'far enough'? That mentality is suicidal at best. If you really want Vartugaul to see peace, then you need to be there to experience it, to help create it. Not give up halfway."

"What makes that suicidal? And who said I was giving up?" she exclaimed.

"That is the definition of giving up, Sulwyn. Making peace with your death now with half-assed honour." Sulwyn could see the tremor run through him as he kept his anger in check. "And you are lying to yourself if you really believe that is your truth. I have seen what happens to people who fly too close to that idealism."

Her tongue was heavy in her mouth. She had always wondered if there was a time that Galahad had considered taking his own life. It looked like she was right. But her story was not his. "I am not lying to myself.

The future isn't set in stone, I could die tomorrow, and that is the reality of the Empire."

"Then why are you so afraid of me?" he whispered, raising his hand and gently touching the base of her neck. Instinctively, she stepped back, but Galahad kept pace with her. It was the first time she had ever seen this kind of menace in his eyes. And while she believed she would always trust him, it did make her wonder why he was called the "Corrupted Prince."

"Did you think I wouldn't notice? Daijiro told me when Eurus grabbed you, your will against his hold dropped completely. You're afraid of death." There was sadness in his eyes as he kept his hand against her until she stumbled into the tree, the bark digging into her back.

"I'm not afraid of death, Galahad. And maybe you are right, my ideals towards dying may be half-assed. I know now that that was an old idealism I set for myself. Before I met you and everyone else. But I'm more afraid of what killing *me* would do to *you*." Her voice was hushed as she looked up at him. She fought everything in her that wanted to flee from his touch against her neck. Because he was right and so was Daijiro. Since that vision, the fear of it could paralyse her when she remembered it.

Slowly, Galahad leaned forwards, taking her by surprise, but unlike before when she anticipated his touch, it confused her. It didn't feel the same way to her now as it did previously when they were back in the tent during the fog town assignment. She wasn't sure if it was her fear mixing into it, changing it. But they had moved passed that. Whether Galahad was aware of it or not, she knew that it wasn't the same between them; she just didn't know what it was now or what she wanted it to be. Because he still managed to send a light thrill through her body.

But Galahad didn't move towards her face or her lips as she thought he would. Instead, he moved to her neck and leaned against her. "You said that the future isn't set in stone." His breath against her neck sending shivers along her skin. "I don't want that future to come to pass, and I don't want to apologise in advance for it in case that also sets it into motion. What I want to apologise for is making you feel it when it hasn't happened."

One hand came to rest behind her lower back, the other hand holding hers. "I've always said I wouldn't willingly hurt you, but that wasn't enough. I don't want to be the person that hurts you at all. And whatever is happening to me will be dealt with, but please, do not fear me. Even if it comes to pass," he pleaded.

Galahad pulled away, taking her in and holding her other hand so that they both stood facing each other. "I am bonded to you, no matter how much you try to suppress it for my sake. You are special to me, Sulwyn, and nothing will change that. No matter what happens." He breathed out softly, his tone bittersweet.

A pressure tinged between her eyes and in her forehead followed by that familiar sting of tears, watching his own eyes blur before her as his tears fell too. She stepped towards him, wrapping her arms around him as he did the same. And they stood together, surrounded by the sweet wind of the trees, holding onto each other. Holding their pieces together. Embracing their hearts.

ço<del>ℓ</del>

| DAIJIRO |

"You don't need to be here," Daijiro said, glancing at Sulwyn in the corner. Galahad took Tarak out of the safe house to stand guard outside, while Eurus knelt before them, the other three Validus kneeling behind.

"I've seen interrogations before." She eyed Eurus, whose focus never left her face.

"You've never seen mine," Daijiro added coldly, and he knew his tone took her by surprise from the slight widening of her eyes even if she tried to hide it. "I don't want your impression of me to change." He tried to smirk but the small movement in her hands let him know she heard the subtle softness in his voice.

"Just because we're on good terms, doesn't mean I've ignored what you've done and what you are capable of," Sulwyn said harshly, and for a split-second, they looked at each other. But he gave her a devious smile, earning one in return before he faced Eurus.

"Eurus, you've already seen how I work, do you have anything you want to say before we get started?" Daijiro asked casually, stooping down in front of him and tilting his head to the side with a smile.

He never used his allure when interrogating anyone. He found it cruel, and though many probably didn't think he had a notion of what cruelty was, it was the truth. He would use it to gain information in passing and maybe to sway things a little in his favour. But he never used it as a form of torture.

That was his only rule.

Because his allure was meant to convince or bring a sense of calm. And to make his enemy feel that type of calm while hurting them was dishonourable to his kind, in his eyes. He wouldn't do what Gwydion did.

But with Eurus, he didn't think this would be an issue. Because Daijiro knew what Eurus truly thought of him, and as he looked at him, he could see Eurus knew that as well.

"I don't have words for a traitor," Eurus seethed, and Daijiro noted the nods of the Validus behind him.

Daijiro stood and went past Eurus to the three men. "Let me tell you men about Eurus. He may be your Leader, but there isn't anyone he cares for less than you," Daijiro spat. He watched the men look at him, then at the back of Eurus's head, and he could see the hesitation and fear in their eyes. "If Eurus did care, he would have fought for you. Would have asked me to question him only. Stand before you as a Leader. Not with his back to you. Eurus doesn't care for anyone besides the ideals of the Empire. Though there is someone else..." He trailed off ambiguously.

"You should keep your lies to yourself," Eurus hissed, turning his head slightly to meet his red eyes.

"Didn't you listen? I don't tell lies. But I don't tell full truths either. This is your opportunity to tell me what I want to know, or things will become a little..." He made eye contact with each man before him. He glanced towards Sulwyn, taking in the way she stood with her shoulders drawn and her hands behind her back. Her hair was tied loosely and her eyes set, keeping her glare on Eurus.

She was right. They had been underestimating her. These were the eyes of someone who had seen a lot more than just torture, who had *been* tortured. But it didn't mean he wanted her to watch him do it. Daijiro stopped, looking at her, and continued to pace around them, hands now folded behind his back.

"How did Nero come to the conclusion that Sulwyn is the murderer of Pandora and Artaxiad?" he asked, calmly watching for a response. The man closest to Sulwyn twitched slightly. He sauntered towards him, watching his shoulders quiver.

Daijiro lifted a finger and saw the man struggled to breathe. *Not too much pressure,* he reminded himself. Just enough to make him feel like there was a heavy weight against him, slowly taking his breath away. Daijiro continued to pace, silence spreading between them.

"No takers?" he asked, maintaining his hold on the man until he finally released it. Watching his shoulders relax in relief. Until he did it again, stronger this time and with a hint of pain in his heart.

"A Captain..." His target exhaled, and Eurus whipped his head towards him. The other Validus remained still.

"A Captain? I'll need more words than that. I'll tell you what. The more words you give me, the more control I'll give back to your lungs. Less words and that control is *mine.*" Daijiro stood right behind him, seeing the tremor of fear run through the man. The sweat that beaded against his neck and soaked into his uniform.

"Hold your tongue," snapped Eurus, but Daijiro increased his hold. The man strained to breathe.

He gasped. "A Captain witnessed the princess..." Daijiro lessened his hold. "Witnessed her go to the room the queen was found in. Before anyone knew." Daijiro removed his hold completely and knelt in front of the man.

"Is that all they saw?" he asked, taking the man's chin between his fingers and staring directly into his eyes. Instead of limiting his breaths, he increased the beat of his heart. The man flushed, only able to nod.

"That is for the queen. What of the king? Where is his proof for that?" The man shook his head. "Are you sure?" whispered Daijiro, leaning closer to him and brushing his fingers over the Validus's ear. The man panted heavily, sweat clinging to his hair and face.

"If we tell you what we know, will you let us go?" he begged, and Daijiro heard the click of anger from Eurus's tongue.

Daijiro stood quickly. "That depends on how much worth you can provide me with." He started to walk around again. "Proof towards the king's death. What is it?" This time he noticed the man on the other end, red haired with a scrawny face, close his eyes tightly.

Daijiro flicked a finger down and dropped the redhead's heart rate, watching the man blink furiously at the sudden change in his body. He swayed somewhat as Daijiro brought it back up to normal speed before gradually raising it faster.

"Nero caught someone from the Pain Cells," said the redhead. Daijiro looked towards Sulwyn. She had yet to move, but her eyes had grown colder.

"Who?"

"The one with blond hair…" He panted, and Daijiro lowered his heart back to a normal speed.

"How did he find her?" he questioned, stepping behind this man and stooping down.

He puffed. "She was caught outside of the Empire walls." Daijiro moved closer. Something about that was wrong.

Daijiro leaned towards the man's ear. "And what did he do with her?" He watched the man try and fail to stay still, his shoulders rising to fight against the shiver.

"He tortured her… before she said she saw the princess kill him."

Daijiro looked up at Sulwyn and could see a faint smile on her lips as she glanced back. Chances were that was not the real Eleri, but Diesirae in disguise. What a person to follow. She willingly let herself be tortured just to frame Sulwyn.

"And what did he do with her after?" he asked lightly, gripping the man's shoulder carefully.

"I don't know..."

"She disappeared," said the man in the middle, and Eurus groaned in annoyance.

"Interesting," Daijiro hummed, standing again and moving in front of Eurus. "Do you not find that suspicious at all, Eurus? That the ones sought after most were suddenly at the Empire's door and then disappeared?"

"I trust Nero and his word," said Eurus defiantly.

"You don't trust anyone, Eurus, so don't try that with me." Daijiro scoffed, continuing to pace again. "Let me tell you the truth instead." He glanced at Sulwyn again, who caught his eye. He watched her jaw clench and knew she understood what the result would be.

"Pandora was murdered by your princess," Daijiro explained bluntly, watching all the men turn towards Sulwyn. She stared at them in defiance, but he saw the look of hurt in her eyes. He knew the truth about Pandora had taken its toll on her. No one here needed to know that. "But let me tell you that Nero is uncharacteristically rash. Unsubstantiated." Daijiro returned to Eurus, kneeling so closely that their knees touched. "Sulwyn didn't kill Artaxiad, though she did injure him." Tension radiated all around the room as everyone watched the two. Daijiro bent closer to Eurus's ear, but not too close, knowing Eurus would bite him if given the chance.

"Galahad did," he whispered, smiling menacingly and they all looked at each other with wide eyes and dropped jaws, but none more so than Eurus.

"That's a lie," Eurus spat, and Daijiro leaned back to look him in the eyes. "Kintana has poisoned him."

"If you ask him, he'll say Kintana freed him. Everyone else in this room saw and heard the truth about Galahad except for you, Eurus," Daijiro replied scathingly, looking at the Validus behind him.

"What truth?"

"That Galahad's clan was murdered by Artaxiad and his army. Tell me, would you love a king like that?" Daijiro's red eyes bore into Eurus's.

But Eurus turned to Sulwyn instead. "The Corrupted Prince has fallen because of you," he snarled.

"He is a prince of many things, Eurus, but the Empire's. And not *yours*," Sulwyn said. Daijiro smiled.

"Now, I only have a day to do this, but really, I don't want to spend the whole time with you all in a room. So, I'm going to make this quick." He stood nimbly and went to the first Validus who had spoken. Though he tried to move out of Daijiro's reach, he held up a palm, paralysing him.

"Please don't," he pleaded, but Daijiro pressed a finger to the man's forehead.

The man screamed loudly, the other two scrambling towards the corner of the room, only to fall onto one another. Soon, the screaming stopped, and the man slumped over to the side, his eyes and ears bleeding.

"That really was all he knew. Shame. The Validus are supposed to have more information than the rest of the Néosan and Captains combined. Eurus, you can save these men if you tell me what Nero's next plans are and what the state of the Empire is," Daijiro demanded, returning to Eurus and kneeling in front of him.

"These men cannot hold their tongues. They are of no use to me," Eurus coldly replied, refusing to look him in the eyes.

"Then what use do you have to me?" whispered Daijiro, and this time he leaned forwards, moving closer to Eurus until his face was just an inch away. Daijiro could see the muscles in his jaw tic and the quiver in his throat when he swallowed. The other men behind him stopped their struggle to stare as Daijiro brought a hand to Eurus's leg, caressing his thigh gently.

"I may not have been in the Uferor long, but I know your *longing* to prove yourself towards me and especially Galahad. And I am not unaccustomed to the look of desire from anyone," he purred, watching Eurus, for the first time, look unsettled.

Daijiro glanced down and behind to see Sulwyn staring intently between them. But she kept her expression in check, her eyes never wavering from them, though he did notice the tension in her own jaw.

"What side do you want to stand on?" he continued quietly, seeing the tightness in Eurus's shoulders as he tried to lean further away from him. Daijiro brought his hand up, fingers dragging across the man's chest and resting his palm against the side of his neck. "You needn't fight against us. Just tell me what Nero wants." But Daijiro moved back swiftly right as Eurus attempted to headbutt him.

He switched his playful demeanour to something cold, and his grip on Eurus tightened. "I'm not here to play games, Eurus. You are on the wrong side."

"What is wrong to you is right to me," Eurus barked, spitting in his face. Daijiro lifted Eurus's black tunic from his torso and used it to rub off the spit. Bunching the fabric in his fist, he stared at Eurus while he trailed his hand under and against his bare chest. Whether he meant to or not, Daijiro had elicited a shiver from the Leader.

"I will make sure you regret your choice. Are you sure you're up for that?" Daijiro warned, moving closer again and licking the bottom of Eurus's lip.

Even though he could sense the desire and strain in him, Eurus held his ground. "And when you are done with me, you will kill me as you have countless others. Regardless of if I do or do not do what you want. Regardless of how I see or want you or Galahad," he hissed, eyes lowered as he leaned forwards and kissed Daijiro.

Until he bit him hard enough to draw blood.

"Daijiro," warned Sulwyn. But he'd already pushed Eurus to the ground, holding him with his knee to his chest, an itching sting running through his lip. The memories of his father's death and his mother's blood were a faded version of themselves in the back of his mind for the moment. He wouldn't let blood control him any longer, but that didn't mean he couldn't continue as ruthlessly as he dared.

"The rest of you will serve as a warning," Daijiro snarled, and within seconds, he crushed their hearts. The two remaining men violently coughed out blood, splattering Daijiro's face and Eurus's head, trailing down their uniforms as both collapsed to the floor. Eyes wide and panic-stricken, the only emotion left on their faces.

Daijiro grabbed Eurus's collar and hoisted him up with sheer strength as they stood together. "Last chance, Eurus," he said, licking the blood from his bruised lip.

"This is weak of you, isn't it? This kind of torture? Kintana has poisoned you all, weakened your hearts," Eurus insisted, satisfied by what he'd done and unfazed by Daijiro's maintained proximity.

He had always known Eurus had some sort of attraction towards him and Galahad, and though he wasn't sure if it was because of power, because of who they were, or if it was strictly physical or more, he wasn't surprised that Eurus wouldn't crack under this. Not unless Daijiro genuinely wanted to kill him.

But that had never been his goal today because he wanted Eurus to send a message.

"You know nothing of the heart, Eurus, so I am going to let you go." Daijiro dropped his collar, but Eurus balanced himself quickly. Daijiro pushed him back onto the stone wall and pulled a dagger out of his boot. He cut the binds of rope around his feet and arms, but paralysed Eurus in place before he could attack. "Nero is smart, and I know he's more than he makes himself out to be. He'll see, eventually, the truth and who the real enemy is. But you should warn him that I am on *her* side." Daijiro stepped back, lifting his other hand in front of him before he made a fist and the bones in Eurus's arms snapped.

Eurus clenched his teeth, clearly refusing to yell, but the sweat and redness was instant around his face, his eyes trying not to roll back from the agony and his body convulsing with every move.

Sulwyn opened the door to the safe house and Daijiro led Eurus out, past Galahad and Tarak, and onto the main path of the forest. "Tell Nero to stay vigilant. That is, if you can even make it to him in time," he whispered, kicking him in the back to move forwards.

Eurus turned to face him, but Sulwyn stepped in front of Daijiro, pointing her sword at Eurus's neck and looking up to the cloudy sky. "It's just before noon. If you're lucky, you'll make it back to a Néosan base or somewhere safe before nightfall. Only if you are as capable as you make yourself out to be."

Eurus bared his teeth, but one look at Daijiro's glare and he was moving forwards until they could no longer see him.

XXXII

A Woman & Two Men Walk Into An Inn

3 departed. 1 possible. 1 returned.

SULWYN and Galahad buried the Validus and left Tarak in the safe house for Wilkson to collect. Once they were on the move, they continued at a slower, more cautious rate, the three of them finally managing to cross back over the border and into Antiqua. Somehow, Sulwyn thought there would be riots or leagues of Néosan waiting for them, but they just continued their desolate path of now-rocky terrain.

"Are you sure this is the right direction?" Galahad asked just as the clouds overhead grew dark. The days had started to grow colder faster now, the harvest moon over, and she was sure it would start to snow soon.

"I'm not too accustomed to the towns of Antiqua, but I am sure this is the right way. It was a small village that we passed through. And though I thought it was only for food, Raghnall had insisted on going here. Why?"

"This is the direction to Eztli's village…" Galahad said.

Sulwyn looked towards the outskirts of the hamlet. She'd never imagined she could be tied to someone she had met from the Empire aside from the king, queen and Galahad. She'd have to tell Eztli when she saw her.

By the time they neared the town, it began to rain, and though it was cold, Sulwyn was grateful for a reason to put up her hood.

"Have you thought of how you will ask anyone if they saw Raghnall without drawing curious eyes?" Daijiro asked just as they passed the village gate, briefly stating their business.

She glanced at him, glad that her eyes were hidden from his. Since interrogating Eurus in ways she didn't expect, Sulwyn had trouble looking him in the eyes without feeling flustered. "We plan to stay the night and restock, right? I'm sure I'll come up with something."

His stare lingered but she chose to ignore it, instead looking through the familiar village. It was early afternoon and all the people huddling about their business moved quicker as the rain picked up.

Once they got to the inn, Galahad paid for a room that all three of them could share. They needed to stay inconspicuous during their visit. Even though Galahad was familiar with the town. They spotted a few wanted posters. Though this village didn't have half as many people as Pliflyn did.

Sulwyn patted Ki gently, giving him her last apple. "You need rest, comply with the horse keeper, okay?" she whispered, and he nuzzled her shoulder in response. She turned to the woman waiting for his reins. "You don't need to tie him. And he'll resist if you try." The woman nodded, a little confused, side-glancing at Ki, who only snorted her way.

The trio made their way to the room, a small but cozy place, well taken care of in the rundown inn. A crackling fire greeted them as they entered the space. There were two beds and a cot, all situated along a wall. A small night table and a long mirror. The bathing room was shared, somewhere out in the hall they had just walked down.

Silently, Sulwyn went over to the cot, dropping her bag onto it and shedding her cloak. Their eyes bore through her back. She knew they were both watching her, but she continued her movements, slinging the sheathed sword off her back and the bow and arrows, and adding it to the pile. If there was one luxury she envied when travelling, it was baths. And before she did anything else, she wanted one to clear her mind and her heart. She wondered vaguely if it was rude of her to ask them if she could have some time alone, but before she could say anything, Galahad tapped her on the shoulder.

"Sulwyn?" he asked carefully, and she realised she had gotten lost in thought.

"Sorry," she mumbled, watching Daijiro and Galahad share a glance.

"We're going to find the things we need before leaving early tomorrow. I have a source in this village, so it should be okay. Do what you need to," he continued, touching her lightly on the shoulder.

She lifted her hand to his. "Thank you," she whispered, earning a nod before he dragged Daijiro along with him. Daijiro cast her one last look before he followed out the door of the room.

Sulwyn sighed loudly as soon as they left, lying back on the cot and staring at the worn, wooden ceiling. She had a lot of time to think to herself on their way here and about what it meant to forsake the name Kintana, especially after facing the Validus.

Going to all these places without hiding her face only to have her face exposed anyway was one thing. But to have so many against her after such a short amount of time made her wonder why she was even doing this in the first place. Why was she going so far?

Everything she and Raghnall had done was negated in a few weeks with the news and bounty and the knowledge that she was their daughter. And maybe it was naïve of her to think that the people would stand up for her name and believe in her just a bit more. But she didn't think so. She'd bled for people she didn't even know. How could that go up in flames in a short amount of time?

Sulwyn huffed, grabbing her cloak and whipping it at the wall, knocking her weapons down in the process. Frustration had been building in her, but this wasn't the time for her to regret her choices. No, that was a lie. She'd never regret her choice. She just wished people had more trust in her.

"A bath. A bath will make me feel better," she told herself as she gathered a towel from the small closet and a change of clothes, and placed them on one of the beds. She took off her boots and started to prod the wooden floor with her feet, banging them along the way with her heel until one shook a little in its place. Prying it open, she shoved her weapons and her bag into it before she picked up her bundle and left for the bathing room down the hall.

It was a small space with two working toilets and another room where a large bath was drawn for the evening. She was just in time as one of the maids finished warming the water, closing the large, coal-filled heater in the corner. She curtsied towards Sulwyn, staring at her.

Sulwyn let her hair down, hoping that it covered most of her face and that the lady didn't recognise her. Or maybe if she did, she would be that small amount of hope she was looking for. Either way, the lady looked at her briefly, hurrying to her next duty.

As soon as she left, Sulwyn located a wooden chair with a sturdy back and shoved it under the handle of the door. She didn't think the place would be busy enough to swarm the bathing room, and the toilets were still open for the rest, but she didn't want to take a chance.

Quickly, she stripped and tossed her dirty clothes to the corner before rinsing with a bucket off to the side and scrubbing the dirt off her dry skin. This water was cold, shocking her nerves, but once she was done, she stepped into the large bath of hot water. As she settled into it, she figured it was large enough to fit six other people.

Being outside for so long had numbed the tips of her toes and fingers, but she relished in the tingle as they thawed, the water warming her to her core.

Sulwyn found a spot in the corner with a ledge and leaned against it, submerging her head underwater before coming back out, her eyes closing. But as soon as she closed them, all she could see was Daijiro and the way he had touched Eurus, and instantly, she became uncomfortably hot. She knew he had a way of reading people, but she honestly didn't expect that kind of plan from him.

Since he displayed that kind of tactic, she wondered even more about him. How he had gotten so skilled to not only be someone of mass destruction but delicate enough to make someone like Eurus expose his intent to him. She was also unsettled by the fact that she had become so desensitized to violence, because Daijiro had killed those other Validus just after trying to seduce Eurus, and it hadn't even bothered her.

What *did* bother her was how irritated watching him made her feel. How her skin tingled as he brushed his hand over Eurus lightly. Or how, for a moment in that room, she wished it were her on the receiving end of his touch, though not as someone being interrogated, but as someone more intimate to him.

Sulwyn growled out in annoyance as the water seemed like it had grown hotter around her instead of soothing. Hot not only to her skin but within her and to her centre. Her heart tremored, and instead of relaxing, she was even more tense.

This was her own fault.

She rarely paid attention to herself when she travelled with Raghnall. And the last time she had been on a mission alone, before arriving at the Empire, was a long while ago. But here, surrounded by warmth and brief safety, the thought of being touched and the increasing irritation… she figured she should use this time to relax herself.

When she got back to the room, even more aggravated than before, Galahad and Daijiro had not returned. Sulwyn stood by the small fire, drying as much of her hair as quickly as she could before she did a quick sweep, taking her bag and weapons out from the floor, donning her cloak and boots and leaving the room, locking it. After departing from her home, they had all agreed never to leave any of their things behind in case they needed to run.

The rain had stopped, but the sky was still dark, even though it wasn't evening yet. There was enough daylight to wander. As she looked up and down the cobblestone street, it seemed like only yesterday when she and Raghnall were running from a band of Néosan. Somehow, the memory made her laugh despite what happened after and she tried to maintain that emotion as she walked down the road.

When she and Raghnall had parted ways in the town, she went to wait near a small bookstore while Raghnall went to gather food. But now that she thought about it, he had only managed to snag stale bread. And even though he said a rotation had come around recently, she noticed that the stores were in decent shape.

If what Galahad said was true and this was Eztli's town, then it was under his protection at the time. As per his deal with Eztli being the main cook, the rotations to this village were retracted. Which meant Raghnall had lied and picked up food from wherever he could to maintain his ruse.

Sulwyn walked towards a small bakery with a mini cart outside the store, selling whatever was left for the day. She made her way directly to it, watching patrons pick up a few things in small baskets or bags. Even for end-of-day bread, they had quite a bit to go around.

Raghnall's bread was stale and plain, so there were only a few places he could have snagged that from without notice. She would start there.

She pulled her hood closer and walked across the cobblestone street to the small cart. A man looked up at her curiously but stayed silent as she glanced at the different breads. But as she looked at them, she realised that their breads were too intricate. Raghnall's bread was pitiful, like something given on the side of a meal.

She waved to the man, shaking her head and carrying on. If the person wanted to meet with him, she didn't think it would be in the bar. A place like that talked far too much, with too many eyes around. If he really did meet with Diesirae, then it would have been somewhere more desolate.

A chilly wind blew past her, carrying the smell of iron and sweet meat. She turned to see a tiny shop that specialised in quick meals. She realised this town must now be a primary rest stop for Néosan. There was no way Galahad could write off an entire village because of one girl. They must have had to earn their keep another way, and serving food would be the best way to do so. It explained why they seemed to be well stocked.

She continued down the street that was now a little more deserted than before with the fading daylight. She watched a young woman with a long torch go around the shop fronts and light the large lanterns that lined the road every so often.

Sulwyn opened the door, a little bell tinkling along, just as the shop-keeper turned to her. It was a younger man, reminding her briefly of Zander from his slender frame to his brown eyes. But she had never seen this man before and chose to stay quiet and take an unoccupied seat.

The place itself was rather spacious, possibly to hold copious amounts of Néosan instead of keeping them outside where they could cause trouble. But the number of seats inside were limited, probably to keep them from staying too long either.

"Can I get you something? We're closing soon, so we might not have much," said the man, looking at her a little warily, but then she noticed a small bracelet on his wrist.

"Where did you get that?" she blurted out.

He looked at her in confusion before his eyes widened in surprise. Sulwyn got up and moved closer to the counter so that the other patrons couldn't hear her.

As she looked at the black cord bracelet, she could see a small circle within a square that held the bracelet together. But it was the symbol she recognised; it was Raghnall's old badge symbol that could be found on his uniform from his High City days. He had shown her the uniform once, and though it was a symbol he kept hidden, she had seen it a few times with people they had come across from time to time. The last one being the dying woman in the lower dungeons of the Empire shortly after she had arrived.

Sulwyn herself never had one, and neither did he or Wilkson and his family. It was something that others wore to signify their allegiance to the Steel Warrior and his cause.

"Oh, you're here! I've got your order in the back. Needed to keep it cool," he started swiftly. Sulwyn glanced over to the few people eating. They looked like men and women who worked outside the village, farmers and herb collectors. She knew this town didn't have much else unless they travelled elsewhere for work.

"I'll pay you when I see it. So many towns get this order wrong," she replied, and he lifted the wooden counter to the other side. She passed through it, and together, they went to the back. But Sulwyn was skeptical, and with his back to her, she pulled out one of the short swords on her hidden waist belt.

As soon as they entered the backdoor, the man turned and reached for her hood, but she pushed him back against the wall and held her blade to his throat.

"Scream, and I'll cut you," she whispered, tossing her hood back. The storage room was illuminated by a small torch, and it flickered angrily across the man's face. But instead of looking like an enemy, he was startled.

"Kintana..." he whispered back, straining away as he tried to swallow. His neck pressed dangerously close to her blade, but she let up a bit.

"Where did you get that bracelet?" she demanded, but he held up his hands.

"The Steel Warrior gave it to me for some bread." He spoke fast. "I didn't understand why. He could have gotten the real stuff from the man up the street, but he wanted this and something else."

Sulwyn pushed the blade closer, keeping her forearm firmly against his chest. "When did you see him?"

"Earlier this year, you both were here. Though I only saw you from down the street."

"What did he ask of you?"

The man kept swallowing, his eyes watering. "I don't really understand what he meant," he stammered.

"Just say what he asked!" she hissed.

"He said 'if Kintana ever comes back around, tell her that whatever she has probably guessed so far is right or close to it. Trust your instincts.'"

"Dammit, Raghnall!" Frustrated, she removed the blade, pushing the man back a little. "When was this?"

"Just before he met with a woman," he answered clearly, happy the blade was far from his artery.

"Did she have deep bronze skin and long black hair?" she asked, putting the blade back, but he reached forwards slowly to stop her.

"Shaved on one side? If that's the one, then yes. There was a moment, though…" he started, but was too afraid to continue.

"Out with it!" Normally, she wouldn't be this impatient, but with how she had been feeling since her bath and being so close to some kind of answer, she was quickly losing patience.

"I'm sorry! Maybe I should have intervened? The Steel Warrior helped my family in the past, and I…" He trailed off, rubbing his hands over his eyes, tears falling.

"Take a deep breath and just explain," Sulwyn said, her teeth clenched while her heart tried to make its way out of her throat.

"There was a moment where the lady got drinks for them both, but before she brought it to him, she spit something into his. After he drank, for just a few minutes, the Steel Warrior looked dazed." His words tumbled over each other. "I thought she must have drugged him. Should I have gotten the Néosan? But they don't help anyone, and they were already causing trouble outside even though they should only be passing through. Anyway, a few minutes later and he was fine again. I didn't think anything of it after that, and she left soon after. But he was fine, took the bread, made a deal with me, then ran after you."

"You foolish man, Raghnall," said Sulwyn harshly. He had put too much trust in her, and in himself, without even knowing what the real threat was.

The man reached for her again, this time grabbing her wrists. But just as he did so, hot pain rushed its way through her right leg and into her chest.

She crashed onto her knees from the shock of it, dazed by how real it felt, as if she had been stabbed. Sulwyn looked up at the man, but he was even more bewildered and terrified than before.

"Please, Kintana, listen to me. There are Néosan hiding here, on the outskirts of town from the north side. If you didn't see them, you must have come from the south. You need to leave!" he exclaimed frantically, eyes wide and tremors of fear running through him.

But when she heard the screams, she knew it was too late to run. Sulwyn stood quickly and slapped the man, grabbing his collar and pulling him close. "You need to calm down, okay?"

The man just nodded profusely. "Okay, okay."

"Do you have any family in this village?" She let him go, gently placing her hand on his chest.

"He saved them once but… no… My family…" He looked away, his face haunted.

"You need to get out of here. Now. Take whatever you need quickly and go," Sulwyn ordered, moving to leave the room but turning back briefly. "Thank you, for not betraying us."

Sulwyn ran out of the room, pulling her hood back on, and exited the store. In the streets, people ran past her, trying to find shelter and barricading doors and windows. About fifty or so Néosan were marching towards her direction, but a commotion of something she couldn't see was happening behind them.

Again, a stabbing sensation throbbed through her leg, her steps faltering as she walked. But with each step, the pain started to recede as she stuck to the edge of the street and made her way forwards. She went around the back of one small building, avoiding detection, travelling the rest of the way hidden in the alleys.

Finally, she made her way to the end of their formation to an open space where the stores ended, and carriages and other large supplies were stored. In the distance, she could see Galahad moving backwards and away from the oncoming barrage of Néosan. He had hidden behind a stack of barrels, clutching his knee.

Sulwyn stared at him, watching as he held his hand over the wound and concentrated. For a moment, a sting pinched her one last time until it disappeared altogether, and he was leaning his head back.

There was no way.

He said himself that she wasn't part of his clan and that the bond would be one-sided. Or so he assumed.

She ducked behind a pile of crates at the sound of someone giving out orders. She waited until their attention was with the Captains and stooped low, running towards Galahad and sliding to a stop in front of him.

"Sulwyn!" Surprise in his eyes and voice, but soon, he moved forwards to kneel. "They have more on the way," Galahad said, getting straight to the point, but Sulwyn just waved him off.

"What happened to your knee?"

"How do you know about my knee?" he asked dumbfounded, but then he glanced at her knee and back to her. "No…"

"I felt it a few minutes ago. What happened?" He looked horrified more than anything.

"My shadow was seen. I didn't expect them, and an archer nipped me. But Sulwyn, just like you blocked me from feeling your pain, I need you to do the same!" he hissed and paused as the Néosan started their march again. He pulled her close against him as they both hid behind the barrels.

"I was going to." She breathed into his shoulder, his chest hot from running. "But you seem less thrilled than I thought you would be," Sulwyn replied, knowing that to bond with someone both ways must be special.

He moved her back a bit, looking at her carefully. "I am thrilled, really I am. The only people I personally knew who were bonded were my mother and her sister. And it helped them out a lot. But when I…"

He trailed off. "When I don't have control or start to lose it, it's painful and disorienting. That can't affect you too."

"It won't, I'll block it, but Galahad, this is good. I don't know how it works, but we can rely on it sometimes. If we ever get separated or captured!" she quietly exclaimed, but an eruption of some kind alerted them to the Néosan and the town that was screaming.

"No," he started, grabbing her arm.

"I need to, Galahad, they will burn this town down to ash until they find me. Someone must have alerted them if they've made their move. I already found out they'd been camping out on the outskirts of town."

"I know. Daijiro went there to try and destroy it. But Sulwyn, you needn't add more to your burden!" he hissed. She just glared at him.

"It's not a burden to save people, and I know you know that. I'll be fine. Running from the Néosan is my specialty. They want me more than you. Can you and Daijiro get the people out?" she pleaded.

Galahad clenched his jaw tightly before nodding. "Fine. But if they get too close, run. Understand? There's a toxic lake a day's journey northwest from here. Let's meet and hide. Few go there."

Sulwyn gripped his hand tightly. "I will. But don't worry." She winked and took off running.

XXXIII

Fire & Carnage, Ice & Happiness.

| SULWYN |

SULWYN nocked an arrow and released it quickly.

On her way towards the Néosan, she urged everyone to either stay hidden or leave. She was happy they were all in the mood to comply.

A strangled cry met her ears as she nocked another arrow and let that fly too. It embedded itself into the back of one of the Néosan and once he fell, they all turned to see her standing in front of them. She only had one arrow left and made a note to get her own set soon.

"How dare you step in the way of the Empire!" cried one of the women, but Sulwyn didn't have time for their banter. She lowered the hood of her cloak, the torches enough to illuminate her face to them all.

Instantly, many froze. But some began to prepare their weapons, ready to try and catch her and claim the reward. She knew that many of the Néosan were forced to be part of the army, knew that given the opportunity, they wouldn't fight for the Empire ever again. She needed to appeal to them and hope the rest would stand down for now.

"It's the fake queen!" cried one man. Sulwyn slung the bow back over her shoulder, placing her last arrow in one of the slots on her belt and drew out her sword instead. The bright Velika metal reflected spots of rainbow in the firelight. The violet swirls and matte black hilt a stark contrast to its shine.

"You must feel so powerful threatening a defenceless town," Sulwyn goaded. "Will Nero give you a reward for that?"

"Silence, mock queen!" yelled others, but Sulwyn had their attention. Fifty or so Néosan wouldn't be too much to handle while she waited for Galahad to get the others to safety. She hoped he found Daijiro on the way so they could get the job done quicker. It would be easier for Daijiro to get them to follow if they were resisting.

"We shall bring peace to the fallen king and queen!" called another, and this caused hype among those who wanted to fight. But Sulwyn still spotted the few reluctant ones around them.

"Peace has never existed *because* of the fallen king and queen!" she returned, catching a couple of the Néosan glancing at each other and slowly stepping back.

"Lies! You murdered our king and queen! Murderer!" yelled a woman, but Sulwyn scoffed.

"You go around murdering the innocent on the whims of their tyrannical words, and *I'm* the murderer?" she exclaimed, but soon an arrow launched itself towards her. Sulwyn deflected it with her sword, but another whistled through, and then another.

Sulwyn deflected as many as she could, but one scratched past her shoulder, another against her thigh. She looked behind her, spotting a few haystacks by the inn, and ran. She hoped Ki escaped outside the village like she told him to if danger was around.

"Face us, coward! Can't you kill us without sneaking around like you did with your own mother and father?" called a man. "Or we will continue our path through this town and make anyone who has seen you talk."

Sulwyn took a deep breath and sheathed her sword. Slowly, she came around the haystacks with her hands up, facing them all. "I will cooperate, but only if you leave this town."

"This town no longer has the prince's protection. A mock queen cannot negotiate that."

"Harm anyone in this town and you will have me to answer to," she warned, slowly walking closer to them.

Many of them laughed or jeered at her declaration, but she continued to walk forwards as they nocked arrows or held up their swords and daggers. If she were shot now, it could kill her, but she just needed to keep them distracted until all the screams of fear could no longer be heard and she knew the people were safe.

"You can't kill me," she started. "Nero wants me alive. How else is he going to prove my hypothetical crimes? And how else will you get your reward?"

"Shut up!" yelled a man, but she saw his bow and arrow quiver.

"You should know the truth about the Empire, though," she continued, gaining the attention of a few. "They were never on your side."

One man roared and shot his arrow. Sulwyn dodged it, but it nicked her on the other shoulder, deeper than the last. Her eyes watered from the air's sting, but she forced herself to ignore it.

"The Empire has been lying to you since the beginning," she went on. "They started those riots years before the fall. Using the civil wars as acts of treason to rise up."

"What lies she speaks!" a woman cried, and she shot an arrow as well.

Sulwyn turned her back quickly, using the sheath to deflect it, but someone else shot one as well and this one she couldn't block.

Pain ripped through her as the arrow scraped deeply past her ribs on the left side. The sting was like fire crossing through her, burning her with the air. Even though it was a shallow wound, the blood fell quickly.

"Only a coward would lie about her own blood after killing them!" cried a man, and many cheers joined him.

"One versus an entire platoon of Néosan seems more cowardly," called Daijiro, stepping out of the alley to her left. "And there are no more townspeople left for you to use as leverage." He walked closer, his smile towards the Néosan bright, but there was murder in his eyes.

Some of the Néosan bowed but many did not, whispers and talk whipping between them. "There are rumours you've become a traitor!" said a man near the middle. If that was true, did Eurus survive?

"Are there now?" he asked, his hands behind his back as he stepped right in front of Sulwyn, before finally, he turned to face her.

"We got them out," he whispered. "Galahad is covering their backs until they get farther away. He's dealing with a smaller squad that stayed at the border first." He faced the Néosan again.

"Finally." Sulwyn breathed heavily, unsheathing the sword.

"Looks like the rumours are true!" said a man. "The Empire won't protect you any longer, Daijiro. We all wondered why you were denounced from All-Command and Leader of Divi. Looks like this is the reason."

"I was denounced? That's unfortunate. I've been with the Empire for twelve years. You think some loyalty would have been earned." He shrugged but turned back to Sulwyn, his eyes glancing over her shoulders, knee and side bleeding through her cream tunic even though she tried to hide it with her cloak. If Daijiro's eyes were murderous before, they were plain monstrous now.

"You can get your honour back!" called a woman. "Capture her alongside us and we can split the bounty. There's more than enough for all of us! Take the mock queen and let us go back to the Empire!" Daijiro began to laugh instead.

"Forget him," said another Néosan. "He's not sheltered by the Empire any longer. Nero took away his titles because he is a traitor! A weak-minded follower!"

"Do you really think the Empire shelters anyone?" he called, his eyes ecstatic. "Do you think they protected me from the traitors and the enemies like they promised you they would?" His voice grew louder, but a hint of a growl stayed in his words. She knew he was losing to whatever drove him into his frenzied state of bloodlust. But she also knew he would regret it more now that he had come so far.

"Actually..." He turned towards Sulwyn again. He pushed her cloak aside, his warm hand passing over her wounded ribs, taking blood on one palm and rubbing it together. "Now that I think about it, the Empire *was* a shelter. It sheltered all of you. But not from the outside." His tone growing a little madder with each word, his blood-coated palms open before him.

"They sheltered you from me."

"Daijiro, stop!" Sulwyn roared, stepping into his back, grabbing his hands and pushing them down. He struggled against her hold, clearly conflicted on how much force he should use on her.

"Take them both!" yelled a man, but Daijiro fought her grip and held up his palm once again. The man dropped to his knees, screaming and writhing in agony. The Néosan around him moved away, startled and afraid of what was happening. Sulwyn knew that unless they ranked high, few in the Empire knew Daijiro's true abilities.

"Half of these people are fighting in fear and you know that," Sulwyn whispered closely. Daijiro bared his teeth but instead of listening to her, he forced ten other men down. They tried to grab the legs of other Néosan as they fell, scraping the skin of their throats and trying to breathe. Though there were fifty or so of them, they all froze, probably wondering if the bounty was high enough to make them face him.

Daijiro closed a fist, keeping it out of her reach. She could hear the crack of bones and watched as the ten men collapsed, their necks broken.

"There is nothing to fear here," started one of the Captains, his dark brown uniform standing out against the tan of the other Néosan. "He is no longer part of the Empire. He is but one man!"

With his call, many roared, raising their weapons, though fear kept them still. But Sulwyn still held onto Daijiro. "It's not worth it to fight here!" she hissed.

Daijiro turned to her, enraged. "They are after you!"

"I know that, that's why we're running! You know we need to keep the deaths to a minimum. There's no point in saving Vartugaul if there's no one left to save!" she exclaimed, but the Captain yelled louder.

"The Empire saved Vartugaul!" he called as he charged right at her. Sulwyn turned and brought her sword to meet his, pushing him back and gaining the advantage. She quickly slipped forwards and slashed at the back of his calf.

The man tumbled to the ground and Sulwyn rushed back to Daijiro, seizing his arms just as he'd raised both hands and forced the Néosan to the ground. But this time, he twisted out of her grip and turned her around so that her back slammed against his chest, her wrists locked in his hands behind her back. "They are here to hurt you." He exhaled heavily, but she didn't want him to succumb to this because of her.

"*You* are hurting me as well, Daijiro." She leaned her head back, looking up at his red irises. His teeth were still clenched and she could see an edge to his eyes. "People change. You've changed. We've both hurt each other in the past as well. There is enough blood on our hands. Don't kill these people."

His grip on her wrists slackened but she could feel his chest heaving, a slight tremor going through him, panicking. Just as he was when he thought she was losing her grip on the task at hand. But she knew what it was like to panic and be unable to control it.

"We don't need to keep killing. We're alive and it is our duty to extend the same to others," she whispered, raising her hand to rest on the back of his neck. Daijiro stared at the Néosan in front of them, his eyes daring them to step forwards. Quickly, he grabbed her hand and ran, turning a corner, through a dark alley, and back towards one of the now-abandoned storefronts.

Looking through the windows quickly, he ushered her inside and to the back, but before she could protest, he trapped her against one of the wooden walls, blocking her with either arm. Sulwyn looked around, seeing piles of folded fabrics and cooking utensils but was soon distracted by his glare of anger mingled with fear and something else. Something rather feral.

"Sulwyn, I can't handle this." His teeth clenched so hard his voice muffled. His hands curled into fists against the wall. "I can't see these people look at you in fear. Like you're some sort of monster. Like Pandora or Artaxiad or me. The bounty on your head is undeserving. They don't deserve your kindness." He stepped closer to her, his head lowering. "They will kill you for a system they still think is in place. They don't deserve you." His eyes were level with hers.

She could see the tremble in his arms, either out of terror or hate, she couldn't tell. But she could see the conflict that shone in his eyes, debating between doing what he knew was right and what he was used to doing for all these years.

"The system will fall in time," started Sulwyn softly, "and when that happens, I want them to remember me, you and Galahad as people who stood by what we believed in since the beginning. If you kill these people, you are no different from Artaxiad and Pandora and who you turned into because of them. You will spread fear through them all and it will be the same vicious cycle all over again." She stood straighter and he moved back, watching her carefully.

"There is no logic in lawlessness. Right now, it is chaos and the Empire still has Nero. They still think Gwydion is one of them, not a Devinal and definitely not a Velyūn. And all the while he's carrying out his plans behind everyone's back. Getting closer to whatever he's striving to achieve."

"I didn't think this would be an easy path, Daijiro. I'm prepared for what's to come!"

"I AM NOT!" he thundered, aiming a punch to the wooden counter beside them. Sulwyn looked at his hand, seeing an instant bruise alongside a small spark of fire. She stared into his eyes, seeing the expression of torment that he carried and having no idea how to break him out of his despair.

Slowly and gently, she lifted her hands and took his now-burnt and bruised one in her own. He looked at her, becoming utterly still as she led his hand to her chest. His brows knitted in confusion, but before he could speak, she cut him off.

"My heart, Daijiro. Feel my heart." She left his hand upon her chest, her own hand atop his. The heat that soaked into her from his touch was maddening but she took his other hand and placed it against his own heart, her other hand just under it so that she could feel the beat of his; quick and strong enough to shake his body ever so slightly.

"You forget who I am. I won't die that easily…" she whispered, thinking of her conversation with Galahad. Knowing he was right and that she couldn't be as reckless as she once was.

Daijiro silently stared at her, his eyes wildly darting back and forth between her own. He took his hand from his own chest, bringing it around her back and pulling her closer. Sulwyn could feel her own heartbeat grow as erratic as his and watched the fear in his eyes fade into something else unsure yet confident. Ever since he had started opening up to her and Galahad, he'd grown a little wilder, but so did his trust. However, with it, a growing paranoia began to take shape. Something that made her think he believed that one day she would disappear once he let her in too much.

Slowly, he moved his other hand away from her chest and to her neck, his fingers moving carefully to the side and pressing. She could feel the pulse in her veins as he pressed a finger against it and watched him relax as if confirming her existence and her words. Confirming her being.

In the distance, she could hear voices coming closer and wondered if the Néosan had decided to regroup and search for them again. But she chose to ignore it, her eyes never leaving his. The smells she had come to enjoy wafted around her. And though she reminded herself that they weren't real, it didn't stop her from anticipating them when they came naturally and subconsciously to him.

Soon, both of his hands were moving along her lower back, heat continuing to seep throughout. He leaned in, his chest and waist pressed against her. His lips gently moving like a flutter of feathers near her neck. Sulwyn realised he was validating her, searching for the beat of life that ran through her. He pressed his lips to where her pulse was strongest, leaning further into her and pushing her back against the wall, his hands moving to her wrists.

Sulwyn could hear his breath and her own loudly in her ears despite the rising sounds outside. And though she knew they needed to move, she didn't want to. Her breathing grew rougher as the heat between them spread further, hearing his own breath echo hers. Until unexpectedly, he nipped her neck just where her pulse sat, and it sent a trail of goose bumps down her collarbone, arm, and leg.

Her shoulders lifted in reflex, only to receive another smaller bite that sent more shivers through her. Trying to tame her wild breathing, she took her hand out of his gentle grip and reached to touch the back of his neck. Running her hands through his fair hair, which had gotten longer in the last few months, reaching past his collar.

His hands were on her back, his lips by her neck, teeth scraping her skin. What was happening?

Instantly, the panic and tension that had been rising within him melted as his shoulders dropped and he kissed her neck softly, bringing her tightly against him and holding her.

After seconds, which might as well have been hours, passed, the yells were growing closer. "Daijiro…" she whispered. They needed to run, leading the Néosan away from the village, and meet up with Galahad. "Daijiro," she repeated, stronger this time. "I will always be here." She hugged him back firmly while he cried into her.

❧

"Ki!" Sulwyn shrieked as the horse galloped to meet her, leading Daijiro's horse with him, keeping to the shadows and away from the Néosan. She realised that Ki had become sort of a leader to the other horses and noticed that they would follow him without prompt. Galahad's was nowhere to be found and she could only assume that meant he had gotten out safely as Daijiro had said.

Sulwyn and Daijiro mounted their horses and proceeded to run straight through the village, passing the Néosan on the way.

"There! Capture them!" yelled another Captain, and soon they were mounting shared horses. Sulwyn turned back, seeing fires in the distance. She hoped the village people could come back to their homes but knew they wouldn't.

The Empire would mark this village as an aid to the enemy and pillage it when the chance arose. She hoped anyone hiding would get out in time before that happened. But until then, they needed to flee.

Daijiro was silent after they snuck out of the abandoned store, and she could not read where his thoughts lay. Instead, she decided to carry on as she normally did and told him the plan to go to the toxic lake nearest. She hoped that Galahad was making his way there now after ensuring the people's safety.

"They're going to catch up with us at this rate if you want to maintain your no-kill plan," called Daijiro, his horse galloping next to Ki.

"We'll have to take the long way and go through Tranquillum's border. Once we reach deeper into the forest, we should be okay. It's night now, they won't be able to follow us clearly, and the closest place to go to is Macil. They will head for that," Sulwyn replied, and though they just had some sort of connection, she found herself unable to look him in the eyes again. Now that she had felt his hands, everything that transpired—plus the incident with Eurus—was burning into her.

She grunted loudly and urged Ki on, trying and failing to focus on the task at hand. But soon enough, they were passing through the trees, their horses coming to a slow trot with the lack of moonlight. Sulwyn pulled out the bandage and strips of fabric from her pack, using this chance to clean and wrap her wounds. Though she had bled quickly, and the cuts were thin on her ribs, it would definitely bruise. The ones on her shoulders and thigh would be fine.

"If we continue north, we should soon be parallel to the lake. I have a vague idea of where it is. Do you know where it is specifically?" she asked quietly. The forest was still, the weather cold but not windy.

"I do. It's not too far, we should reach it by tomorrow afternoon at this pace and a night's rest." He dismounted his horse, taking its reins. Sulwyn followed suit, taking the reins from Daijiro's hands and tying them to Ki's saddle so that he could lead.

She could sense Daijiro's eyes on her in the silence even though she couldn't see well, but the stare was boring into her, flustering her again.

"What?"

"Since that safe house, you've been avoiding my eyes."

"Not really, we had a lot of eye contact in that shop..." she said quietly, her words becoming lower and lower.

"Does it bother you?" he asked mildly.

"Does what bother me?" She tried to see him but could only see his outline and the white that mixed into his hair as it shone against the faint moonlight.

"What I did with Eurus."

Sulwyn didn't answer, annoyed that Galahad and he both knew how to read her openly. Is this what she was like with Raghnall? It was no wonder she was always getting into trouble.

"Did it bother you?" he repeated, and his tone was different now, almost hesitant.

She frowned. "In what way? You did a lot of things in that room that could fall under being a bother."

Daijiro stopped and turned to her. She stopped as well. "That isn't normally how that goes. It's usually a little more..." He trailed off.

"Violent? I was in the room, Daijiro. I understand that Eurus seems to be attracted to both of you. And I did think he held you both on some kind of pedestal from our interactions." She sighed. "I wasn't bothered that you were seducing a Leader, if that's what you're asking."

"Are you sure?"

Sulwyn just stared at him, taking in his eyes that appeared dark burgundy in the night. "Does it matter? You were interrogating him. And though that was a whole different kind of strategy, that didn't even work well, by the way. I think it managed to stir some kind of emotion in him."

"That's not only what I meant." He sounded frustrated and this annoyed her. He had irritated her this whole time, but he continued to stare. "Remove the part about it being an interrogation. Did seeing me with him bother you?"

"I don't care if you've been with several types of people, regardless of who they were or what your relationship was with them. Man, woman and anyone else or no one at all, it doesn't matter. You're fishing for a reaction or answer. Just ask me the damn question," she demanded. Having him talk about it did nothing to deflate the confusion that rose in her again. Sulwyn was glad it was dark. She was sure her expression would give her thoughts away.

But Daijiro smirked, only the whites of his teeth catching the light around them. "I see."

"What do you mean 'I see'? Why are you asking me this in the first place? We're wasting time standing here." She turned to move forwards, Ki waiting patiently to follow, but they both stopped as Daijiro remained in front of her.

"Were you jealous?" he whispered, the smell of mint stronger now.

"I wouldn't be jealous of his position," she stammered, slapping herself internally for how it came out.

"I said forget about the interrogation part..."

"What do you want from me?" She took a step back. The conversation was just going in circles.

"I'm not unaccustomed to looks of desire," he repeated the words he had whispered to Eurus. The heat and frustration rose within her. But instead of succumbing to it, she pushed past him, continuing their path.

"Do not insult me," she snapped, but he kept pace with her, the horses following behind.

"Since we left that place, you haven't looked at me except for just now and the moment before. I want you to express yourself," he continued, but she was becoming more exasperated and embarrassed at the same time.

"I told you to ask your damn question and stop fishing." She rounded on him. "Don't make fun of me, Daijiro. Unlike you, I am not accustomed to the look of desire or anything of the sort. I chose to ignore that part of life." She watched the teasing in his eyes diminish.

"I apologise," he muttered, silence spreading between them.

Finally, after four hours of walking, they found a clear space deep enough into the trees for a fire. Faint moonlight shone over them, briefly illuminating the area and their breath in the air.

It was Galahad's horse that carried the tent, so they would have to sleep in the open with just the blankets they had on them. But Sulwyn didn't mind. She liked the crisp air, and the night was dry. This way, she could sleep under the stars.

But as the silence between them continued, even after they made a small fire and tea to warm themselves, she started to grow increasingly anxious. Without Daijiro distracting her about her feelings, her mind strayed to Galahad and the people of the village.

Were they safe? Was Galahad safe? Now that they were both bonded somehow, she would have felt if he lost control or was injured. Or would she? Was there a distance to this thing? Or was there a limit to what they could feel? But Galahad was Galahad, and she needed to trust that he was safe.

He *had* to be safe.

"Cailín?"

Sulwyn's gaze focused over the fire and back on him. Instantly, she looked down but cursed herself for it. There had been a question she wanted to ask since his time with Eurus, and it only grew after their moment in the abandoned shop and from the discussion they just had.

"Ask me," he whispered softly.

"I have no experience in this ..." Her voice hushed, feeling like a child towards him. "Not the way you obviously do."

"That isn't a question... And a lot of what I have done was for survival, for money and for pure lust, and nothing more." He trailed off, his eyes boring into hers, the red reflecting the fire between them.

"I'm not going to ask you," she started angrily. "You are seven years older than me and have lived a life not unlike my own. But what you have done or needed to do is your choice, not mine. Who you've been with—" She stopped, thinking of his hands trailing along Eurus and then on herself.

"No one else can smell mint, Sulwyn..." His words deeper, more serious than she had ever seen, standing from his perch on a tree stump and kneeling beside her. "And I don't think anyone else ever will."

"That can change." There was a lump in her throat, trying to prevent her from what she was thinking. "Earlier, I felt Galahad's injury to his knee." His eyes widened and he leaned back a bit. "Galahad never thought that was feasible. But his feeling my pain is already unheard of to him. Now that I can feel his, it means that things we didn't think were possible are. Someone else may smell mint one day."

"It doesn't work that way with me. His clan is different. They bond because they're meant to travel and stay together as a group. They thrive in numbers. Velikat are different. We're just a race of evolved people. We don't have those kinds of ties to one another, not like that." His voice hushed. "There is mint *because* of you. It only manifests because. Of. You. I've already told you how I feel. And I know now is not the best time, but seeing you get hurt for something you didn't do, watching people look at you with unfounded hate... It put everything into perspective.

And I apologise for being insensitive before. I just felt you should be a bit more open with yourself. You already have so many things on your mind, and none of them are you."

A chill rippled through her; a fever was building. But she ignored it, wanting to respond to him but stopping because she didn't know how. However, Daijiro reached forwards and pulled her off the stump she was sitting on to join him on the hard ground.

"Tell me what you felt..." he whispered.

Sulwyn looked down, the late night weakening her resolve to keep her thoughts to herself. His warmth ruined the thoughts that she tried to hold back. Red eyes that showed her nothing but safety and care and the willingness to show it to her.

"Jealousy." She sighed and watched the corner of his lips lift in a smirk, knowing she had confirmed his thoughts.

"He doesn't smell anything from me. No one really has until Galahad, probably due to our ties to the All-Mother. But he doesn't smell it the way you do."

"If he smells it, doesn't that mean you hold him in deep regard?"

"Yes, it does. And maybe I always have, even though we barely got along before then. But my heart won't change. Not anymore. There is no reason for you to feel jealous of anyone, let alone Eurus of all people."

"How do you know?" But her question was met with an incredulous stare. She was aware that they'd both been leaning just a bit closer to each other with every word they spoke. The fire hot against her skin, warming her even though the chill of the fever was rising.

"I can't control who makes me feel what." Her voice was hushed now. The only sound besides them was the soft crackle of the fire and the slow breaths of their horses sleeping.

"I can make that worse," Daijiro said coyly.

Sulwyn looked down again, a mix of shame and embarrassment and annoyance at her own inability to tame whatever it was that was rising in her. But Daijiro pulled the blanket off himself and tossed it onto the ground behind her. She stared at him as he leaned forwards, leading her to lay against it. That same unfulfilled tingling sensation she felt in the bathing room travelled through her again, her stomach light and twisted and warm, but in anticipation not discomfort.

Daijiro braced his forearms against either side of her, lifting a hand to unwrap the blanket around her. Her fever mixed with the cool air and the heat from the fire elicited a shudder that travelled down to her toes. And though the fever was rising quicker, she still chose to ignore it and hoped he'd think it was their proximity to the fire that her skin was so warm.

But Daijiro didn't move further. Instead, he just hovered over her, his knees still on the ground and a space that she wished wasn't there between them. Against the rioting heart in her ribcage and the numbing pain of her incoming fever, she closed that space and pulled him onto her.

Just like the first time he'd kissed her, his lips were warm but maintained a tame control over her own. But unlike the first time, instead of the light ember tingle that went through her then, it was stronger. It was like ice and fire mixed into one, and she wanted more

But Daijiro was upholding his painfully slow movement on her lips, and though she had brought him closer, that space was still too much. She he didn't have the same experience he did, she'd just have to make it.

Sulwyn pulled the collar of his tunic, bringing him down against her so that the twigs and rocks of the forest floor dug into her back just a little from his weight. But the huff of surprise from him made it worth it.

"This is a little more than I was expecting from you, Cailín." He breathed onto her skin, but this intensified the burn in her. She looked into his eyes, seeing caution in them as well as fire, and still, she wanted more of it.

"This is *less* than I was expecting," she countered, and was satisfied with his smirk against her lips. She figured he was considering her emotions, but if she wanted the fire, she'd have to create it.

Sulwyn drew her tongue over his lips, surprising him enough that he responded in kind until she bit his lip just over the healing cut Eurus had caused. Daijiro stilled, and she opened her eyes to find his dangerous as she tasted the blood.

"I said I was jealous," she hissed, earning a low growl and the intensity she was looking for.

His lips parted, making way for her tongue and the fire she wanted him to give. Up until now, he had been restraining his kisses, but it had disappeared, and in its wake was something a little primal with a mix of longing she didn't realise he had been holding in.

But when she let herself think about it through the tingling and the fervor that now passed through her skin and nerves, she knew he had been waiting for her for a while. And it gratified her, empowered her. So, she tightened her grip around his collar before moving her hands along his back and to his chest, tugging and loosening the red sash he wore around his waist, much to his surprise. His eyes widened in alarm and then in fear.

The fever finally coursed through her, and she froze.

He pulled back and lifted her along with him so that she was in between his arms and cradled to his chest. The agony of it coursed through her, erasing the fire and leaving behind needles and glass in her veins and under her skin. She wanted to scream but she silenced herself, biting down hard on her hand until it was pulled away and replaced with Daijiro's.

Sulwyn tried to pull away, but he held her still. "It's fine. Just let it pass," he whispered calmly in her ear, holding her carefully.

Soon, her skin was numb and instead of fire and forest, she saw ice and snow. Everything around her was cold, the wind strong and the path they walked on was narrow. The threat of mounds of snow piled around them as they walked one by one over the path that Galahad led. Sulwyn looked behind her, and relief of the strongest kind passed through her as she not only saw Daijiro, but Taru, Eztli, Arsinone, Nori, Kione and Riko. All of them were alive and all of them together. And though they were all freezing, they spoke low among themselves, trudging their way through.

There was a soft whistle of frigid air around them, clean and crisp, and on the horizon, she could see the sun, clear of clouds, reflecting tiny diamonds onto the snow around them. But wherever they were, she couldn't see a single patch of greenery. The only place she knew that was like this was Mortui Gemma. And as Galahad was in the lead, this only confirmed her thought.

"I'll die before we make it there," Daijiro called, but Galahad just silenced him with a look. It didn't work. "I don't handle cold well, unlike you, ice boy. I am practically fire." And Sulwyn saw the layers of clothes over Daijiro as if he took every sash he owned and wrapped them all around himself.

"We're almost there. This is the fastest way, so stop bitching." But Galahad looked back at him again with a bright smile, though his eyes were a little sad.

Sulwyn opened her eyes, tears streaming down her cheeks, seeing the ghost of their smiles and the pure happiness that radiated from Galahad despite going home to a place that had seen fire and carnage.

That Horse Holds Grudges

| GALAHAD |

GALAHAD paced restlessly atop a slab of tall rocks he'd taken shelter on. From it, he could see the surrounding area. The toxic lake, coloured cobalt and rust, below him to the left; and far to the right was the bordering forest of Tranquillum that he stared at every minute, though unable to see too far due to a damp fog.

Briefly, far past midnight, a fleeting pain coursed through him, similar to the time Sulwyn had her vision in Wallasyn. But it only lasted for a few seconds before it was gone completely, Sulwyn doing her best to keep it from him.

He didn't understand much about the bond and how it worked. He didn't feel any of her pain when she was taken by Gwydion and wondered if that had to do with her forgetting herself completely. But it did surprise him to feel it over such a distance now. As he was too young at the time, he never learned much about that part of his clan. He didn't know how common it was or what it was like for different people, and at this point, he might never know unless he went back home. But he didn't want it to burden her.

Since then, he hadn't felt anything else, which he figured must be a good sign. But now it was late afternoon and he had yet to see them. Impatience clawed within him, but he tried to keep it down with his trust for her and Daijiro.

After they met up in the village, Daijiro managed to convince everyone to escape, and they quickly got them out before the Néosan could notice. Galahad urged Daijiro to go after Sulwyn, and instead took his chances with the small group left at the border.

The reaction was expected. And they all wanted his head for the reward. But Galahad maintained his control and managed to disarm and knock out every single one of them before leading the people towards the coverage of trees. The same trees he figured Sulwyn would go in as well to hide.

But it had been long enough now. Why weren't they here yet?

Impatience finally won out, and Galahad began to climb his way down the small peak of low mountains, earning a whiff of dizzying air that skimmed off the top of the lake. He picked this place knowing no one came here for the sheer danger of it. At least this way, they could hide while still having eyes on all directions of Antiqua.

When Galahad finally reached the bottom, the neigh of a horse reached his ears from a distance. He turned to see both Daijiro and Sulwyn coming towards him out of the fog, looking worse for wear but alive. Somehow being separated from them, then being reunited, brought on a whole wave of tension and relief in one go.

"You look alive," Daijiro said, jumping off his horse and walking towards Ki. The horse neighed loudly, shoving Daijiro away and moving towards Galahad instead, lowering onto the ground. Sulwyn only sighed but slid off slowly, wincing with every movement.

"Don't look at me like that. I've just got a couple of well-placed bruises." She smiled tightly at him, raising the side of her tunic to expose a large purple bruise along her skin.

"They sometimes use poisoned arrows, not lethal, but it explains the result..." Galahad explained slowly, still confused at Ki's reaction to Daijiro. Galahad spotted a violent-looking bite on his hand that also started to turn purple. But the more he stared at it, the more he realised they were human teeth marks.

"It's not nice to stare," Daijiro purred, raising his hand for him to see. "I needed to silence her somehow, otherwise the entire Empire would have flooded that forest."

"Excuse me?" Galahad raised an eyebrow, unsure of what to make of that.

Daijiro smirked. "Not everything is about sex."

Galahad rolled his eyes. He'd have to admit he wasn't expecting to hear what transpired, but relief washed over him and he moved forwards, bringing Sulwyn into a tight embrace.

"Bruises!" she exclaimed, moving his arm up so that it rested higher on her back than on her wounds.

"I'm glad you're safe…" he muttered into her hair, and she nodded, hugging him tightly.

"I'm glad you are too, which I'm assuming means the people are as well?" She pulled back a bit, looking at him carefully.

"Last I left them, they were making their way south towards Uhuru. Thought it would be the best place to take shelter since the population is much lower. Are you going to tell me why your horse looks like he wishes nothing more than to stomp on Daijiro?" he asked, and she turned in his arms to look at Ki.

Ki was definitely tramping around having a stare down with Daijiro, and though Galahad knew Daijiro could easily control that, he found it interesting that he chose not to.

"He thinks Daijiro hurt me while I was experiencing a vision." She shrugged but he noticed she wouldn't look him in the eyes.

The way Daijiro looked at her had changed, no, evolved, into something deeper. Galahad let her go and instead motioned for her to lift her tunic again.

"You don't have to heal it," Sulwyn protested, but Galahad gave her a stern look. She gave up, pulling away the material as he worked to remove the bandages.

"Shouldn't we move out of the open?" suggested Daijiro. Galahad saw him edge away from Ki and closer to them.

"No one comes here," he mumbled, peeling off the bandage and revealing a shallow but sticky wound.

"This would have gotten infected if you left it," he reprimanded her, but proceeded to heal it. "Can't you heal injuries?" he asked Daijiro, who had taken up sitting on the ground behind them, using them as coverage from Ki.

"Only myself, or at least, that's all I've ever tried..." He trailed off, looking at Galahad intently. But Galahad turned his attention back to Sulwyn as she lowered the tunic and pulled down the sleeve off both shoulders.

As he proceeded to heal the wounds there, he spotted a small, red bruise on her neck. Sulwyn looked up at him, turning her head the other way so that he couldn't see it. Galahad took a deep breath, an inkling of bitterness mixed in is heart. He lifted the fabric back up to cover her shoulders, placing a hand over it instead.

"I meant what I said," he whispered, aware of Daijiro staring at him. "I will always be next to you."

She looked at him, her grey eyes bright, and he knew she was boiling over with unspeakable amounts of emotions. But they were hers to hold and he would not force them out. Instead, he trusted that she would always stay open with him.

"Galahad... I'm not afraid anymore," she whispered. He found it odd to hear the word "afraid" come from her, but realised she was talking about her other vision.

"What did you see?" he asked, but she shook her head.

"I won't tell you. And I didn't tell Daijiro either. I don't want to tell anyone anymore unless I must," she started, but Galahad stopped her from moving back.

"Is it sad?" he asked, hoping she wouldn't keep anything distressing from him.

"No, actually. But I don't want to somehow alter the things that may or may not happen because I've seen a future. I want to believe it's not always set but I have accepted if they are," she said firmly, her gaze fierce.

"Okay." He nodded, moving back and ushering them to follow. "Okay. I trust you'll tell us if you have to. But don't shy away from them either." And he led them up through the longer path so the horses could follow.

ღ

| SULWYN |

"Nice little cave you've got here…" Daijiro said once they made it to the top. By the time they reached inside, it had gotten even darker. Sulwyn plopped onto the ground, lying on the cold stone.

"We need to rest… At least half a day. For the horses more than anything," she said, looking towards the cave opening at the sky. It was a cold grey and the temperature was steadily dropping with each passing day.

"That might be for the best…" Galahad replied, taking a seat next to her. Daijiro joined them but made sure to stay on the farthest side away from Ki. Sulwyn looked at the horse disapprovingly and sighed.

"Did you see the Néosan?" asked Sulwyn.

"In the distance. I believe they split up at one point. I know some are going to Macil. I'm not sure about the others."

"I thought they would," she muttered, thinking deeply.

They had run out of time.

From where they were now, it would take about twelve days to get to Antac, and they would only lessen that by two if they took the risk and went straight through the Empire. While a part of her found that idea recklessly thrilling, the other part of her knew that it was beyond idiotic. But there was a backup.

"I want to get to Antac as soon as possible," Sulwyn said, sitting up. "If the towns in Guāngcǎi have our faces coating the walls, imagine what the towns in Antiqua look like. And though there isn't anything visible to tie the others to us, all it will take is Nero losing some patience and adding their faces to the ranks. He knows who was with me at the time. I wouldn't put it past anyone from the Empire to use them against me if they already haven't."

"I understand, but you told them to linger for five days then leave and come back in ten," Galahad started. "If they do that, then they should be able to stay low until we get there."

"Look how much has changed in just a few weeks after we escaped the Empire! Another two weeks could be their death. No, we'll have to use another way. We'll have to—"

"Shift to them," Daijiro added from his spot on the ground.

"How did you..." Sulwyn trailed off, watching as he sat up and turned to her, his eyes just as wide. She didn't tell any of them about the vials she received from Wilkson except for the one to pass notes. When it came to Wilkson being a Devinal, she was cautious about who she told; her small party knew, and that almost felt like two too many.

"How did you know?" he asked, but Sulwyn was just as confused.

"I was going to say shift to them with the vials I got from Wilkson, but I don't have many and it's not accurate. Not to mention, we can't bring the horses... But how did you know I have them?"

"Oh..." he started, and for once, he looked like he'd said too much, but Sulwyn wasn't having it. Not after all of that.

"What are you keeping from us?" she demanded, crawling over to him. Galahad looked mildly concerned but Ki interrupted all of them, neighing loudly and pawing at the ground as if he wanted nothing more than to back–kick Daijiro.

"I'm not keeping anything," he said rather defensively, but as soon as he caught her eye, he looked down.

"We're past this," Galahad said, looking between them both. Sulwyn could see that hint of anger in Daijiro's eyes again, restless and a little unhinged.

"The more we interact with Gwydion, the more similarities I see," Daijiro said irritably, and they looked at him with concern. "I told you before that shifting magic costs the user tremendously. And I know you picked up on my words..." He glanced at her again.

"You can shift..." Sulwyn said slowly, but she was still confused. She knew he had more magical capabilities than her, but she also knew he wasn't a Devinal. She knew very little, only that shifting was such a high-costing ability, that if someone who wasn't a Devinal attempted it, it either wouldn't work or they would die.

Daijiro held out his hand, palm up and flat. Soon, a tiny ball of fire grew in the centre of it. Just like the one he showed her during their mission in Macil.

"Even though it's not by magic, it still costs a lot to use it. Shifting isn't fair. It bends the balance of nature," Daijiro explained, and his tone held that ghost of a fear that came with his past. The fear he hid with carnage. "Fire's allegiance and the gift of shifting from place to place. That is what was passed down to me." He sighed in defeat. "My ability to shift is different and more taxing. The vial would be a better option, so I'm glad you have them. I can only take one person with me at a time, and depending on the distance, I will be knocked out for an hour to a day. It's only recently that I learned this. It's how I returned to the Empire so fast before the coronation, shifted to the back of the stables. Was out for a few hours."

Galahad glanced outside the cave and to the ever-darkening grey clouds. "I know what it's like to not be able to understand what your power truly is. Be it from being unable to control it or being stunted because of your environment. But either way, it isn't something for you to be frightened of. Not anymore."

Daijiro focused on him, the tiny ball of fire fading into a wisp of smoke.

Galahad continued. "Since I've known you, to who you've become now and what we've learned about each other, I think you've grown tremendously from when you first came to the Empire. No longer are you trapped by what your father has done to you. Stunted in growth from his hate and the fear you harboured for him. I can see it in your actions, and every time fire comes out when you didn't mean for it to, to protect. It is your power to harness." Galahad reached forwards, clapping him on the back.

Daijiro laughed a bit, wiping his eyes and looking up at the cave ceiling. "Out of all the people I could have cooped up with, it had to be with you two, didn't it?"

Sulwyn reached forwards, taking his hand and placing her palm against his. The skin was still hot from where the flame hovered over it. "No one can hurt you anymore, Daijiro, especially not if we're around…" she said softly, heat rising along her neck, maintaining her stare on his crimson eyes. But the way he looked at her now froze her blood, yet set a blaze under her skin, and soon she was letting go and looking out of the cave again to the now darkening sky of the setting sun.

We're Both Very Tragic

NIGHT quickly fell over them, the air cool against her skin and the smell of poisonous wind less prominent in the near stillness. The three of them remained hidden by the tall rocks on the ground. Ki paced restlessly behind them. Sulwyn finally managed to get him to stop acting hostile towards Daijiro and instead gave him a mission of his own.

"Are you sure you want to leave him behind?" Galahad asked. Sulwyn stroked Ki's mane, trying to fill him with positivity.

"We don't have a choice. We've run out of time. I trust he'll remember his way back to the safe house..." she whispered, hoping to impart what he needed to do clearly. Daijiro stepped up to her.

"Do I have permission to ensure he knows what he's doing?" He looked pointedly at Ki, who turned his large head to face him, his coat gleaming a gentle auburn.

"Be nice, Ki," Sulwyn warned, stepping back and watching Daijiro touch the side of the horse's neck. Soon, they were both still, a pull different than what she was accustomed to floating around them. Ki neighed softly, nuzzling the side of Daijiro's head, throwing him a little off balance.

Daijiro smiled widely, turning to Sulwyn. Dazzled briefly by a youthful smile she'd never seen, he nodded confidently.

"He knows exactly where he's going. He should get there safely." He touched her shoulder reassuringly but Sulwyn could only nod.

Taking out the small notebook and the vial of blue ink, Sulwyn wrote a note to Wilkson:

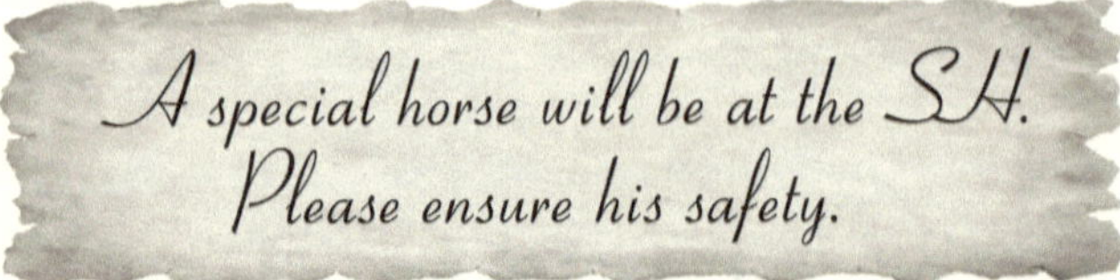

"What is the point of magic if it can't even work properly..." Sulwyn muttered bitterly, tucking away the blue vial and the notebook, and taking a yellow one out of the pouch, bitter that she must leave her friend behind.

"You should know that magic in itself is a cheat. Shifting even more so," Daijiro started, turning to Galahad. "Honestly I'm surprised you have so little background in it."

Galahad shrugged. "I was never taught, and though I have tried a few times, I think the blood of the First Father rejects it."

"But if you have ties to the All-Mother, shouldn't you be the perfect candidate?" he asked as Sulwyn walked forwards and led Ki to the other two horses.

"The All-Mother wasn't a Devinal..."

"She is the source of them, though."

But Sulwyn was no longer listening. She loosened out the reins as far as she could, creating a good amount of space between Ki and the other horses, tying them both to his saddle. After a few minutes of buckling and knotting, she stood in front of him again.

"I will come back for you," she said, watching his intelligent eyes on hers. "I've rigged the reins in a way that if for whatever reason, danger is around you, you need only stomp on the chains holding them to you. Don't travel too closely or you will get tangled."

She reached forwards to pat him again, leaning her forehead to his muzzle. With one strong neigh and a stomp, he started to trot forwards, leading the other horses with him, and going back the way she and Daijiro had come and into the night.

Sulwyn watched him until she could no longer see them in the distance, finally turning to face Galahad and Daijiro.

"I've never done this before, I only know in theory what to do," Sulwyn started, holding out the vial. It was hard to believe they could bottle the ability to shift in this small, yellow liquid, but she'd take whatever Wilkson gave her. "He also said the vials were shatter–proof, but Diesirae and Tiamat smashed theirs to the ground to activate it."

"I'm sure that if you chuck it hard enough it will be fine," Daijiro replied, picking up his bag and slinging it over his shoulder; Galahad doing the same.

"We all need to think about Antac." Sulwyn fixed her bag as well. "Have you been there before?" she asked Daijiro.

"A few times some years back."

"Did you go to the coast? Where the small houses are?"

His eyes bored into her own knowingly, but she kept her face impassive. A lot of time had passed since she thought of the events that transpired there. From when she found the impersonators and the family dead at their hands. At Caldwell and his sister. And Galahad standing with her by the coast, pouring his life story into her, while the ashes of the dead flew into the sea. Her eyes found Galahad's, knowing he was thinking the same thing.

Daijiro looked between them. "I know of the coast, is that good enough?" he said softly, and she knew he could sense there was a bond he could not step between, regardless of her feelings between them. Both were important to her. There was no going back now.

"Should be." She took a deep breath putting her right hand out, the black ring they all wore glinting from the weak moonlight. They took her hand in theirs, gripping it tightly. "This magic is finicky and unsteady. At least from my understanding," she continued, "Focus on the coast of Antac and if we are lucky, we will shift close enough to it. My target was the basement of a house, but close to it might be okay. This is our only option now. We wasted too much time." Her voice a whisper.

Galahad squeezed her hand, gaining her attention. "They will be fine. We will be fine. Ki will be fine." He smiled gently.

Sulwyn took another deep breath. "Okay. Ready?"

They nodded, faces concentrated. Sulwyn nodded to reassure herself, and with as much force as she could muster, tossed the vial onto the rocky ground beneath them, her eyes closed.

The smell of the toxic lake still wafted gently around them. She looked down at the vial lying innocently between their feet, not a crack in sight.

"Really, Wilkson?" Sulwyn exclaimed exasperatedly, but Daijiro tugged on both their hands.

"Concentrate on the coast of Antac." Before she could say anything more, Daijiro brought his heel down onto the vial, the glass shattering under it.

Instantly, the temperature around them dropped, and with it, a pale puff of yellow mist enveloped them. Soon, the night sky and the stars above them were swallowed into nothingness. The cool air different, stiffer, if that were possible. Sulwyn couldn't see Galahad or Daijiro, but she could sense them, the warmth of their hands seeping into her own. Within a few dizzying seconds, they appeared in the middle of a snowy bank, snow falling gently around them, and the pale-yellow mist evaporating.

Sulwyn crashed into the snow, legs collapsing under her and the world spinning. White and blue mixed with black dots clouded her vision and nausea ebbed within her stomach. Disoriented, she looked up, the sky still night but the air much colder and fresher. Quickly sitting, she looked around spotting mountains, a snow-covered forest in the distance behind her, and the trail of the coast far in front of her.

"This isn't Antac..." she mumbled, bracing herself to stand.

"It's not too far," Galahad said, standing as well and looking towards the coast. "We're near the mountain edges of Mortui Gemma. I haven't been here since I was a child..."

She turned to him, longing in his eyes as he looked up to something she couldn't see.

"Daijiro?" Sulwyn looked down to see him in a ball, still in the snow.

"Have I ever mentioned that I hate the cold?" he chattered finally, sitting up, and starting to pull out any article of clothing he had. Sulwyn stifled a laugh, thinking back to the vision she had.

"Well, we're still a day away by foot. So, you better get used to it," said Galahad, holding his arm out for him to take. Daijiro gripped it, standing with all his clothes in hand before one by one he put them all on. Sulwyn also reached into her bag, pulling out the wool, burgundy cloak and a thick, woolen scarf she hadn't worn since last year.

"Are you not cold?" she asked, watching Galahad put up his hood, seemingly content.

"Surprisingly enough, even though I spent years away from here, I retained my tolerance to cold. My clan isn't normally cold in the first place."

"Because you're made of ice?" Daijiro asked, arms wrapped around himself tightly. Galahad shrugged, leading the way while trudging through the ankle-deep snow and making a beeline towards the edge of the forest.

"We can take this way. Past these trees is a trail we used long ago that opens to a small forever-frozen lake we can cross. It should still be sturdy. The temperature here is almost always the same."

"Used for what?" asked Sulwyn, keeping pace with his quick strides. Daijiro lingered behind them, frozen and grumbling.

"Though we could grow a lot of the essentials, we did need to come and stock up occasionally in other resources. Antac is where they would go to until the High City fell. After that, they would stray further and visit other places randomly to ensure we were never found. So much good that did…"

Sulwyn took his hand, squeezing it tightly. He was right, the cold didn't affect him at all, his hands were still warm. "What's done is done. All we can do now is hope that we can stop this so that no one else will need to go through what you or Daijiro have."

"Can I touch you too?" Daijiro asked, hurrying behind them and grabbing Galahad's other hand. "Oh, warmth!" He sighed, rubbing Galahad's palm on his face.

Galahad gave him an incredulous look but didn't move to take his hand back.

ꙮ

| GALAHAD |

Galahad could feel Sulwyn's and Daijiro's hands growing colder with each passing hour as they continued past the thin forest to the edge of the coast and straight across the small lake. Both fell silent some hours before, concentrating all their energy to make it to the other side where they could finally build a fire and rest.

It was twilight, dusk soon to arrive with a hint of light on the horizon. Galahad glanced to either of them. Both nodding to him every so often, until soon, Sulwyn let go of his hand to put it inside her cloak against her chest. Daijiro, too, let go moments after to wrap his arms around himself properly. And together they continued like this.

"It's not far now," he started, after another hour, raising his hand and pointing to the thicket of trees in the upcoming distance. Even he was starting to fill the cold now.

But as they walked, an eerie foreboding passed through him and soon after, a loud crack resonated around them. Galahad stopped, eyes wide, turning next to him to see Daijiro, his expression the same. Another crack rent the air and he turned to face Sulwyn only to find she wasn't there.

"Sulwyn?" called Galahad, maintaining as much stillness as he could. But numbing waves of panic erupted within him. Daijiro shuffled closer, eyes wide in fear. Fear in a way he didn't know Daijiro could express.

"Sulwyn!" roared Galahad again, and ever so slightly, they both heard a thud.

He immediately looked down at the ice around him just as another slow thud made its way towards them. "Daijiro, wait!" Galahad reached to grab the back of Daijiro's cloak, but grabbed air instead.

He watched Daijiro skid forwards, falling to his knees some feet away, bending down. Carefully, Galahad made his way over, stopping halfway, spotting an uneven hole large enough for Sulwyn to fit through in the cracked ice.

Again, they heard a thump, and soon, Galahad saw the glimmer of her sword just below his feet. Daijiro slid over and shoved him aside, crashing onto that part of the ice instead. And without any plan or caution, started to bang the side of his fist against the ice.

"That isn't going to do anything!"

"Do you have a better idea?" he yelled, still banging furiously, until finally, he aimed his fist directly at it. His knuckles scraped on the ice leaving blood behind. Galahad could sense the dread rising in Daijiro, never had he seen him look so erratically terrified in all the years he knew him.

He looked around, watching as more and more cracks started to crawl across the ice. They weren't too far from the bank now. If they could get her out and run, they would have a chance. Galahad pulled out his sword, pushing Daijiro aside with his foot.

With as much strength as he could muster, Galahad smashed the hilt onto the ice, creating a hefty dent. But the current shifted and Sulwyn was dragged further down. They followed her as she steadily floated closer to the edge. But even if they got closer, that wouldn't matter if she ran out of air first.

Galahad tried again and again, managing to take out chunks of ice. But still, it was not enough. Daijiro moved in front of him, his eyes wild and his face concentrated, until finally, he pulled a small dagger from under the many folds of his clothes and enveloped it in fire.

Galahad moved back, the raw heat of the flame emitting from Daijiro. Unlike when Sulwyn was in a coma and he had cauterised only her wound, the fire burned his skin instead. But Daijiro didn't seem to care. And with great strength, he slammed the hilt of fire straight into the ice, creating a huge hole. Ice fell away instantly from the heat of the flames and Daijiro jumped straight in. Galahad slid forwards, grabbing onto one of his sashes at the last second.

∽◌∾

| DAIJIRO |

Daijiro couldn't hear anything Galahad said once he realised Sulwyn was under the ice. And now that he was in the water, feeling the tug on his sash, he confirmed that he truly detested the cold. But that didn't matter now. Even as the ice filled his lungs and froze his limbs, it didn't matter as long as he could reach her.

Sulwyn's eyes were closed, the grip on her sword still tight, and her burgundy cloak that looked black flowed gently around her. An image that jarred him so much, he gasped, letting water rush in and choke him with a vengeance. But with one last pull against Galahad's hold, he managed to wrap his hand around her wrist and pull her to him.

As he swam up, the tug on him became more urgent until Galahad was gripping his shoulders and pulling him out on top of the ice, grabbing onto her sword before it was lost forever. Icy water seared his throat as he vomited what he had swallowed before, gasping for air.

But it didn't end there.

The deep vibration of cracks continued to echo around them. And before he realised it, Galahad was pulling him to his feet and pushing him along while the ice started to fall behind them.

Sliding more than running, Daijiro—with Sulwyn over his shoulder and Galahad behind—moved as quickly as he could until finally, he leapt onto the edge of the bank. Daijiro's foot slipped back into the water but Galahad was pulling him onto the solid ground again just as the ice and lake whirled around them in a current he didn't expect.

∽◌∾

| GALAHAD |

Galahad pulled Daijiro forwards towards a bigger clearing, dropping the sword onto the snow and helping him place Sulwyn down gently. He immediately realised she wasn't breathing.

"Go start a fire," Galahad commanded urgently, and though Daijiro did not seem focused, he turned around and started to clear the area, searching for anything dry enough.

He had never resuscitated anyone before. Never had the need to and didn't even really know how. He checked her pulse, the blood within beating slowly but strongly under her skin. They had no idea how long Sulwyn had gone without air, but he needed to get her breathing.

Carefully, he pulled the cloak off her, placing his hand over her chest to try and sense the water in her lungs. If he could just move it with his energy enough for her to cough it out... But fear was clouding his judgement, and instead, he fell back one pressing her chest hard in rapid succession. He moved his hands to her cold and pale face, tilting her head back and pinching her nose to breathe into her mouth. He prayed to anything that listened that he wasn't doing this wrong. Hoped that what he witnessed and read about was enough for this moment.

Her lips were cold and swollen from his attempts, but he breathed anyway, moving and pushing his hand up her torso to try and force the water out. Over and over he did this, until finally, she coughed, water spilling out of her mouth and onto her chest.

Sulwyn sat up wildly, her eyes disoriented before finding his. Galahad wiped her face with his cloak before taking it off and throwing it over her. Daijiro stumbled forwards, his hand burned and leaving a trail of blood. But before any of them could say anything, he dropped to his knees and wrapped her in a tight embrace.

"Let her catch her breath." Galahad coughed, leaning back on his hands as relief flooded his nerves. He watched Sulwyn raise her hand to stroke the back of Daijiro's wet hair. His body trembling just as much as Sulwyn's, be it from the cold or fear or both, he wasn't sure.

"I'm alive, Daijiro..." Sulwyn whispered, her voice hoarse.

ॐ

|SULWYN|

The first thing Sulwyn saw when she opened her eyes was the millions of multicoloured stars above her in the night sky. The second was Galahad's haunted but relieved expression, his lips red and tears in his eyes. And the third was Daijiro's burned and bleeding fist that matched the dark scarlet of his eyes, before she saw nothing at all as he pulled her into an embrace that made her already congested chest tighter.

Daijiro was soaked, shivering as she was, in more than just cold. She wasn't sure if Galahad could hear him, but he said the same thing over and over again in a garbled whisper. "I'm sorry, I'm sorry, I'm sorry." She lifted her hand to the back of his neck, trying to pass some calm into him.

"I'm alive, Daijiro…" Her throat hurt. The water was so cold, it burned her insides in shards of ice. His hand intertwined in her hair and against her neck, finding her pulse and leaning into her neck checking for himself once again.

She had seen Galahad on the other side of the ice as she tried and failed to break it with the hilt of her sword. His face as pale as the ice she was under. Had seen when Daijiro dove into the water just before everything faded into darkness.

"Thank you. To both of you really. The ice gave out before I could move and the cold silenced me," she whispered, still trying to calm Daijiro down. Galahad shuffled closer to her, pulling Daijiro back.

"I said to let her breathe," Galahad urged, agitated. Daijiro moved back ever so slightly, insisting that he touch her at all times.

"You'll both get hypothermia, stand," he demanded, prodding Daijiro, and together they carried Sulwyn to the blazing fire. Galahad helped her lean against a tree. "You'll need to get out of your clothes, both of you."

"I'm wearing all my clothes." Daijiro wheezed in disbelief.

"Then wear mine, you both will have to." He turned to her. "Your bag went into the water as well. I'm glad it didn't get lost." Galahad helped

Sulwyn remove said bag and take off her cloak and tunic. She yanked off the boots and pants that clung to her skin, shivering as the wind went through the long undershirt she wore before she pulled that off too. The snow numbing against her naked skin, but Galahad pulled out a brown, long-sleeved tunic, rolling it up and putting it over her head.

"I'll take everything out of your bag and hang it, okay?" he said softly, taking out pants and passing them to her. Sulwyn only managed a nod, the chill seeping into her, but the warmth of dry clothes on her skin couldn't have been better.

"Wait," she called, reaching for the bag. He brought it back, holding it open as she fished out the small sack that Wilkson had given her. Rifling through the vials, the notebook and the journal from Pandora, Sulwyn pulled out the vial of clear liquid. Thinking about her vision, she didn't want to use two vials. It might dampen the effects, but half of one between her and Daijiro should help.

She put the sack into her bag and gave it back to Galahad. He stood still, watching as she unsealed the vial and drank half. Instantly, a lukewarm heat travelled down her throat and into her stomach, spreading thinly to her extremities. "Give the rest to Daijiro."

Galahad nodded, taking her bag and splaying out the contents by the fire. He then walked over to Daijiro and handed him the vial while pulling out another long-sleeved tunic and pants from his bag to toss at him.

"Strip, dammit," Galahad said, but Daijiro was too cold to function even after he downed the vial, sitting with his arms around his knees and as close to the fire as he could get. Just watching them both.

"I think he needs your assistance too." Sulwyn smirked, watching Daijiro scowl.

"Arms up," Galahad said, exasperated, and Daijiro did as he was told. But because he put on everything he brought, it was more like unwrapping a shivering, uncooperative gift. Sash after sash, tunic after tunic. All pulled off, until finally, Galahad could take off every layer of clothing he had.

"How is this better?" he hissed, but paused when he caught Sulwyn's stare. To be fair, she hadn't seen him without clothes before as he did with her at the pond, even if she did still have a thin slip all that time ago.

He had a lot of scars, just like she and Galahad. But there were two spots that stood out strikingly as the firelight flickered onto it. One along the front centre, a jagged, horizontal scar that she couldn't see clearly from her position. And another along his right leg that was deep, and travelled from the top of his thigh to the bottom of his knee. Almost as if...

"Do you like it?" he whispered darkly, and Galahad, too, looked down at the scar. "When I was thirteen and becoming a little more rebellious, Tamesis caught me in a trap. A long, metal hook scraped across me and hung me upside down by the knee. I don't know where he got it from, but it was coated in poison that couldn't be healed easily. I hung there for an entire night before my mother was able to come and take me down."

Sulwyn and Galahad were stunned into silence. But Daijiro scoffed, smoothing his hair back and taking the clothes Galahad handed to him.

"Both of you..." Sulwyn started, anger lacing her voice. "I am so sorry..." She looked up at Daijiro and Galahad.

"I'm over it. You both said it, there isn't anyone who can hold me back. Not anymore. And I'm sure the same is for you?" Daijiro turned to Galahad just as he pulled on the pants and the tunic.

Galahad looked at him seriously, with affection she had never seen him direct towards Daijiro. "We're both very tragic, do you want a hug?"

Daijiro's face fell in shock, something stirring in his eyes, until he roared with laughter, more than she ever heard before. She was beyond perplexed, but there was a shared sort of understanding between them. Without a word, he continued laughing, pulling Galahad into a strong hug and patting his back.

XXXVI

The Town By The Shore

| SULWYN |

SULWYN never really thought too much about what it would mean to try and yell within her own mind. But as she tried it, she realised it was rather frustrating.

Regardless, she tried.

She called Arsinone's name, imagining it as loudly as she could while they edged carefully along the coast, the sun marking the day just before noon; Antac in the near distance. But the closer they got, prickles of fear ran through her, over her skin and into her hair and down to her fingernails.

Did they ever make it to Kione?

Were they even still alive? Based on her premonition, they should be, but she couldn't trust that wouldn't change.

Or had they been captured, locked in the Empire and tortured on her whereabouts?

"Sulwyn, she'll know if we're here." Galahad's voice piercing her thoughts even though it was low. And though he tried to reassure her, she could hear the underlying worry in his words. The tremor of fear laced within them.

"We should have set the meeting point in the forest we just came from," Sulwyn hissed. "Antac is an important town. Whether they followed our trail or not, they would have sent higher security there, wouldn't they?

I should have picked the forest." She berated herself not for the first time since they woke and resumed their trek towards the town.

Once they had reached the other side of the not–so–frozen lake, the snow started to lighten, and the temperature became a little more bearable as they travelled through the trees. Just like everywhere else in Vartugaul, the weather was chaotic and random. But Mortui Gemma was always cold and always snowed until one made it out of the shadow of the mountains. Now they were trekking along dry, hard ground mixed with sand and still-present grass, the air not as cold yet.

Sulwyn looked back at Daijiro, silently trailing behind them, his focus elsewhere.

But she stopped, turned to face him and managed to catch him off guard. Hurriedly, he pushed his hand into his pocket but knew it was too late.

"I thought you said you could heal it," Sulwyn snapped, marching right up to him. Galahad, too, stopped, glancing around the area before coming next to him as well.

Daijiro angrily tutted, yanking his hand out of her reach, but Galahad caught his wrist and held it firmly in front of them. The wince of pain didn't go unnoticed.

Daijiro's hand was wrapped in layers of bandages, but blood still managed to seep its way through. Carefully, Sulwyn unwrapped it, holding the bundle of bloodied fabric between her fingers as she took in the state of his hand.

"This is…" she hesitated. "Is it broken?" Her eyes met his, and for once, he didn't want to look at her. His hand was crumpled. Badly bruised and cut from the ice the night before, tears around the skin of his knuckles, raw and red. But somehow made worse surrounded by pink, burned flesh that reflected in the sun.

Galahad took Daijiro's hand out of hers and examined it, moving his fingers gently and touching his skin gingerly. Then his wrist, bending it slowly. Watching carefully for any reaction from Daijiro. "I don't think it's broken. Fractured maybe. It's hard to tell. Why can't you heal it?"

Daijiro glared, his eyes angry—but not at them. "I lost control of the fire. I could have destroyed everything if I had lost a little more. As punishment, I cannot heal it myself."

"What kind of rule is that?" exclaimed Sulwyn. "Now isn't really the time to decide self-imposing rules."

"It's the phoenix's rule. Since I have no guide, it's decided to take it upon itself to become one instead."

"Since when?" Galahad asked, fascinated by the whole thing.

"Since last night when I first used the flame properly on my own."

"But you used a whole lot more of it in Macil," Sulwyn pointed out.

"That wasn't me, not alone. It was the phoenix finally awakening. The control then wasn't mine. It was hers. And any time before were small bursts from my own concentration. The only reason it didn't fully go out of control this time is because the phoenix took over instead. I'm the only heir left. When I die, she dies too, unless I can pass it onto a blood heir. So as punishment for losing her allegiance in my panicked state, I can't heal it, and neither can anyone else. The damn bird is a sadist."

"Fitting," Galahad said, earning a kick to the shin from Daijiro. But they were both distracted by Sulwyn who was now rummaging in her bag and pulling out a fresh roll of bandages that had dried a little crinkly.

"It's too bad I like to cheat." She winked, also pulling out a purple vial. Carefully, she uncorked it and slowly poured it into the bandages. Handing the vial to Galahad, she motioned for Daijiro to hold his hand out.

"Open your hand as much as you can." She directed and he complied, stretching his palm out, albeit the visible pain that ran through him, his hand shaking. Gently, she wrapped the damp bandage around and around his hand until it was properly bound.

"It tingles. Is this for burns?" he asked as she sealed the half bottle tightly, dropping it back into her bag.

"It is and I don't have many. Let's try and maintain 'fire's allegiance' for the rest of the journey."

He smirked, flexing his hand with a bit more comfort than before. "Once the burn heals, I should be able to do the rest."

"Sulwyn?"

She froze, looking back towards Antac. It was faint, and still too far from Arsinone's proper radius, but she had heard it. Fleetingly so.

"I heard her," Sulwyn whispered, eyes wide. And before waiting for either to respond, she crouched and took off at an odd run. Hoping beyond hope that the voice was in surprise and not a call for help. Galahad and Daijiro quickly followed after her.

But as she got closer, she could see the front of the town, and in the distance, there was a blockade of Néosan. Just as one moved to turn into their line of sight, Sulwyn skidded to a halt, turned back around and tackled both Daijiro and Galahad off the edge of the coast wall and into the blue-green water beside them.

Galahad and Daijiro spluttered for a second, but Sulwyn was already swimming closely to the edge of the ocean walls. She wasn't even paying attention to how strong the current was and thanked the moon that it was calm for now.

"Well, so much for healing my burn," Daijiro said, a little annoyed, but Sulwyn just waved him off.

"If you think Wilkson lets water ruin his magic then you're in for a surprise. Did you see them?" She turned the Galahad.

"There's about fifty or so. That's about the same from the other town. They probably sent a platoon to each nearby town. Just in case."

"Can we swim from here to the coast behind Antac? We aren't that far."

"But will the coast remain this calm?" asked Daijiro, looking to the sky. Sulwyn did as well, the sky crisp, blue and clear for the time being.

"We only have to make it far enough until Arsinone can hear us," Galahad said, and with that, he joined Sulwyn near the wall, keeping one hand firmly upon it while he urged her to swim forwards.

"I like the parts in our journey when we're not freezing or soaking wet. Or both," Daijiro muttered, swimming behind Galahad.

"Is it just me or is the ring becoming hot?" Daijiro asked, beads of sweat along his forehead.

"No, I feel it too," Sulwyn said excitedly, but a tremor of worry flowed over her. Was it worry, or was it actually the cold? Her wet hair whipped into her face, the wind picking up and the current starting to grow. But more than that, she was tired. All three of them were. They had been slowly swimming for an hour and it was starting to take its toll.

"We need to get out now, any longer, and we risk being taken by the current," warned Galahad. "Hold on." And without word, he placed both hands along the coast wall of rock and dirt. Sulwyn and Daijiro stopped, watching him carefully climb up until he was at the edge of the wall of earth. He looked around briefly until an intake of breath caught Sulwyn's attention.

"Oh." His voice mildly surprised before he dropped back into the water between them. Something like hope in his eyes. "We've made our way closer than I thought. The Néosan can't see us from here if they've stayed at the town entrance. The only problem is the high walls. But..." This time he smiled. "There's a hill just over this bend that we can climb up unseen and it goes right behind where I think Azhar's bar is."

"Then what are we waiting for," said Sulwyn, and with all the energy left in her, she swam forwards until they reached a small curve along the wall.

Once past it, the hill was just before them, and soon, their boots could touch the wet sludge as they awkwardly hobbled forwards and up the slope, staying low to the ground. With each step she took, heaviness and exhaustion ran through her. Her legs and torso like lead bound in chains, but still, she continued. The wind blew past them, freezing her once again, as the current finally picked up behind them. She crept forwards slowly and carefully, seeing the familiar rooftops of Antac dusted in light frost.

The heat that seeped through the black ring on her right index finger brought a sense of elation.

"Can any of you hear Arsinone?" she asked, the elation fading. They should be close enough by now…

"I haven't…" Galahad said quietly, and Sulwyn noted the silence that pressed around them.

Dripping, tired and cold, Sulwyn pushed the weariness aside, trying to bring forth any energy she could muster, trying her best to sense anything. Something was wrong here. But before she could think any further, blackness seeped into her mind like an oppressive fog, and she fell hard onto the ground.

XXXVII

Back To The Beginning

| SULWYN |

SULWYN inhaled deeply, the sounds around her mixed and intangible; hadn't she been in a situation like this before? She tried to move, but struggled in her seat against bindings. Blackness still surrounded her, but instead of the strange fog that had filled her mind, it was fabric, and almost pressed against her now-open eyes.

Before she could speak, someone shushed her. But panic flared, chest tightening and her body stiff. If the others were taken and tortured it would be all her fault. If they died it would be her fault. Sulwyn tried and failed to keep calm, taking deep, shaky breaths but her heart continued its quick, hard beats.

Despite her efforts, she made a quiet, sort of desperate sound while she fought against coils of rope. With every pull, it rubbed angrily against her skin. And then she stopped, hearing a sort of muffled response. Was someone gagged?

But soon, so was she.

Rough hands lifted the fabric up over her head enough to force her jaws open and shove a damp cloth into her mouth. She tried and failed to yell, her voice just as muffled, but in that moment, she caught a glance of her surroundings, though there was barely any light.

Her wrists were bound in old, dry rope. The floor wooden, clean, but worn down from brown to mostly grey. And part of a wooden chair leg off to her right. Someone else gagged and bound as she was.

She tried to call out to Arsinone but got no response. Fine. If this was how they wanted to play, she would play. Sulwyn took a deep breath through her nose and exhaled heavily. There was no time for her to panic, not after all of this. Everyone knew the risk they were taking, and with the Empire around, everything was a risk.

It was now, she acknowledged, that finding out more of the truth had weakened her. Made her vulnerable and tired. But her fight was far from over, and it wouldn't end here. She took another deep breath, calm forcing its way through.

The wet cloth in her mouth was fresh cotton and the water clean. Just like the bit of floor she could see before they pulled the fabric back down. Something about the floor was familiar, but she couldn't place it, not yet. Another breath and she noticed the smell of salt in the air. They were still close to the coast. Inside somewhere nearby, then. And her clothes were no longer soaking, only slightly damp. Either she had been unconscious for a long time or.... Fire. Warmth slowly crawled its way on her back. Unnoticed before in her panic and the small source of light.

She knew where she was now.

It was one of the abandoned houses from her first time in Antac. Which one, she wasn't sure, but either way, it was somewhere familiar. And then the smell of sweet rain, burnt wood and mint drifted over her. Faint like a whisper. Daijiro was near her, and based on how erratic the smells were, he must still be in and out of consciousness. But he was quiet, or maybe unable to speak just like her.

She clenched her fists and realised the ring on her thumb was gone, but the ring Raghnall gave her was still on her index.

With a smirk, realisation hit her, and with it, she remembered the ropes on her wrist. Old and dry. So she tugged hard. The rope burned into her skin with each pull, but no one moved to stop her. Did the person leave?

Perfect.

She yanked harder.

Now, she was glad for the gag, biting down on it as she strained against it, the burn on her wrists like splinters all shoved into her skin at once. A slight tearing sound met her ears, and her right hand gained more space, until finally, the rope snapped and thumped softly to the ground.

Swiftly, she pulled the fabric off her head, removed the gag from her mouth and took in her surroundings. The house looked the same since the last time she was in it. The one where she had entered from the basement all those months ago. The personal effects still strewn on the floor from what she could see. The sofas covered in blood from her kills, though the bodies had been taken out. The house was untouched since they had left. Probably marked as bad luck by the town.

She turned around, the sky dark through the cracks of dirty windows that hadn't been boarded, and the only source of light was the dying embers some feet behind her—barely enough to see properly. The sofas had been pushed back, making room for her and the other two chairs beside her. And though she couldn't make out their clothes, she knew one was Galahad and one Daijiro. Sulwyn tossed the fabric bag onto the floor and pulled at the other rope until it snapped. Her wrists stung more now, but she took the damp cloth and pressed it onto either wrist for a moment. Soothing the burning and wiping the blood.

Sulwyn wanted to speak but decided against it, and instead, bent forwards searching into the inside of her boot for the small dagger she kept there. With it, she slashed the rope around her ankles and stood.

Instantly, waves upon waves of vertigo hit her. Her knees buckled and her body swayed until she landed on one knee hard against the floor. The person next to her jolted abruptly, but quickly, she reached forwards and touched their leg, realising it was Galahad. He was quiet and still, but something was off about him.

Disoriented, she stood and pulled the fabric off his head. But Galahad couldn't see her. His eyes remained shut and his face an expression of torment, seeing something within that she could not. Quietly and a little unsteady, she bent low near his ear, his body tensing when she spoke.

"Galahad... you're okay." She spoke in barely a whisper. But it was enough. His eyes snapped open, exposing their half-coloured, half-black hue. But there was that black fog she had seen in her own mind, fading from within his eyes just as the black of his own also crept back.

Stunned, he breathed in sharply, looking down and around in continued shock. Sulwyn cut the rope at his wrists, handed him the dagger, and pressed a finger to his lips. As she moved onto Daijiro, the vertigo passed with each quiet step towards him.

Gently, she brought her hand over his and his breath stilled. Gradually, she reached forwards, lifting the fabric off his head and tossing it to the floor. Like Galahad, his eyes were closed but sweat clung to his face, reflecting in the faint light. As soon as she cupped his neck, she staggered for a moment, the familiar smells overwhelming her senses. Steadying herself, she bent low to his ear, whispering softly, "You are safe, Daijiro..."

His eyes opened, and in the bare flicker of dying flames, she could see a dark fog pass over his eyes until his crimson ones caught the light of the embers. Galahad passed her the dagger as he stood, also swaying from violent waves of vertigo.

She motioned for Galahad to sit while she cut Daijiro's binds. As soon as he was free, he tried to stand, but Sulwyn pushed him down. Seeing the waves rise in him too, his gait unbalanced, even from his small movement. Sulwyn kept her hand on his shoulder, urging him to stay put. But he reached up, clenching her hand with cold fingers. She could see the fear in his eyes, watch as it started to pass now that he was awake. But she needed to move. She squeezed his hand back, then let go.

Before either could do anything more, she crouched, looking around the room. Their bags had been taken, weapons as well. Nothing else was in the room but she couldn't be too sure due to lack of light. She turned to Galahad and tapped him. Without word, he nodded, and in the faint light, she watched his tricoloured eyes fade to black.

Slowly, he stood and scanned the room, shaking his head.

She didn't need weapons anyway. Sulwyn motioned for him to sit back down, watching him totter slightly. For whatever reason, the vertigo left her far quicker than it did them. So she would make the first move.

Maintaining her crouch, she motioned to Galahad to keep Daijiro down, and then walked forwards. Though she had only been in this house once, she memorised everything she had seen before. It was clear to her as she navigated the sitting room with barely any light until she reached the hall where there was none.

To her left was the cellar, to her right the entrance to the house. In front of her were the stairs to go up, but she hadn't searched up there the first time. Sulwyn stood still for a moment, closing her eyes and listening to the house. She could hear the faint cracks of the dying embers. The sound of both Galahad and Daijiro breathing deeply to steady the vertigo. And if she listened carefully, she could hear someone pacing on the second floor.

Edging her way around, she placed one boot on the step. Then another. And another. Slowly and carefully, gliding her hand over the railing that curved along the wooden stairs. She wasn't sure if she was just lucky or if the floors were in good shape, but not one creak sounded as she went.

Finally, she reached the top, and here there was a sliver of light leaking through a closed door to her left. Crouching again, she stepped closer and closer, pausing every few steps and listening carefully. She had no weapons besides the small dagger that she left downstairs. If her assumption was wrong, she could be in for a struggle. And though normally that wouldn't be the worst thing, she didn't want to draw extra attention to the house from the Néosan. Unless she was completely wrong, and Néosan themselves were in the room.

The footsteps in the room halted, and all too soon, the hallway was flooded with light, blinding her momentarily as the door swung open. Swiftly, she dove onto the floor just as a fist launched at the now–empty spot.

"I knew it." Sulwyn smiled, swiping her leg forwards and knocking Kione off balance.

"Impressive," a soft voice said somewhere behind him. Kione stepped back just as Riko walked forwards. Sulwyn stood, brushing the dust off her clothes. Not that it mattered. She was already covered in everything else at that point.

"I'm so glad you're alive," Sulwyn said, pulling Kione into a strong embrace. His arms wrapped tightly around her, squeezing her hard enough to lift her a little off the ground.

"What gave it away?" he asked, his voice muffled against her hair.

"There was no reason to take the rings off," Sulwyn explained as he set her back down on her feet. "The only reason would be to stop resonating with the others. But in case I was an impostor, I wouldn't have known that."

Sulwyn finally gave the room attention, a bitter sadness welling in her as she thought about the owners of the house. This room clearly belonged to one of their children. It was neat and modest. A small desk and chair in one corner and a small cot in the other. Shelves lined the wall with little trinkets, collected or found. The other chairs within the room were added recently, scoured from the rest of the house to here. She took a seat, bidding the memories away.

Normally, she would have suggested the basement, but she was sure all of them would have sensed the malice within it and chose this room instead. It had no windows and was safe from light seeping to the outside. The living room, too, had been boarded, but fire would still eventually draw attention once it was dark. She figured they lit the fire for their benefit since they were soaked, then put it out around the time she had awakened at sunset. The rough hands and the shushing had been Kione.

Behind her, Galahad and Daijiro finally made their way up. She glanced at Riko, eyeing her suspiciously. But Riko shook her head, her eyes pleading as she mouthed *soon*. Whatever magic Riko had used on them affected Daijiro and Galahad in a way she did not approve. And by the looks of it, neither did Riko. But somehow, she didn't seem to have control over that.

"Is there a reason you knocked us out and poisoned us with magic?" Daijiro asked scathingly, his eyes on Riko. Sulwyn never did learn what it was that was between them, but somehow Daijiro was not thrilled to see her again. A reaction that both Daijiro and Riko were surprised at.

Tutting, Daijiro looked away, stretching his neck and moving to pat Kione on the shoulder instead. Sulwyn had many questions, but they would have time.

"I assume you did this because Arsinone isn't in Antac," Sulwyn started, dread in her heart.

But Kione smiled. "She's with Taru. They went scouting for information. They'll be back soon. Nori and Eztli are on food duty and should return shortly."

"With Gwydion able to use magic to disguise pretty much anyone, this was the only way I could make sure you were you," Riko explained softly.

"How so?" Galahad asked, taking a seat on a chair beside Sulwyn.

"From what I have heard, Kintana is sensible," Riko started, nodding to Sulwyn as she also sat. "If it were anyone in relation to Gwydion, or even Diesirae herself, they wouldn't have assessed the situation this way. We were ready to escape if need be. But we were sure it was you, so I put trust that you would figure it out. And of course, if it were Gwydion, my magic wouldn't hold him long."

"Gwydion is a Velyūn," Daijiro spat, glaring at Riko.

"A what?" Kione asked, but his voice fell silent when he saw Riko's mouth agape, brows furrowed.

"That..." she whispered, looking at anything but Daijiro, or any of them, and ever so subtly, she reached the back of her neck. Sulwyn kept quiet, watching her expression turn from disbelief to frustration to apologetic, before finally, she looked up at Daijiro again.

Just like Sulwyn had her bond to Galahad, it appeared that Riko had one to Daijiro. Unintentionally, Sulwyn scoffed, earning a glance from everyone in the room. But Daijiro barely registered it and walked straight up to Riko, his posture rigid and full of rising anger.

"How could you not tell? Shouldn't *that* have been the first thing you told me?" he hissed, but Galahad stood and tugged him back, turning Daijiro to face him.

"She was a prisoner finally in the light of freedom. I don't know what it is that's between you, but you have no right to judge her." Galahad's tone was tight. If anyone understood what Riko had gone through, it was him.

Kione glanced at Sulwyn, but she shook her head.

"I can judge whoever I like. A Devinal who is full of herself couldn't even recognise a Velyūn in front of her. She didn't seal her mind off from the beginning. There was plenty of time to figure it out."

"I didn't even think of that!" Riko snapped, but her eyes were wide in disbelief and regret. "I didn't realise. If I had known, I would have—"

"What?" he seethed. "What would you have done? Could you do anything? Or was all that talk about being different even for a Devinal for show?"

"Daijiro," Sulwyn muttered quietly. He froze, his eyes wide as if remembering his place. "Few people know about Velyūn to begin with. Some only hear the name. She was taken a long time ago. How can you expect her to fully recognise one when you were barely into your abilities as a child?"

Daijiro turned to her, his face falling. "How...?"

The corner of Sulwyn's lips lifted ever so slightly. "Ability to assess situations, isn't that right, Riko?" She looked at her, Riko's eyes widening in understanding. Sulwyn turned back to Daijiro. "You've met in the past, but it would have to be sometime before she was captured. When you were both young and when you barely had a handle on your true self. How could you expect her to recognise one in front of her when the only one she had ever met was barely one himself? One thing confuses me though." She faced Riko again. "He had no recollection of you when we first rescued you. It wasn't until the night we left that something changed. But due to the following events, I assume you didn't get to fully talk about it. Not after it digested properly."

"She returned my memories," Daijiro said in a tone she couldn't place.

"You stole them?" asked Galahad, looking from Daijiro to Riko.

"My mother did, we had no choice..."

"You had a choice," Daijiro barked.

"It's in the past," Sulwyn concluded. "It doesn't matter that they were stolen. What happened to you would have still happened."

"It matters to me!" Daijiro bellowed, but Sulwyn stood quickly, dashing over and covering his mouth.

"This house may be at the far side of town, and the ocean may hide our voices, but still. Have some self-preservation!" Sulwyn hissed, but he yanked her hand from his face, snarling at her.

"My past was shit for as long as I can remember but I could handle it. Those memories would have been important to my mother. Then, at least she would have died trying to defend herself."

Sulwyn took a step back, his bandaged hand tight over her wrist that still burned from the rope, but she pushed that pain down. The smirk he was giving her now was similar to when he was torturing Tiergan. in the fog town. His eyes were wild and full of hatred and bloodlust.

"Did you think you knew everything about me? Did you really want to know how absolutely destroyed my mother really was after dealing with Tamesis? How her love for him ripped her apart?" He pulled her against his chest, Sulwyn listening to him with bated breath. Everyone's eyes on them.

He moved close to her ear, his lips just a breath away from her, eliciting a shiver as he whispered. "She *let* him do it. The village was burning, and everyone had been killed. And she let him kill her. Without a single thought to my existence." His jaw clenched so tightly she could see the muscles moving.

"I thought..." Sulwyn started, that original fear from the first time she ever met him thrummed through her. The one that made her question why everyone feared the Empire when this man existed. But this time it wasn't for herself. It was for him, knowing that he became this way from his own fear.

"That's not what you told me either ..." Galahad said, his voice almost as quiet. Sulwyn glanced at him, his brows furrowed, and then at Daijiro again, his eyes bright and red and furious.

"Do you really think that's something I want to relive? Why? Do you want to understand me more? Do you think you can fix it?"

"That was never my intention." Sulwyn's words were as thin as air and not enough to drag him out of what only he could see.

Daijiro chuckled bitterly, his eyes darkening, damp with unfallen tears and madness. "If you want to know so badly, and I didn't lie to you either, if that's what you're thinking. I omitted it." His eyes pierced hers, his fury almost tangible. She knew it was directed not only to his past, but to disappointment in how he was acting now. How easily he could fall back into who he thought he was. "I said I came in the morning from hunting and found him in our home and that he had killed her. I *was* gone hunting, and I did come back to the village in ruins. But instead of doing anything about it, I hid. Watched what was happening, trying to find the enemy. It wasn't until I returned did I learn that Tamesis was the one who brought the Empire to our door. Because it was then I was captured and bound and forced onto my knees in my own home, by Néosan. Silenced and unable to call out to her. Her back to me as she faced him, unaware that I was even there, not even wondering where I was and what I would come back to. And I watched her. Watched her hug him tightly as she blithered and cried. Watched as he looked at her with disgust and all she said was, 'If it will make you happy, then I understand'."

"That's... You could have been blinded by the emotions and shock," Sulwyn stuttered.

"He *told* her he was going to kill her, that he wanted to slice her head from her neck and watch her die. And she said she understood!

Her entire village was burning before her eyes, and you think *I* was blinded?" His voice cracked, raising higher with each word.

There was nothing she could say that could erase what he had seen and felt and been through. And even though dread tingled through her while she looked at him, she could also see the agony he carried in his eyes and shoulders. The vulnerability he went to such lengths to hide.

Sulwyn pulled him forwards, his grip still on her wrist, and reached up holding the back of his neck. "There isn't anything that can bring her back." Her voice soft and tender. "There isn't anything any one of us can do now for what you have suffered. But we can make sure that this won't happen in the future to anyone else. It's why we fight." She gently brought Daijiro closer, touching her forehead to his and looking into the depths of his eyes.

He loosened his hold on her wrist, the throbbing a little nauseating at this point, but she ignored it. "The rest of us don't know the full story, but Riko and her mother did what they thought was right at the time. And even if they had left the memories, you can't know that would have made a difference. Because by the sound of it, she was already lost long before."

But as Sulwyn said those words, an ominous chill crawled deep into the pit of her heart and up her spine. No one loved someone so blindly. Not to the point where they would give themselves over fully like that without a care for their child, themselves or their people without some sort of remorse or thought. Especially to someone so cruel. She clearly loved Daijiro but something about his mother always sounded off to her, and now even more so. She glanced at Galahad, and when their eyes met, she knew he thought so too.

Kione raised his hand. "Is... anyone going to tell me what a Velyūn is?" He was sitting quietly in the corner, his voice a tad shaky.

Daijiro sighed deeply, the sound a little frustrated, but another deep breath and he was hugging Sulwyn. And then another breath, breathing her in deeply. She stayed still, keeping her arms lightly around him as the pain now affected both wrists, growing agony sent bright spots dancing in her eyes. She would worry about her thoughts on his mother when the time came. For now, they needed to worry about the present and what to do next.

"A Velyūn," Daijiro started, letting go of Sulwyn and taking both wrists between his hands and frowning, "is a half-breed between a human and a Velikat. Born with abilities far stronger than a Velikat. Zalika is one, and so is Gwydion."

A cold tingle passed into her skin like mint, soothing the throbbing pain. She watched the skin begin to heal itself with a gentle blue fire that wrapped warmly around the red and raw rope burn. Astounding. This was nothing short of outstanding. His small, confident smile confirmed that this was the first time he'd ever managed to heal someone else.

"I've never seen anything like that..." Riko said timidly, her eyes bright and watery. Sulwyn gave her a reassuring glance just as the blue flames turned white before fading altogether.

Daijiro shrugged. "I've never seen it either." He lifted Sulwyn's wrists to look at them closely. The skin was red and irritated, but the cuts from the rope were healed. He unwrapped his hand, gingerly handing the bandage to Sulwyn.

"Wilkson is rather good at what he does," he mumbled, stretching out his fingers. The bruises and cuts were still there, but the burn had turned a light pink and was well on its way to healing. Taking another deep breath, Daijiro held his right hand over his left and the same light-blue fire coated his knuckles and skin until it was healed completely.

"You'll give him a run for his money with tricks like that." Sulwyn sat on the chair again. The tension rose and cleared the room as Daijiro took a seat on the floor.

"We should wait for the others before we continue this," Galahad said, sitting back as well and leaning against the chair. Sulwyn could see the exhaustion clinging to him. Clinging to all three of them. Clearly, she had given the others the better route.

"Not the better route. Any route you are a part of is bound to be messy."

She stood, relief coursing through her just as they heard a door quietly squeak open. Sulwyn grabbed a lit candle from the table and took it with her towards the stairs, careful to keep it low and away from any windows. Taru was closing the basement door behind him just as she spotted Arsinone walking to the foot of the steps.

"Oh, I'm so glad..." Sulwyn whispered, all the energy she had just gained seeping out of her once more. She was exhausted but refused to rest until the last two returned. She needed to see them. Needed to purge herself of the constant fear deep in her body.

And soon enough, just as Taru and Arsinone made their way up the stairs, the basement door opened again and in walked Eztli and Nori, each with a small basket of what she assumed was food.

"Sweetness!" Eztli squeaked, hopping on the spot. Nori looked up as she closed the door, relief flooding her face.

"I told you they would be all right!" Nori said.

"There's too many of us to sit in the room," Taru added from behind Arsinone just as she tackled Sulwyn, her arms wrapping around her waist. She hugged the girl tightly while trying not to drop the candle.

"I'm not going in that basement," Sulwyn said sternly, but Taru glanced at her as horror dawned on her. "Can you speak to..."

"It's fleeting. Pitiful and heartbreaking," Taru grunted, annoyed and saddened by the thought alone. "All that is left is the last thoughts they had before they died. And some flitting from the All-Mother's Garden. Those ones were a bit better."

"How so?"

"They thanked you for what you did." He smiled sadly, moving to the side and gesturing for her to go back down the stairs. Sulwyn pulled Arsinone along with her, and together with the others, they relocated into the kitchen.

Though the kitchen also had windows, now boarded, it faced the coast where no one could see it unless they walked right up to the house from the side. But even then, they kept the candlelight minimal and in the centre of the floor as they all crowded around it.

They ate in comfortable silence. The food and drinks given to Eztli from Azhar who had been supplying them since they came to the town four days prior. Sulwyn would need to go talk to him before they moved on. She needed to know what Raghnall did when he came here and how he looked. But she would do that tomorrow. Her thoughts were lulled by the peace of those around her and the food now settled within her.

She had always been running.

Running and running nonstop since she chose her path nearly eighteen years ago when she was only six. But for the first time in her life, she was content. For just a small moment. Just a small second in time where she even felt a little safe.

XXXVIII

The Best Disguise Is Me

| SULWYN |

"TELL me about Raghnall," Sulwyn said quietly. Azhar turned, dropping his ring of keys, looking this way and that along the empty cobblestone street. Sulwyn had been waiting since before the sun peaked over the horizon for Azhar to open his bar and inn. Waiting and waiting to hear anything at all about Raghnall.

He studied her, but a sound in the distance startled him into motion. Swiftly bending down, he picked up the keys, unlocked several locks then ushered her in quickly.

"You're just as hasty as he is, let me say that," he grumbled, motioning for her to go behind the bar while he opened all the curtains and shutters. She watched as he proceeded to go about his daily ritual. Darting back and forth to prepare the bar and kitchens as he normally would. Making sure to avoid suspicion at any cost. He looked just the same as he did the first time she met him.

His hair had grown even longer, now past his shoulders, though some of the brown was mixed with grey. His clothes were not as well kept as before, and there were more golden scars that shone against his dark skin. Azhar looked like he'd been through the wringer; his brown eyes were tired and puffy, but she could see the strength that shone in them. The determination that kept him going for himself and others. Sulwyn waited patiently, or as patiently as she could, stepping back and forth along the length of the old, worn-down, wooden bar. She watched his eyes follow her every so often, until finally, once he was done taking all the chairs off the tables, he came behind the bar with her.

"Down," he muttered, watching as someone passed by the windows. She did as she was told, and took a seat on a low stool, hiding behind the bar completely as he grabbed a bin of spoons and proceeded to rinse them in a bucket of water.

"When did you get here?" he grunted, and because of the concern that laced his voice, she conceded.

"I'm sorry to come at you like this. I arrived last night, but I don't plan to stay long. We'll all be gone soon." Sulwyn glanced at his hand, seeing the bracelet with Raghnall's symbol of a circle within a square. He didn't have that bracelet when she first met him, and if Raghnall could trust him, so could she.

"As you should. Artaxiad's men might be dull, but they will eventually catch on. I've been more active recently. Soon, they will realise that's not part of my schedule."

"How long have the Néosan been here?"

"About two weeks now? Your face is plastered all over the town, as is the prince's. Never thought I'd see the day."

"And the people..." she started, unsure if she wanted to know. But Azhar answered.

"Divided. Some remember you from that day. The few that were in here were shocked about who you were, in all aspects. There are people who loathe Kintana now." His voice was gruff, but she could hear the notes of annoyance. "Idiots, if you ask me. Been too scared for too long."

Sulwyn looked at him. "What makes you different then? Why don't you just hate me with the others? Even if you helped Raghnall at that time, he's being made out to be a traitor as well."

Azhar stopped. "You saved me and my family's lives. Long ago." Sulwyn stared at him, unable to draw his face from her memory. He just laughed.

"You were younger." He eyed her a little. "Some ten years ago? What were you then?"

"Almost fourteen…"

"Fourteen? Geez, he's trained you well. No. More than that. You are something all on your own." He laughed again, now moving on to butter knives. "I didn't use to live here. Lived back in Guāngcǎi. In the farther areas. But then our town was destroyed by some kind of blast."

"Oh! I'm so sorry…"

"Not your fault, is it? Them bleeding Néosan and their nasty ways. We all needed to leave Shā. But if you and Raghnall hadn't been there, I don't think any of us would have gotten away."

"Shā …" She didn't remember much from that time, but the blast was something she had never seen and would never forget. "But they burned your town… There wasn't anything we could do. I'd never seen anyone use the toxic water from the lakes as weapons. To make it explode like that…" But even as she said it, something in her stirred. She sat straighter. "Did you ever encounter that again? Or hear of it?"

Azhar paused, thinking and shaking his head. "No, actually. I just assumed they deemed it too dangerous for the Néosan to use ever again."

Sulwyn didn't believe that. If the Empire cared about anyone at all, it would have been the Captains and the Validus, at the most. At least in the way where they weren't as expendable. But the Néosan… not so much. And though it would look bad to have their army injured from their own weapons, she didn't think that was the case. After seeing the impostors, were they even real Néosan during that time in Shā? And if not, wouldn't that possibly mean they were also tied to Gwydion? He would be the only person who would be capable of creating an explosive.

"You all right?" asked Azhar, his hand waving in front of her face.

"Yes, sorry. But thank you." She reached forwards and touched the black leather bracelet around his wrist.

He looked down at it, smiling ever so subtly. "It was an honour to be given this, really. I was younger during the High City reign, but I still remember it clearly. Remember what freedom really meant." He sighed. "Raghnall was a mess when he came. How he even survived is plain luck in my opinion."

Sulwyn clenched her teeth. "I heard they were here for three weeks."

"About that, Wilkson brought him to me. We've met in the past, so it was a shock to see him alive, to be honest. I don't think I'd seen him since before the fall. Took me a while to even recognise him. But I knew he was a secretive man. And the fact that he was in front of me proved how dire the situation was."

Azhar moved on to forks now, looking out the window as more and more people started to pass. Though his bar wasn't open yet and the other staff had yet to arrive, he would need to open it soon to start serving breakfast before the townspeople went to work.

"Raghnall was out. Barely responded. No feeling in his left arm and leg. Pale as death. I still don't understand what he did. And I won't ask. The less I know, the better. I just know he got you into Valens. But it was easy enough to hide them. Wilkson knows how to fit in, and Raghnall stayed in the rooms upstairs. I barely had to feed him, which was both a good and terrible thing. Then one day, after about two weeks, he was awake. Fully awake. As if he hadn't just spent the last few days on his deathbed. He was weak and looked like right old shit. But his eyes...." He paused as if unable to catch the right words.

"His eyes?"

"They looked like yours." He turned to her, smirking just a little. "Fierce, determined. It's been a long time since I've seen that kind of defiance in someone. The Steel Warrior still lives in him, but he *is* crippled. And that's a fact."

"How badly...?"

"He never regained proper feeling in his left side. He is partially blind in the left eye and has a slower gait now, a limp and a stiff arm."

Sulwyn sighed. "I guess it's good he's right-handed." She rubbed her face but Azhar just laughed.

"That's what he said, the fool." Azhar dried off his hands, taking the crate of clean mixed utensils to distribute across the tables. Sulwyn stayed low, listening to the clink of metal. "He came to me the day he left. Early in the morning before Wilkson was back from gathering information. This was some time after you left. And, about that, I am sorry for not telling you. I couldn't. When you showed up in town, Wilkson warned me that whatever Raghnall did would be for naught if you didn't learn about it yourself."

"Raghnall's always pulling people into half-assed plans without anyone understanding what part they play. If anything, I apologise to you."

Azhar chuckled. "You both are really similar. Different too. It's nice, but yes. So, he came to me before he left, gifted me this bracelet and told me to pass on a message to you if you ever came by again asking questions." Sulwyn stood slightly, only enough to peep over the wooden bar and look at him. He turned to face her, and she could see he expected her reaction. His eyes warmed as he repeated Raghnall's words. "I have the best disguise. Me as I am. Burned, hobbled, old and reported dead. The next time you see me, be ready."

"What the hell is that?!" Sulwyn sputtered, but she ducked down just as there was a sharp rap at the front door window. She listened to Azhar place the crate down off his hip and onto the table to go open it.

"Not open yet, sir," he said sternly, but Sulwyn could hear the slight wobble in his voice. It was a Néosan in front of him.

"A bit off schedule, aren't you?" The man's voice was loud and searching.

"Not really. Once my utensils are set, I open the doors. I think you're just early."

"Are you talking back to me?"

Sulwyn tensed, listening hard.

"Just telling you like it is. But if you're really that hungry, you can come in. The stove should be ready."

Silence followed until the man spoke again. "Keep your head down, dog. We'll be back again when the other animals aren't out for food." The Néosan chortled at his own words as he left. Azhar remained silent until the door closed and Sulwyn heard footsteps going back to the table.

"You better leave now," he muttered, all trace of humour and warmth gone from his voice.

"I will fix this, Azhar. Somehow," she announced, edging around the bar, the legs of the tables blocking her from the front entrance. She knew he was following her movements until she made it to the backdoor. The hill by the ocean where they had climbed out of right before her.

"It's not really your responsibility, you know," he said off–handedly. She turned to him, his eyes kind but sorrowful.

"Maybe, maybe not. But it needs to be someone's. And since I've already been vying for the lead spot, I might as well continue." She winked at him, earning a smile, before she turned and ran out the door.

৯০৹ঞ

Sulwyn made her way through the shadows, people and stores until she found herself back at the small house and in front of the cellar door.

In the early morning when it was dark, she was able to exit out a side door, hidden and unseen, but now that the sun had risen, she had no choice but to come back through the cellar. To come back through the path were she first let herself become entirely intertwined in the Empire's business from the other side of the mirror.

For her entire life, she had always looked at the Empire one way. From the side of the weak and silent. The side who couldn't fight back or take charge of their lives. The side that battled for those who could not, protecting anyone she could.

Now, she faced these old wooden doors again.

A different person.

Coming from a different side.

From those who shoved aside the others and bled words of hatred. The ones that had armies to stand for them and protect their lives. The side that needn't battle for their spot, and instead, sit and watch those who fell before them.

But this side was broken.

Unlike the side she was from, this side was twisted and rotted and black. Full of loathsome souls who crushed one another to stand atop the rest. Digging their feet into the backs of others. Rising above the pools of blood and torturing those around them. Though unsurprised at how sick the Empire really was, she was surprised by the few that had been tainted or pulled in.

This side was broken, with shards like Caldwell, Galahad and Daijiro. So shattered that they cut anyone around them. Pieces like Nori, Eztli, Arsinone and Riko; all wanting and needing someone there for them but who had no one when they needed it most.

But if there was anything Sulwyn learned, it was that there were no sides. Not really. Instead of a glass mirror, the Empire and the rest of Vartugaul were an image of still water that had shattered under heavy rain. A rain caused by Gwydion. Though she was unsure of how exactly, she knew this was the truth. The truth she was reaching. She just needed to find Raghnall and figure out the rest.

Sulwyn closed her eyes, breathing out softly, and opened the doors to descend into the dark basement.

The smell of rotting had vanished, leaving behind a faint, musty smell of wet stone, mould and traces of ash. Plunged into darkness when she closed the doors, she chose to navigate her way without light. She didn't think she could face seeing the stains of torture that would forever be imprinted below this house.

Her boot brushed the edge of the wooden step, and she climbed up quietly, hoping she was back before the others awakened. But her hope was thwarted when the door quickly opened and a rather upset Arsinone stood in front of it.

"You are very lucky," she started, her eyes rising as Sulwyn reached the top. "My radius has extended quite a bit, but not near enough to hear you all over this town. Half of them wanted to go on a search party for you until I could convince them that I could finally hear your fleeting thoughts." Arsinone crossed her arms, staring her down, though her head was tilted up to look at her properly.

Sulwyn knelt in front of Arsinone and wrapped her arms around her tightly.

"Oh…" she mumbled, surprised. But Sulwyn couldn't say anything. Her throat constricted with the effort of holding back her tears, with the effort of holding back everything she ever wanted to scream. Sulwyn sat in the middle of the hall, pulling Arsinone into her lap, and just continued to hold her. Seeing nothing but the darkness she left in the basement.

Eztli, Kione and Nori all came out from the sitting area, most likely the ones who wanted to search for her, stunned into silence. But still, Sulwyn kept her cries in, unable to understand why she felt the way she did. Unable to form the words even in her mind, let alone aloud.

Sulwyn knew the others moved into the open now, coming from upstairs until the brief passing of mint washed over her. Evoking something in her to let everything down and out until anguished tears came freely. From all the anger and rage exploding within. From all the despair and emptiness. All the love and happiness from those around her, and the fact that Raghnall was still possibly alive. Oh, what a journey they had in front of them.

Arsinone eased back, Sulwyn's hold on her lax, arms falling to the floor. Someone moved next to her, but she wasn't paying attention anymore. She just wanted to sleep. Just a little bit. She hadn't slept since arriving. She just needed that and then she would be ready. Or at least, that's what she would tell herself for now.

"Please let me sleep…" she whispered, not aware of wanting to say it aloud, but glad for it either way. Everyone watched her carefully, their stares heavy, but she wouldn't look up. Someone knelt before her, moving her hair back and out of her face. Their hands were warm as they rested on either cheek.

"I have a plan…" Galahad said softly. "And I know you will agree with it. I promise we won't discuss everything until after you have rested and joined us. A few more hours won't do us any harm. Not now. Go."

Sulwyn looked up into his tricoloured eyes. Warmth and rest shone through him, something she hadn't ever seen in him. He smiled gently, brushing tears off her cheeks before turning his head and nodding. He gripped her shoulders in reassurance before he got up, stepping back as another set of legs stood before her.

With ease, Daijiro helped her stand before lifting her across his arms. Sulwyn plopped her head against his shoulder as he parted through the others and took her up the stairs.

The Soul Can Heal

| SULWYN |

THERE were no dreams. No thoughts or words flitting in her mind. It was empty and warm and relaxing.

Until she woke up and it all rushed back to her.

Sulwyn gasped, sitting up in a panic until an arm pulled her back down.

"It doesn't surprise me that I can't even subdue your mind long enough for you to sleep peacefully," Daijiro said.

Sulwyn turned, her head resting against the side of his chest. He had changed from the clothes Galahad had given him back into his own. She had done that the night before after they had finished eating. Revelling in a bath of cool water before she sat in front of the dying fire until sleep finally came. But she couldn't sleep longer than a half hour at best. Thus, she left before the rest awakened and made her way to Azhar. Sulwyn blamed irritation on her earlier behaviour.

She sighed, leaning back and relaxing into the pillows. Trying not to think about whose room this once was. The windows were cutained here, cracked open ever so slightly so that the deep brown fabric fluttered, sunlight streaming in with every crack the wind made. The room itself was like the others. Simple, old but well-kept. The upstairs rooms were untouched, though there wasn't much value to begin with. Probably in attempts to keep anyone robbing them out of their rooms.

Hoping they would take what they saw downstairs and leave. It was too bad that it didn't work.

"You're tensing again."

"Are you on guard duty?" she asked softly.

"Who am I protecting?"

"Everyone else…" Sulwyn replied darkly, her mind on the Néosan at the edge of the town. She could hear the whisper of a laugh from Daijiro.

"I'm not for hire for a job like that. My goal now was to get you to sleep. But alas…" His shoulder nudged her as he shrugged.

"Tell me…" Sulwyn started, unsure of how to ask about Riko.

"Are you jealous?" She could hear his smirk as he asked, and found herself smiling.

"No, would you rather I was?"

"Not really. I've seen you jealous, it's very… scratchy."

"Zalika enhanced my jealousy. It's not normally like that."

"How about *you* tell me about that time first?" he countered. Sulwyn sat up, turning to face him as the thin blanket fell off her shoulders, sending a shiver through her.

"What time?"

"While I was surprised that you held jealousy in regard to me, it wasn't only towards me… Tell me about when you first met."

"Are *you* jealous?" she asked, brow raised.

"A little. There is something there I could never touch. I wonder if that would have changed if I had received you when you first came."

"No. It wouldn't have," Sulwyn said, a gentle smile on her lips. Daijiro's dark red eyes bore into hers. "Ah, I think that's more than just a little jealous, but I asked first."

"You're supposed to be sleeping."

"Sleeping and resting are the same in my books. Speak," she demanded, now sitting up properly and bracing upright on the pillow.

Daijiro glanced at her silently until he took her hand in his. A thrilling surge sparked through his touch, his hand hot. But when he finally spoke, she tried to focus on that instead.

"Riko and her mother used to travel. They met my mother, became friends and came to our small village when I was ten. As she would go back and forth between her travels, Riko stayed with us, and for two years, it was like that. She was my only friend. But times were different then. *Everything* was different then…" He trailed off.

"Had she not left, what do you think would have happened?"

Daijiro sighed, closing his eyes and leaning his head back against the board as well. "I think the village would have been attacked regardless. And if it had been, there's a chance they would have died sooner. Or they could have survived. But you are right. I don't think my mother's reaction would have changed, so neither would mine. My heart isn't kind, Sulwyn. And though I've learned to make space in it, that won't change. Not fully. I have learned patience, but my core is blood."

"Why did you fight then?" Sulwyn whispered, noting that his hand had grown tighter over hers while he spoke.

"Revenge. Injustice. Despair. I wanted to fill the hole Tamesis had created. Instead, I became just as bad as him, filling it with blood." He moved to let go of her hand, but Sulwyn held on tighter.

"Why do you fight now?" She looked at him and he opened his eyes to face her, realisation dawning on him. She smiled. "Growth doesn't happen overnight. And it doesn't stop overnight either. We've all done things we are not proud of under titles we tried to find justification in. But it's about knowing when to do so and when to stop that makes us different."

Daijiro huffed, reaching over and taking her other hand. "Your turn. Why wouldn't it have made a difference if I met you when you first came here?"

Sulwyn looked at the sunlight streaming across the dark wooden floor and onto the bed. "I met Galahad for the first time when I was six, not here."

Daijiro stared at her, eyes wide. "That was even before he was brought here."

"He saved me from being choked to death by a Néosan."

"That's pretty low…" muttered Daijiro.

Sulwyn shrugged. "Not really, I've seen worse. However, I did attack the Néosan first and stabbed him in the thigh, so…"

Daijiro roared with laughter. "Why am I not surprised. That's brilliant. And then?"

"Galahad came and stabbed him in the back. Quite sure he killed him now that I think about it. But then he ran off once Raghnall arrived."

"Why wasn't he with you?"

"He was getting our provisions. I ran off on my own to help someone else."

"Ah, now there's our true Sulwyn." He smirked, turning her to face him. Sulwyn avoided his stare, embarrassment and warmth wrapping around her. His hands were even hotter now, forcing her to truly realise how close they were, and on a bed, of all things.

"How long have I been up here?" Sulwyn asked, trying to lean back again.

"Not nearly long enough that I can let you go," he whispered, and though she tried not to look at him, she did anyway. Regretting and revelling in her decision all at once. He pulled her hands up, resting them along his shoulders and behind his neck, then brought his lips to hers, capturing her breath of surprise.

An incessant need rose in her all at once, like it had been sitting there in the pit of her core, waiting and waiting until it had this chance to pounce. And though she could feel the tension in Daijiro's shoulders, understanding that he wanted nothing more than to show her how he felt, especially after she had fallen in the ice, he maintained a sense of gentleness. Touching her neck softly, carefully pulling her closer.

Her premonition had interrupted them last time, but because of it she burned on the inside, wanting so much to engulf him. To know more about him. It was the only reason she cared about what was between him and Riko. Not because of jealousy, but because she wanted to know that there was a time in his life when he'd been happy, at least once. They all had that moment, and she had always wondered if he had his.

His lips were soft. His tongue even softer. Warm hands weaved through her hair until she found herself pushing him back to lean over him, her hair framing his face and her arms on either side of his shoulders.

Sulwyn kissed him again, carefully, trying to hold back whatever was in her. But Daijiro wasn't having it. He leaned forwards and wrapped her legs around his waist, pulling her right against him. He paused for a beat, gazing into her eyes, double-checking her response. She kissed him deeply this time. Eager to feel his tongue on hers, to inhale him. Savouring everything because there was a soft nagging in her mind that she was trying to ignore.

Daijiro was equally eager to do the same, further deepening the kiss between them until his hands started to roam. The tapping in her mind growing more incessant. But she gained a stronger distraction when his hands began to slowly roam her back and then around to her breasts.

Goose bumps ran over her skin, she was unbelievably sensitive, responding with a small jolt of her hips that only fed his curiosity more. And still, the tapping grew.

Just a little more, she wanted to give herself just a little more. Sulwyn tugged his sash, pulling him so that he pushed her down onto the bed. When she opened her eyes, the blaze in his own nearly ruined her. She could see the hint of hesitation, knowing that this wouldn't end the way they both wanted it to.

They both stilled, breaths mixing as they took each other in. Gently, he brought a hand towards her cheek, grazing her skin with hot fingers. Pushing her hair away from her face and behind her ear. The act was tender. More than she thought he was capable of. But she clearly had so much more to learn.

Daijiro moved his hand a little lower, brushing a thumb over her bottom lip and taking her chin between his fingers. The kiss he gave her now was delicate but also a bit mournful. But he still kept his lips against hers before pulling away as little as possible. Sulwyn clung to his back, trying to memorise every movement. Brushing her hands over his shoulder blades and the width of his back. Skimming lower, eliciting a quiet groan as she softly moved from his back to the front of his chest. She wanted to go lower. She wanted him to go lower as well. But the tapping only warned her further.

Sulwyn wanted to do more, have more time with him, but she could no longer ignore the warning inside her.

Their mingled breathing was the only sound around them, both staring into the other's eyes again. She never realised that his irises weren't pure red but had small flecks of gold in them that glimmered a little in the light around her.

Earlier, when Sulwyn was sitting in the middle of the floor, and her heart was plummeting into darkness, she saw nothing. Try as she might, she couldn't find an anchor to bring her out until that instance when the mild scent of mint spread through her. And she wondered briefly if that was what he meant when he thought of her. As the person who kept him down in this storm. And if the storm wasn't there, would it be the same?

Daijiro's brow furrowed, and though he stayed silent, she could see growing concern. There was an answer forming in her, but she needed to know. "If the Empire didn't burn Vartugaul and our lives did not become this, would we be here like this?" Her voice barely audible, afraid of his response.

His expression changed to serious in the split–second it took her to blink. "No." A cold drop of reality fell into her heart but he continued. "If they didn't plan to burn Vartugaul, you wouldn't have been here. You wouldn't be you, and I wouldn't be me. But despite my life, and selfishly the lives of everyone else, I wouldn't change what I've been through if it meant I wouldn't find you. The past is the past. We are here now. Isn't that what you said? You aren't some temporary fix to the problems

I face. You are the guide to the person I want to be for myself, and for you. I may not be kind in the way you are used to. But don't question how deeply I've come to love you." A growl tinged the last words, his eyes blazing so strongly she might as well be engulfed by fire.

Sulwyn inhaled.

There, he said it again.

The second time since he said it back in Wilkson's bar.

"Daijiro…" was all that came out. She wanted to give him the time they deserved, the words and thoughts he deserved.

"I know your answer, Sulwyn, even if you won't voice it yourself," he whispered, sitting up and taking her with him. "But I also know you are duty–bound. I don't expect you to do anything you aren't ready to, especially when the setting isn't ideal."

"I don't only mean *that*…" Sulwyn said, the heat prickling her neck.

"Neither do I," he whispered. "I am content with what we have and what we will have whenever you want it, if at all."

Sulwyn continued to look at him. To really see the man in front of her and how far they had come. She knew it now that she would trust him with her life, wherever it took them. She leaned forwards, pulling his head down slightly, and softly kissed his forehead.

Sulwyn finally managed to get her mind to relax enough to let Daijiro help her sleep, soft fingers over her forehead the last thing she remembered. And when she woke, the sun had risen high into the sky, the bed warm with sleep and rays of sun.

She rolled off her side and onto her back to find Daijiro still next to her, his eyes opening slowly from her movement.

"How do you feel?" he murmured deeply. He raised a hand to her cheek, his touch feather–like.

"Rested… I haven't felt this rested in such a long time. And clear. I feel… light," she confessed, sighing as she did so. All the thoughts from the morning and all the thoughts since she left her home had settled for now. This was the time she needed. And there was a goal to achieve.

Daijiro sat up, stretching wildly as he stood. His boots had been tossed unceremoniously to the side just before he placed Sulwyn onto the bed, taking off her own in the process. She watched him make his way over, putting a foot in each before a sharp knock vibrated off the door.

Daijiro stepped over her own boots, pulling the door open. Eztli rushed in with a pitcher of water. She gave him a sidelong glance then jerked her head for him to leave. Sulwyn could only stare at them both, Daijiro obviously itching to say something but deciding against it. He gave Sulwyn a tender smile and walked out the door and out of sight.

"Explain," Eztli said, giving Sulwyn a glass and hefting the pitcher up to pour water.

"You'll need to be a bit more specific…" She trailed off, taking slow, deep gulps. She forgot how refreshing water was.

"Do ya know," she started but stopped. Sulwyn could see how flustered and annoyed she was getting. Knowing what she was truly referring to but choosing to watch this reaction instead. "Look, I know ya were havin' a tragic moment downstairs, and my heart was literally breakin' watchin' ya, but do ya know how surprised most of us were when Daijiro took ya upstairs? Like that? Daijiro? *Daijiro?*"

"Who wasn't surprised?" asked Sulwyn, a smile growing on her lips at the frustration in Eztli's eyes.

"Really? Is that the question 'ere? Arsinone, Galahad and Riko. Riko! This girl just got 'ere, and she's not surprised?"

"She's not surprised because I've already told her where I stand," came Daijiro's voice from the hall.

Sulwyn's chest and neck were melting at this point, but she was distracted when Eztli huffed, "Are ya eavesdropping right now?"

"Tying my boots, since someone kicked me out before I had the chance. Wouldn't want to trip now, would I?" Humour laced his voice, but irritation rattled through Eztli.

She leaned forwards and slammed the door shut, turning to face Sulwyn again. "Are ya sure?" Her voice was low, eyes glaring daggers.

Sulwyn looked at her carefully. "Sure, about what?"

"This? That?" She jabbed her thumb towards the door. "Him? Sulwyn. I don't know much 'bout him on a personal note. But there are so many rumours of what he has done."

Sulwyn stared at her straight in the eyes. "I know what he has and hasn't done. I know and don' know who he is. But I know where he draws the line, no matter how far away it may be. We've all done things to survive or when we were lost."

Eztli whimpered. "He's terrifyin', Sulwyn."

"I know, but I'm not afraid. If that's what you're getting at."

"And you shouldn't be."

Arsinone's voice resonated in her soul, and by the startled jump of Eztli's, hers as well.

"What makes you say that?" Sulwyn asked, drinking more of the water.

"His soul is slowly healing." Sulwyn's eyes widened, looking up at Eztli even though she didn't really know what that meant. But Arsinone continued, *"Are you ready to come downstairs?"*

Sulwyn stood, Eztli handing over her boots. She was ready.

Opening the door, Daijiro was nowhere to be found. Sulwyn stepped forwards out of the room and into the hall before making her way down the stairs. As she reached the bottom, Galahad came out from the kitchen and wordlessly wrapped her in a hug.

Sulwyn closed her eyes, her arms tight around him as emotions like nostalgia and peace came over her. It resonated like a beat between them, and by the way his back tensed, he felt it too. She looked up, seeing the confirmation in his eyes.

"If the bond between us leaves room for things like this, I'll keep that part open." She smiled, overjoyed by how content he looked.

"Somehow you have more control over it than I do." He chuckled, taking her hand and pulling her towards the kitchen. Eztli quickly went to the living room, bringing Nori and Kione with her.

This kitchen was larger than the one in the house across from them. Everything coated in a thin layer of dust, vaguely reminding her of Pandora and Artaxiad's house. All the chairs had been brought into this room while she was sleeping, set up in a large circle before them.

"I think it's about time we finally talk and plan our next step," Galahad started, taking a seat and motioning for the rest to follow.

Sulwyn sat across from him, the curtained window to her back as the others sat around, and finally, they all stared at her.

In all her travels, she had never sat in a room with this many people regarding the future of Vartugaul and themselves. She was only ever used to being with Raghnall, and sometimes Wilkson and Kai. But having eight other people waiting for her to start their odd meeting was a little jarring. She would start from the beginning.

"Over half a year ago, I was brought to the Empire as a prisoner held captive and announced the Blood Princess. Both Kintana's and the Steel Warrior's names were slandered, and Raghnall's death was announced to the world as a traitor. I should explain a little about that first." Sulwyn hesitated, looking at everyone around her. She was sure of her trust in everyone here. And if worse came to worse, she would have to kill anyone who betrayed them. Raghnall made this plan for a reason, the longer Gwydion was kept in the dark the better. Sulwyn glanced at Daijiro, a glint in his eyes. She knew he was thinking the same.

"As ludicrous as it sounds, Raghnall faked his death to bring me to the Empire."

"Excuse me?" Kione asked, leaning forwards. "Is that even possible?"

"With magic…" started Riko thoughtfully. "Risky magic and a lot of skill and madness, it would be possible…?"

"Something he has access to in all aspects," Sulwyn said, happy that this seemed to digest well. "I don't know the details, but on a bet of all things circumstantial in his plan, his goal was to get me in, and if all went well, get himself out. That way he could properly find the true threat he was looking for without anyone knowing. Hoping the real threat would show face at his death thus allowing me to find them regardless."

"Real threat?" muttered Taru, looking at her carefully. Sulwyn glanced at him. Seeing him as calm as she left him when they escaped still unsettled her. She wondered if he was keeping an active effort to ignore all the objects around him, or if it came naturally to him. She wasn't sure how old he truly was, but he must have a handle on his power by now.

She continued. "Based on what I've discovered so far… Gwydion is the real threat."

"Isn't he a scholar or somethin'?" asked Eztli. "Part o' the Triarchy?"

"It's a cover," said Sulwyn darkly. She caught Galahad's eye but shook her head; she would tell her story. "I mentioned a bit of this to Kione and Riko when we first arrived last night. But I discovered two things during the time we separated. One, Gwydion didn't come to the Empire thirteen years ago. He helped create it. He's known Pandora and Artaxiad since way before. Hold on a second."

There was nothing better than proof, so Sulwyn got up and walked to the living area to get her sack. Sitting back down in the kitchen, she rifled through it and found the damage-proof pouch of vials and pulled out Pandora's journal.

Sulwyn pried apart the pages carefully, turning to the spot where the painting sat between its pages. Before she could say any more, Taru reached forwards. Sulwyn handed him both items and watched in silence.

"Taru…" Galahad warned, glancing at Sulwyn and then at Daijiro. Taru silenced him with a shrewd look, closing his eyes and holding the journal and image closely to his chest. Silence settled over them, giving Sulwyn the chance to gather her thoughts further. In the distance through the sliver of open window, she could hear the waves of the coast wash over the rocks.

A clatter, and the journal fell to the floor. The portrait fluttering after it. Taru looked at her quickly, his eyes full of sadness and another emotion she couldn't read, but she was sure he was actively trying not to look anywhere near Daijiro.

"Teenagers," he said with a heavy breath. "They met when they were in their late teens. That portrait was drawn a few months after to commemorate their growing partnership, for lack of a better word. But Sulwyn, he's—"

"Second thing, he's a Velyūn *and* a Devinal," Sulwyn finished, seeing the faint horror in Taru's uneven eyes. "I don't know the details and I don't know who truly started the rebellion. But I know that they were together, plotting to bring the High City down years in advance."

"Seventeen years to be exact," Daijiro said, looking between all of them. Sulwyn could see his suspicion growing, but he held his tongue, sitting calmly.

"Yes, seventeen years of planning…Then he disappeared from the public eye, changed his appearance and showed up ten years after the fall as if they had never met before, even though it seems they've been together for almost forty years. That in itself is odd to me, but without any more details, I can't say more. But for those years absent, I think he's been working on a plan of his own while Artaxiad and Pandora led the Empire." Sulwyn leaned forwards, hands on her knees. "Pandora knew Gwydion was a Devinal, but I don't think either of them knew he was a Velyūn. And based on how rare you are," she waved to Daijiro, "it doesn't surprise me. However, I think part of his goal has something to do with what I think his ability is *as* a Velyūn."

Eztli raised a hand. "A what? Ya keep sayin' this word and I have no idea what it means." She crossed her arms.

"Me. I'm a Velyūn." Daijiro stood. "A half-breed between a human and a Velikat. The Velikat were a race of elite humans that evolved sometime after The Shift that destroyed the Lost World. I don't know the history, but I know, like Galahad, we have a connection to the All-Mother."

Eztli gawked at him—they all did—and then Sulwyn could smell the sweet rain, burnt wood and mint envelop her gently. But where it only floated around her, it subconsciously enticed everyone else. Everyone except for Galahad, and to her surprise, Taru. Sulwyn stared at him, but he put a finger to his lips ever so subtly.

Daijiro stepped closer to Eztli kneeling in front of her, his allure strong, though not as strong as he could make it. Sulwyn vaguely wondered what the effect of that would be. But she continued to watch the rest of them as they stared at him, waiting for him to say or do anything.

"My ability is to allure all genders, no matter their preference." He spoke softly as she leaned closer to him. "To sway them my way, in any way. It's not the most dazzling thing, but it's perfect for information gathering or getting what you want." Daijiro was now inches away from Eztli who did not move back in the slightest until Sulwyn could feel the pull lessen ever so slowly, and with it, Eztli's rising expression of horror.

"What did ya just do?" she hissed, jumping back when the allure fell completely.

"Exactly."

"So, you can sway emotions... That's a little..." Kione hesitated. Sulwyn tried to shush him, but Daijiro turned to him smiling wildly. "You've worked at the Solus. You've heard the rumours. But I don't think you've ever witnessed it. Or better yet, *experienced* it."

"Daijiro," Galahad warned.

Daijiro smirked. "Hush, prince." He glanced at Sulwyn, and she knew he wasn't going to do anything dangerous. Because she knew he was well aware of how much she would beat him if he tried. His smile widened as he held out a palm in front of Kione. Sulwyn watched Kione's eyes widen in surprise, and then fear, as he tried and failed to move.

Daijiro swiftly dropped his hand and went back to his seat. "I have control over every nerve and muscle of a person. Again, useful for interrogation on the off-chance that gently swaying them isn't enough. That is a Velyūn. Or at least, my power as one."

"You can breathe, Kione," Sulwyn said. Nori, who had been still the entire time, reached over and patted Kione gently on the shoulder.

"I told ya he was scary," Eztli whispered, finally leaning back.

"Gwydion is a Velyūn and a Devinal," reminded Sulwyn, and now she watched as that fact sank in. "I don't know what Gwydion's true abilities are but based on Pandora's journal and what I have experienced myself, I think it has something to do with desire. Bringing out a person's deepest desire, allowing them to act on it. Kind of like Zalika's ability to bring out jealousy. And yes, she's a Velyūn too. And I don't like that we have no idea where she went. Or where Zander is for that matter...." She trailed off, something nagging at her once again.

"Ya just said they be rare and now we know three of 'em?" Eztli asked, still reeling from her encounter with Daijiro.

"The rare do tend to come together," Taru muttered.

"Wouldn't that be a good thing? To bring out desire?" asked Nori.

"If a person's desire was innocent, possibly," Taru explained. "But if a person was darker or twisted and just needed a little more ambition, then it would be an extremely dangerous thing. If what you say is correct, it makes sense in Artaxiad's and Pandora's actions thus far."

"Near the end of Artaxiad's life, his desire changed from ruling the Empire to creating a stronger heir and ruling the Empire alongside me for more power." A shiver of disgust crawled over Sulwyn. "Whatever he did, I think it broke Artaxiad's mind just as it did to Pandora until pure desire was the only thing left." She mulled over her thoughts. Pandora clearly showed defiance when she was pregnant, and at the end when she warned Sulwyn. Taru did say her strong willpower derived from Pandora. How fitting.

"Then why is someone like that in the shadows?" Kione asked, loathing in his eyes for Gwydion and that his sister was with him.

"Daijiro once explained to me that people wanted to extract the power from Velikat. And in turn, Velyūn. But the power doesn't exist in the blood or anything like that. My guess is that he is trying to recreate his own ability to allure, or part of it, using magic and science. I've been under the influence of his prototype, thanks to Artaxiad, and to a poison in its final stages. One that he said is ready to work on individuals, but they seem to be struggling with mass production. Which brings me to you." She turned to Taru, and his body sagged as if expecting this moment.

Taru sighed, looking at anywhere else until finally he turned his uneven coloured eyes on her. "I was waiting for you to ask since the first time you came back. I could smell her on you, but since the times were chaotic, we never had a chance to speak. But yes, Tiamat is my sister. My twin and other half. I am thankful that you didn't harm her, though I am sure you wanted to." He cast a glance at Galahad.

"I had a horrible feeling that if we did, something would happen," Sulwyn whispered, seeing the sadness in his eyes.

He smiled gently. "I guess it's my turn to share a little?"

XL

Two Sides Of The Same Seed
|SULWYN|

SULWYN just stared at Taru. This tiny man before her, wispy and tottery, though not at this moment.

This man was born from a tree.

"I think that's enough for a lifetime," said Eztli, eyes wide in disbelief. "Devinal and Velyūn are one thing, but now we have tree people."

Taru smiled lightly. "We are Rízes, but I am still a person like you, but my sister and I were grown in the roots of a tree. Not fully in existence until the right person passed us. This tale is easier to digest if you just accept it." He leaned forwards and patted Eztli on the knee.

Galahad glanced out a small hole in the window behind Sulwyn. "I don't think we should stay past a couple more days in this town. The sooner we get to the planning part of all of this, the better."

Taru nodded. "Two women, a couple, came to the tree one day to admire it. It was a magnificent tree. One of a kind. Large and full of orange flowers and indigo leaves. Even after we left, it continued to bloom each year. I was told we were presented to them in the trunk of the tree as they sat against it. It opened itself to them to show us as infants. They took us and raised us." Taru's tone was light and nostalgic, and truly seemed like an old man reminiscing. "For years we grew and learned as one normally does. The only difference is that our knowledge of the world and the people was vast even at a youthful age, and with it, our power." He looked at Sulwyn. "As you know, I can read the history of a soul. While Tiamat can control a soul."

"That's not equal," said Nori quietly.

"No one said it would be," Taru replied sadly. "But we both have advantages and disadvantages. Tiamat grew nightmarish with age. The more she takes a soul, the more she loses some of her own, because with each soul she takes she needs to put a little of her own in it to control it. Of course, she can take it back once she's done with it. But like anything that breaks, it's not whole the same way again."

"She told us it's easier for her to take control if a soul has been read by you," Galahad said solemnly.

"This is true. Though no threat to you, letting me read you does bare the soul to the skies. The only one who can take advantage of that is her. That is her disadvantage to me. Mine to her is that any soul she has tainted I can purify. Break her control and heal it as long as there is still something to heal."

"Fascinating..." Galahad mused, looking at him pointedly. "So then, what was this tree and where is it now?"

"Ah, this tree was incredibly old. So much older than I. So old that it was born during the time of the Lost World."

"You mean a hundred thousand years ago?!" exclaimed Sulwyn, finally letting the story sink in.

"Probably just a little more, but yes. This tree absorbed the good and bad energy of the world and when The Shift happened it grew even more. As the centuries passed, it, too, evolved like many other things. It survived The Shift and lived through The Dragon Reign, The Battle of Teeth, all the way to the Armistice Period one thousand years ago when the High City was first established by the Zalman clan."

"Was this tree planted by the All-Mother?" asked Daijiro, his curiosity overriding his suspicion of Taru. Sulwyn glanced at Galahad, his eyes relieved for now. Sulwyn never actually asked Galahad why he, and clearly

Taru, wanted to keep his soul reading a secret from Daijiro, but something in her was starting to agree.

"Yes and no. The All-Mother was created by the land itself, and in turn, related to the tree. A living manifestation of the tree's original purpose. But instead, she would take the negative energy, convert it into positive energy, then give it back to the land. Which is how clans like the Velikat and Kurome came to be along the way."

"So, you're… a hundred thousand years old?" Kione asked, his eyebrows practically at his hairline.

"No, no. I am only three hundred and fifty-two. Give or take a few years."

"Only?" Kione wheezed at that, all of them staring at Taru incredulously. The old man only shrugged.

"No wonder you're so…" Sulwyn struggled to find a word that could encompass Taru's entity. "…different."

Taru hiccupped in laughter, a bit of the twinkle she was used to when she first met him back in his eyes. "Oh yes, so very different."

"Then what about the little one?" Daijiro asked, pointing at Arsinone. She had been silent the entire time. Listening to all of them, only watching.

"It's hard to be alive for so long on your own," said Taru in defeat. "I did settle down at one point. She is blood. Descendant of my own, with her own gifts that manifested differently than I could have imagined. She is a little of both of us in some respects. Arsinone can hear the soul of a person or animal and project her own soul forwards to communicate. But she can also project emotions that can lead to a semi-controlled state of another person's soul."

"Ah, so you're a half-breed like me." Daijiro smirked. Arsinone smiled at him, her eyes a little brighter.

"Are you okay?" Sulwyn asked, turning to face her properly. "You've been quiet the entire time."

"A child is still a child, no matter the gifts they carry," said Taru warmly. "She is afraid."

Arsinone only nodded, holding her hands in her lap. "I'm okay. I don't have much to say, so don't mind me while I listen." She gestured for the rest to continue.

"What happened to the tree then?" Sulwyn asked, and Taru's eyes grew dark and a little malevolent. Here he was briefly identical to Tiamat.

"I destroyed it." His voice was harsh. "Tiamat and I parted ways when we got older. She became too much for me to control. But it was my mistake to let her go on her own. And I will fix that mistake. We can only die by the others' hand, lest we upset a balance. But as atonement, I cut down the tree and burned it so that it could never create another one like us again. The only thing was…" He glanced at Daijiro now, giving him his full attention.

"What?" he snapped, but everyone turned to look at him too.

"When I burned the tree, a bird of fire erupted from the ashes," Taru continued, but Daijiro just looked as if he had never seen him before now. Eyes wide, jaw clenched. "I couldn't smell it before. Didn't recognise it at first. But each time I saw you, the smell became stronger."

"What smell?" Daijiro's voice was low, the others watching carefully.

"The smell of ash, of Innominatam. The phoenix born of my tree." Sulwyn wasn't sure what kind of emotion was running through Daijiro, but his eyes were fierce and his body rigid.

"Taru… We will continue this another time," Galahad started, breaking the growing tension between them.

"He's right," Sulwyn said. "But now you know the main facts at hand. Gwydion is the true threat. Or I sure as hell hope so because if he isn't, I don't think I'd be prepared for what is."

"Did you all learn anything on your side?" asked Galahad. Sulwyn caught him sharing a hardened glance with Daijiro. But Daijiro sat back, crossing a leg over his knee and listening.

"Well," replied Eztli, "I think our journey was far less adventurous, jus' my own thoughts, but that's why we're still alive. We were travelling from Illa when we saw the Néosan move out. A smaller platoon spotted us, but we managed to lose 'em once we passed some frozen lake. A bunch of them went o'er it, but it started to crack, so they left it and went back."

"That's why it broke…?" Galahad whispered in disbelief.

"What?" Eztli's eyes wide with bewilderment.

"That lake has been frozen for so many years. Before I was born. We know how to navigate it and how many people can go at a time. Frozen for years…" he huffed in despair.

Sulwyn frowned, encouraging Eztli to continue.

"I'm sorry abou' the lake?" Eztli mumbled in confusion, but Galahad waved her on, his fingers pinching the bridge of his nose. "Taru suggested we go to Zilwunt first just in case, ya know? But once we go' there, the town was already buzzin' with activity. We stayed for about a week, ya? Just before the full platoon of Néosan came through. Posting yer faces everywhere! We were sure ya'd get caught. But we had hope. What we did learn, though, is that Nero is pushing everyone to find ya. The Empire is in a fit state. Riots are happening now. Platoons being sent to each major town across Vartugaul…" She fell silent, staring at Sulwyn. "But everyone is now targeting one person. And it's Sulwyn." She pointed to her; unable to meet her eyes.

"Kintana is the enemy, the Blood Princess is the enemy." Sulwyn sighed. "Raghnall is the enemy. But no one sees the truth. And even if they don't know about Gwydion, and originally bought Zander being the scapegoat for killing Pandora, or the prisoners for killing Artaxiad, it doesn't stop the fact that people are turning a blind eye. And now choosing to see me and Galahad as the perpetrators."

"Of course they would," said Galahad. "Gwydion helped a lot of the Privileged and helped with the Diarchy at the time. They've already lost Artaxiad and Pandora, convinced now that you somehow poisoned them. They won't lose him too. Not yet."

"And what of Nero?" she demanded. "I thought he held some sort of regard in their minds?"

"He does, but he's not a Velyūn and a Devinal cheat, is he?" Daijiro asked. "We have no idea what he's done to gain so much popularity among the rest."

"If Artaxiad's army is spreading out to find you, I think it's best you disappear for a while. Lure people into thinking you're dead or missing," Galahad said, and now they all looked at him. Sulwyn turned her eyes to his. Seeing the thoughts she knew were coming from his lips. "We need to go into hiding. Just for now. Just until we can further figure out what we can do. With them in high security, it will be hard for us to move and stay safe."

"But others will be at risk if we do that," said Sulwyn, torn between hiding to bide time and fighting now. But he was right. They would be plunging themselves into a losing battle. No one was on her side, and the ones who were didn't have the strength to aid her.

"I'm not worried about that as much as I normally would be. You forget that Ildri and the others haven't been found yet, either." Galahad smirked.

"But the Néosan are everywhere. And in time, there will be nowhere to hide," said Nori quietly.

"We could always go to Malumagri," Kione suggested, but shrugged when everyone stared at him as if he had two heads.

"I think that's an adventure for another day…" Daijiro sighed, humour in his eyes.

"No. There is one place that few can go to. Not without a guide of some kind, be it in person or by careful instruction," Galahad said, and here Sulwyn waited. Knowing what was coming and she smiled when their eyes met. Understanding flit through him as he took a deep breath. "We will go to my home, to Mortui Gemma."

XLI

Blood Doesn't Equal Family

"WE have our tasks," said Sulwyn. "I want us to be ready by tomorrow night. Riko, come help me?" She smiled as the others got up to prepare for the upcoming trek to climb along a snowy mountain.

Riko looked mildly surprised but followed Sulwyn as she made her way back up the stairs. Neither speaking until Sulwyn led her into the bedroom she was sleeping in before. With a snap, she closed the door and gestured for Riko to sit.

"I am trusting you, Riko," Sulwyn started. "But in order to do that, I need to know a few things."

"I promised I would tell you. There is no need to question me." She smiled sadly and patted the bed for Sulwyn to sit next to her.

"Why didn't your magic affect me the same way it did Daijiro and Galahad when we first woke up, and what did you show them?"

"Oh, is that the first question? Ah ha, I can breathe a little." She laughed nervously. Sulwyn looked as Riko tried to fold her trembling hands in her lap, but she kept her light green eyes firmly on Sulwyn's. "It's a night fog. Meant to cause darkness to the one it is cast on and held in said darkness by playing out recent memories of unpleasantness. But you woke rather soon compared to the others."

"Recent?" Sulwyn asked, her voice raised just a tad.

"But it was a very weak version of itself." She held up her hands, waving frantically. "It shouldn't have dug deep enough to find anything scarring to any of you. But..." She started to trail off, but Sulwyn grabbed one of her hands and kept her focused.

"Does it have to do with the black-looking veins on your neck?" Sulwyn asked carefully.

Riko looked down, taking her hand back and rubbing the side of her neck slowly. Her hair usually covered it, but once Sulwyn was aware it was there, she always managed to spot even a little part of it.

"Devinal hold magic. We are able to hold and convert it to do our bidding, store it for later. But unlike others, Nori and I rely on our hearts and health, with only some help from the light of the moon and sun like other Devinal. It's extremely rare according to my mother. But as mentioned before, the All-Mother can be said to be the deriving point for the evolved... with that in mind. Depending on my state of mind, if I am not careful, magic will backfire, and instead, I will absorb the negativity around it. But unlike the All-Mother, I cannot convert it back into the land."

"Is magic negative?"

"No... but intent is, once you use it against someone it merges with them and becomes tainted before the job is fully over. But for me, when that happens, it stings me." Riko moved her hair aside, turning her neck.

Just under her right jaw, a small web of black threaded its way down behind the base of her neck. There, it bloomed out, turning into a twisted flower seeping into her skin like ink until it faded.

Sulwyn reached forwards to touch it. She flinched. "It's cold!"

"It's dead." Riko let her hair fall.

Sulwyn tilted her head in confusion. "Dead?"

"Unlike most... The more I use magic against someone, the more it corrupts me because I can't naturally let it go. And because I haven't figured out how to release it, it holds in my body. Tainting my heart."

"And that would kill you?" Sulwyn's voice was hushed. She had never heard of this happening to anyone before. Did Wilkson know of it, could he help?

"No, it corrupts. Corrupts until I no longer exist, and I am a shell for magic to walk on its own. Guided by the negativity it's absorbed."

"And Nori...?"

Riko looked down now, tears welling. "She doesn't know about it. But Sulwyn... I found the beginning of the mark on her back."

Throughout the rest of the day, everyone was quietly busy getting as much as they could packed and portioned and ready to go. Kione and Eztli gathered more food to add to the provisions they had been collecting slowly since their arrival.

Nori and Riko went to find warmer clothes, something that wasn't too difficult now that the winter weather was fast approaching. Unlike just a week ago when it was brisk only in the morning and at night, now it was cool straight through the day with bits of sun to give some comfort, much to Daijiro's dismay.

As Galahad's and Sulwyn's faces were posted nearly everywhere, they were confined to the house until it started to grow darker. That was when Sulwyn would go to gather a few more weapons and any other bits of supplies that needed replenishing.

But Sulwyn had been waiting until it was dark enough to finally go to the house across from them. The house that held Caldwell's last memory of his sister in her last moments.

Breaking in through the cellar door, this house had more of a crawl space than a basement. Slowly and carefully, she made her way along the rough stone until she met the door at the end. After a few awkward kicks, the door gave way and Sulwyn crawled in.

Standing straight, she looked at the bleak house. Here, the windows hadn't been boarded, in fact, some had been broken and the house was now a shell of what it once was; robbed and cold. Sulwyn walked in, the wooden floor creaking gently with every other step until she found her way to the kitchen.

The scene was left untouched. The chair where his sister was found still sat in the centre, dried blood coating the cut ropes, and the knife Caldwell used to kill her still on the floor. Sulwyn never did learn exactly what had befallen his sister. She didn't even know her name. But here, a ghost of her memory lived in this house forever. A reminder to Sulwyn of what the Empire was truly capable of. She bent down and picked up the rusted, silver dagger. Plain, no markings, something anyone could get.

Regardless of who truly started the rebellion and who truly ruled the Empire, the corruption was real. The violence was real. All the hate and anger that carried over the land was a disease caused by the people. Killing the innocent to crawl higher to the top.

How dare they.

"Sulwyn?"

Arsinone's voice resonated within her, bringing her out of her thoughts once again. She seemed to be getting lost in them a lot lately. There was just so much to think about. So many more people to worry over. And though she saw it in her vision, was it really in her best interest to leave into hiding?

Nero wasn't stupid and neither was Gwydion. They would know she was biding her time. Taking a step back. Hiding. And she was sure they would suspect Mortui Gemma. But like Galahad said, there was no one left to guide them. The whereabouts of the remnants of his clan were unknown and Tiergan was presumably dead. And though according to Galahad, while Nero had been there in the past, they barely made it there. She didn't think Nero or Gwydion were fool enough to risk the journey.

No, they wouldn't do that because they knew, just like she knew, that she wouldn't be able to stay hidden long. Not when Gwydion was out creating something unknown and Nero out to rip apart Vartugaul to find her.

"Sulwyn?"

But still. How could she let these people cover for her? Fight for her? Wouldn't it be in everyone's best interest if they went with Galahad, and she went alone? She needed to find Raghnall anyway.

But could she leave?

There was something happening to Riko, and now Nori. Daijiro was suspicious of everyone, and somehow keeping him from Taru's soul reading seemed logical even though she didn't know why. And the longer Galahad was exposed to all of this, the more chance he had of losing control completely. If she left, would that get them to go into hiding without her? Could she leave before they could stop her?

Sulwyn sat up. Completely unaware of when she had slumped against the wall and slid onto the floor. If she left now, she didn't need anything with her. If she kept to the shadows and went back into the Empire, they could take her. Call off the search. Call off the terror going through each town. She stared at the underside of an old sofa. Dust clinging to the remaining fabric, coating the floor, and now wrapped in her hair. She was lying down again, unaware of when she had done that.

She needed to leave.

Sulwyn stood swiftly, looking around the house for anything of use as the dagger was now useless. As she walked around, she located a small, dirty short sword. That would be enough. Tucking it into the side of her waistband, she moved to one of the broken windows on the side of the house.

She stumbled—an odd creak in the distance distracting her—she looked down, a burning tingle rising in her arm. "Really?" she hissed, looking at the deep scratch the jagged glass cut across her skin. Briefly stunned by the sting, Sulwyn jumped off the ledge and landed quietly onto the ground. Just another injury for her to ignore.

The lanterns in the distance were lit, casting everything around into long, dark shadows. Sulwyn ducked low, running across the frosted grass and onto the slick cobblestone.

She looked beside her to the other house, dark and silent. Good. They had done well to hide there. With haste, she went forwards, darting between the houses and stores. Slinking into the shadows all around her, running and running as her breath rose in small puffs of white, the sting along her arm numbing in the cold.

She did wish she had her cloak. The only thing she had on was a black wool tunic and brown fur-lined pants. But if she gathered some things along the way, she would be fine. Within an hour or so, she was at the front of the town.

Just outside of the border, a platoon of about fifty Néosan were stationed and camped. All patrolling the areas, taking turns to walk through the now-resting town along the centre of the street. How foolish. If only they applied themselves better, they might have found her.

Sulwyn stepped behind the last building; a small shed that held food for the travelling horses. She peeked around the brick wall, looking into the distance and preparing to take off when a hand covered her mouth, and she was yanked back instead.

"Are you insane?" Galahad hissed, pulling her into the shadows and letting go. Sulwyn bit her lip, trapping the sound she was about the make. Her heart pounding in her chest, she turned back, the Néosan unaware of any commotion around them.

"Are you?" she challenged, reminded of a time in the past, in a bush outside the Proelium Terra. "I need to go, Galahad." Her voice harsher than she meant.

"*Go where exactly?*"

"To the Empire. Please listen to me. I can't ask any of you to do this. Not for me. No one deserves this. They are after me and me alone. They only added you to the portraits *because* of me."

"Do you hear yourself?"

"I'm serious! I can't run anymore. If they take me, Nero will call back the Néosan. It'll go back to normal."

"Normal? *This* is normal? Vartugaul as it is now, is normal to you?" She watched the blackness begin to creep around the edges of his eyes, but he ignored it.

"Take them with you. Take them home with you and keep them safe. I will find Raghnall, and we can regroup from there."

"Is that what you've spent this whole time living for? Either die along your path and leave us in charge or ultimately let the Empire take you back?" She could see the frustration shake his shoulders, chest rising. While he was fantastic at remaining impassive most times, she had learned to read his subtle changes. But that wasn't enough to deafen the battle in her mind from her choices made and unmade.

"No. It's not. But I didn't spend this whole time fighting so that I would lose the people close to me. Not again. The people hate me. I spent my entire life fighting for them and in just a few weeks my name and everything I've done thus far was tarnished. If turning myself in helps them, shouldn't I do it?"

"And when they kill you, when does it end?" His nostrils flared. "Whether you like it or not, you are the start of the next revolution. Have always been the start. Similar yet so incredibly different from your parents. Don't you see the point of what Raghnall has done thus far? Of what even Pandora did thus far?"

Sulwyn had been so lost in her thoughts that she hadn't really let that sink in. Not properly. Galahad pulled her closer, holding her shoulders as the black in his eyes cleared. "Raghnall helped you be who you are today. But Pandora also set the groundwork of another plan set in motion from your birth. As insane as it sounds, she, too, sacrificed something on a whim. On a chance that you would show up in front of her and seek the true enemy. Do you see that? Do you fully understand that? There is no crime in biding your time. Stepping back is not giving up."

The clomp of heavy boots stopped him. Galahad stepped into her as they both leaned into the darkness, waiting in silence as the footsteps passed, and they stayed silent for just a bit longer.

"I want to leave tonight," said Sulwyn, Galahad's argument joining her own in her mind. "Before I do something stupid, let's go. I can't stay here anymore. Tonight or tomorrow night. We won't be ready any more than we are now."

"Sulwyn…"

"I can't do this, Galahad!" she hissed. "This wasn't how it was supposed to be! Raghnall wasn't supposed to dump me at the Empire to fulfil a reckless plan. His expectations were too high, and for what? I don't even know if he's alive!" Galahad tried to shush her, but the numbness in her was overflowing. The build of hysteria was always sitting in the back of her mind. Whether it was when she first confided in Galahad in the middle of his garden room, or when she screamed into the night in the middle of a pond. After seeing a bedroom made just for her arrival and read Pandora's journal, everything had been waiting to overflow. And while drowning in her own mind she figured running to the Empire was the right idea? Clearly, she needed to go up in the mountains more than anyone.

"I spent my entire life hating Pandora and Artaxiad. And my hate was justified up until I realised that Pandora was just as much a victim as anyone else. And though she chose her path, she had another one laid out in front of her. They both did. There was a time, a small but serious time they considered quitting it all… and…" She halted; her throat tight. "That desire in them wasn't strong enough."

"I'm sorry, I truly am. And there isn't anything I would want more than to give you the answers you are looking for, but we will get there in time. You've discovered more than you expected in such a short time. We will get there." He gently held her face between his palms. A caring warmth seeping through her. "We can leave tonight. Once everyone sleeps a bit we will go. Okay? But you were never meant to do this alone, Sulwyn. When Raghnall gave you to me, I didn't understand the look he was giving me then. Because I was so blinded by the anger of him betraying you, I didn't realise until learning what we have now. But Sulwyn. There was relief when he saw who I was."

"What?"

"In a moment of clarity, he registered who I was when he saw my eyes. So briefly. Until he was unfocused again and he went on his way. At the very most, he knew you wouldn't be alone. If he managed to predict that much into his plan, who knows what else he thought of. Who you would meet and what you would discover. Allies are everywhere, hidden in plain sight as you've discovered. Don't let them undermine you. Even I did that, and it was my mistake. You didn't get this far on name alone, Sulwyn."

More footsteps sounded around them. He was right—she couldn't let them find her now. How could she be so stupid for so long? There was a limit to foolishness, and she was at the point of passing it again for the millionth time. They both listened carefully, waiting for the footfalls to fade before she looked at Galahad. "Slap me."

"I'm sorry?"

"Please, just. Slap me. You've done it twice before, might as well make it a third."

"That was for very different reasons at a very different time. And your arm is currently bleeding."

"It's fine, just another injury. Besides a slap is for the same reasons, really. Me freaking out, you needing to knock sense into me, right? Please?" She threw in a pleading smile.

Galahad gave her an incredulous stare, looked around briefly, then swiftly slapped her. As gentle as always, a light tingle emitted in her cheek. But the sound still resonated and with a wide smile, Sulwyn grabbed his hand and pulled him to run.

Sulwyn's eyes opened to the sound of stillness and light breathing. All nine of them decided to rest in the living room. The fire burned low to embers, giving a slight heat to the space. It was the dead of night now. Cloudy, and limiting the amount of light that would be around them.

When she and Galahad came back, she was berated by Eztli and Arsinone, something she had expected. But when she told them she wanted to leave tonight, no one argued. They were as ready as they would ever be. So, they decided to have a proper final meal and time for themselves.

Sulwyn faced the nagging in the back of her mind, represented by the family that had died in the house. When she illuminated the basement with firelight, she saw the remnants of blood and leftover ash. And something in her closed. She started in Antac with the Empire, and she would end it here as well. She didn't know how long she had sat on those stairs, but only moved once the small fire burned out.

After that, she wandered the house, readied her bag and helped the others with theirs. Everyone had a portion of food and clothes to carry in the off–chance they were separated for too long. They each carried at least three weapons of varying sort, medical aid and supplies to camp. Galahad assured them that the path they would take had multiple caves stocked with other supplies that no one should have discovered and pillaged. This was a sense of joy for Daijiro, who intended to wear all his clothes again.

Sulwyn sat up slowly, careful not to wake anyone around her. But when she looked around, Taru was already up, looking absently into the grate of embers, the only source of light. He nodded to her lightly and smiled reassuringly. It still surprised her he was born from a tree and almost four hundred years old. But this explained why the DrvaMørk were reverting into wood, something that didn't make any sense to her beforehand. How curious.

She pulled the blankets off herself, stretched and gently padded around the others, making her way to the small bathing room in the hall, picking up the bundle of clothes she had left earlier at the side of the door. Sulwyn stared at her dark reflection, ran her hands through her hair with icy water set aside in a bowl before tying it back in a loose braid, and prepared to change her clothes. She pulled off her nightwear, something she wanted to give herself the luxury of wearing at least once before they made it to Galahad's home, and folded it carefully onto the counter.

A shiver crawled along her skin, hurrying her to pull the red woolen tunic over her undershirt. Reaching over for the fur-lined black leather pants, Sulwyn paused, turning to see Kione behind her.

"Did I make noise?" she whispered, looking past him, trying and failing to see into the dark hall.

"No, I woke when you did." His voice was low and tired with sleep. He looked at her carefully. She returned the look, donning pants before giving him her full attention.

"What do you want to know?" Sulwyn asked, taking her night clothes and leading him to the kitchen. Kione followed her silently, each of his steps heavy with dread. His was a conversation she had been avoiding.

"Who is she... really? My sister... What has she done?"

Sulwyn turned to him, eyes solemn. "How much do you actually know?"

"Nothing! No one is telling me properly!" he hissed. "When you returned to the Empire in a coma, Daijiro told me she was the one who ambushed you on the way back. But after that, I never learned more. No one wants to answer me."

"I can answer you," Daijiro said, stepping into the kitchen, his eyes dangerous, but Sulwyn would not have it.

"*I* will answer you, Kione. Daijiro, shut up," she snapped, watching his eyes narrow. "Diesirae, or I assume her alter name is Ubusuku, carried on a cult that I think you know of? They believe that sacrificing strong individuals and drinking their blood, can make them all stronger."

"Is that cannibalism?" Daijiro asked, but Sulwyn glared at him. "What? I've been asking that for a while now, and I'm not getting an answer."

Sulwyn ignored him completely.

"I told Daijiro and Galahad before that we have never had a tribe or clan like that. Blood is only used during the weapon ceremony to bind the weapon to their owner. And blood purification when someone dies so they may pass to the Land of Hope. Whatever it is that she has been experimenting with has nothing to do with our people. It has to be something of Gwydion's. Diesirae always kept to herself, but she always fought for others. Her betrayal didn't make sense to me. Is there a chance he is controlling her like with you?" Kione's voice was hopeful.

She knew it wasn't related to his clan, but she needed to hear it anyway. Because now she wondered what did they achieve with the blood of the Kurome clan? She bit her lip, Kione's voice bringing her back to the moment at hand. "No, Kione... I don't think so. She's definitely not what you think. Even the first time I met her with you, to the time I met her in the cave when I was first taken, she felt like a completely different person. It goes beyond desire."

"Then what about me? Does she have any care for me?" he asked desperately.

Sulwyn was at a loss for words. She didn't think Diesirae didn't have love for him, but that her love wasn't greater than her goal. Maybe just like Pandora. Though where Diesirae was concerned and the way Gwydion trusted her, she didn't think their partnership was like that. Diesirae seemed to stand on equal ground in Gwydion's eyes.

Daijiro stepped forwards, moving closer to Kione. Sulwyn was about to stop him, but Daijiro spoke first.

"Even if she loves you, it doesn't mean she's right. Her goal and purpose are separate from whatever bond she has with you. And though it didn't faze her when we asked about you, it did seem to bother her if you found out. I think she planned to keep this from you for as long as possible." His voice was deep but gentle.

"Regardless, she has betrayed me. Betrayed all I stood for and all I thought she stood for. If it weren't for Gwydion stepping in, which he may have done at her request, I would have been slaughtered just like the other men and women they used at that trial. She brought harm onto all of you and I don't even know how to ask you to forgive me for that," Kione countered angrily, but Daijiro reached forwards, placing his hand behind Kione's neck and pulling him lower to eye level with him.

"You are you. And your sister is of no concern. I do not see her when I look at you," Daijiro said fiercely. "I see a young man who's been thrown into a little more than he was expecting, but I see the strength you have to overcome it. Besides, if you betrayed Sulwyn after all of that, I'm quite sure she would kill you. If I didn't do it first." He meant it, though he had a crooked smile. "Let's get ready to face some snow."

❧

Sulwyn waited alongside Taru and Eztli in the shadow of Azhar's inn. The night sky was pitch-black, cloudy and perfect for sneaking out of the town unnoticed by anyone. The fading sweet air of dinner and food left room for the tangy salt around her, the ocean in the distance.

They had decided to split into three groups to avoid suspicion and notice. Nine of them at once was too much, even if half of them were used to sneaking around. They were all to meet in the forest away from Antac and towards Mortui Gemma. Galahad, Nori and Riko left first, two hours ago. Daijiro, Arsinone and Kione left an hour later, and now Sulwyn, Taru and Eztli were meeting their hour before they could take off. By the time they walked halfway, the sun would begin to rise, but they wouldn't be visible to the camp in front of Antac, thanks to the curve of the coast.

"Are you ready?" asked Sulwyn. Taru and Eztli nodded, looking around one last time.

"It's been years since I travelled like this past month," Eztli said, sighing. "It's so much more work than I give ya two credit for."

"It's about the journey, my dear," said Taru happily.

"Taru, what happened to Hana and all the other horses?" Sulwyn exclaimed, only realising this now.

"Hana took them to safety, not sure where, though," he said pleasantly and not at all concerned. She stared at him but was also glad he was starting to show his true self again.

"Ah, I did the same with Ki!" Sulwyn said brightly. She hoped Wilkson found him.

"Are we goin'?" asked Eztli, looking at the cloudy night sky.

"Yes, until next time…" Sulwyn whispered towards Azhar's bar.

The three of them moved down the hill along the coast. Navigating without much light was a bit risky, but they had no other choice. Careful to avoid falling into the ocean, they continued at a brisk pace. Sulwyn glanced at Taru every so often, but he had no qualms with keeping up, and in fact, seemed to be slowing down for Eztli's sake.

Quietly they went, stopping every so often to listen and ensure no one was following them or spotted them in the distance, until finally after a few hours, they made their way past the bend with Antac out of sight.

The sky was brightening on the horizon now, the pinks and oranges of dawn bleeding into yellow and green. Here, they decided to stop and rest for a moment on a spot of dry grass and sand near the stone wall.

The ocean breeze sent shivers through her but also brought calm. The sound of the crashing, unexplored water lulled her into a peaceful state of mind. Eztli moved closer to see it, sitting along the stone wall while Taru and Sulwyn remained a short distance from her on a slope.

"Your hair is buzzing," said Taru, looking at the waves.

"Buzzing?"

"You have questions," he noted.

Sulwyn closed her eyes, listening to the waves. "Why does Galahad want to stop you from reading Daijiro's soul?"

"Because I made him. Galahad is wise. Wise beyond his years, and though I haven't explained anything to him, he carries through," Taru started. "I don't know much about Daijiro in terms of who he truly is, but there is one thing I found oddly fascinating about him." He looked at her. "I can't hear his clothes."

Sulwyn stared at him, confusion rising until she remembered that one time when Taru noted Galahad's clothes didn't like him. "What does that mean exactly?"

"I couldn't tell you since I can't hear it. Either his power blocks my ability to hear their souls or they are silenced in submission to him. But I can tell you that there is a lot of history to him. As a Velyūn, that's already expected. I, myself, have only ever come across five before this in my time of life. Velikat were always quiet and hidden. Unbonded and different from Galahad's clan, they existed away because they didn't think others would understand them. But life does happen and sometimes they would meet other regular people and fall in love."

"I don't think Daijiro's mother and father were properly in love."

"Maybe, I don't know anything about them. But Daijiro was born and that is still something good. As for why I don't want to read him..." Taru hesitated, finally looking at Sulwyn with his uneven grey and brown eyes. "I think it's a feeling. An instinctual decision on my part, if you will, but it seems like Daijiro is far too perceptive to let that last for too long. Sooner or later, I will have to read his history. But for now, we can delay it with the hassle of it all."

"Hassle?"

"I slept for a week straight after Galahad's reading. I have a feeling his will be no different."

XLII

The Search Is Over

HOURS passed until finally, Sulwyn could see the trees in the near distance. She was beyond thankful that just for once, they weren't being watched or chased. And just for once, everything was going according to plan. By the time the three of them walked to the edge of the forest, the sun had already set. Bringing with it a cold drop in temperature.

"Do ya know where to go?" asked Eztli, exhaustion all over her face.

"We're close," Sulwyn replied, walking further and further through the forest, until finally, they heard a light crackle of fire. Slowly, she moved forwards until the light illuminated the others who were sitting and chatting.

"Finally!" Nori sighed, running towards Eztli and hugging her tightly. Sulwyn eyed them carefully, the hug more tender than she had seen between them. But Arsinone stepped forwards, to hug Sulwyn and then squish Taru.

"I told them you were in the forest. Tea is ready!" Arsinone announced happily, handing her a steaming metal mug and pulling Taru with her.

Sulwyn held the handle gingerly, the heat warming her hands immediately. In the distance and through the trees, she could see the lake they had crossed. The wild current had settled with large ice blocks floating peacefully like she didn't almost drown in it.

They would need to go around now, extending the time. They would also need to be careful. She was sure the Néosan would keep their eyes around this area now that they knew someone had gotten past it. But she hoped that if they spotted the cracked lake, they would assume whoever they were chasing had fallen in.

Sulwyn dropped her bag onto the ground realising that Daijiro and Galahad were nowhere to be seen. She looked at Arsinone, but she only pointed into the trees by the very same lake. Nodding her thanks, Sulwyn waved to the others and walked towards the icy water.

She was unsure of what she was walking into but was pleasantly surprised when she spotted both men sitting by the edge, drinking warm mugs of tea. Daijiro was wrapped in a ball in his large blanket; the only thing visible were his hands and his head. Galahad, on the other hand, had no blanket, legs forwards and out. Both sitting on a dried fallen tree–trunk.

"It was definitely Eztli that delayed you, wasn't it?" Daijiro asked, turning to greet her. His smile caught her breath. Somehow, she wasn't expecting it. It was vulnerable and ecstatic all at once as soon as he laid his eyes on her.

"She did her best," said Sulwyn, standing behind them. As the sun finally set, the multicolour stars began to shine brighter. The sky had cleared with a light chill. The moon was a sliver of itself and illuminated little in the distance.

"He can't say anything," Galahad started. "They took turns carrying Arsinone on their back. They caught up to me sooner than they should have. It was good we were already past the bend."

Sulwyn laughed. "That would count as cheating."

"It's practical. She's little. One of our steps is three of hers. You'd have passed us," retorted Daijiro, sliding over and making space between them.

She stepped over the tree–trunk, taking a seat and holding the cooling mug between her hands. "A lot is going to change by the time we come back down," she whispered, taking a sip. It was full of berries and honey and warmed her insides enjoyably.

"This way, we can at least keep the others safe if we need to go down first," Galahad said, his eyes on her. She always loved it when the multicoloured stars reflected into his eyes, blending into a rainbow of colours. "What?"

"Nothing. I just feel… reassured." Sulwyn smiled.

"I wish you felt that way before you almost gave yourself to the Empire," Daijiro said scathingly.

Sulwyn turned to him. "It is still a plan of last resort, but we hadn't tried all our options yet and I didn't see that earlier."

"I don't care if it's a last resort," he said quietly. "It isn't a plan you'll see through without resistance. Heed our warning."

She turned to Galahad, who only shrugged. "You two get along so well, considering you couldn't stand being near each other." She scoffed.

"We never really interacted until he became the All-Command. Then his clan was under threat," said Daijiro. "Practically raging. Who would welcome that? Killing a bunch of Néosan in anger. He threatened my position. *I'm* the Leader most feared. I take that title seriously."

Sulwyn raised an eyebrow at him before turning to give Galahad a disapproving look. "What exactly did you do anyway? Everyone kept alluding to you becoming a mass murderer or something. And I know you killed a chef, according to Kione."

"That man was pretty vile," said Daijiro in Galahad's defence. But Sulwyn ignored him, keeping her eyes on Galahad.

There was regret in his eyes, and in turn, Sulwyn lost her next words to berate him somewhere in her throat. "My clan was threatened. But so were you… Some of the Captains thought Artaxiad wasn't fond of you. A rumor was spread that you were an illegitimate child from a man Pandora was seeing. Being so dedicated to their king, they wanted to…" A slight quiver went through him, a ghosted wave of anger.

"So, you killed them?" Her voice was quiet, barely carrying across the wind.

"They deserved it," Galahad said harshly, tracking the chunks of ice floating by unbothered.

"Though at the time I wasn't aware of the situation. Nor did I care then either. But I do agree with him," Daijiro said. "Don't feel bad for them. They aren't worthy of it."

"I don't feel bad for them. It's just I know acting out like that isn't something you would normally do if you had more control at the time. Thank you… and I'm sorry." Sulwyn took Galahad's hand in her right one. "Besides, we've all done things we aren't proud of, isn't that right, Daijiro?" She turned to him now, his expression sorrowful. Daijiro raised a finger to the scar on the side of her head from when he had accidentally hit her. He nodded, taking the mug out of her hand and holding her left. "New start," said Sulwyn. "We know the threat now. We need to be better than him. Better than the Vartugaul Pandora and Artaxiad left behind. Better than who we were before." She squeezed their hands, a new–found calm within herself.

⚘⚘

A few days had passed since they started their trek towards and into the mountain. The vision Sulwyn had seen was already fulfilled by the second day, exactly as it was when she first saw it. Since then, they had managed to find a cave every night preserved by the cold and disuse. The knowledge of the terrain was still fixed in Galahad's mind.

The cave they were in tonight would be their last until they made it to the centre. Unlike what she thought, they weren't climbing to the top. They were slowly making their way to the actual centre of the snowy mass. Each cave detoured further in, like layers and layers within the mountain. It sort of reminded her of the Solus and how there were tall walls cut out like a maze. She knew the Solus was made sometime during the High City, but was it made by someone similar?

"Yes," whispered Galahad, his eyes on hers as they all sat around the fire.

"What?"

"Someone from my clan helped make the Solus." He smirked at her wide eyes, always able to read her openly.

"You didn't say that before!"

"I couldn't tell you about myself then. Then it just slipped my mind." He shrugged.

"Are you sure this is the last cave?" Daijiro whined, practically on the fire.

"Are you not carrying a bird of *actual* fire? Shouldn't you be hot all the time?" Galahad asked. The others just stared back and forth between their friendly banter that happened constantly and to no end during their climb.

"He's cold *because* of the fire," said Taru randomly, looking up from the rock he was holding. Everyone stared at him instead. "Innominatam is a bird of fire only when it is in use or in flight. Otherwise, it eats heat."

"So, you're telling me that this bird steals my heat?" Daijiro asked incredulously. Taru only nodded, now petting the rock.

"That's a small price to pay to have a fire bird," said Kione from his side of the circle. Daijiro scowled and grumbled something unintelligible.

"It is the last cave. We will get there by midday tomorrow," said Galahad. Though he sounded excited, Sulwyn could see the apprehension in his eyes. "I'm not too sure what will be left of the place. I don't know how long the fires raged after or if anything will be salvageable. At this point, nature would have taken over instead. If we're lucky, some of the crops may still be okay. They were usually self-sustainable as long as they didn't burn too."

"Are you nervous?" Riko asked next to him. He turned to her and Sulwyn noticed the way he glanced at the black patch by her neck, his eyes curious but wary.

"A little... It's been so long I'm not sure what I should feel."

"Well, look at it this way," Eztli started, "at least it's going to be a safe haven for a while. I'm sure yer clan would be happy."

"Why didn't the survivors just come back here?" Sulwyn asked.

"After the attack, the area was patrolled for a long time. Believing it unsafe, they let go and moved on. But before they left the fog town, they said they wanted to repent. Even those that weren't part of Diesirae's group. They still housed them. Said they didn't deserve to share the space of my father, a man they had misjudged."

"This is why all the special clans ended up dead," said Daijiro, "because they always have these stupid laws and regulations among themselves. Everyone is equal in the eyes of the Empire. They're going to kill you either way."

"That's what I've been saying every time someone tells me to rest," said Sulwyn, downing her tea and standing. "I'm ordering bed for everyone. I want to get us there even faster." She whipped the excess liquid out of the mug and dried it with a rag in her bag before putting it away.

Unlike the other caves, this one was larger and had much more left in it to aid their exhaustion. And just like each cave, it had a small slope within that linked up to the others, taking in tiny amounts of snow to be melted by fire for water. There were also a lot of dry foods that were stale but filling enough. And even though they had brought their own provisions, they tried to use a little of both.

Sulwyn moved her blankets to the side in a corner, her back to the cave wall as the others picked a spot elsewhere. She never slept with her back to the opening. No matter how far in they were, she knew she couldn't sleep otherwise. Now that they were in the innermost cave, the wind here was less, the draft coming in almost a whisper.

Just as she was starting to doze off, a shuffle near her woke her, and soon, she was staring up at Eztli. "Are you okay?" she asked sleepily.

"Fine... I just... I wondered if we could talk for a bit. Then I'll go back to my spot," she asked timidly, something that just didn't suit Eztli.

"Sure, come," Sulwyn replied, patting the spot next to her. Eztli laid down next to her, facing her so that her back was to the cave opening a few feet away.

"So... this. This'll sound a little unexpected, but I'll just go righ' in," she started, her voice so quiet Sulwyn actually had to strain to hear it. After a few seconds of silence, Sulwyn urged her on.

"When we separated..." Eztli paused, looking for words, but Sulwyn now realised she was nervous. And like Sulwyn, who couldn't visibly flush due to her complexion, she could feel the heat radiating from Eztli's hands and face from nerves.

"During our travels. I've come to realise something... about someone. And I haven't addressed it since, but I also can't stop thinking about it. And I know this isn't really the best time, but yer the only one that's close to my age and I thought maybe ya would have some sort of insight on this kind of thing?"

"Eztli... I need to know what happened before I can help you."

"I kissed someone."

Sulwyn took a moment to process this fact.

Eztli was travelling with Taru, Arsinone, Riko, Kione and Nori. Sulwyn really hoped that Taru was not interested and honestly didn't think so. Arsinone was too young and not even a consideration and Riko was still, to her understanding, in love with Daijiro. So, the person in question could only be either Kione or Nori. Both of whom were good people. Why was there a problem and why would she know any more than her? If anything, she knew less, but Eztli's eyes were wide and nervous, so she would have to do the best she could. "Okay?"

"I wasn't expecting it. It came out of nowhere! And..."

"Did it upset you?" asked Sulwyn, concerned.

"No. No! Quite the opposite, actually. I loved it. At first, I was too surprised to really register it, ya know? And then I was into it, and then it ended. And that was it. Never again after that! And now I'm left all bothered... and, uncomfortable because I'm not bringin' it up, and neither are they. And I'm just burning."

Sulwyn laughed. "I understand that." Eztli eyed her, but she would divulge nothing else. "So, what's the problem? Since when do you hold back?"

"Well. I'm older," Eztli replied, looking away.

"Does that matter?" Sulwyn was waiting for her to tell her who the person was, but now she really had no idea.

"I don't even know if it was like a 'maybe we are going to die tomorrow' thing or a 'I've wanted to do this for a while' thing."

"Both are proper questions. Who was it?"

"Nori… It was Nori…" Her voice a wisp of air at this point.

Sulwyn smirked. "She took you by surprise, then? Was it really her or Duri?"

"What? Duri? No, no, it was definitely Nori. Her face was on fire after that, and then she ran away. But we only stopped because her sister came into our room. And then after that…"

"So, what exactly did you want from me?" Sulwyn asked, smiling. "I don't see a problem, and I don't think you'll be rejected. I think you might be surprised at the outcome if you decide to be open. You may not have noticed the signs before, but if you're feeling this way now, maybe somewhere deep down, you were hoping for this. The cave is huge. I think you should go ask her." Then Sulwyn shoved her off her blanket. Eztli was scandalised, to say the least, but her expression was brighter than when she first came to her.

"Good night, sweetness." Sulwyn winked, using her nickname against her. Eztli's face was priceless, but she nodded with renewed vigor as she got up to go back to her spot. It was conveniently near Nori, now that Sulwyn looked at it. She watched a little longer, seeing Eztli hover near Nori's blankets until she was lying next to her.

Sulwyn readjusted to face the cave opening again. Sleep burned her eyes and finally came to her, until again, she was interrupted. Opening her eyes, she was met with red ones looking down at her.

A ball of blanket, Daijiro sat next to her. "I'm cold."

"I just want to sleep..." Sulwyn grumbled, but she shifted back a bit and lifted up the blankets. Daijiro smiled gently, lying down next to her and wrapping them both in his blanket. Sulwyn tried and failed to stop the heat that flowed through her entire being at their proximity. But she accepted it anyway because sleep kept calling to her.

Gently, Daijiro turned on his side, facing her and stroking the top of her head. Try as she might, her eyes kept closing, until finally, the warmth enveloped her.

ﱢﱢ

"You knew," Galahad said as they made their final trek through the snow. Sulwyn turned to him, his eyes bright. "You had a vision of it."

"I did. But I didn't want to influence the flow in any way," Sulwyn replied.

"What did you see?"

"That moment a few days ago, when Daijiro called you 'ice boy'." She laughed. "It was beautiful then, and it's still beautiful now. The snow is so bright and untouched."

"And COLD!" Daijiro complained from somewhere behind her. Sulwyn could only roll her eyes. But she did agree even if she wouldn't tell him.

By now, they had been walking for hours, and though the ground had flattened out, the snow here was deeper. Coming right up to their knees and slowing their progress greatly. Try as she might, she could see nothing but snow in every direction. Hills upon hills of it rose around them in the carved-out path that had remained for all these years. Galahad said they used to be cleared out and easier to navigate, but if this was as bad as it got, Sulwyn was okay with it. She was expecting the journey to be much more difficult, but she understood now why they needed a guide.

If anyone else came and didn't know about the caves, they would wander endlessly with no sense of direction and nothing to mark their path.

Not to mention that there was no shelter or means of food, and of course, the cold.

"Did you know that Artaxiad's right arm was permanently damaged?" Galahad asked casually as they trudged on.

"From... when they came here? No..." But as she thought about it, there were times when his grip or the movement of his hand was stiff.

"He had frostbite. Part of his arm received nerve damage. Though Tiergan told them where to go, there was a storm, and it was night. Without an actual guide and the use of the caves, the fact that they made it was impressive in itself. Though I do know a lot of Néosan perished that night." But Sulwyn could see the ghost of hatred etched in his emotions, wishing that they *all* had died that night in the storm and snow.

"I'm glad we have a guide like you then," said Sulwyn, patting his back and accidentally adding a ton of snow onto his cloak.

"I don't want to sound like I'm complaining," Kione started loudly behind them, "but I actually can't feel my legs anymore."

"We're almost there, and we can make as much fire as we like once we arrive," Galahad answered.

Silence fell around them as they concentrated on making their way through the cold. And as marvellous as the ice was, she was done with travelling in it. Though, she assumed that once they made it within his village, it would just be more snow and ice built in a livable fashion. Assuming it survived the fire and years of negligence.

With each step, the cold started to freeze her lungs. Ice sticking to her lashes and the hairs in her nose with each breath. At this point, she was also losing feeling in her legs and envied Arsinone just a little for being small enough to be carried.

Sulwyn looked back at the rest of them. All pink in the face from the cold, bundled in scarves and woolen hats, and in Daijiro's case, every-thing he owned. She could see the tiredness in all of them, and still, she was surprised by Taru's unchanging demeanour throughout their travel. Maybe sturdy like a tree meant something.

"Sulwyn," whispered Galahad, stopping abruptly.

She looked at him, seeing the fear in his eyes as she spotted the snowy arch in the distance. Though the tunnels of snow stopped them from seeing beyond, she knew what he was feeling.

"It's okay. We're with you. And no matter what you see or remember, I'll be next to you. And if you need to leave, you can do that too. Maybe step outside and climb down a few caves back."

He laughed nervously, taking her hand in his.

"You were right. This was the best choice," she whispered, squeezing his hand.

"I know. I know…" he repeated, standing and staring at the arch.

Even though the others were beyond freezing, they kept quiet, watching Galahad carefully. Soon, it started to snow, and finally, he was ready to step forwards.

But as they walked through the arch together, the high snow walls encasing them in a windless tunnel, a maddening sense of foreboding rose in Sulwyn all at once like a heavy mass, warning her.

"There is another tunnel after this, and then we will be in the centre as soon as we pass this antechamber," he continued, but the warning in her grew; someone was here.

"Galahad, wait," she hissed, letting go of his hand just as they entered the large, empty space of snow. The air was exceptionally fresh and the afternoon sky was clear and bright yellow and green above them. But Sulwyn reached for her bow, quickly nocked an arrow and aimed it at the next entrance tunnel across them shrouded in shadows.

She figured his lack of reaction was due to how lost in thought he was, but Galahad finally tensed, sensing what she had. The others stopped behind.

Daijiro stepped forwards alongside Kione, both coming up beside her and Galahad as they watched and waited. But Sulwyn stayed firm, keeping the bow taut, waiting and going through the list of people in her mind of who would be here and why.

Had Gwydion predicted they would make it here? Did he know how to get here? Given his prowess, it wouldn't be beyond him to find someone from Galahad's clan and force them to lead the way. But all along their journey, it didn't look like anything had been touched. Unless he didn't use any of the caves. As a Devinal, maybe he knew magic that could protect him. And though Sulwyn asked before, Galahad confirmed it's not possible to shift here because of the land being protected, something she didn't understand. But maybe Gwydion had found a way around it.

Until Sulwyn dropped the bow and arrow completely, letting it sink into the snow while her breath came up short. Her already cold body was numb to everything around her as a figure walked slowly out of the large snow tunnel and into the light before stopping and leaning on a great ornate wooden cane.

With a smirk on his face, Raghnall announced, "Took you long enough."

TO BE CONTINUED IN

THE BONDS THAT BIND US

BOOK III

Names, Words and Terminology of Vartugaul:

Characters: *Note: This is how I pronounce them.**

Sulwyn*: SUL-win – *our main protagonist, daughter of Queen Pandora and King Artaxiad.*

Raghnall: RAE-N-aeL – *The Steel Warrior, former High Captain of the High City and Sulwyn's saviour and mentor.*

Galahad: ga-la-Had – *the adopted prince of the Empire and Leader of Validus Uferor San.*

Daijiro: die-JEE-rOH – *Leader of Validus Uferor Divi and Interrogator of the Solus.*

Artaxiad: ar-TAX-ee-ADD – *King of the Empire.*

Pandora: PAN-do-RAH – *Queen of the Empire.*

Caldwell: KAWld-wel – *Leader of Validus Uferor En, the first Uferor group founded.*

Eztli: ezz-li – *A maid and head chef in Valens Muros.*

Arsinone: ar-SE-non – *A maid of Valens Muros and Soul Reader.*

Nori: NO-ree – *A maid of Valens Muros.*

Duri: DOO-ree – *The alter identity of Nori.*

Kione: KEEY-on – *A Common One and Protector in the Solus.*

Diesirae: DEZ-ah-ray – *Sister to Kione and Common One.*

Tiergan: tEAr-gin – *The spokesperson in the fog town.*

Taru: TAA-roo – *A whimsical old man and Soul History Reader.*

Zalika: ZA-li-Kaa - *A servant of Tiergan's.*

Gwydion: Gwid-ee-ohn – *Member of the Triarchy and scholar.*

Nero: NEE-row - *Raghnall's younger brother and founder of the Triarchy/Diarchy.*

Ildri: iLL-dree - *Prisoner in the Pain Cells of the Solus, also known as number Thirty-Six. A Devinal. Part of Raghnall's Guard.*

Eleri: eL-lar-REE - *Prisoner in the Pain Cells of the Solus, also known as Twenty-Seven, Raghnall's second in command during the High City reign.*

Thirty: Prison Number - *Prisoner in the Pain Cells of the Solus, part of Raghnall's Guard.*

Forty-Two: Prison Number - *Prisoner in the Pain Cells of the Solus, part of Raghnall's Guard.*

Names, Words and Terminology of Vartugaul:

Wilkson: WILK-sin - *The last son of King Zelmir of the Zalman.*

Amalthea: AH-MaL-THEE- ah - *Wilkson's Wife.*

Kai: KA-ee - *Wilkson's son.*

Lelia: LEE-lee-AH - *Wilkson's Daughter*

Demir: DuH-MeeR – *Validus in Uferor En.*

Sibril: SIB-ruul – *Validus in Uferor San.*

Elian: EL-lee-IN – *Validus in Uferor Divi.*

Tiamat: TEE-AH-mat – *Taru's twin.*

Tarak: TEH-Ra-K – *Leader of Validus Uferor Vier.*

Eurus: ee-UR-iss – *Leader of Validus Uferor Fimm.*

Riko: Ree-kou – *Nori's sister, a devinal once captive of Gwydion and childhood friend of Daijiro.*

Azhar: AH-zar – *Townleader and barman in Antac.*

Zander: ZAAN–derr - *Pandora's missing brother.*

Zelmir: ZELL–mur - *The last King of the fallen High City.*

Names, Words and Terminology of Vartugaul:

Places:

Vartugaul: var-TU-gaal - *The name of the entire land.*

Antiqua: an-tee-gwa - *The continent where the Empire resides.*

Guāngcǎi: gang-kai - *The largest continent in Vartugaul. Where Nero and Gwydion govern.*

Mortui Gemma: more-too-ee gem-mah - *The snowy continent, harsh winter conditions all year–round.*

Uhuru: oo-who-roo - *The sandy continent where Kione, Diesirae and Ildri are from.*

Antac: an-TAAK - *The town responsible for making weapons out of Neuore.*

Tranquillum Forest: tran-QILL-um forest - *The forest that borders all Vartugaul.*

Valens Muros: VAL-eez moo-rose - *The main castle of the Empire where the King and Queen reside.*

Eques Muros: eh-qwess moo-rose - *The secondary castle where all military personnel train or live.*

Proelium Terra: pRO-eel-i-UM tear-RAH — *Colosseum–like structure dug out of a mountain to hold tralis and battles or major announcements.*

the Solus: the SOUL-Uh-s — *The prison of the Empire built by the High City.*

The Fog Town: *A mysterious town hidden from the Empire. Now abandoned.*

Wallaysn: WALL-AH-sin - *A getaway/vacation town for the Privilege of the Empire.*

Pliflyn: PUL-if-LIN - *A larger town in Guāngcǎi.*

Paraga: PUH-ra-gaah - *Near Sulwyn's home.*

Staultbrand: sTUH-lt-ber-an-d - *Wilkson's home town.*

Shā: shh-AH - *Azhar's previous home town, mysteriously bombed.*

Slave Bases: - *Four total. One in Uhuru they collect sand for glass. One at the base of Mortui Gemma where they mine crystal and ice. One to mine Neuore, used to develop weapons and armour. One on the border of Malumagri, they collect poison and chemicals from the border.*

Macil: MA-sill - *A town Sulwyn, Daijiro and Eurus (with their Validus groups) visit.*

Synd: si-IN-d - *A town Galahad and Tarak (with their Validus groups) visit.*

Names, Words and Terminology of Vartugaul:

Titles:

Néosan: NAY-oh-san – *Artaxiad's Army, lowest level.*

Captains: CAP-tins – *Above Néosan, lead large platoons of fifty or more.*

Validus: vAL-ee-doS – *Above Captains, smaller platoons of ten.*

Uferor: U-for-er – *Consists of four Validus and one Leader in teams of five.*

Leaders: Leed-eers – *Higher than all army personal, only five.*

All-Command: Ah-ll Ka-mand – *Overseas and controls all army personal.*

Protectors: pro-tek-tours - *On par with Validus, govern over the Solus.*

Triarchy: try-arr-key - *Group of three that govern over Empire business.*

Races, Clans and Tribes: *Note: This is how I pronounce them.**

Devinal: dee-vine-all - *People born with the ability to hold magic.*

Kuvuli: coo-vuu-lai - *An honourable tribe, with old history from Uhuru.*

Kurome: coo-row-meh - *The clan of black eyes.*

Velikat: vel-ee-cat - *Race of elite humans that evolved sometime after the Lost World.*

Velikai: vel-ee-kai - *The term used for female Velikat.*

Velika: vel-ee-kaa - *The term used for male Velikat.*

Velyūn*: veel-yuun - *The term used for a Velikat half-breed.*

Rízes: RYE-zez - *Tiamat and Taru's species.*

| ACKNOWLEDGEMENTS |

First for making it this far, I thank you! It's been a long journey and though the Corrupted Prince was delayed by an entire year, it is finally here! But as always, I wouldn't have made it this far without some very special people...

Theodora, my silly, bright, wild, free spirited, clever, hilarious, perceptive and everything in-between little. When I published The Blood Princess you were closer to two than one. Now you're almost three and a half and I feel like I meet a new you every day. The "threenager" phase is not for the weak, but seeing you grow and learn and express things all on your own is far more worth it than the frustration of a screaming and defiant toddler that loves to be naked. You are kind and understanding and I can't wait (but also can) to see who you truly become. I love you to the stars and back and all the way to Gallifrey.

Steven, my husband of six years and partner of sixteen. This year hasn't been easy for either of us. But being by your side through it all will always be worth it. You are an amazing friend, partner and Dada. Thank you for always encouraging me and this dream no matter how tough it gets or impossible it may seem. We'll both find ourselves again soon, it's just going to take a little longer since we're also guiding a brand-new human. (She just got here!)

Le mama, you've been with me since birth so thanks for that (lol XD) thank you for (finally) reading my book and then becoming obsessed with it. As well as advertising it to anyone. You've helped give me time to write (by sacrificing yourself to Theo and her shenanigans.) As well as just being around and support us. And also, being a strange being. Since your strangeness has passed onto me, it's why I am the way I am and I'd never change it. Probably why Theo is Theo as well to be honest.

KATIE! I absolutely adore you. I will forever be thankful for the bookstagram community for introducing us. And I guess The Blood Princess because you were my beta reader first, then we became soul besties. We may not have physically met yet, but you've moved just a little closer. One day! Thank you for being there in all aspects. From book things to baby things to poop stories and other random ass shit (take the pun).

Maddie. The first person (that I know of) to basically make a mini shrine or my book and be my first hardcopy order for The Blood Princess. Your understanding of my own characters is wild and a little scary. And it's great to have someone who is as invested as I am to talk about plot. Thank you for always supporting me and these characters, and for the best memes.

To my forever artist, Bree. Guuurrrrrllllllll. GIRL. Your art is the shit and I will keep you forever. Thank you for always bringing my characters to life, but more than that, thank you for letting me into your life. I am so proud of you and extremely happy my book brought another awesome person into my life.

To all my beta readers who took interest and read The Corrupted Prince. First, I apologise for even having a deadline since I ended up postponing the entire thing. Second, I'll be sending swag stuff soon! Aside from my lack of organization, I am super thankful for you all. And I hope you'll beta read for book three as well!

Rashida; my next-door neighbour and friend. Thank you for always being there and reading my emotions way too well. You are a bright star and I'm so happy we moved next to you. It's also a bonus that Theo has other littles to play with! I hope to read your book one day about the adventures you've had thus far. And thank you for the warm hugs and letting Theo basically walk into your house uninvited.

Gen and Soraya, thank you for always taking care of Theo and giving me time to work on this book or to give me time for when I need to do something. You guys are fantastic mother and sister-in law and I continue to wish the best for you both.

Susan; an unexpected partnership and friend. While you strive to make Grendel Press the best it can be, you also are a hard worker with a dream that I respect. Thank you for loving my stories so much, and even if we get short with each other, I know this will continue to be a fantastic ride.

To everyone at Grendel Press, while I don't know any of you personally, you've helped polish and given love to this book and I couldn't have asked for more.

As you get older, people come and go into your lives. Many of the people who were with me during the very beginning of this journey are no longer involved with my life for various reasons. Though this can be unfortunate, sometimes these things happen for you to grow and find who you were meant to. When a door closes, at least a window or something opens, right? So, to all the new yet deep friendships I've made in the last couple of years…you are my people, and I will always be there. For accepting me as I am, despite our differences or struggles, I thank you.

To anyone who gave this book a chance and is back for more…I thank you with all of my being. I love this book and it's world and characters with my life. And to see it grow and read by strangers is so surreal. To have people who talk to me about their theories or thoughts. Who take the time to get to know these characters that all live within me. There is no higher honour. I only hope that as I continue to write and grow, that you continue to be by my side, (as well as make everyone you know read this series XD)

Lastly, to those who struggle with mental health. I will always be here for you. I understand the struggle so well, as I too try to heal and grow. And I also understand what it's like to have people not understand. Regardless of these people, I want to be here for you. I have setbacks, and relapses into old habits. But I'm starting to see that there are more positive days than negative. Even if that day is just getting out of bed. As always, I'm open to talk or listen. My DMs are always open, even if I don't get to it right away. I see you. You are doing great. You are loved. And you matter.

If I forgot anyone, just let me know and I'll give you a shoutout. I tried to think of everyone I could want to thank, but it is always when you least expect it (in my case, showers and driving) then you remember.

| ABOUT THE AUTHOR |

S.A. Gonsalves is a Canadian author from Ontario.

With the second book of The Bonds That Bind Us series out and about, she still can't wait to bring you more. With two more books planned for this series, this isn't the last of Vartugaul and its characters. But it is possible, she will be able to work on another different story entirely. Along with the other stories waiting to come out, this is far from the end of this author's journey.

Now equipped with some ADHD treatment and other things, she may procrastinate much less, but is still behind on her TBR list, anime list, game list and more. She is also still trying to battle balance mom life and fitting in date time with her husband. Alas.

She also thoroughly loves talking to readers, so send her a message and discuss her ear off!

Follow her unorganized process on Instagram:
@writer.stepfanie

www.sagonsalves.com